"WHEN DO WE START BEING RICH?"

"That's something we've got to talk to you about," Harry said as he and Emma came into the room. "We need some help with the next phase and you strike me as the kind of man we need."

"What kind of man?" asked Lord Carnarvon. "A money man, a seaman, a banana farmer, a diver, a mechanic? What?"

Emma knitted her brows, then said, "The kind of man who, when he says, 'Do what I say or I'll kill you,' people will do what he says . . . Or he'll kill them."

THOMAS PERRY

"Masterly at combining high humor and total terror with awesome splendid audacity!"
Chicago Tribune

"One of the best thriller writers to swagger down the pike in a long time"
Philadelphia Inquirer

THOMAS PERRY

AVON BOOKS NEW YORK

AVON BOOKS
A division of
The Hearst Corporation
105 Madison Avenue
New York, New York 10016

Published by arrangement with The Putnam Berkley Group, Inc.
Library of Congress Catalog Card Number: 87-7188
ISBN: 0-380-70663-6

First Avon Books Printing: May 1989

Printed in the U.S.A.

K-R 10 9 8 7 6 5 4 3 2 1

For Jo

We asked him many questions concerning all these things, to which he answered very willingly; only we made no inquiries after monsters, than which nothing is more common; for everywhere one may hear of ravenous dogs and wolves, and cruel man-eaters; but it is not so easy to find states that are well and wisely governed.

—THOMAS MORE, *Utopia*

1

LOS ANGELES

Emma sat stiffly on the big plush seat of the Cadillac, looking small and faint, hugging the little suitcase as though it could protect her. "Are they still following us?"

"Of course they are," said Harry. "With any luck they'll follow us all the way to Tierra del Fuego. We'll be on a plane to Paris or someplace before they remember they lost us on the San Diego Freeway."

She looked at Harry long enough to see his face illuminated by a streetlight that passed overhead, then another. His jaw was working, and his eyes glowed with an idiot excitement. "Harry, there's still time to stop this. We can deliver the money right to his house."

"We took our shot, and it's too late to go back and act like nothing happened. He knows already."

"How? How can he know we stole his money when he's not expecting it until tomorrow?"

"He knows," said Harry. "Think about him. He weighs more than the king of Tonga, but did you ever see him eat anything?"

"What does that have to do with—"

"Even a potato chip? Ever even hear of him eating anything?"

"No."

"Well, the same way he keeps his weight up—that's how he knows."

"Come on, Harry. You act like he's Moby Dick."

Harry glanced at her, his face suddenly serious. "You know, I think he is. You ever notice that he tells you all about what somebody told him in some bar in San Francisco last night, when you were with him in Los Angeles last night?"

"You're giving me the creeps."

"Don't worry. Even if they catch us, they won't kill us. There's absolutely no—" Suddenly there was a deafening bang from somewhere behind, and the rear window of the car was blasted into fragments that swept over the back seat and clattered against the windshield like shards of ice. Harry yelled, "Yaah!" and stomped on the gas pedal.

The Cadillac tore down the quiet street toward the airport, flashing through the first intersection as the light turned red and the driver of a car on the cross-street slowly nosed his red Porsche into view. There was a blare of a horn that sounded loud for only a second, then faded into the past behind them.

"You hit?" asked Harry.

"No," said Emma.

"Then for God's sake, say something."

"I'm scared."

"Not that," said Harry. He steered with a maniacal concentration, every touch of the wheel sending the speeding car too far to one side, so he finally straddled the white line in the middle of the road and aimed the car straight ahead. He could see the next light was red, so he hit the brake and skidded into a right turn between two cars in the intersection. The second screeched its brakes, but the Cadillac was already well beyond its reach by then, the bundle of metal and broken glass and desperation moving faster than the reflexes of a man who was merely indignant.

Harry turned onto the long, winding drive under the sign marked "Arrivals," weaving from lane to lane among the slow, purposeful buses and taxicabs that rolled forward in vast, docile herds toward the terminal.

As Harry approached the first cutoff on the left, Emma said, "The car is a problem." Harry danced the car across one lane, then another, then swung the car up into the cutoff and up the ramp into the parking structure. He pulled a ticket from the automatic dispenser, already gliding under the gate as it rose to admit him, and dropped the ticket on the seat beside him. He turned into the first empty space, and switched off the engine.

"Now for the fun part," he said, brushing the stray shock of sandy hair out of his eyes. "Haven't you got better shoes than that?"

Emma studied his face. It bore the same expression of alarmed concern that he used in the days when he was selling bogus credit-card insurance, only now the expression must be sincere. There was something surrealistic about using your face and your capacity to express emotion to rob people. At the end of it, you still had to use the same face for other things. "No, I don't," she said, and got out of the car.

Harry came around the rear of the car and took the briefcase in one hand, and Emma's arm in the other. "It's a good thing we're going on vacation. This is the worst bail-out we've ever done." He hurried Emma to the elevator, pushed the button, and pulled her inside.

"I didn't plan it this way," said Emma. "If you'll remember, I was dressed to go out to dinner, not out of the country."

"That's the problem. We didn't plan it at all. No tickets, no clothes, no guns, no—"

"Guns?" she said. "Guns, Harry? Maybe it's time to quit."

"Well, they might have gotten us to the damned airport without having to drive like a lunatic. People would have a lot better chance if I were shooting at them than aiming that Caddy at the space between them."

The door slid open, and an elderly man pushed a large blue suitcase halfway into the elevator. "Excuse us," said Harry, and stepped past it with difficulty. The man paid no attention to Harry and Emma, so engrossed was he in pushing his two other suitcases into the elevator. The automatic door began to close, then hit the blue suitcase and opened again, then began a series of peristaltic twitches against the heavy immobile obstacle.

Harry and Emma entered the international terminal and scanned the crowds as they moved to the ticket counters.

Suddenly Harry grasped Emma's arm and steered her in a graceful arc, then released her as her slow trajectory propelled her out the side door.

Harry hurried Emma down the sidewalk, past travelers who emerged from the baggage area and stared expectantly for a moment, then set their suitcases on the pavement while they tried to formulate plans that would end in their not having to lift the heavy luggage again.

"Did he see us?" asked Harry.

"I don't know. I didn't see him," said Emma.

"Come on. Let's get with the program. Are you sure something didn't hit you?" He looked down at the back of her coat. "Nope. It's probably just shock."

They hurried across the street with a group of freed passengers carrying suitcases, then skirted the fenced parking structure to the other side of the loop. Harry paused, standing behind a pole, and then peered across the drive and up it at the approaching traffic. Then they dodged between two cars, rushed into the wake of a passing bus, and slipped into the American Airlines terminal.

In the gigantic foyer they moved to the pair of television screens marked "Arrivals" and "Departures." Harry said, "It looks like Cleveland is first, then Miami, then Chicago. Three should be enough."

"I'll buy the Cleveland tickets and meet you in the gift shop," she said.

Harry moved to the ticket counter and stood in the line of people, stepping forward a pace each time someone turned away from the counter, but always scanning the people who entered through the glass doors that ran the length of the huge room, until at last his turn came. He bought two tickets to Miami. As the ticket man looked up to establish eye contact with the next person in line, Harry said, "And two for Chicago." The man looked confused, but Harry added, "My in-laws. What can I say? They grew up there, and they hate Miami."

"Yes, sir. Names?"

"Mr. and Mrs. Millikan."

Harry glanced at the gift-shop window a hundred feet away. He could see Emma standing in front of a row of salt and pepper shakers in the shape of movie cameras, pretending to look at them while she kept watch. Harry felt a barely perceptible tightness in his chest, and decided he wouldn't allow it to go on long enough to develop into an attack of guilt.

Harry slipped his tickets into the inside pocket of his jacket as he strolled toward the gift shop and nodded to Emma through the window. As she joined him on the open floor, she saw two men walk through the doorway on the end of the room near the hall that led to the departure gates. "I see them," said Harry. "It's Benny Costa and that big guy that never says anything except 'How you doin'?' "

"Were they the ones in the other terminal?"

"No. They're not just going around checking. He's got men watching all the terminals." Harry stepped into the alcove beside the gift shop and whispered. "He's out there himself, sitting in the dark somewhere, waiting. I can feel him."

"Maybe this is where he eats," said Emma.

Harry glared at her, then flicked his eyes to his wristwatch. "We've got about five minutes before the Cleveland flight. We've got to get past them and onto that plane."

Emma opened her purse and looked at the ticket folder. "Gate Eighty-nine."

Harry and Emma looked at each other, then turned and walked quickly across the floor to the little wooden archway where men and women in identical suits like those of waiters operated metal detectors. Harry and Emma stepped under the arch, and joined the stream of passengers moving down the hallway. Emma could see the people beginning to form a line to Gate 89, and she took a step toward them, but Harry jerked her back. "It's not going to be that easy."

"It's already not that easy," she said. "You keep grabbing me." She followed him to the waiting area, then around to the corner of the wall, where Harry leaned out to peek back up the hallway. Benny Costa was approaching the barrier of the metal detector. He stopped, studied the operation for a second, then walked to the right and out of sight.

"Costa is going to come in here after us," said Harry. "He's getting rid of his gun."

Harry pulled Emma out into the hallway, then back past

the checkpoint. "Are you sure this is a good idea?" she asked.

Harry moved on in the direction he'd seen Benny Costa take. They passed a men's room, and Harry moved to the next alcove beyond it and waited. He counted to twenty, then cautiously looked down the hall. He could see Benny Costa walking toward the metal detectors. Harry stepped forward toward the men's room, but this time Emma jerked him back. "You're not going in there for that gun.

"I know right where it is," he said. "There's no place to put it but the trash."

"Come on," she said. "We can just make the Miami flight."

Harry hesitated, then followed her. They ran along the hallway and down an escalator, then across the foyer and up another escalator. When they reached Gate 22, the new crowd was already filing into the tunnel to the airplane.

As they joined the line of passengers, Harry turned to Emma. "It's kind of strange, isn't it? You walk through the door into this sort of dark, carpeted, winding tube, and that's the end of you."

The man in front of Harry turned around, frowning. "Please."

"I mean in the good sense," Harry assured him. "Not literally." He let the man get a few paces ahead before he started to walk. He said to Emma, "It's true. It feels like you're going to come out of the cave and discover America or something."

Emma buckled her seat belt and watched Harry stand up to put his coat in the overhead compartment. His eyes flicked toward the rear of the airplane, scanning the seats for a face he knew. He lingered, folding his coat, then looking dissatisfied and folding it again as he watched the stewardess greeting the passengers at the doorway. Finally a man outside swung the big hatch shut and latched it, and Harry sat down.

"We're still a few steps ahead of them," he whispered. "If they didn't see us leave, it could take them some time to get this far."

Emma's eyes closed, then half-opened. "It'll take them about an hour."

"If everybody who wants us dead stays an hour behind us, that's a pretty good life," said Harry. "We're in terrific shape." He let his eyes drop toward the suitcase under his seat and grinned.

"What are we going to do when we get to Miami?"

He considered the question. "Well, I don't see Miami as a final destination, do you?"

"Not if you put it that way."

"I think we have the funds to go somewhere better. In fact, we've got enough, when you think about it, to live like royalty in some places—places where the Fat Man isn't likely to stumble on us as he goes out one day to pillage and plunder."

Emma looked at Harry in amusement. "Live like royalty? Harry, we've only got five hundred thousand." Then her amusement turned to alarm. "Oh-oh. We're talking Third World, aren't we?"

Harry put his hand on her arm. "We're talking about places where people go on vacations."

"Harry," she said. "There is no place so benighted and godforsaken that some moron won't go there on vacation. People could be living in an open sewer and swallowing dirt to stop the hunger, and there'd be a couple from Larchmont wearing comfortable shoes there to take pictures of them."

Harry patted her arm. "Come on, baby. We've been through everything together over the last ten years. This is nothing. We've been to hell and back."

"Not back," said Emma. Then she saw his face muscles slacken, and the energy seemed to go out of him. He leaned back in his seat and brushed the long strands of unruly sand-colored hair back off his forehead wearily. She added, "I didn't say I haven't enjoyed it," and Harry's smile returned too quickly, as though a shutter had clicked and now there was another picture. Harry was always Harry, she reminded herself.

Harry studied Emma. She was a miracle. The bright, clear green eyes seemed to glow with unquestioning love and admiration as she stared at him, her smooth white brow completely untroubled. Her skin was like fresh milk and the dark chestnut hair seemed to flow down from her head in shining rivulets that tried to caress her beautiful face before they rested on her shoulders.

He'd met her at college. He always told people that much, and although it wasn't true, it wasn't exactly a lie. In fact, he had been in Virginia trying to sell the semiliterate scion of a rich Tidewater family named Bradleigh a bogus early-eighteenth-century letter in which the first Duke of Marlborough gave an early Bradleigh title to a small estate in gratitude for saving his life in the War of the Spanish Succession. Emma had been a promising graduate student in the English Department at UCLA. She'd been spending the summer in Washington so she could do some research in the Folger Shakespeare Library. She'd tried at first to support herself by tutoring, then posted a notice on a bulletin board offering services in research and typing, which she later admitted to Harry was an encoded offer to write term papers for dull undergraduates at Georgetown. Since she was so far from home, her first step into crime seemed somehow beyond a geographical statute of limitations, like things the British colonizers did in India. But Mr. Bradleigh came one day to ask that the staff of the library authenticate Harry's bogus letter, and noticed Emma's little index card posted on the board by the door. When he spotted the offer of "research," he saw it as a godsend. He had been dreading the fees that rare-book experts might charge, but he couldn't afford to let the matter rest. His own investigation, subtly directed by Harry, had shown him that the "small estate" had been small only by the standards of the Duke of Marlborough, and had had a nearby city grow up to swallow it since then, and the city was called London. Mr. Bradleigh had no clear idea of how to proceed, but Harry had set the hook. Bradleigh's imagination had now galloped from the simple vain wish to prove he had ancestors to a lust to reclaim their diverted millions and their usurped titles. He called the number on the index card and hired this young female graduate student to begin the lengthy and tedious bookwork that would eventually make him the Duke of Something-or-Other.

Harry had orchestrated this particular scheme a number of times in different parts of the country, and had found it an easy way to pick up a bit of money. Generally people who came from families with this kind of pretension were educated in very old prep schools with a great store of tradition but rather lackadaisical instruction, followed by some time served in universities sufficiently well established to be able to tolerate a few inmates whose only talents were dressing well and drinking a great deal without getting unruly. Such people tended to grow up overconfident about their ability to evaluate something as simple as a holograph document from another century, and its historical, legal, and sociological implications. Harry had also counted on the fact that such people are usually unaccustomed to doing much actual work, so they tended to pay him off and send him on his way long before they'd progressed far enough in their studies to discover they'd been fooled by a blatant forgery. Upon making this discovery, some of them tore up the letter and pretended the whole thing never happened, while the others had the letter framed, knowing that their friends were no more qualified to dispute its authenticity than they had been to prove it, but so far none of Harry's victims had caused Harry any embarrassment.

But this time, when Harry went to deliver the forged letter and receive his hefty reward, Mr. Bradleigh was not alone in the drawing room of the former plantation where he lived. There was with him a beautiful young graduate student with bright, predatory green eyes and chestnut hair, who took up the letter with exaggerated care, put on a pair of tortoiseshell eyeglasses she didn't need, and pronounced the document genuine. She would, she announced, begin the authentication process immediately. But since all the necessary supporting documents were housed in England, she'd need the sum of twenty-five thousand dollars to fly there and begin her work.

In those first moments, Harry had recognized a kindred spirit and fallen in love with her. He had followed her to her apartment, and they'd come to an understanding that had unaccountably shaded off into a honeymoon in England that had lasted nearly a year and cost them only an occasional letter to Mr. Bradleigh. It might have lasted much longer, if Harry hadn't watched a Granada Television broadcast of the American series *Dallas,* and been inspired to suggest to a British banker that he might be heir to a Texas oil fortune by virtue of a Mexican land grant.

But in a sense, Harry had met Emma in college, so when he told people that, he often felt he wasn't really lying and could say it with more than his usual conviction. He looked at Emma, who had turned away to stare out the airplane window at the lights that already were beginning to flash past, faster and faster as the plane began to lighten and lift off. "Don't worry," he said. "We're on our way to someplace interesting: 'The Land of Adventure,' they call it."

"Where's that?" she asked.

"Damned if I know."

She almost hoped he was telling the truth. The place didn't much matter, as long as all the people who wanted them both so badly they probably had dreams about them were looking somewhere else. There must be hundreds of people by now, all demanding each night that Harry and Emma make a visit to their dreams. There must be some price for that, she thought, some price she paid in her own sleep, so that she woke up a little tired each morning, drained of energy by all of those visits.

Emma watched Harry as he settled back in his seat and closed his eyes. As always, Harry would be able to sleep. His thin sand-colored hair would begin to fall onto his high forehead in a moment, and then he'd sleep blissfully until a few minutes outside of Miami, when he'd sit up, perfectly rested. She envied him for that, and couldn't help wondering how Harry had gotten to be Harry. It occurred to her again that Harry might not even be the name he'd been born with, as Erskine almost certainly wasn't. His name had probably been taken as Harry took everything he needed, from someone who would probably never notice the theft. But it might not have been stolen: his name, and therefore hers, might well be one of the things he created one day out of nothing.

2

Eighteen Hours

MIAMI

Harry and Emma walked along the deserted docks, looking at the boats tied in the marina. The sun had already set, and a few yacht owners were sitting in lawn chairs on the decks of their craft, drinking various concoctions and watching paid crewmen hosing seawater and fish guts into the harbor.

Emma said, "I feel a little out of place. What are we looking for that we haven't already seen?"

"The right kind of boat," said Harry. "It's got to be big enough to get us someplace safe. And it can't belong to some retired realtor."

"It'll be dark soon," said Emma.

"That won't matter to the boat I'm looking for."

"It'll matter plenty if my heel goes through one of the cracks between these boards."

Harry stopped suddenly and pointed at an old schooner moored nearby. "That's the sort of thing." At the stern of the schooner, he could see that once there had been a name, but at some point it had been painted over. Lower down was the home port, "Kingston."

The hull was white, but it had obviously seen some hard service since it had last been overhauled. There were black, oily streaks that streamed from the scuppers to the waterline, and even the ropes that held it to the dock looked frayed and dirty. Emma frowned. "It's just about the worst-looking boat for miles. And it's a sailboat. We've got to get out of here faster than five miles an hour.''

Harry walked toward the boat, almost hypnotized. As he approached, the cabin door closed, and a small ray of electric light appeared on the deck from a crack beside the top hinge.

Harry stood at the edge of the dock and called, ''Hello.''

There was a rustling inside, but nobody appeared on deck. ''Hello,'' he called again. Then he bent over and knocked on the deck.

The cabin door opened, and a small, dark man appeared. He had coarse, straight black hair that seemed to flare out as though he'd just come in from the wind, and large Oriental eyes set on a broad, flat face. ''I thought I heard something,'' he said. ''You lost?''

''No,'' said Harry. ''We wondered about hiring your boat for a trip.''

The man chuckled, but the only sound that came from him was a series of shallow breaths. ''Sorry,'' he said. ''I don't do charters. And I'm leaving tonight for Jamaica. Tomorrow morning go to those slips over there by that building.'' He pointed, but Harry didn't turn his head to see what he was pointing at. Then the man looked at Harry's sport coat. ''And wear something''—he hesitated—''something old.'' He turned away to go into his cabin, but then he realized that Harry had stepped onto his deck.

''It's important that we go to Jamaica with you,'' said Harry. ''I'll give you ten thousand for the trip. Cash.''

The man's eyes narrowed. ''Are the police after you?''

''No,'' said Harry. He stared over the man's shoulder, and saw something in the cabin. ''If you leave that door open, they'll be after you. I just hate Miami.''

The man stepped to the door and closed it, then said, ''So you're not cops.''

''No,'' said Harry. ''And I'll raise the price to twelve thousand if you'll get us out of here now.''

The man looked at them for a moment. ''After you help the lady aboard and cast off the lines, go into the cabin and make yourselves comfortable. I'd rather not have you on deck until we're out of sight.''

Harry helped Emma onto the deck, pulled the stern line free, and went to join her in the cabin. As Harry opened the door, he saw Emma sitting on a bunk, looking around her. The cabin was spacious, but was furnished with only a table and two chairs, and two bunks built like shelves into the wall. There was a small, bare electric light bulb that dimmed for a second as the man on deck started the engine, then brightened again to reveal what Emma was looking at. What Harry had seen before had been only a sample. The whole cabin was packed with identical cartons covered with red lettering that said "SONY TRINITRON" and "THIS END UP."

"Interesting," said Emma. "I think there's something in the Girl Scout manual that says 'Don't go anywhere with a man who has more than twenty television sets.'" They both felt the vessel sway a little as it left the calm, dead water of the harbor. Emma added, "Of course, when the ship has sailed, make the best of it until you throw up."

Harry opened the suitcase and counted out twelve thousand dollars onto the wool army blanket on the bunk.

"What are you doing?" asked Emma. "What's he going to do with money out here?"

"If we get stopped, they'll take it anyway. I'd rather they took his money." He closed the suitcase and put it under the bunk. As he did, the engine died, and they could hear the water rushing against the hull of the schooner as the wind caught the sails.

Harry opened the cabin door. "Is it okay to come out yet?"

"Sure," said the man. "It's just when we're leaving the harbor. By now they can't tell if you're Bigfoot or the Prince of Wales."

Harry stepped onto the deck. The lights of Miami were beginning to come on, but they were already fading into the hazy distance. "My name is Harry Erskine. This is my wife, Emma."

The man shook his hand, but kept his eyes forward. "I'm Lord Carnarvon. And I already know it's a funny name."

Harry said, "Can you make much money smuggling television sets?"

"I get by. I bring cigarettes and liquor in from duty-free ports, and take out whatever I can pick up that's the right temperature. What about you?"

"We're the right temperature."

"How did you absorb the heat?"

"Don't worry," said Harry. "Once we're away from the mainland, we're not a liability. We've done a lot of things—sold franchises, mail-order self-help kits, that kind of thing. We made the mistake of allowing someone to invest quite a bit of capital in an idea we had. Our accounting systems differed."

"I see," said Lord Carnarvon thoughtfully.

"Here's the cash," said Harry, holding a thick stack of bills out to Lord Carnarvon.

Lord Carnarvon took the money and stuffed it into the pockets of his shirt, his jacket, and his jeans. "Thanks. It'll keep me warm when the breeze kicks up."

Harry looked out into the darkness before them, then a chill seemed to lodge itself between two disks in his spine. "Where's your compass?"

"There's one in the cabin. Help yourself."

"Not for me to look at. For you. How the hell can you tell where you're going?"

"I don't have to tell where I'm going. I just go there."

"How do you do that?"

"I'm a Carib."

"You're pulling my leg, aren't you?"

"No."

Harry thought for a moment. "Why do you have a compass at all? And maps . . . there are maps in there too."

"In case I have to tell anybody where I've been."

Harry stood beside him and tried to follow the angle of Lord Carnarvon's eyes to the place where he seemed to be looking. But there was nothing but deep, unending, unvaried black. Harry patted his arm in a friendly way. "Keep up the good work." He moved into the cabin, and studied Emma, who was lying on the bunk, her eyes closed for the first time in thirty hours. Thank God she hadn't heard.

It was well after midnight when Lord Carnarvon set the wheel and stepped into the cabin. Emma was asleep on the bottom bunk, but Harry was sitting at the table, staring at a large nautical map. Lord Carnarvon could see there were several others that Harry must have studied before he set them neatly aside on the top bunk. When Harry heard him come in, he looked up with glazed, eager eyes like a man who has just come up from under water. Harry said quietly, "I can hardly wait until Emma wakes up. I just had an idea that's going to make us all rich."

Lord Carnarvon sat in the rare-book room of the Jamaica Institute and watched as Mr. Baines, the curator, walked quietly in and set two more ancient leather-bound books on the table beside Harry, then looked down at him for a moment. Mr. Baines's eyes expressed a sad longing, a terrible, suppressed wish to be allowed to speak, but Harry didn't seem to notice him. Mr. Baines turned on his heel and walked toward the door. As he opened it to go, Harry looked up. "Thanks, Mr. Baines," he called.

"You're welcome, Mr. Erskine," said Mr. Baines eagerly. "I believe you've nearly exhausted our collection, but I'll keep searching the catalogues. Perhaps if—"

"Thanks," said Harry. "Anything you've got."

Baines subsided into his customary resignation, went out, and closed the door behind him.

Lord Carnarvon opened one of the big books. It smelled like dust combined with some stale crackers he'd left in the cabin of his schooner once, and had ended up eating late one night after they'd gotten soft from the sea air. The leather binding was flaking into an orange dust at the edges, and the paper shaded into darker beige as it neared the margins. But he could recognize the crude hand-drawn representations of places he knew as he looked at the ornate old maps. They were seamen's charts of the western Caribbean, complete with shoals and forgotten wrecks and the carefully noted sites of fierce battles between navies whose own descendants probably didn't know they'd ever been there. "He wants to play too," said Lord Carnarvon.

Harry looked up from his book, puzzled.

"Mr. Baines," said Lord Carnarvon. "He thinks we're

looking for a treasure ship on the reefs. He's bored sitting in this place all day, and we're driving him crazy by not telling him what we're after."

Harry frowned. "What kind of idiot looks for sunken treasure ships?"

Lord Carnarvon shrugged. "The guy who found the *Atocha* and hauled up a couple of billion dollars in gold ingots."

"If it makes you feel better, tell Baines we're looking for the Seven Cities of Cibola." Harry looked at his book again.

Lord Carnarvon leaned back in his chair, propped his feet on the table, and closed his eyes. He'd been at this now for nearly a week, and had missed the chance to deliver a load of duty-free malt Scotch to Miami in that time. Harry and Emma had made up the money, but he'd still paid a price by spending the week on land and indoors, answering questions about weather and currents, shipping routes, and the many kinds of people who lived on the sea.

Lord Carnarvon opened his eyes for a moment and they settled on a glass-fronted bookcase across the room. The furniture in this museum reminded him of the polished wooden fixtures of a Frenchman's yacht he'd once manned on the Petit Cul-de-Sac Marin off the head of the butterfly-shaped island of Guadeloupe. That was where he'd learned about polish. He'd learned to polish the woodwork until the captain could hold a ruler next to it and read the ten-centimeter mark in the reflection, and he'd spent the rest of the time polishing himself. He'd honed the French patois he'd learned on the Carib reservation of Dominica into a language the Parisians who came to stay on the yacht would admit they understood. And then he'd gotten tired of the polish and gone home.

But the life on the island of Dominica was dull. When the Frenchmen on the yacht had said they were bored, their ennui had nothing to do with the despair he felt in the Carib village he returned to at the age of nineteen. He felt a sense that things were as they had been for a hundred years before he was born, and as they would be a hundred years after he died. There was no chance that anything interesting could ever happen to him or to anyone he would ever meet. They would all fish, and harvest bananas, coconuts, or oranges. Then one day they'd get too old to work, and stay home until they died. He decided he had to gamble on a fate that he hadn't already witnessed.

Since in those days Dominica was still one of the remaining crumbs of the dismantled British Empire, he had little trouble making his way from one place to another. He'd gone first to the British Virgin Islands, then to Bermuda. In Bermuda he found work on a cruise ship returning passengers to Canada. When he arrived in Canada, tired of another month of polishing wood and brass, he jumped ship and stayed.

Lord Carnarvon immediately learned that he had no legal right to be where he was, and that he couldn't use his own name. But he also learned that in Quebec they spoke both French and English, as Dominicans did, and that if he told people he was an Ojibway Indian they seemed satisfied and stopped asking him questions he couldn't answer.

In Montreal he found work as a busboy in a coffee shop where they also sold books and where a blond lady came twice a week to play the harp while people ate their pastries. He loved the great, sophisticated city, with all its strangers constantly moving from place to place creating an impression that important activities were afoot. There he greatly enlarged his familiarity with serious books, learned to speak with urban North Americans, and had joyous, lighthearted sexual intercourse with the lady who played the harp. He had won the friendship of the lady, whose name was Hélène pronounced Elaine, by telling her who he really was and agreeing with her when she expressed her distaste for the shoddy record compiled by the British imperialists in the Western Hemisphere.

She introduced him to other people who mistakenly took him for a fine example of whatever they considered themselves to be, on similarly scant grounds. Among them had been the Couvrier brothers, two young men who smuggled things in and out of the United States for reasons which had something to do with radical Canadian politics. Lord Carnarvon never really understood the intellectual implications of their acts of defiance, but noticed that they were making more money than he was, and eagerly apprenticed himself to their trade.

His satisfaction with this new life had lasted only until the middle of the winter, when the harpist moved to Vancouver to play in a hotel restaurant, the Couvrier brothers were arrested for putting an explosive device in a mailbox in Ottawa, and Lord Carnarvon found himself hospitalized with pneumonia. It amazed him that in a few short months the green glory of the Montreal summer had turned to an iron, pitiless cold that pierced the seams of his clothes and clapped his chest so he couldn't breathe. He had known before he'd come that Montreal was cold, but he hadn't fathomed what that really meant: that it was not just a place with an unpleasant climate, but a place where a man would die if he simply stayed outdoors from one dawn to the next. On the evidence that so many people seemed to live there, he had erroneously assumed that the place was inhabitable.

When he left the hospital he still had a little money. He decided he had a choice of flying home, or keeping what he had. So he used his skills as a smuggler to work his way south. His first accomplishment was to smuggle himself and a hundred boxes of Cuban cigars across the Rainbow Bridge at Niagara Falls, and sell them in the parking lot of the Trap and Skeet Club in Buffalo to a trio of sportsmen who included the owner of a chain of restaurants, a famous orthodontist, and a minor politician. Supplementing his tolerance for manual labor with a talent for sensing an opportunity for profit, he arrived in Miami in the spring with enough money to buy a boat and join in the thriving tropical smuggling trade. He had, over the years, met thieves and confidence tricksters without number, but he felt instinctively that there was something special about Harry and Emma. To him they smelled like luck.

Suddenly he felt something touch his arm, and he opened his eyes. The light had changed, so he knew he'd been asleep. He looked around, and saw Emma sitting in the chair beside him.

"Sorry to wake you," she said. "We're finished here."

"How does it look?" he asked.

"Harry's satisfied. It looks as though we're going to be rich."

"When do we start being rich?"

"That's something we've got to talk to you about," said Harry. He was standing on the other side of the room looking out the window at the fading afternoon sun. "We need some help with the next phase, and you strike me as the kind of man who might know the kind of man we need."

"What kind of man are you talking about?" asked Lord Carnarvon. "A money man, a seaman, a banana farmer, a diver, a mechanic? What?"

Emma knitted her brows, then said, "Well, the kind of man who, when he says, 'Do what I say or I'll kill you,' people will do what he says, or he'll kill them."

3

Two Weeks

KINGSTON

John Vickers stood alone in his room in the Cane Palace Hotel. He had done his two hundred sit-ups and his two hundred pushups, and walked down the creaking corridor to stand under the tepid, rusty trickle of the communal shower. Now he was dressed again, and it was time to perform the ritual of cleaning and oiling the Browning P-35 Hi-Power nine-millimeter pistol he kept wrapped in a cloth under the spare pillow of his bed.

He sat on the bed and heard the familiar click of the chain-link springs, but right after it he heard the rap on the door. His hand completed the motion of reaching under the pillow, touched the heavy piece of metal, and then withdrew. Vickers stood up and opened the door.

In the hallway stood a tall, heavyset man with a dark, bushy mustache and close-cropped hair. If Vickers had needed to find him, he'd have said he looked like an American football player. It had been years since he'd seen McManus in a suit, or in anything but the tailored, heavily starched fatigues he affected even in settlements fifty miles from the sound of gunfire. He decided the suit was no improvement. McManus wore it with the same look of an animal dressed in human clothing and about to tear his way out of it. "Hello, Mike," said Vickers. "I figured we'd run into one another soon.

"Good," said McManus. "I wouldn't put anything big together without giving my old friends a shot at it. I want you, and maybe Chinese Gordon, if he can pull himself together and soldier without running a card game."

"I don't think I want to go back to Africa just yet," said Vickers. "I thought it over when I heard you were looking for people. I like Jamaica."

"What rank did you carry last time out? Major?"

"Colonel. Last two times out."

"I think I can get you brigadier. You'll be in command of a regiment of rangers. You train them yourself. We've got six, eight months. The men are waiting just over the border in established bases. Morale is high, and they can't wait to get back in."

"I read the papers. They're not eager, they're hungry. And those aren't bases, they're refugee camps. Who do you think you're talking to?"

"It's a good job. The place is loaded with valuable minerals. Silenium, titanium, semiprecious stones, petroleum, all right under the topsoil and ready to go. And they haven't been able to market any of it since the troubles started. We stroll in and accept the gratitude of the provisional government, and fly out. We hold on to the key players until they're sufficiently grateful, of course."

"No."

"Why not?"

"I'm thinking of retiring."

"Don't give me that. You haven't worked since Chad. You're living in this fleabag hotel in the worst part of Kingston and you're two months behind in your rent. The manager tried to sell me your suitcase."

"He's acting as my agent."

"You signed with the other side, didn't you? The government hired you."

"No. I'm staying out of this one."

"Why?"

"You, Mike. You're wearing a five-thousand-dollar wristwatch."

McManus slipped the expansion band over his beefy fist and waved it at Vickers. "I'll give it to you. Here."

"I don't want your watch," said Vickers. "Somebody gave you money to set this up, and you're already looting the fund. You're offering a quick jab over the border with rangers because you haven't set up a resupply system."

"We'll live off the land. The peasants are pissed off at the government and they'll—"

"Peasants don't have nine-millimeter ammo, Mike, and you can't live off the land in a country that's been at war for two years. The crops didn't get planted this spring. In eight months they'll be digging roots."

"You're a soldier, Vickers. You can't sit here forever in some dump waiting for your investments to pay off. You're almost out of money, and when you are, Jamaica will deport you. Canada's not planning any wars at the moment, even if they would have you back."

"I'll manage," said Vickers. "If you're going to find yourself some fresh meat, you'd better get out of here and start looking."

McManus started to say something, but the futility of it seemed to settle on him. He took a business card out of his pocket and placed it on the old, nicked dresser, then went out, closing the door behind him.

The Cane Palace was an ancient wooden hotel with an ornate white facade that created the impression of some grand and illusionary aspiration of a long-dead proprietor who'd let his false premonitions of growth and prosperity take visible form. Harry and Emma followed Lord Carnarvon between two baroque half-columns that were bolted on both sides of the ten-foot doorway. At some point the columns had begun to crack and splinter, and since then spikes had been driven in to pin the pieces together in only an approximation of their original shape.

In the lobby they followed Lord Carnarvon's white shirt through the sun-bereft gloom, straining their eyes to detect possible obstacles that might loom up suddenly from the tile floor.

As Emma's eyes adjusted to the light, she saw Lord Carnarvon disappear into another portal at the end of the lobby. It was still darker, like a cave, and had a damp, rank smell that owed something to cigarettes and something to spilled beer, and as she lifted her foot to take a second step into the tunnel, it first resisted and then gave an audible, sticky crack as it came off the floor.

At the end of the little corridor, Lord Carnarvon turned left, and when Emma followed, she entered a room that was bright, with sunlight streaming through tall, old-fashioned windows with open tops, and a big arch opening to a patio. Lord Carnarvon sat down at a table with his back to the wall, and she and Harry joined him. Only when she was in the chair did she look around her. There was an old mahogany bar, with hundreds of liquor bottles lining the wall behind it in six tiers that reached to the ceiling. On cabinets in the corners of the room were glass cases, unlit and in shadows. She peered at the nearest until she realized that what she was looking at was a display of stuffed baby alligators arranged with perverse precision to look like a tiny orchestra from the big-band era. The little alligators were propped up behind podiums, holding little trombones and clarinets to their snouts with their claws, and there was even a bandleader in white sport coat and wire-rimmed spectacles, the leathery skin stretched back above his teeth to approximate someone's idea of a swing-era smile. She shuddered, and looked the other way.

In that direction there were two large young men who wore tight white T-shirts with the sleeves rolled up as though to relieve the pressure on their biceps. They seemed to divide their time between playing cards and drinking boilermakers. As she glanced in their direction, one of them leaned his head back to gulp down a shot, and under his close-cropped hair she could see a roll of skin form at the base of his skull, then disappear as he tapped his shot glass down on the table. When his companion nodded, Emma realized that the drinking had something to do with the card game, but the rules weren't comprehensible to an observer.

"Is he here?" asked Harry.

Lord Carnarvon shook his head, and Emma felt relieved. Lord Carnarvon added, "He's on vacation, sort of. He doesn't keep regular hours."

Harry glanced at a large table on the patio, where three men, one black and the others white, sat drinking what looked like screwdrivers. Each had his feet up on the chair across from him, and from time to time they closed their eyes and held their faces up to the sun. "You know anybody else in here?"

Lord Carnarvon's eyelids lowered as he nodded. "Wait for Vickers. He's the one you want to talk to. It'll be easier if we have some margaritas."

Lord Carnarvon caught Emma's sidelong glance at Harry and protested, "You need the salt in this climate." He got up and walked to the bar, and talked to the old black bartender, then returned with three bulbous glasses on a tray. "The waitress quit," he said. Then, under his breath he added, "They tip big when they're drunk, but she had to work like hell to get them that far gone, and then she had to get them to leave."

They lifted their glasses, and Lord Carnarvon took a sip, then quickly set his on the table. "There he is."

Emma half-turned to see a tall, rangy blond man at the bar. He wore jeans and a plain blue oxford shirt with short sleeves. He accepted a draft beer from the bartender and turned to walk toward a table in the darkest corner of the room beside one of the hideous glass cases. She could see that his face and arms were a reddish brown that looked like a permanent sunburn. There were wrinkles around his pale eyes, as though he spent a great deal of time squinting. The wrinkles accentuated the sharpness of his features, and Emma decided that if he lived to be fifty, he'd look as though he'd been carved out of wood.

Vickers sat at his table, sipping his beer and staring at the little glass box beside him. Inside it were thirteen little stuffed alligators arranged at a table in the positions of the figures in *The Last Supper.* He studied the glass box and considered the man who had spent hundreds of hours doing this. There was terrific premeditation, and relentless persistence, employed in a cause that made no sense.

He glanced away from it, and spotted Lord Carnarvon emerging from the gloom across the saloon and coming toward him. He smiled and pushed a chair out with his foot.

Lord Carnarvon stopped and grasped the chair-back, but made no move to sit. "Vickers," he said. "See those people at that table over there?"

Vickers looked. There were a man and woman in their thirties, obviously together and probably married. The woman lived somewhere in the borderlands between being merely pretty and being strikingly beautiful, but in this light he couldn't decide which he would call it. She had obviously made some kind of decision herself, as women who worked for a living often did. She didn't dress as though she wanted to be stared at. The man with her had a friendly, open, wholesome face, as some doctors had. "Who are they?"

"They're Harry and Emma Erskine. I want you to talk to them."

"What are they?"

"I guess you'd have to call them investors, or something like that."

"What do they want?"

"Come listen to them," said Lord Carnarvon. "They've got a plan, Vickers. It's going to make us all millionaires. You've got to hear these people talk."

"Oh, Jesus, L. C. I'm having a bad day."

"Ten minutes. Give them ten minutes." He paused, as though calculating. "Listen to them for their whole pitch and they'll pay your bar bill."

Vickers chuckled. "You don't know what you're saying."

Lord Carnarvon leaned forward and said in almost a whisper, "They've already paid me twelve thousand in cash."

Vickers sat back in his chair, his eyes on Harry Erskine. Harry moved his hands only from the wrists, his forearms resting on the table as though he were attempting to keep himself from using all of his power to invoke his vision, because there wasn't enough room in the bar to hold it.

"Imagine yourself sitting on an island," said Harry. "A Caribbean island with long, beautiful white beaches and—" He hesitated, and asked, "Do you like girls?"

"Of course I like girls," said Vickers irritably.

"Then there on the beach are hundreds of fantastic, smooth-skinned young women of all shapes, sizes, and colors, there on the beach wondering if anything exciting is going to happen to them during this vacation.'' Harry paused and watched Vickers.

''Well?'' said Vickers. ''Is anything exciting going to happen?''

''That could be up to you. In fact, the whole idea, the beaches, everything, can vanish like so many bubbles in a tonic, or you can be there.''

Vickers looked at Lord Carnarvon, his face beginning to set itself in a cold, rigid expression. His eyes narrowed as he turned back to Harry. ''You may have come to the wrong place to tell this particular story. As it happens, we are on a Caribbean island with long, beautiful white beaches.'' He waved his hand in dismissal. ''And the rest of it.''

Harry held up his hand, smiling. ''But it's their island, not yours. This is your fantasy we're building here.''

Vickers said to Lord Carnarvon, ''Did you tell them I don't have any money?'' He looked at Harry, and then to Emma. ''I don't have any money.''

Harry called to the bartender, ''Another round, please. We'll be over to pick it up in a minute.'' He smiled and leaned forward on his elbows. ''There. That's taken care of.''

''I mean,'' said Vickers, ''that I can't be swindled.'' Harry's face slackened, as though his feelings had been hurt, but Vickers went on. ''Not that I'm too smart or anything like that. I've been fooled and cheated lots of times, and I'm sure you're good enough to do the job. Nothing personal. I just can't invest in real estate, or unreal estates, or whatever.'' He leaned forward until his face was a foot from Harry's. ''I'm not sure yet if my clothes and I are going to check out of the hotel on the same day.''

''You've got it all wrong,'' Harry protested. ''It's not a swindle.''

Emma corrected him. ''Well, actually, it's sort of a swindle, but we came here to find out if you'd like to take part in it. We're making an offer of partnership.''

''I'm going for it,'' said Lord Carnarvon. ''They convinced me.''

Vickers' eyes were on Lord Carnarvon as he said, "In spite of that, thanks for the offer. I could use it."

Lord Carnarvon appeared to think for a moment, but then he noticed that the new drinks were standing on the bar. He stood up to retrieve them.

Harry grinned. "We'd like to leave in a day or two."

Vickers lifted his glass to them, and drank the last inch of beer. "Good luck."

Emma's eyes widened. "You mean you don't want to go with us?"

"What does it pay?"

"I offer you," said Harry, "a vision of your own gardens and beaches, sanctuary from harm—deserved or undeserved, we make no distinction—power, comfort, freedom . . . leisure, even . . . great wealth, and friendship."

"What does it pay in the numerical sense?"

"That's the beauty of it. As much as we can take," said Harry. "We are going to be the people who take high finance around the corner from science to alchemy."

"Why do you need me?"

"Our problem," said Emma, "is that we're basically weasels. We need something like a big dog to pull this off."

"Pull what off?"

"A traditional Caribbean industry."

"Raising limes?"

"We are going to take over a tiny island in the sea, and make it into a haven for tax evasion, money laundering, and generally hiding assets from the authorities, ex-wives, and all the slings and arrows that outrage fortune. We'll get very rich on the rake-off."

"What island?" asked Vickers. One of his blond eyebrows slowly arched.

"The island doesn't have a name," said Harry. "Or I suppose it does, but we don't know what the natives call it, if there are any. I've been very careful about picking the place out. It's about two hundred miles southwest of here, roughly equidistant from Jamaica and the mainland. In fact, if you go a few hundred miles in any direction you'll hit land, and most of the places you'll hit don't get along very well with the people to the left and right of them. It's in open sea, and none of the old European explorers seems to have landed there and claimed it for his inbred, syphilitic king. If we can just land and subdue the locals, it's ours.''

''How is that possible?'' Vickers said with a chuckle. ''Every inch of dry land and half the sea lanes in the world have been fought over a hundred times. Somebody owns everything.''

''Not anybody we have to worry about,'' said Lord Carnarvon. ''We just spent a week in the Jamaica Institute down on East Street looking at old maps, ships' logs, everything we could find. No country has claimed this island yet. It's not even on the maps.''

Vickers blew a breath of air out through pursed lips in a silent whistle. ''You mind telling me how you found it?''

''It was marked on a chart I bought from an old marlin fisherman a couple of years ago,'' said Lord Carnarvon. ''He used to put in lots of things in pencil: places where he'd caught marlin, uncharted reefs, but only one island. And Harry spotted it.''

Harry interrupted. ''What he meant to say was that it's not on modern, printed maps. We're living in a haphazard age. The old explorers put it on their maps. They put everything on their maps, because they never knew if some little mole on the ass of the ocean might be made of gold or have the fountain of youth or be the place where the lost tribes of Israel decided to settle down. They had no capacity for surprise because they were confident that anywhere they went, what they'd find would be bizarre. Besides, they sailed around in ships that weren't much more than a big wooden barn being blown downwind, so any land at all might either run them aground or save them from drowning.''

Vickers smiled. ''And you're sure it exists.''

''It has to,'' said Emma. ''We found it on three old maps besides the marlin fisherman's—one Spanish from the sixteenth century, and two English drawn fifty years apart two hundred years ago. These are not a bunch of old liars who swapped stories. They all had to have seen it.''

Vickers thought about it for a moment. ''It's an interesting thought, but I'm not really looking for a long-term job."

"Long-term?" Harry repeated with distaste. "Who said anything about long-term? We can't get involved in anything like that. We have things to do, places to go. What I want to do is pop in, get the place in shape for a quick sale, and get out." He pointed to Emma. "Look. This is a beautiful young woman. You think she wants to spend two or three of the best years of her life marooned on a desert island like Robinson Crusoe's girlfriend? No. She wants to dance, travel, wear strapless evening gowns. This thing will take a couple of months, six at the most."

Vickers nodded. "I turned down one job today. There might be another one along presently, but I'd better not count on it. I'll do this much: I'll take a look at the island with you, and see what we're up against. After that we can decide if it's worth the risk."

As they walked out of the dark cavern of the Cane Palace, Emma put her hand on Lord Carnarvon's chest and stopped him. "How do you know he's the one we want?"

Lord Carnarvon shrugged. "I've known him for six or seven years. He always seems to get out alive, and then later the other ones, the ones with the big cars and the bodyguards and the sunglasses, come and offer him more money to go somewhere else. That means he must be good at it."

"I just hope he's not some kind of psychotic who starts murdering people as soon as he's out of sight of a road."

Lord Carnarvon shook his head. "They wouldn't hire him a second time . . . would they?"

4

One Month

THE CARIBBEAN SEA

The warm night air seemed to flatten the black sea as though the world were compressed inside a gigantic balloon. Harry Erskine stepped back and glanced up the tall mast of the schooner at the place where it disappeared into the darkness.

Emma leaned close to him and asked, "What is it—airplanes?"

"Feel the air. It's so full of something, it's got weight. It feels tight in your chest."

"So what's up there?"

"The possibility of signs and portents. Lightning. Saint Elmo's fire. Flying fish. A dove with a sprig of parsley in its mouth."

From the dim cabin came the voice of Vickers. "I make it sixteen north, eighty west. We should be past the Rosalind Bank." There was a rapid series of clicks as Vickers loaded the rifles and laid them in a row on the bunk beside him.

The faint glow from the cabin shone upward on the dark, Carib features of Lord Carnarvon at the helm. He scowled at the invisible horizon, then leaned over the port gunwale to study the imperceptible movement of the water. "Right on the money," he announced. "Cue ball in the side pocket."

Vickers emerged from the cabin and joined Lord Carnarvon at the helm. As the tall Canadian tugged his black beret lower to cover his blond hair, his face assumed the same watchful expression as Lord Carnarvon's. "Ideal weather for a night landing."

Lord Carnarvon shrugged. "We won't drown. High humidity and low ceiling, though. They'll hear us in Jamaica."

"We'll just have to keep the noise down. We can't hit the beach with our weapons on full auto and hose down the first thing that goes bump in the night."

"No noise. I'm going to murder dozens of sleeping civilians, rape villages, eat babies, that sort of thing. But I'll be quiet about it."

On the foredeck, Emma whispered, "Why doesn't he ever sound like he's joking?"

Harry smiled. "There's no reason to believe anybody lives there. You know that."

Lord Carnarvon raised his head and called, "Land ho, I regret to say. Three points off the starboard bow, coming at you like a bad dream courtesy of ancient Carib know-how."

"I don't see anything," said Vickers.

"Neither do I." Lord Carnarvon winced. "But I sure smell it."

"What are you talking about?" asked Harry. He moved to the bow of the schooner and stared into the darkness. After a few seconds he said, "Wait. I can hear waves. It must be the beach. Cut the engine."

Vickers wrinkled his nose. "I smell it too." He sniffed the air with flared nostrils. "I say if anyone lives there we find him and kill him. Only decent thing to do."

Lord Carnarvon shook his head. "I'll shoot him, but I'm not going to eat him. Filthy bugger."

Emma said, "You said it would be an unspoiled island paradise, Harry. It smells like a cow pasture."

"Relax, everybody," Harry said. "It's low tide. Of course it's a little fishy. Malibu smells a little at low tide. St. Tropez smells a little. Once we're set up we'll take care of it."

"How, Harry?" demanded Emma.

"Same way they do. With money. L.C., how close would you say we are?"

"A quarter of a mile, maybe a little more. There's some chop to the surface ahead, though. It looks like shoals."

Vickers said, "The chart shows deep water on the leeward side."

Lord Carnarvon spun the wheel and brought the schooner about. "It's also got pictures of sea monsters on it. And the wind is a fat cherub with his cheeks puckered up."

"It's very old," said Harry. "Just get us around to the other side. The island isn't that big."

They moved slowly in a circular course, the engine throbbing over the sound of the surf. After a half-hour Vickers pointed ahead. "There. You can see the shape of it in the moonlight."

Emma studied the sight. "It reminds me of something."

"Pancakes," said Harry. "Warm, luscious, right there on the plate ready for us to gobble up."

"That's right," said Emma. "But not a stack of pancakes—just one, sort of a thin one."

"All right," said Vickers. "Let's get to it." He disappeared into the cabin and returned to hand out the rifles, first to Harry and Emma, then to Lord Carnarvon, who left his on the roof of the cabin.

Lord Carnarvon slowly moved the schooner toward the island, scanning the surface of the water as they glided on in the night. Every few minutes he would leave the wheel and lean over the side to study the water. Now the shore was closer, and he said, "Shoals to the right, shoals to the left, but Harry's luck is holding out."

"What do you mean?" asked Vickers.

"It's a natural harbor. Drop anchor anytime you get around to it."

Vickers lowered the anchor into the water carefully, as though he feared it would break. Lord Carnarvon reversed his engine to let the craft tug against the chain for a moment. "She's set," he said. "Let out fifteen feet more slack so she'll stay that way while we're having our invasion."

"It's not an invasion," said Emma.

At the stern, Harry had removed the chock from the

capstan, and was cranking the dinghy to the water. The others gathered around him. Suddenly he turned and said, "This is an historic occasion. You can feel it. The atmosphere is charged."

"You can smell it," said Vickers. "Watch those muzzles as you go over the side, now. No casualties."

Harry blocked the ladder. "Wait a second. Before we even go ashore, we should say something. We're all equal partners in this forever. No backing out, no unilateral decisions by anyone, ever. Agreed?"

"Agreed," said Vickers.

"We swear," said Lord Carnarvon. "A solemn, momentous moment." He dropped to his knees on the deck, spread his arms, and called to the sky, "Lord, for what we are about to steal, we thank you, amen."

Harry rowed the dinghy while the others sat quietly until the keel scraped on the sand and stuck. Vickers and Lord Carnarvon hauled the dinghy up onto the beach, then tied its rope to a large rock.

"Well, let's see what we've got," said Harry. The four walked up the soft sand to the low, jagged rock ledge at its border. Harry kicked at it, and asked, "What do you think? I'd say volcanic, with some overlay of coral."

"I'd say a million years of bird shit," Lord Carnarvon answered, "with a beach of kitty litter."

"Watch your feet. It's slippery in places," said Vickers.

The four stepped up to the rock shelf and fanned slowly out from the beach to walk inland. Harry moved in a straight path, counting his paces: "Three hundred and one, two, three, four . . ." The moon was high now, and they could see that the flat rock shell stretched from the windward end of the island to where they stood. There was not a tree or bush, no rise or fall appeared before the shine of the moonlight on the ocean began again a few hundred yards away.

Lord Carnarvon spoke. "Yessiree, looks like corn country to me. Flat as a pool table and nearly as fertile."

Emma nodded. "It looks like the surface of the moon."

Harry muttered, "Three-ninety-three," and stopped walking. "Quit worrying. Did you ever see pictures of Palm Springs or Las Vegas before they were developed?"

"Is that possible?" asked Vickers.

"Three-ninety-six. You know what I mean. And we've got the sea and we've got rain." He trotted to catch up. "Ninety-seven, eight, nine, four hundred."

"Hey," Emma said. "Look at that." She pointed off to the left, where the light of the rising moon gleamed on a higher shelf of rock. Perched on that layer was another prominence. "It looks like the pat of butter on the pancake."

Vickers said quietly, "It's a building. Let's go."

"Four-twenty-six," said Harry. "Wait a minute." But the others had already veered to the left, and were cautiously making their way toward the rise on the rock. "Four-twenty-seven," he said, taking a step forward. He gazed at the ocean in the distance. "Twenty-eight, twenty-nine, oh, shit." He trotted after the others.

At the foot of the rise, they all flocked together again. "It looks like a little fort," said Emma. "It's all stone, with no windows."

Lord Carnarvon turned to Vickers. "What do you say, Rear Admiral? It looks to me like Hitler's special bunker in the West Indies."

"How do I know?" said Vickers. "Let's look around."

Lord Carnarvon said, "Shall we fire a few warning shots first?"

"There's nobody here, you idiot."

"The cowards."

They climbed to the next level, and walked around to the other side, where they found an empty doorway. Vickers stepped forward. "Wow. Place is a little gamey, isn't it?"

"Turn on a light," said Emma.

Harry pulled out his flashlight and shone it inside. "There's nothing in there," he said, then looked up. "There's no roof, either." He switched off the light.

"Wait," said Emma.

"Come on," said Harry. "I'd like to get some spikes from the boat. We can post our claim along the shore."

"Just a second. Shine the light on the wall."

Harry clicked on the flashlight and let the beam dance

randomly in the little enclosure. "My God," he whispered. "Is that—?"

Lord Carnarvon stepped inside, taking Harry's flashlight with him. He began to chuckle softly as he moved the light close to the wall, then turned and swept the other walls slowly. "Yes it is, Harry. That's exactly what it is."

"What?" asked Vickers.

"Well, a little of everything," Lord Carnarvon answered. "They go from the floor clear up to here." He shone the light on the wall at the level of his knees. "Mussels, anemones, but mostly barnacles."

"The smell," said Emma.

"Harry was right about that. It's low-tide smell, just like the French Riviera. Only difference is, at high tide France doesn't go under."

"So this place is—"

"That's right, Emma. We've got ourselves a real bonanza here. Just like the lost city of Atlantis."

Harry planted his feet in the doorway and said, "It's just a little setback, a little bit of a challenge to show we can handle ourselves. It's a couple of feet less elevation than we'd like. People run into that all the time in Beverly Hills."

But Emma wasn't listening. She was watching as the first small rivulets of the ocean appeared on the rock and trickled toward Harry's heels.

Vickers leaned unmoving with his shoulder against the doorway and gazed out onto the vast expanse of dark unbroken sea. He cradled his rifle in his arms comfortably, as though the years of watching in rain forests and desert villages had made him unaware of the weight of it. He seemed not to notice the splashing sound of Lord Carnarvon's approach.

"Can you see the boat yet?"

Vickers shook his head. "In another hour it'll be dawn, and we can check."

"What are you looking at?"

Vickers shrugged. "A while ago I saw something big break the surface. Maybe twenty feet out."

"Big?"

"Too big to get his nose in the door, I hope."

"The wading is better in here anyway. The water's gone down a lot. You can sit down without drowning."

Vickers kept his eyes on the open sea. "I'll wait. What do you suppose this place was?"

"I'd say somebody wanted to build a marker on the shoals. All you'd need is enough dry space at high tide to see it."

"Your people?"

"Hell no. Caribs didn't give a shit about shoals, and they didn't build anything out of stone. They were too busy paddling around in canoes looking for somebody to eat."

"Who, then?"

Harry splashed toward them. "Who cares? The Spanish, French, Dutch, British, Mexicans, Colombians, Americans, people from Saturn who like to walk around with their asses wet all the time."

"I thought you were over there contemplating suicide," said Vickers.

"Me?" He laughed. "I was just thinking this through. I know it's a little empty right now, but—"

"Not empty enough," muttered Vickers, stepping into the doorway.

Lord Carnarvon said, "Harry, there's a fish about the size of a school bus swimming around on the patio, and he's here because his species has evolved to smell the sweat in your sneakers."

Harry grinned. "No matter. Once we've adjusted the landscape a little we'll kick his butt out of here. There's plenty of room for him in the ocean."

"Harry, this is the ocean," said Emma. "We're in it."

Harry hugged her, then began to pace back and forth, the water washing up to his shins at each step. "You've got to see with your minds, not with your eyes. Don't you think I know we're standing up to our ankles in seawater two hundred miles from the nearest land?"

"One wonders," said Vickers.

"This is just our *Noche Triste*. In a little while we'll be on dry land again, and feeling ready to do the next thing."

"Next thing?"

Harry held his palms upward. "It's no good to us like this."

"That's exactly what I've been thinking," said Lord Carnarvon. "We needed an island, and I'd say what we've got is a shoal."

"No, don't you see?" said Harry. "It's a thousand times better for us. There aren't any inhabitants to get in the way. There's no chance any country has a claim on the place that we missed, because half the time there isn't any such place. We're in the money. It'll just take a little longer to collect than I thought."

The others stared at Harry in amazement. He was wet to the knees, his hair was disheveled from the sea breeze, and his eyes were bloodshot and tired. In this light, his skin looked a little gray, and his hands shook when he gestured, perhaps from the exhaustion of standing up all night to keep from drowning. But his voice was deep and clear, resonant with the confidence of a madman. Emma watched him, and felt a little tremor of fear. This was Harry at his most vivid, and he was going to talk them into something. She had no hope that any of them would remain unconvinced, only that it wasn't something that would destroy them. She listened for his next words, and when they came, she wasn't surprised.

"What do you do when you find a choice empty lot?" asked Harry. "You build. Our only problem is where to get the materials we need without giving anybody any money. . . ."

Lord Carnarvon spun the wheel and headed the schooner out of the harbor, feathering the engine's throttle. Harry and Emma leaned over the two sides of the bow and stared down into the water.

"It's beautiful," said Emma. "It's so clear and bright you could read down there."

"Someday you will," said Harry. "For now let's just watch the bottom. If there's a wreck sticking up I want it to be a sight rather than an experience."

Lord Carnarvon turned to Vickers. "Have you got a heading for me yet?"

"I'd say our best bet is Limón, Costa Rica."

Harry called, ‘‘Will they have what I want?’’

Vickers said, ‘‘Harry, anybody who’s got anything has what you want. Nicaragua and Honduras are out. They’re busy flipping a coin to see who will invade and who will be the home team.

Lord Carnarvon said, ‘‘It looks like open ocean from here out. Time to unfurl the sails and preserve the precious petroleum reserves of the Republic of Stink Island.’’

‘‘You can’t call it that,’’ said Emma.

‘‘We’ll think of something,’’ Harry said. ‘‘Vickers, what’s the reason for Costa Rica?’’

‘‘It’s the ideal place for your kind of shopping. It’s on the mainland, so there are plenty of other suspects. But best of all, their armed forces consist of five thousand farmers with rifles in their corn cribs.’’

‘‘For the whole country?’’

‘‘That’s right. They’d lose an all-out war with the Philadelphia Police Department.’’

LIMÓN

Harry, Vickers, and Emma walked along the docks of Limón, studying the ships at anchor in the harbor. Harry pointed to a freighter that rode low in the water, with great black mounds overflowing the hatches in its midsection. ‘‘Cargo looks like coal. That would do fine.’’

Vickers shook his head. ‘‘She’s too big for the three of us to operate. Besides, anybody who needs a shipload of coal is bound to be somebody big enough to own factories.’’

Emma said, ‘‘Let’s stay away from the big freight lines anyway. They’re not going to sit back and write off a zillion-dollar ship.’’

Harry threw up his hands. ‘‘If you’re going to steal, you have to choose the people who own things. That’s the way it is. It’s a law of physics.’’

‘‘Don’t be impatient,’’ said Emma. ‘‘Shop around a little before you decide.’’

Harry walked along the wharf, staring seaward. ‘‘Oil

tankers. Shit. Half the ships in the world must be oil tankers, and the other half are part of some damned navy."

"Be patient, Harry." Emma put her arm around his shoulder. "We don't want to make a mistake, do we?"

Harry sighed. "We never should have left Lord Carnarvon with the boat. He knows the sea. It's in his blood."

Vickers said, "If you'll remember, that's what you said when we were deciding who should stay with the boat."

"I suppose so. But there aren't many like him."

"That's because when there were, nobody else in this part of the world was safe from them. If we had fifty, we could steal the whole country."

"But we don't," said Emma, "so we've got to be selective." She stared up past the line of docks and warehouses. "I think I see something we can afford now."

Vickers held his wrist close to his face to catch the light of the moon. "It's after three, but I still don't see any sign of the crew. Either there's a fantastic whorehouse in town, or they've put in for a long stay."

"As long as the boat isn't broken we'll be fine," said Emma. "Everything else is perfect."

Harry studied the short, broad-beamed vessel. "It looks clean and it's sitting high in the water. I don't hear any pumps, do you?"

Emma listened. "No. All I hear is the radio. It sounds like a baseball game."

They sat behind a crate on the wharf and waited a few minutes before Vickers spoke. "How can it be a baseball game at this time of night?"

"Who cares?" said Emma. "Maybe it's a quadrupleheader."

"More likely a tie going into the seventy-third inning," said Harry. "I just wish we had a getaway plan."

"We do," Vickers said. "Lord Carnarvon will be back on the spot tomorrow."

"I just hope we don't have to tread water waiting for him."

Emma smiled. "Are we agreed that it's time to start, or do you want to synchronize your watches and put on false noses first?"

"We're agreed," snapped Vickers.

"Then let's go." She moved quietly along the moonlit pier, keeping in the shadows of the cargo containers stacked in ranks behind her. Vickers followed at a distance, scanning the area around Emma for signs that someone was awake to see her.

She reached the tugboat's gangplank, scampered aboard silently, and disappeared behind the bridge. Vickers waited for thirty seconds before he slowly made his way to the foredeck.

Harry sat on the pier between two crates, and checked the magazine of his pistol for the third time. He craned his neck to stare down the pier. The long concrete pavement seemed endless and white in the darkness. He counted to a hundred, then did it again to be sure, and then moved.

He crept to the edge of the pier, then stepped quickly along it to the first piling, tugged the thick rope off, and let it sag into the water. In the calm, sluggish harbor he could detect no change in the position of the barge. Harry stood up and made his way to the second barge. This one was so close to the pier that he could see its cargo gleaming in the darkness like polished silver. He felt his body lighten a little with the excitement of the moment. Someday people are going to wonder what this felt like, he decided. He slipped the spliced noose off the piling and walked to the third barge. As he was freeing its line, something on the stern of the barge caught his eye. It was a large diamond-shaped sign with the numeral four in black. He looked up the line of barges to the tugboat. Three barges, and one tugboat to pull them, he thought. That made four, but why would anybody have to put up a sign to count to four?

But he could already see the silhouette of a person standing outside the cabin of the tugboat. As he watched, a cigarette lighter flickered, and he could see a yellow-orange aura of light that made Emma's face and shoulders appear. Harry trotted up the pier to the tugboat, cast off the two lines that held it, and scrambled up the gangplank.

Emma met him on the deck. "One man aboard, Harry. You'd better talk to him."

Harry climbed to the wheelhouse and entered. Vickers was standing with his pistol pointed at the deck, staring at a tall, burly black man who sat scowling at Harry.

Vickers said, "This is Captain Pettigrew, Harry."

"Pleased to meet you, Commodore." Harry smiled. "We're . . . well, at the moment we're pirates."

The Captain's eyebrows raised slightly. "Pirates?" He paused, and a thought seemed to enter his mind and grow, rapidly branching outward to reach for a series of variations and implications. Vickers flicked off the safety catch of his pistol, and his knees seemed to bend slightly and lock.

The Captain's chest heaved as he took a deep breath, but he let it out in a cough of laughter. "Pie-rats," he said. "I thought you were after my wallet."

"Nothing so practical as that," said Harry. "No harm will come to you or your tugboat."

Captain Pettigrew folded his arms. "That's right."

Harry continued, happily. "In fact, we wouldn't bother you at all, but we're here to steal those barges, and you happen to be in the tugboat that's tied to them.

The Captain's mouth slowly opened to reveal a row of large, even teeth, as his eyes narrowed. "The barges?"

"Yeah," said Harry. "If you haven't noticed, you're being followed by three barges crammed full of cars."

"You're here to steal those barges?"

"Yes," said Emma, who was now at the window behind the Captain. "So let's get on with it. By now we could have stolen the whole—"

But Captain Pettigrew was shaking now, giggling helplessly.

"What's he laughing at?" asked Vickers.

The Captain waved a hand at him. "You're not pirates, you're just taking out the garbage."

Harry stepped closer and stared into the Captain's gleeful face. "Tell me about it."

The Captain collected himself. "Those old leaky barges are loaded with junk cars. They're not worth anything except to me. I got a thousand American dollars to tow them out to deep water and scuttle them."

Harry showed no surprise. "They're worth something to both of us.

"Oh?" said the Captain. "You spend the evening out there kicking the tires? It's a trick question, because there aren't any tires. Around here they figure a car is only good for twenty-five or thirty years, then the damned thing quits and they strip it."

"What about the barges?"

"They used to haul bananas about the time Moses crossed the Red Sea. The wood's so rotten you can't haul anything but salt water. If they stay in the harbor they'll sink."

"We can't let that happen," said Emma. "Start the engine."

Captain Pettigrew didn't move.

"What are you waiting for?" said Vickers.

Pettigrew's scowl returned. "I said nobody gives a shit if you take the barges."

Harry turned to Emma. "How much cash did we bring?"

"About four hundred."

"Done," said Captain Pettigrew.

When the waves in front of the bow were visible, Emma decided there was no choice but to call it morning. The sun was still somewhere ahead, beyond the fog. The droning engine of the tugboat had filled the dead hours that someone might have felt the need to fill with words. She realized without interest that she could see Vickers' face now, not just the shape of him. He was still sitting in the corner, watching Captain Pettigrew watching the compass. Harry was asleep in the crew's quarters.

She asked, "You holding up, Admiral? What do you usually do about breakfast?"

The Captain looked ahead. "We used to cook it up on board. Now that I'm a pirate I suppose we'll have to steal it."

"Sometimes the old ways are best. Is there a galley?"

"Down aft where the bunks are, we've got a cooler and a propane stove. Are you up to that?"

She grinned. "Life with Harry is only about half room service. I can cook a polar bear with a blowtorch."

She made her way down the narrow steps into the dim cabin. As she entered, she could already smell the bacon frying, and Harry was breaking an egg into a pan. Harry turned. "Good timing. I seem to need a hand here. Can you keep an eye on this stuff while I pick the shell out of this egg?"

"Get out of here," she said. "You know you'll just kill us all."

"I thought the experience might improve my skills."

"Stick to hot dogs. You can be the waiter and busboy." She snatched the pan and spatula from his hands and examined them. "Come to think of it, you can wash the dishes. It'll be a new experience for them."

Harry sat back on the bed and watched as Emma fried the eggs and drained the bacon grease with a practiced ease. In a few seconds there were four plates of hot food on the narrow counter. Emma said, "Okay, let's deliver."

They each took two plates and a handful of silverware and climbed to the bridge.

"Wonderful," said Vickers, passing a plate to the Captain. Then his eyes narrowed. "Harry didn't cook this, did he?"

Emma was holding the forks up to the light and scrutinizing them. "Don't worry. I caught him before he got too far. Here's another clean one." She handed it to Vickers.

The Captain ate standing at the wheel. "It will be a fine, calm day," he announced.

"Have we got enough gas to get to the shoals?" asked Emma.

"An odd time to ask that," said the Captain. "I work up and down the coast, so I've got reserve tanks. Some of the places I go, you can't be sure they'll have it when you get there. You have to pay a lot of attention to details."

"Like the fourth barge," said Harry.

"Fourth barge?" Vickers looked confused.

"Yeah. He's got three barges, and the third one has a big sign on it that says 'Four.' "

Vickers stood up and stepped to the open port to stare

back at the trailing barges. "Explosives," he said. "What the hell are you doing with explosives?"

The Captain smiled. "How did you think I was going to sink them?"

Vickers hesitated. "I don't know. An army of woodpeckers." He thought for a moment. "What is it?"

"Just dynamite."

Vickers seemed to get used to the idea. "Is it all in the last barge? That's the only one with placards."

"Sure. I like it a hundred yards away. Don't you? Just in case I have to bump things around a little."

Vickers set his plate beside him. His expression brightened. "This must be my lucky day. A man with common sense. Captain, why don't you take a break? I'll watch the wheel."

Vickers could see the schooner a mile off, riding at anchor, its white sides glistening as it dipped and rose with the lazy swells.

Captain Pettigrew was studying his maps, his brow furrowed. "I don't much like towing three barges and a crate of dynamite onto a shoal that's not on the charts."

"Wrong, Captain," said Harry. "This is its last day as a shoal. Tomorrow it'll be an island."

"A pile of old car bodies isn't an island," said Pettigrew. "It's a junkyard." He pointed into the distance at the schooner. "Is that fellow a seaman?"

"Lord Carnarvon? He navigates by sniffing the air and dragging his toes in the water."

"Lord Carnarvon," the Captain sighed. "Another one."

"He's not what you think," Emma said. "Everybody in his family is named Lord Carnarvon, even the girls."

Vickers added, "He's a Carib Indian. After the big uprising in 1930 the British Army penned them up on a reservation in Dominica and gave names to the troublemakers. Tut's tomb was still big news in those days."

"Good enough," said the Captain. "I'll take a chance that he's in a safe anchorage." He spun the wheel and moved toward the schooner, watching the barges slowly swing into his wake.

As they closed on the schooner, Lord Carnarvon appeared on the foredeck, stripped to the waist. The Captain waved to him and said, "He's a Carib all right. You don't see many of them this far west.

"There aren't many of them anywhere," said Vickers. "But one will hold us for now."

The Captain studied Vickers for a moment, then seemed to be satisfied. Lord Carnarvon was now walking along the gunwale of the schooner with effortless balance, and pointing to the spot where he wanted the tug to come abreast of his boat.

As the tug slowly edged up to the schooner, Lord Carnarvon stepped aboard and climbed to the bridge. He gave a shrill whistle through his teeth in imitation of a boatswain piping an admiral onto a battleship.

Captain Pettigrew was the only one who understood. He held out a large, callused hand. "Welcome aboard, Lord Carnarvon."

Lord Carnarvon grinned and shook the hand. "I was expecting a hapless victim with a bullet in his leg. A red Dutchman that kept shouting 'Swine.' How did these three get you?"

"This is Captain Pettigrew," said Emma. "We hired him to help."

Lord Carnarvon asked, "What did you bring us?"

Pettigrew shrugged. "Just the three or four hundred junked cars. They weren't worth the counting, so nobody did. The barges are for scuttling."

"What's your draft?"

Pettigrew answered, "Three feet for the tug, two for the barges, but they shipped water on the way out."

Lord Carnarvon nodded, then picked the pencil from its holder above the map table and drew a picture of the island. "High tide is an hour from now. We've got a lot to do." He drew an arrow across the thick end of the island. "We'll move the barges in like this, then anchor them. It won't be deep enough for you beyond here." He drew a line at the edge of the submerged island.

The Captain studied the map, then stared at the rocky

pile on the end of the island to get his bearings. "I'll want you in the aft barge to set the anchor."

"Right," said Lord Carnarvon. "I'll lower the dinghy."

As Lord Carnarvon turned to go, the Captain said, "Wait. What are you people really doing out here?"

Lord Carnarvon smiled. "Didn't they tell you?"

"They said they were building an island."

Lord Carnarvon shook his head as he left the cabin. "That's ridiculous.

"What are you really doing?"

"Building an island."

Lord Carnarvon tugged to set the anchor in the rock ledges on the windward edge of the shoal, then watched the chain slowly tighten as the barge drifted into position and held. He looked along the line of barges, and he could see that they were perfectly strung in a sweeping arc across the center of the submerged island. The battered, rusted hulks of the old cars huddled in the barges looked like toys, the bottom layer pushed together touching bumper to bumper, then others piled on top at strange angles, until the weight of them had made the loaders stop for fear that the barges might sink before they reached deep water.

Lord Carnarvon climbed down into the dinghy and began to row toward the tugboat. He leaned hard into each stroke, then let the light boat glide on the water for a few feet, with a methodical ease. As he rowed he quietly sang a secret song to himself. It was a song about dividing time into the proper number of breaths and paddle strokes in a war canoe on the open sea. It was sweet and tranquil and reassuring, reminding the singer that the ocean was limitless and every piece of land in every direction was full of enemies who would still be there when the canoe reached them.

It was dark when Vickers cast the towline off the last of the barges and Captain Pettigrew started the powerful engine of the tugboat. He moved away from the island to the anchored schooner, and waited while Lord Carnarvon stepped onto the schooner's deck and weighed anchor. Then he slowly towed the other vessel into open sea.

A half-mile out he cut the engine again.

Emma said, "Will we be able to see it from here?"

Captain Pettigrew shrugged. "There's not much to obscure the view."

Vickers scanned the ocean with the Captain's binoculars. "It won't look like much. There will be three little flashes, and a few seconds later you'll hear three little pops, and the barges will sink a couple of feet. In the morning they'll be on dry land and we can go look them over."

Behind him, Emma saw the first of the flashes. It lit the surface of the water for an instant, then faded, leaving a blue-green afterimage. She closed her eyes and it still floated in the darkness like a flower, but around it was something like a splash.

Harry was saying, "Holy—" when the pop reached Emma's ears. It was loud and sharp like a gunshot, and it made her look again. As she did, the other sound reached her. It was a deafening roar, and now she could see that the whole barge was ablaze, the billowing flames rolling into the sky.

"It's the cars," Vickers snapped. "Didn't they drain the gas tanks?" Behind him, Emma saw another flash, and a flaming automobile did a double somersault in the air and bounced once on the barge, then flopped into the ocean beside it.

Captain Pettigrew tried to answer, "It doesn't look like they—" But two more explosives flashed, and they seemed to obliterate the need to speak.

Just before dawn the last of the automobiles exploded. Its tank had been almost empty, so it blew with a vicious bang that tore the truck lid off and bent the sides outward before the surrounding flames engulfed the chassis.

In the bridge of the tugboat the five occupants leaned on the windowsills and watched the fire that stretched across the three barges in an unbroken line.

"The ocean is on fire," said Emma. "We seem to have made sort of a bad start."

"It's just seepage," said Harry. "There are hundreds of leaky oil pans, greasy parts. It'll be burned off soon." He squinted at the wall of fire. "It seems to be burning lower already, doesn't it?"

Vickers shook his head. "No, it doesn't."

"It won't spread over this far, will it?" asked Emma.

"Not a chance," said Captain Pettigrew. "Those barges are riding on solid rock. If they're not where you want them, you'll have to learn to live with it." He tilted his head slightly and held his breath. "Listen."

They could hear a low rushing sound like a steady wind as the fire scoured the barges and cars in the distance, but now there was something added to it, a higher, droning sound.

Vickers stepped out onto the deck and pivoted slowly on his heels, then pointed to the sky. "It's an airplane. See his lights?"

Pettigrew moved to the radio and turned a knob across bands of whistling and crackling until a tiny voice with a British accent broke through. "Have not heard your Mayday, but will try to transmit to Kingston, Jamaica. . . . Repeat, coastal vessels. I have—"

The Captain snapped into his microphone, "Whiskey Zulu Alpha six-nine-five-eight to aircraft. We have sent no Mayday. Negative. Do not send Mayday."

The voice on the radio was clearer now. "I can see three ships on fire. What the hell is going on down there? Have you picked up the survivors?" As the man spoke, the sound of his engine nearly drowned him out because he was swooping low over the tugboat.

"All souls are safe aboard," said the Captain. "We are out of Limón, scuttling barges to mark the shoals."

"Well, you picked a damned fancy way to do it. It looks like a volcano from a hundred miles off."

"That's very good news," said the Captain. "The route along here should be very safe for shipping."

There was a muffled voice in the background, and the pilot answered without releasing his transmitter button. "Just some idiots—" Then his voice faded.

Captain Pettigrew broke in. "Thank you for your concern. Whiskey Zulu Alpha six-nine-five-eight out.'' He hung the microphone back on its hook.

The bridge had a dull gray light now that didn't flicker and move with the distant burning. Emma said, ''I'm going to get some sleep.'' As an afterthought, she added, ''I'm not going to get undressed, so anybody who wants can take a bunk if he doesn't snore. Wake me up when the island is cooked.''

As she moved to the gangway that led down to the cabin, she glanced at the fire again. It was still burning furiously, but now she could see that the tide had gone out and the stranded barges were on dry rock. The eastern sky was beginning to glow with a dim light of its own that made her tired eyes squint. But to the north, above the blazing island, a thick cloud of opaque black smoke rose a mile or more straight up into the sky, then trailed off in a sickening smear that stretched eastward toward the Lesser Antilles.

Behind her, Lord Carnarvon was saying, ''It's probably better this way. Now maybe the place won't stink so much. It'll be sterilized.''

Emma made her way down the narrow steps, wondering how much time she had to sleep before the first ship saw the smoke and arrived to rescue them. She decided it didn't matter. Anybody could see it wasn't the kind of fire that burned for a few hours and then died. It was the kind of fire that would burn for days and nights until every speck of paint, drop of oil, piece of plastic or wood or fabric or rubber was consumed. After that, Harry would think of something else.

5

One Year

THE ISLAND

Harry closed his eyes and sniffed the air as Captain Pettigrew eased the ancient tour boat into the pier in the harbor. He could just feel in his ankles the gentle bump as a ripple in the water nudged the boat into the rubber tire nailed to the pier. Harry decided that finally, after a year, the smell was gone. The fire had incinerated the dead animals, then burned off the grease, and left a place as clean and empty as the moon. Then there had been the load of rocks from the road-building in Guatemala, and after that the cement that hadn't been stolen from the hotel construction on the coast of Belize: it had just been bought from a contractor who wore three diamond rings on each hand, and offered to throw in a load of steel I-beams if they could be taken the same night.

Harry had spent the past year ranging about the hemisphere looking for any form of detritus that could be had for nothing and would raise the level of the island a few inches farther above the sea. Captain Pettigrew had helped him recruit a gang of laborers from the poverty-stricken ports of the Central American mainland, men who were used to starting work as soon as there was enough light to see, and continuing until they couldn't see anymore. He had taken these men wherever there was any waterproof substance piled up and ready to be disposed of. They'd hauled tons of crushed shale from an experimental shale-oil refinery in Mexico, a mountain of scallop shells from an old fish-packing plant in Bermuda, a mound of broken glass from a bottling factory in Jamaica, a load of stone blocks from a sixteenth-century cathedral destroyed by an earthquake in El Salvador. They'd leased a ship to transport a whole junkyard from Trinidad—a load of bathtubs, bicycles, bedsprings, rubber boots, vinyl phonograph records, plastic sandals without mates, tin cans, window blinds, broken crockery, and what appeared to be the remains of an entire establishment devoted to the preparation and sale of East Indian cuisine, from the metal sign that once hung above the door, to the broken cash register. These items were brought to the island and anchored with cement poured in random trails over them, and then covered with dirt stolen from the remote islands in the Banco Gorda and the fringes of the Caymans.

Harry and Emma and Vickers and Captain Pettigrew had brought in extra men from all over the region as they needed them, hiring them wherever they were at the moment when they realized they couldn't move so much stone or dirt with the men they had. They offered to pay the men a little more than they were making in their dusty villages and their overcrowded slums, which was virtually nothing, housed them in whatever shelters the most experienced of them could teach the others to build, and fed them from a common kitchen that served simple, cheap food brought in on the same vessels that brought the men and the rocks and the dirt and the lumber.

And there were more of these vessels now. To Lord Carnarvon's smuggling schooner and Captain Pettigrew's tugboat had been added a fleet of converted fishing boats acquired with the crews who manned them, an elderly freighter of some ten thousand tons that had arrived with sailors but no captain and could never dock in Panamanian ports, and the tour boat that was now bringing Harry's newest load of tourists to the island.

The tourists had been one of Emma's ideas. Building and supplying the island required a regular schedule of arrivals and departures in any case, and usually there was room for passengers. When Emma had read in an American magazine that a charter company in New York was actually charging people huge sums for the chance to relive the hardships of Darwin's voyage on the *Beagle*, she had suggested that Harry look into the possibility of selling a competing set of hardships that could be experienced in shorter doses and much closer to home. So Harry had rented a post-office box in Jamaica and sent a few thousand copies of a brochure to travel agents in American cities. The brochure had emphasized what a bleak, empty, forbidding place the island was, and consequently, the island had become a rage among the most perversely adventurous of tourists. They clamored for the chance to spend a week or two on this bit of parched rock protruding from an alien sea, eating rations in a mess hall they shared with a hundred sweating laborers, some of whom looked as though they might cut a throat for a wristwatch.

Everything was arranged so that the tourists paid for the expenses of the island. To Harry it sometimes seemed that the island was building itself, and only required that its five principal residents rotate in a continuous cycle, each spending a few weeks on the island, then a few weeks scouring the surrounding territories for supplies, tourists, recruits, or money. This time Harry was returning with all of those precious commodities, and he was feeling like an explorer sailing into Genoa with a shipload of spices, silks, and rubies from the Orient.

Harry threw the bowline to the dark, square-faced man on the dock, and stepped onto the thick, rough boards beside him. Harry asked, "Are you another one of Lord Carnarvon's cousins?"

The man answered, "Not me. I've got cousins in New York, and cousins in San Juan. That's plenty. You Harry?"

"That's right."

"I'm Augustino Cruz. I'm supposed to take your herd over to the sheds and get them settled."

Harry moved close and whispered, "Augie, take good care of them. And don't call those things sheds. We're calling them cottages now."

Augustino smiled. "I'll remember." He stepped aboard and nimbly climbed to the afterdeck, where the two dozen people waited, staring in awe at the tiny island.

As Harry moved off, he heard Augustino beginning his speech. "Welcome to Carib Island. As our brochures tell you, this is one of the few islands in the region that Columbus didn't discover. It was known only to the fierce Carib Indians for centuries, until Dr. Harry Erskine, our host, deciphered the texts accompanying sixteenth-century Portuguese maps in the collection of the British Maritime Museum. Fortunately, the descendants of these same Caribs had preserved in the legends of their forefathers a record of a sacred island that came and went with the phases of the moon. As we walk to the cottages, please feel free to ask questions . . ."

Harry walked until Augustino Cruz's voice faded into nothing. He climbed the breakwater and walked along the causeway toward the end of the island, where he could see a crew of men placing stone blocks to raise the wall one more level. As he approached, he picked out Lord Carnarvon's voice. "Steady, steady. All right, perfect."

The stone rested in place, and one man, who seemed to be a competent mason, slapped mortar on the next space, while the others pushed another stone onto a set of rollers. Lord Carnarvon stepped from among the crew and said, "Here's Harry."

The others paused to glance at the lone man, and two of them waved, so Harry waved back. He could see they were Lord Carnarvon's cousins, which meant he knew them by name, but felt worse for it.

"Hello, Lord Carnarvon," he said, and all three nodded.

The one Harry thought of as the real, original Lord Carnarvon walked with Harry along the breakwall.

"It's not bad," said Harry. "Every time I look, it's three steps farther along."

"You should look more often. I've had everybody working full days since you left."

Harry stopped and stared out over the stone wall at the long row of waves breaking a hundred yards out on the shallow sandbars. "How long has Vickers been gone?"

"A month. He went a week after you did. One night he started raving about how the basis of all true civilizations was dirt, and then he took Captain Pettigrew's men in the tugboat."

"Did he have something in mind, or did he just crack? He'd been here a long time."

Lord Carnarvon shrugged. "He helped to finish the causeway around the island before he got restless. He worked with both crews from sunup until sunset. A good time was had by all."

"What do you mean?"

"He was the founder of the Sunset Games. Every night when the sun started to go down, he'd gather everybody at the east end of the island and hold shooting contests until it got dark. Then there was knife throwing by lantern light in the big barracks.

"Jesus. Did anybody get hurt?"

"Not this bunch. By the time they got tired of it, just about any of them could hit a beer bottle floating in heavy surf a hundred yards out. It scared the hell out of the last bunch of tourists. At least the knives were quiet."

"What stopped it?"

"After they all got too good at it, there wasn't much point in it."

"We can rotate them out, starting now. We brought six new men from Bermuda this trip. I don't want anything to annoy these tourists. Every damned one of them is paying a hell of a lot of money to rough it on a desert island for a few weeks. If they want to get shot they can do it at home."

"We can talk to the men tonight, and see if anybody wants out."

"Now that we've got enough altitude to keep our feet dry, we could pay them all off and concentrate on the tourists."

"What would that do for us?"

Harry walked on, surveying the rocky interior of the island. "They pay the expenses already. If we told them this was an archaeological site we could get them to move the terrain around for us. I haven't got it worked out yet, but—"

"Forget it, Harry. The first one to move five feet of rocks finds a burned-out fifty-six Chevy."

"How about the offshore work? There are wrecked boats out there. We could sell this as a chance to dive for treasure. Or we could say there's a sunken city. They'd help lift the rocks and bring them to shore."

"No. It's too hard for them, and it's dangerous. Sure as hell we'd end up losing some."

Harry nodded. "I suppose." He walked on, and added, "I hate to sell them short, though. These are people who'll pay big money just to be marooned someplace where they can't get a fancy meal or talk on the telephone. Just think what they'd pay if we made them do hard labor too."

Lord Carnarvon held Harry's arm and said slowly, "I vote no. And you know Emma would vote no, and Captain Pettigrew. Vickers would probably vote yes, but you can't prove it."

"Oh well," said Harry. "There's always something wasted. It's my month to work the island, so I'll have plenty of time to think up something better."

"Just get as much work done as you can while I'm gone."

"We'll plan it all out in the morning before you leave. And don't forget, I'd like to pay off anybody who's bored enough to be dangerous, and ship him out with you."

"You've got to remember that these guys are making more money in a month than they'd make in a year in the villages they're from, and there's no way to spend it."

Harry said, "So what?"

"So I don't think we'll get anybody who wants to leave, this trip. Strange as it seems, a few months on Stink Island make a hell of an investment in their futures."

"We're calling it 'Carib Island' now, remember? It makes the tourists happy. Just make sure I don't get stuck here with some maniac from Venezuela who's about to go berserk after Vickers trained him to use every damned weapon known to man."

"If you're worried, I can leave my cousins here with you."

"I'll take my chances with the maniac."

Lord Carnarvon looked at Harry, then at the ground, and then at Harry again. "Has it occurred to you that a whole year has come and gone? We've been on this island a year, Harry."

"Not really. Hell, I just spent two weeks in Miami. I

don't count those two weeks, or the time any of us spend away." He paused, and then sighed. "Okay. You've got me. I said this would only take a year."

"Actually, you said six months."

"Look at me. I'm caught. I'm embarrassed. From here on, this is going to be easy. The hard part is over. Vickers knew that, or he wouldn't have gone off on vacation."

BARRANQUILLA

Vickers sat in the wheelhouse of the tug watching the tall concrete-and-glass buildings move past the window in a slow procession. Vickers' eyes swept up a double file of buildings that had edged so close to the wharf that they looked like palisades. He could see the broad street between them stretching up and away from the river, with red and green traffic signals diminishing to the horizon. He sighted up the street like a surveyor, and held the image after the angle had closed and the street was replaced by others.

A week ago he'd exhausted his Spanish explaining to Joaquín, the tugboat pilot, the nature and importance of his idea, and had stretched his Spanish to a new proficiency listening to Joaquín explain the difference between a tugboat pilot and a ship's navigator. In the end they'd set out westward on the theory that they'd hit the coast somewhere and Joaquin would find out where he was and turn left or right as needed. Since moving into coastal waters, they'd sometimes used English, and Vickers would ask, as cities, harbors, and landmarks floated past his window, "Where the fuck are we?"

This time he hadn't needed to repeat it, because Joaquín had told him it was coming as soon as they'd crossed into Colombian waters. It was a place, he'd indicated, that was invented by God's foreknowledge that Vickers would be born, develop a grand obsession, and decide that he needed such a place. What Joaquín had really said was that God, knowing the joke that Vickers would be, had revealed the punch line two hundred years before, as He sometimes liked to do. This was Barranquilla.

The Magdalena River began high in the Andes and flowed hundreds of miles through fertile plains and thick jungles, picking up minerals and rotting vegetation and rich soil and—here Joaquín had added "drowned cattle and sewage and the excrement of people long dead"—carried them downriver past the thriving metropolis of Barranquilla solely for the purpose of depositing them in the sea at Boca Ceniza to make the harbor impassable.

If the authorities knew what Vickers had in mind, they would line up to greet him on the docks, said Joaquín. As the tug edged up to berth at the wharf, Vickers could see the authorities standing in a line, dressed in bright green uniforms. Their leader spoke through an electronic bullhorn. "Please tie up at berth number three. If you do not, you will be shot."

Vickers watched as Dave, the able-bodied seaman, tied a rope to a big iron ring on the dock. Then three men in uniforms swarmed over him, threw him down on the foredeck, and handcuffed his hands behind his back. Four others jumped to the deck and clattered up the steps to the wheelhouse. The first through the door sidestepped to the left and the second sidestepped to the right with admirable precision, their submachine guns held at the hip. After a pause of four seconds, the third man entered, followed by the man with the bullhorn.

Vickers glanced at the man's shoulders and gritted his teeth. In all of the seven armies that Vickers had joined in different parts of the world, the worst men had always managed to come packaged in the uniforms of colonels. "Welcome aboard, Colonel," he said. "What can I do for you?"

"You and your crew will come with me, Captain. You will bring only your papers."

"I'm not a captain, actually," said Vickers in English. "I'm a colonel. Retired, of course. And about the papers—"

"Bring them," the Colonel snapped.

Vickers turned to Joaquín. "Do we have any papers? I sure hope you know where they are."

Joaquín was busily pulling some tattered, cellophane-wrapped certificates out of a tackle box in the corner of the wheelhouse.

The Colonel stepped out onto the deck, and Vickers followed, with Joaquín at his heels. Then one of the soldiers pushed Vickers against the wheelhouse and frisked him, and then did the same to Joaquín, while the others stood guard.

The army truck was already below on the wharf, backing up to take on its prisoners. When it stopped, two soldiers trotted around to drop open the tailgate to reveal the darkness inside.

Vickers sat on a straight wooden chair, acutely aware of the handcuffs on his wrists, but more acutely aware of a bee that had somehow found its way through the labyrinth of hallways to his cell. Now it was flying in little circles along the whitewashed wall, but in time, he knew, it would exhaust the geometric possibilities of the three solid stone surfaces and find its way out through the bars, or set off across the empty room and notice that Vickers was the best thing to land on. Since Vickers was handcuffed to the chair, he would be exactly like those people who believed that the way to respond to bees was to remain perfectly still: the bee would land on his face or his testicles.

Since Vickers' record of joining the army that was going to win its war was less than perfect, he'd been in jails like this before. The tiny physical details were often indications of what was to come. They were actually only matters of degree, but in the small spaces between those gradations, prisoners disappeared. If there had been stains on the floor, it might mean someone had been beaten to death during an interrogation, or it might only mean that the soldiers had thrown chicken blood there to frighten him, but wouldn't think of torture. As it happened, the floor and walls were quite clean, and that was more problematical. The worst regimes in the world had the cleanest interrogation rooms, which had to be hosed out and disinfected after each customer was dragged out. He tried to remember whether Colombia was that sort of place, or the other sort.

Then he heard the clicking heels of the soldier's boots approaching in the hallway. The cell opened and closed, and he heard the Colonel's voice snap angrily, "Sergeant." Vickers sighed. The voice was cold and edged.

"Yes sir?" said the sergeant.

"They forgot to take the handcuffs off him."

Vickers felt the handcuffs fall from his wrists and heard the sergeant scrape them up off the floor. Vickers knew that didn't mean he was supposed to move.

The Colonel added, "And there's a bee in here. How are we supposed to talk with a damned bee flying around our heads?"

Vickers heard a thump, then another, then the sergeant ran across the room in front of him carrying one shoe in his hand. Then Vickers heard three quick thumps, and the sergeant said, "Got him."

"Thank you," said the Colonel, who moved around into Vickers' field of vision. "Now, Mr. Vickers. What brings you to Colombia?"

"Well," Vickers began, "we're here to—"

The Colonel held up his hand. "Think before you answer. Your tugboat was observed from the air moving along the coastline into Colombian waters last night. You were moving eastward toward the Guajira Peninsula. When you stopped at Barranquilla today your vessel was searched."

Vickers shrugged. "It's *Great Tugboat Journeys of the World.* I'm scouting locations for a BBC television series. No doubt you found the cameras."

"We found some of the things we expected to find—guns and ammunition."

Vickers studied him. "Expected to find?" He thought for a moment. "Since most of the ships that dock in a port this size probably carry some kind of firearm, let's assume that isn't a capital offense unless we took them ashore, which we didn't. In fact, we didn't even land until you told us to." The Colonel's face showed nothing, so Vickers continued. "I admit the firearms are on board and belong to me. Now what?"

The Colonel looked puzzled. "Now what?"

Vickers said, "I'm the prisoner here."

The Colonel straightened. "I know that. What do you expect of me?"

"You're supposed to say that I've just pleaded guilty to hunting without a license, or that you suspect me of something else, and ask me questions. For Christ's sake, I can't interrogate myself."

The Colonel paced back and forth in front of Vickers, his boot heels clicking on the concrete floor. "I have always believed that it was best for a man's psyche to open his mind to another. That way he may lighten the burden he carries."

Vickers nodded eagerly. "Terrific. Me too."

"Yes?" said the Colonel. He seemed to brighten.

They both took three breaths, waiting; then they both looked at the floor. The Colonel turned and walked to the corner of the room, and sighed.

Vickers asked, "Do you mind if I stand up? I'm not violent or anything, and I've been sitting for over an hour."

"No, go ahead," said the Colonel. "You can't run anywhere."

Vickers said, "Just thought I'd ask. Sometimes they don't care, and sometimes they shoot you for resisting arrest or something." He stood up and walked stiffly across the room. When he turned, the Colonel was just sitting down in the chair.

He noticed Vickers watching him, and said, "You don't mind, do you? I've been on my feet a lot today." Then he added, "It's the boots."

"The boots?"

He pointed to his shiny calf-high black leather boots. "A remnant of the days when the officer was the one who rode the horse. Some traditions die hard."

Vickers walked up to the Colonel. "I have an idea that may speed things up a bit. You arrested me and my men today, right?"

"Of course I did," said the Colonel.

"By the way—they haven't been harmed, have they?"

The Colonel scowled. "What do you think I am? Do I look like Mussolini?"

"The boots aren't your fault," Vickers admitted. "At

any rate, since you made a special trip just to pick us up, you must have had something in mind.'' Vickers walked across the room, then turned on his heel and walked back. ''There must have been a specific crime around here—a robbery, maybe. Right?''

The Colonel grasped the arms of the chair. ''No.'' Then he wavered. ''Well, yes. I arrested you for a specific crime, but not for just one specific act of crime.''

''Very good,'' said Vickers. ''Now—what was that crime?''

The Colonel stared at him in amazement. ''This is Colombia.''

''Not good enough,'' Vickers said. ''You can't blame me for that one. I'm a Canadian citizen.''

''This is Colombia,'' the Colonel shouted. ''You sneak into Colombia on—of all things—a tugboat, in the middle of the night, heavily armed, a tugboat-load of heavily armed foreigners, one of you a North American at that. It leaves me speechless.''

''The crime!'' shouted Vickers. ''Tell me the crime.''

The Colonel's eyes seemed to burn with the clarity of a private vision. ''Drugs. I suspect you of smuggling drugs. You say you're Canadian, but you must be from Mars if you don't know. It's the only crime that foreigners come to Colombia to commit. Maybe they're coming from Mars now to get drugs, and you're only the first. In a week there will be spaceships landing at Riohacha.'' He bared his teeth and said, ''Well, I'll arrest them too.''

Vickers patted his shoulder. ''That's a relief.''

The Colonel took a deep breath as though to collect himself. ''What's a relief?''

''Well, you searched the boat, didn't you?''

''I admitted that.''

''And there weren't any drugs aboard, and not much money.''

''Yes,'' said the Colonel. ''That's right.''

''And no local person in the drug trade around here would just give me a load of cocaine to put in a tugboat, and say, '*Adiós*, John. Send me a check if you make it to Miami,' right?''

"Then what in God's name are you after? Did you come here to drive me mad?"

Vickers grinned. "I'm glad you asked. Joaquín told me the authorities would be interested in my plan, and you're the first one to ask about it. I appreciate that. What I came for is dirt."

The Colonel set his elbow on the arm of the chair and leaned his chin on the palm of his hand. He wondered why he was listening to this. But the alternative was to ask questions, and it might have taken weeks of questions even to learn about the dirt.

THE ISLAND

The spotter plane appeared first. Harry might never have seen it if Mrs. Doulton hadn't mistaken it for a high-flying seabird resting in a warm updraft over the island and insisted that everyone join the game of taxonomic identification. Harry was ten feet in front of the group, having ventured so far into an improvised lecture about island history that it threatened to degenerate into a sermon through repetition of the two odd bits of information in his possession. He intoned, "The main thing to remember about our Carib forefathers is that they were primarily fighters, not settlers. We can think of the island as a remote space station in the middle of a vast—"

"Birdie!" shrieked Mrs. Doulton. "Up there!"

The other members of the group instantly stepped backward, craning their necks to squint into the sky, shielding their eyes from the sun. Mr. Doulton obediently aimed his Nikon into the empty blue and snapped two pictures of the tiny dot above them. The only ones who didn't immediately look were Harry and Mr. Hazlett. Harry was watching to be sure none of his tourists tripped on the rocks and tumbled over the newly completed seawall, and Mr. Hazlett was, as always, engaged in mute contemplation of his ascetic project of going two weeks without smoking a cigarette. "Two more days," he whispered.

By the time Harry had rushed with outstretched arms to guard the perimeter, the tourists were in the middle of the race to find a name. "Albatross!" was shouted and echoed, then attacked and defended. "Gull?" asked someone.

But now Mr. Doulton had accomplished the first rapid-fire salvo he'd always planned in case he was ever in the presence of The Truly Remarkable. He sighted this distant phenomenon through his camera's viewfinder and adjusted the focus of the four-hundred-millimeter lens. "It's an airplane, dear," he said, but snapped the picture anyway. There was a collective sigh.

"It is?" shouted Harry. "It is? Where?" He stepped forward and snatched Mr. Doulton's camera, which tightened the strap around Mr. Doulton's neck so that he and Harry looked as though they were leaning their heads together to sing a duet into a single microphone. Mr. Doulton stood awkwardly at an angle to let Harry look for a moment, then straightened as Harry let the heavy camera swing back against his sternum, where it made a destructive thud he believed might be audible as well as painful.

Harry tried to formulate two theories, one to explain the presence of this small twin-engine airplane to himself, and one to explain it to his flock. It was now circling far above them. He decided his own curiosity could wait, and concentrated on lying to his guests. "It's probably a friend of mine. They fly high to keep from disturbing the—" He could think of nothing they might disturb, since there was no living thing on the parched and empty rock except these tourists and the work crew. But Mrs. Canby was a compulsive interrupter, so she was already saying "—delicate ecological balance." That seemed sufficiently predictable to satisfy everyone except Mr. Hazlett, who was no longer able to decipher words from outside, and didn't care about either birds or airplanes.

They were able to walk a hundred yards before the squadron of four fighter planes appeared low on the horizon, then came toward them fifty feet above the ocean like gigantic bullets.

Harry stared in disbelief as they approached. At first he heard only a dull roar, but as they streaked closer the sound deepened until his own stomach seemed to vibrate. They pulled upward at what seemed to be the last possible instant before they would have sliced off his scalp, and shot into the sky, turning over and climbing in a pattern that made them diverge. "Sweet Jesus," he said to Mr. Doulton, who was kneeling now, snapping pictures in his practiced drill, which involved hitting the winding lever and the shutter button with a single motion of his thumb.

Harry turned around three times, not knowing what to look at. He looked at the four planes, now banking upward in the distance, then at the little band of tourists, then at the empty ocean in the other direction, then at the planes again.

"They shouldn't come so close," said Mrs. Canby. "You should tell them."

Harry's terror was about to be transformed into rage, but he didn't allow an image to form in his mind of anything specific happening to Mrs. Canby. Instead he said to the group, "I think it's time for a break. I'll bet lunch is ready."

Augustino Cruz was running across the stone flats at the far end of the island. Harry watched him sprint toward the group for a few seconds, and thought: Go back, don't scare these people. They'll stampede like lemmings and jump in the sea.

But Augustino didn't seem to feel Harry's telepathy. He kept coming, running hard. Harry smiled and waved at him, then said, "See? Augustino is on his way."

"What's the matter with him?" asked Mr. Doulton, aiming his camera at Augustino.

Harry forced a chuckle. "He's new on the island, and I keep telling him he works too hard. Nice boy."

"Nice boy," Mrs. Canby repeated.

Then Augustino ran into the center of the group, panting. Harry grabbed him firmly, whispered, "Don't say anything or I'll kill you," then announced, "We'll catch up. Go on ahead, everyone." The group strolled on toward the shacks at the end of the island, occasionally staring into the sky, as Harry held Augustino.

"You've seen airplanes before. What's the problem?"

"We're being invaded." Augustino stopped to take more deep breaths, leaning over with his hands on his knees.

Harry spoke in an even tone. "Don't say that in front of the suckers. One of them will have a heart attack."

"You'd better do something fast."

"I can't do anything about fighter planes," said Harry. "All pilots are crazy. They just do things like this and then go somewhere to get drunk."

"It's not the planes I'm worried about. It's the ships."

Harry straightened and stared to the southeast. His first thought was to wonder why he hadn't seen them before. There were at least a dozen of them strung out along the horizon in some kind of formation. Then, even as he asked himself the next question, he knew it must have been asked a number of times by other people. "What do I say to a fleet of ships that will make it go away?"

Harry sat on the stone wall beside Augustino watching the ships through Mr. Doulton's camera lens. He'd also snatched Mrs. Canby's copy of the *Travel Guide to the Caribbean and South America* from her straw handbag.

"Fourteen ships," he said. "Only a few of them have dropped anchor so far."

"Let me see," said Augustino.

Harry handed him the camera, and turned to the guidebook. "It's not doing me a hell of a lot of good. Our only chance is if they're not planning to come ashore. Maybe they think it's too shallow."

"How much depth do they need?"

"How should I know? Just look for a flag."

"I can see a couple. Yellow on top, then blue, then red. Three stripes." Augustino offered the camera. "See?"

"Keep looking. That can't be the flag of a country." Harry leafed through the guidebook. Each chapter started with a crude map of a country with a little flag stuck in the capital city. After a few pages of flags with three stripes in various shocking colors he said, "I guess it can. What was it again?"

"Big yellow stripe, small blue, and small red."

"Colombia. They're a long way from home." Harry scanned the chapter entitled "Colombia, Emerald of the Spanish Main," then tossed the guidebook on the rocks behind him.

The sudden motion startled Augustino, and he asked, "What's it say?"

"Bring a raincoat, and get a shoeshine for ten pesos." Harry took the camera back and peered at the long line of ships. The first three seemed to be warships of some kind, but the others were a strange array of freighters and scows. This had to be some sort of task force commissioned to accomplish a deranged mission to further the obscure interests of one South American government at the expense of another South American government. "You know," he said, "even the British used civilian ships to move troops to the Falkland Islands."

"What do we do?"

Harry stood up. "Surrender. Maybe we can get them to shoot Mrs. Canby."

They stood and watched as the tiny uniformed figures on the deck of the largest gray navy ship scrambled back and forth. A moment later a small green helicopter rose into the air.

Harry took off his shirt as he walked inland to a flat, open stretch of rock. As the helicopter approached, he waved the shirt at it in great, sweeping motions of his arm. The helicopter came in low, then hovered above him for a few seconds, the downward rush of air blowing the shirt out of his hand. When he turned to chase it, the helicopter came down in an unsteady, pendulum motion, then dropped the last six inches. The big rotors churned to a stop, and Harry decided it was safe to put his shirt on. The far door swung open, and around the helicopter came two figures. When Harry saw the first man, his breath caught in his throat. He was tall, dark, and thin, with high black boots. Harry quickly buttoned his shirt and tucked in the tail. Then the second man came around, already talking. "Harry, say hello to the Colonel."

Vickers paced the length of Harry's shack, his body throwing a long, wavering shadow in the lantern light. Harry lay in his bunk and stared at the ceiling. He closed his eyes and listened to the distant throbbing of the pumps, then said, "How long will it take?"

"I figure five days, six at the most. By then they'll have

emptied the mud onto the island, everybody will be exhausted, and they'll be ready to go home."

"I still don't see what they're getting out of it."

"Everything, Harry. The Colonel gets to prove to everybody that his men can move so many inert tons onto ships and land it someplace hundreds of miles away. The navy gets a chance to sail someplace. The mayor gets his harbor dredged using military labor, and gets the sludge taken so far away that it won't ever seep back in."

"Are you sure they don't have something else in mind?"

Vickers sighed. "I'm telling you, there's nothing else. Colonels want to be generals, and mayors want to be governors. The only way they can make it is to do something that sounds like it's complicated and didn't cost as much as it would have if somebody else was doing it."

"But it's the most inefficient thing I've ever heard of."

Vickers stared at him. "I'll try it again. The army has a lot of men and money, but not much to do. The city has a harbor that keeps filling up with mud, but it costs a lot to keep dredging it. The Colonel wants to show off. The mayor wants to show off. Besides that, either one of them could be president someday, and then the other one will have a friend who is the president. What do they have to do, write it down?"

"Tell me honestly," said Harry. "How do you feel about golf?"

6

Six Years

WASHINGTON

"It's a complicated situation, sir." The Assistant Undersecretary opened his file folder and looked at his notes. Whenever he had to see the Senator he always went first to the stockroom and picked out a fresh, clean manila folder and placed a few sheets of paper inside. Sometimes the papers bore detailed information, and sometimes, like this time, most of the sheets came from the stockroom.

The Senator frowned and looked down at the six black-and-white photographs on his desk. His head moved from left to right in six separate little jerks. "Why is it complicated?" The Senator's bright little eyes narrowed as he leaned back in his chair and focused on the Assistant Undersecretary's mouth. The Senator had observed during the Assistant Undersecretary's first year as liaison with his committee that the right corner of his mouth was the place where the knot was tied. In his years as a poker player, the Senator had learned that when some people experienced tension, the entire force would find its way to a single muscle and grip it like a claw. No matter how smooth and relaxed they made the rest of their physiognomy, they could never control that twitch, the one spot to which they banished their anxiety. He had put himself through law school on the strength of this knowledge and the fact that his own knot was tied where it couldn't be seen by an opponent.

The right corner of the Assistant Undersecretary's mouth

was nearly paralyzed today, so that the left side opened wider. "We weren't informed of the existence of the place until a week ago, for one thing."

"Well now," the Senator began. "That's interesting. This photograph I have here says it's eight years old. That's kind of hard to reconcile."

The Assistant Undersecretary seemed, unaccountably, to relax. "If you'll notice, Senator, in the eight-year-old picture there's nothing actually penetrating the surface of the ocean. At that time it was, technically speaking, only a shoal."

The Senator looked at the second picture. "It's dry as a tennis court in this one, and that's six years old." He watched the Undersecretary's lips tighten again, and anticipated that something comprehensible was about to be said.

"Yes, sir," said the Assistant Undersecretary. "You have to understand that those are satellite photographs, and therefore the property of Military Intelligence. They're classified even now. We had a hell of a time getting them, and of course the military didn't think they were pictures of anything at all."

"If nobody thought they were anything, why the hell were they classified?"

"Because of the equipment, Senator. It's the capability of the equipment that's classified. Even if the picture were worthless, it would show what sort of quality we're getting from that particular surveillance satellite."

The Senator said, "Tell me more."

The Assistant Undersecretary relaxed, but the Senator decided he probably wasn't lying, so he let him. "The military satellite took hundreds of these photographs over the years. The standard nautical charts indicated that there was a shallow reef at those coordinates, which was visible at low tide. Each time a photograph was interpreted, it was assumed that the photograph was taken at low tide."

"Why did they assume that?" the Senator asked.

"Because the reef was visible."

"You're kidding."

The Assistant Undersecretary's brow wrinkled. "In their defense, I should say that it didn't seem important to them.

They were looking for the things they look for—the building of airstrips on land, ships and submarines at sea. That area was one of the few places they felt confident about, because it's too shallow for a nuclear submarine to operate in. There was also a workload problem, I understand."

The Senator was beginning to feel uncomfortable, so he stood up and stared at the photographs again, as the Assistant Undersecretary continued. "It's sort of interesting to contemplate. The photo-interp people were working three shifts, because at about that time the Caribbean and Central America were getting to be worrisome. So each shift assumed that one or both of the others were seeing these coordinates at high tide, when no land was visible. Of course, they were, only the land was still visible, and—"

"I get the idea, or all I'm going to get today," said the Senator. "I'll let them make the rest of the excuses themselves. Tell me how the rest of it happened."

The Assistant Undersecretary studied the older man, took a deep breath, and savored the last moments of his tenure in the State Department. In a year he would probably be vice-president of a bank, and look back on these days as his period of adventurous youth. "I'll be very frank. We dropped the ball. No excuses." For once, he felt free of the facial tic that had plagued him for years.

"I appreciate that," said the Senator slowly. "Tell me."

The Assistant Undersecretary smiled. "If it hadn't been my own career, this would seem almost funny. We thought we had a shoal in a godforsaken stretch of ocean, and it was slowly being built into an island. You know why this landed on my desk? Because it's an 'emerging nation.' "

The Senator watched him, and realized that the man had made some kind of transformation. He sensed that the time had come to see if the new man was useful. "Hard to deny that."

"They played a very good game. They came in low with the sun at their backs and outsmarted everybody."

"How?"

"Treaties, mostly. First it was a treaty where everybody agreed not to destroy the environment of Antarctica. The way these things work is that the major nations negotiate and sign. Then over a period, a lot of other countries, one by one, add their names. It's one of those things where anybody who wants can join. You pay very close attention while the first few signatures go on. If they sign, it doesn't much matter if the others do or not. If the twenty most powerful countries agree that nobody is going to strip-mine the south pole, it's damned well not going to be strip-mined."

"They signed it? How did they know where to go, what to say?"

The Assistant Undersecretary shrugged. "They read about it and sent a letter agreeing to the terms. The people who saw it probably didn't want to admit to anybody that they never heard of the place. You don't make it in diplomacy if you say 'Where the hell is that?' "

"Then what?"

"They agreed not to do a lot of things. They won't hunt whales, they won't test nuclear weapons aboveground, they won't torture political prisoners, import the skins of endangered species, or have a war in outer space."

"Damned agreeable of them, considering they're a chunk of rock the size of an avocado farm."

"They're actually pretty selective. They became official signatories of twenty or thirty treaties the same way. They picked most things they could sign without actually meeting with anybody, with a real preference for agreeing not to do things they couldn't do if they wanted to. After the first few, the name started to look familiar. Then it got a little more serious."

"What do you mean?"

"Over the past six years there have been quite a few changes. We averaged about twelve revolutions a year. They started recognizing governments. Whenever a new government came to power, they'd officially recognize it."

The Senator lowered himself into his chair and looked at the Assistant Undersecretary. "Where do we stand now?" He added, "No bullshit."

The Assistant Undersecretary repeated, "No bullshit. They're signatories of treaties with ninety-seven countries that I know about. Without exception, the foreign ministries of those countries will be more reluctant than we are to admit they were fooled. They were among the first to recognize the governments of about twenty countries, so they have some equivalent of our 'most-favored-nation' status. I'd say that, to the extent that diplomacy is a practical art, they mastered it. They got what they wanted."

The Senator's jaw clenched. "What's to stop somebody—I'm not saying us—from landing a battalion of marines and gobbling that island up?"

"Geography."

"Geography isn't much of an advantage in modern strategy."

The Assistant Undersecretary produced a map from his file folder and pointed to a tiny mark he'd made on it. "The island is halfway between Jamaica and the Honduras-Nicaragua border. Equally close to the north are the British Cayman Islands, and to the south, Isla de Providencia, which is Colombian. Cuba and Haiti are a little farther away, as are Belize, Costa Rica, Panama, Guatemala, and Mexico. And of course, none of these countries would make a move anyway, nor would any still-more-distant country."

"Why not?"

"They're afraid of the reaction of the United States."

NEW YORK

The Assistant Undersecretary sat in the special council chamber beside Jody Caldwell, the American deputy representative. Caldwell slouched in his chair, looking as though he might be asleep, but the earphones on his head were pulsing the English translation into his brain. He closed his eyes tighter as though it kept the words inside his head.

Ambassador Bayoum of Maldives was just beginning his speech. The language he spoke was Deviki, a dialect of Sinhalese, so in the chamber his was the only head not clamped by earphones. He had been chosen to speak for the Intergovernmental Maritime Consultative Organization, not only for his knowledge of nautical issues but also for his passion about islands. The Republic of Maldives consisted of two thousand islands comprising a total land area only a third the size of New York City. The population of 135,000 might well have been gathered under a dome to decide on all governmental issues, if they could have afforded a dome or had differences to discuss. The single issue was that the average person made a hundred dollars a year, and everyone felt the same about that.

"The Intergovernmental Maritime Consultative Organization recommends that the report of the Trusteeship Council be abrogated and set aside." The translator paused, breathing hard into his microphone after that effort. What the Ambassador had said was, "I yearn to piss on this paper." Then he launched into a discussion of islands in general. Although Ambassador Bayoum's country consisted of two thousand islands, only about two hundred were inhabited, and the rest served mainly as places to have shipwrecks. The idea that anyone could be greedy enough to argue over possession of a tiny island seemed to him to be an outrage. Anybody could have an island if he were willing to live on it. He noted that the usual punishment for treason in the Maldives was exile to a remote island for three or four years. It was clear to him that the only reason a great power ever wanted an island was to build a military base on it. In his own experience, it had been the British base on the island of Gan. When the British had withdrawn in 1975, the Soviet Union had graciously offered to occupy it. That offer had been declined. Now, said Bayoum, the same thing was being offered in the Caribbean. "I demand," he said, "that this issue be settled in a vote of the General Assembly."

Next Danyankin was allowed to read his statement. "The Soviet Union will ignore the Ambassador's suggestion of ulterior motives in the affair of Gan Island," he said. "But there is complete agreement on the present issue, the disposition of the island in the Caribbean. The majority vote of the Trusteeship Council was to appoint the United States trustee. The Soviet Union was the lone dissenting vote. At present the United Nations administers only one trust territory, the Pacific Islands, with the United States as trustee since 1947. I will remind my colleagues of only a few things concerning the administration of that trust. First, these islands are being used as military bases for the U.S. Pacific fleet and the U.S. Air Force. Second, the islands of Bikini and Eniwetok have been demolished by nuclear tests. Third, the World Health Organization reported that the health conditions in the chain, after twenty years of American colonization, were atrocious. Finally, I remind my colleagues that Palau and the Marshall Islands have requested independence from the United States, but have been blocked for many years from achieving it, despite referendums and promises. The record is not good. If additional territories are to be placed in trust by the United Nations, then they should be administered by a nation other than the United States.'' He sat down and compressed himself into his suit like a crouching cat.

''Damn,'' muttered Jody Caldwell. ''He would bring that up.''

''Say something,'' said the Assistant Undersecretary.

Caldwell looked at him. ''What am I supposed to say? It's all true. We didn't do those islands any favors.''

''But the reason we were there was to save them from the Japanese.''

Caldwell scowled. ''I'm supposed to say that with Aritomo sitting across the damned table? In an hour I've got to convince him to kick in three billion to the International Fund for Agricultural Development.''

''Come on,'' whispered the Assistant Undersecretary. ''I can't tell Washington we gave up.''

Caldwell sighed, and pressed a button on the table in front of him, which lit up another button on the console in front of Mr. Jugwartha, who was presiding. Jugwartha nodded at him, but called instead on the representative from Djibouti, Mr. Kanomi, who stood and said in his British accent, ''I would like to speak for the World Intellectual Property Organization.''

Mr. Jugwartha raised his eyebrows. ''Have you been chosen to speak for the WIPO? I haven't been informed of that.''

''Been chosen?'' said Kanomi. He and Jugwartha had been at Cambridge together in the fifties, and each had a benevolent contempt for the other's native intelligence. ''Of course not. I have merely chosen to take the point of view of that organization, of which all concerned nations are members."

"How can that be?" asked Jugwartha.

"WIPO's charter is to protect literary, industrial, scientific, and artistic works, is it not?" He didn't wait for an answer. "This island is a manmade contrivance. It is both a scientific and an industrial work, is it not?" He smiled. "It is intellectual property."

The Assistant Undersecretary clutched Jody Caldwell's arm. "That man is crazy."

Caldwell slowly pulled his arm away, and said quietly, "Do we really want that island? I mean, we've got three thousand of them in the Pacific trust, we've got fifty-three Virgin Islands, six Samoan islands, Guam, the Aleutians, Puerto Rico, Wake, Midway, Hawaii . . ."

"Of course we don't," hissed the Assistant Undersecretary. "But we can't let people go around building the damned things wherever they feel like."

Mr. Jugwartha was saying, "Mr. Kanomi, this is a serious matter, and you are trying to solve it with mechanisms designed to protect trademarks and patents. Surely—"

Kanomi interrupted. "Surely a man who saves a baby from a pack of wolves by whacking them with his walking stick should not be criticized for faulty equipment."

Jugwartha snapped, "He should be criticized for being an idiot." He switched off Kanomi's microphone. Only those who spoke English understood Kanomi's shout: "I have broken no rule. This is an infringement."

But the representative from Saudi Arabia was speaking. Ali Hiraz spoke softly, in a high nasal voice that indicated that he had never in his life wondered if people would listen carefully to what he said. "The island's existence is undeniable. Its ownership is unquestionable. It is, and it will be."

The Assistant Undersecretary gazed at Jody Caldwell with a kind of intellectual despair.

Caldwell leaned over and whispered, "You want to tell him he's crazy? You'd better have one of those cars that run on chickenshit."

Ali Hiraz seemed to speak even more quietly now, and

Mr. Jugwartha fiddled with the volume knob for the microphone. "The island has been built as a perpetual homeland for the native people of the region, the Carib Indians. There is no danger that this tiny remnant of an indigenous group slaughtered three hundred years ago will pose a threat to the vital interests of any nation. There is no argument for a trustee. A group that can pull land out of the sea can surely live on it." He prepared to sit, but then as an afterthought he tossed a piece of paper on the table in front of him. "Here is a list of ninety-two nations who agree." Then he sat down.

The Assistant Undersecretary whispered, "You've got to save this."

Caldwell saw the signal from Mr. Jugwartha and rose to his feet. "The United States has always supported the rights of all regions to determine their fates. I propose that a free and fair ballot be held on the island to establish the will of the people."

Mr. Jugwartha looked puzzled. "But that's already been done. Twice, in fact."

"Thank you," said Caldwell, and sat down.

The Assistant Undersecretary gaped at him in disbelief. After a few seconds Caldwell muttered, "At least we've got that behind us."

THE ISLAND

It was only by chance that Harry saw the shape of the big yacht moving into the cove after sunset. He had been studying the size of the waves that boiled over the knife-edged reef at low tide, wondering if the coral or rocks or whatever the substance was that made it so dangerous could be strong enough to serve as a foundation for another extension of land. The sun had gone down before he'd made up his mind, and he'd stayed at the water's edge long enough to see the big boat float soundlessly through the rift in the reef and drop anchor.

It was long and white, with huge enclosed cabins and a professional crew that wore identical white pants and blue coats like the navy of some small but solvent country.

There was a thicket of antennas and dishes and electronic gear on the roof, and there were portholes that revealed nothing of the interior.

Harry ran toward the nearest building, which was Lord Carnarvon's new barracks, a small, sturdy white box set on blocks because Lord Carnarvon had never been able to decide where he wanted to put it. Harry climbed over the plateau of new ground they'd built on the slag of an Argentine steel mill and the shards of a pottery plant in Veracruz, and sprinted for the barracks.

The lanterns were still lit, and he could hear the sound of hammering. As he flung the door open, he saw two Lord Carnarvons fitting a new handle to a sledgehammer, one pounding the heavy metal head onto the clean blond wood, while the other held it, his fingers half an inch from the spot where the second hammer hit. They looked up at Harry and smiled, unconcerned, as the hammer hit again.

Harry spotted the original Lord Carnarvon lying on a top bunk at the far end of the big, empty room, his leg hanging down and swinging back and forth as he turned the pages of a catalogue with a picture of a boat on it. "Lord Carnarvon," Harry gasped. "You know where Vickers is?"

"No. Where?" He went on reading.

"I asked because I didn't know."

"He's probably out doing some Vickers thing." Lord Carnarvon looked up at the ceiling. "I'd say he's figuring out how to kill somebody with a thumbtack."

Harry grabbed Lord Carnarvon's leg and tugged. "Come on. We've got trouble."

Lord Carnarvon kicked his leg free, then swung it down, and then he was off the bunk and standing beside Harry. There wasn't so much as a thump, just a slight depression of the floorboards as he eased his weight onto them. "What sort of trouble?"

"There's a big yacht in the cove. I think it's Fat Jimmy, come to cut my ears off."

One of the other Lord Carnarvons moved closer, carrying the new sledgehammer at the neck. "Fat Jimmy? Sounds like somebody we can eat."

The real Lord Carnarvon shrugged. "We'll see. Go find

Vickers and meet us here.'' He walked to the wall and opened a cabinet, then handed Harry a black M16 rifle and two loaded magazines. He handed another to the remaining Lord Carnarvon, who started to go with them to the door, but Harry held his arm.

''Emma's alone at our place,'' said Harry. ''If Fat Jimmy had her, he'd kill her.''

''I'll bring her,'' said that Lord Carnarvon. ''He can get you both at once.''

Harry, Emma, and Lord Carnarvon moved out of the cover of the Guatemalan forest that had been brought in and planted intact four years ago, then crossed the open lawn beyond it, and descended to the plateau of new ground, leaving Lord Carnarvon's cousins on the heights. They kept low, crouching to keep their profiles from showing above the rocky shelf that protected the beach from the sea at low tide. Finally Harry knelt behind an outcropping, and the others joined him. He pointed out at the yacht in the cove. ''See? It's got to be the Fat Man. He's here to collect.''

''Collect what?'' asked Lord Carnarvon. He studied the yacht in the cove. There were a few lights glowing through portholes on the side, and a uniformed man was visible in the pilothouse reading something. He didn't seem to be armed, or to be watching for anything more sinister than a change in the wind that might shift the anchors out of the sand and set the huge craft adrift.

''The Fat Man will collect whatever he can collect,'' said Harry. ''He's like a vacuum cleaner, moving through the world sucking up whatever he can get.''

Emma sighed. ''What Harry means is that we stole some of his money. He was the one we were trying to avoid when we met you. You might say he financed a lot of this island.''

They stared out at the white shape in the cove, watching the gentle ripples expend their energy against its unmoving side. Lord Carnarvon turned to Emma. ''Is that who you think this is—this Fat Jimmy character?''

''No,'' said Emma. ''I can't picture Fat Jimmy actually

getting into a boat and coming down here to break our legs. I mean, what does a boat like that cost?''

Lord Carnarvon thought for a moment. ''It's hard to do an assessment in the dark. A million or so, I guess. How much did you take?''

''Satisfied, Harry?'' asked Emma.

''It's got to be him. Who else would need a million dollars' worth of boat to ship his butt down here to take over an island that's not even breaking even yet?'' Harry sighted his rifle on the man in the pilothouse.

Lord Carnarvon looked at the seaman. The man sat back in his chair and put his feet up on the console astride the wheel, holding his book in his lap. ''Is that Fat Jimmy?''

''No,'' said Emma. ''Does it look like somebody named Fat Jimmy?''

''Do you know that guy? Have you seen him before?''

''No,'' Harry admitted.

''Then I wouldn't murder him just yet.''

''Why not?'' Harry lowered his rifle.

''Just a hunch. Look at the stern of the boat. The home port is Corpus Christi. It doesn't look like the sort of boat you'd pick out to go kill somebody, and he doesn't look like the sort of man you'd pick to help you.''

''That's true, Harry,'' said Emma. ''You've got to admit that nothing about this looks like Fat Jimmy.''

''All right,'' Harry muttered. ''We'll wait.''

''Hell,'' said Lord Carnarvon. ''It might even be one of those rich investors you said would come along.''

Nathan Packer stood before the mirror in his stateroom and tugged the cuffs of his plain white shirt to ensure that exactly a quarter of an inch of cuff was visible beyond the sleeve of his navy-blue blazer. He'd rejected the regimental tie of the Scottish Borderers. Stucker, his valet, had ratified the decision, on the grounds that people in the tropics didn't wear neckties. But Packer hadn't considered what other people did. Nathan Packer did what he did, and other people damned well got out of the way if they had time, and if they didn't, they picked themselves up off the ground and said, ''So that's Nat Packer.'' But this was a very special set of negotiations, and Nat Packer never negotiated at a disadvantage. He'd never in his life met a confidence man who didn't know by heart every set of British regimental colors, every school tie, and at least one member of every men's club in the English-speaking world.

He moved out of the stateroom into the carpeted hallway, and closed the heavy mahogany door behind him. He nodded to his head accountant, Sam Fish, who was coming down the hallway toward him carrying a hard-sided leather briefcase. Fish pivoted on his heel and fell into step with Packer, then held the briefcase out to him. "Here it is, Nat. Would you like to check it?"

"Did you check it?" Packer walked on without looking at it.

"Yes, I did," said Fish.

"That's always been good enough for me, Sammy." Packer accepted the briefcase and started up the stairway. "By the way," he added, "if these people are a disappointment, you'll have to run things at home for as long as it takes. I've already told everybody who needs to know. Melissa is to stay in Los Angeles until the whole thing blows over and I come to get her or . . . or I don't. Make sure she has everything."

Fish nodded, and Packer disappeared up the stairs. Fish thought about the words "if these people are a disappointment." If they were smart, they'd come to terms. If they were simply too greedy to control themselves, they'd put Packer in a bottle like a genie and try to extract hundreds of millions of dollars out of him in exchange for the promise that they'd let him go. The very existence of a man like Packer was too much for some people. Professional thieves, terrorist groups, prostitutes, blackmailers, and tax men followed him from one continent to another, looking for an opportunity. Cabdrivers expected hundred-dollar tips, as though they'd carried, not a hundred-and-eighty-pound man, but the weight of his empire and enterprise and notoriety in their cabs. And the people on this island, he thought, were probably a bad gamble. They seemed to be everything at once.

In Sam Fish's reading of history he'd never come across a set of founding fathers of any country anywhere who hadn't been heavily armed and a little crazy. And what Packer was proposing now was, Fish knew, a turning point in the man's life worthy of a character in a William for-God's-sake Shakespeare play. He'd fallen in love with a woman who'd been about to get divorced anyway, but you couldn't prove that part of it to the envious set of mean-spirited fundamentalists who handpicked school textbooks and congressional candidates for West Texas.

It had been the night of the state convention, and Packer had still been in his office waiting for the telegram that was going to say, "Nat, I just realized that some fool forgot to invite you," even though Packer had put up a full third of the overhead. Sam Fish had been there when Packer had picked up the telephone and told his pilot to button up the plane for the night. Then Packer had said, "Well, that's that. Sam, do me a favor and see what you can find out about the people who have themselves that little island down in the Caribbean."

His social and political aspirations for Texas had just gone the same way as the telegram. Maybe they were together somewhere with the formula for turning lead into gold and the plans for the perpetual-motion machine. But at that moment, Nat Packer's life had changed. It was, Sam reflected, right out of John for-God's-sake Milton. "Evil, be thou my good." Only people in offices late at night didn't say it that way. They said things like, "Well, that's that." And then they set out to do something different.

Nat Packer took the dinghy ashore, cutting the outboard motor just after he'd climbed over the crest of the first of the beach breakers. He tipped the motor up to protect the propeller's shearpin and drifted to the beach. He managed to step off the bow as a wave receded, so his feet stayed dry. Then he began to haul the dinghy up onto the sand. He saw the shadow on the sand beside his feet, but he didn't turn around until the boat was secure. When he did, he found himself looking up at a tall blond man wearing the tinted aviator glasses of a tropical dictator and a shoulder holster with a military-issue .45 automatic stuck in it too loosely for Packer's taste.

"How do?" said the man. "Off course?"

"No. I came to look around, and to talk to you folks." He held out his hand and the man shook it. "My name's Nat Packer."

"John Vickers," said the man. "You want to bring that little suitcase with you?"

"We'd better," said Packer. "I'd hate to have it wash out of the boat. It's full of money."

Vickers looked at the briefcase for a moment, then at Packer. "Oh. That Nat Packer. The one you want to talk to is Harry. Or maybe Emma. Come on." He walked up a long sloping rock ledge that jutted up from the sea. Then he looked back at the briefcase Packer carried. "Harry said somebody like you would be along. Glad I lived to see it."

Packer sat uneasily on a bunk bed in the little wooden building at the narrow end of the island. His gaze ran along the shelves that covered every wall, and his mind was so used to expressing abstract ideas in numbers that it didn't need to go beyond the estimate that about sixty percent of the containers on the shelves contained food, and forty had brand names: Remington, Winchester, Savage.

"Just happen to be in the neighborhood?" asked Emma. Packer shook his head. "Well, at least I can offer you some lemonade. Or would you like something stronger?"

"I'll have whatever you're all having," said Packer. "And thank you very much."

Harry said, "Then it's lemonade. In this climate you can't drink until sundown. That sun hits you and you start to get too comfortable around bulldozers and cement mixers. Steel gears and flywheels start to look soft and friendly."

Emma placed a pitcher on the table and poured glasses of lemonade for Packer, Harry, and herself. As she handed Packer his glass, she said, "Vickers said your suitcase is full of money. What for?"

Packer lifted the briefcase to his knees and opened it toward Harry and Emma, to reveal the orderly ranks of hundred-dollar bills. He spoke as he closed the briefcase and set it aside. "I'm just trying to be reasonably businesslike. It doesn't take much to figure out why you're on this island or what the take will be once you're established. I'd like to be one of the people who know you, and it sometimes saves me time to show people I'm not wasting their time being hypothetical."

"It's interesting," said Harry. "I always thought I'd have to do some kind of advertising after we got things started. There's a magazine that's only for the members of the British peerage. They get it for free, and nobody else can buy it. I thought I'd take out a full page."

"You are advertising," said Packer. "When you get a godforsaken piece of rock landscaped and planted like a botanical garden and recognized as a country, you're saying 'I'm open for business.' "

"I hope other people are as astute as you are," said Emma. Then she looked a little concerned. "But not many are, are they? You're Nat Packer, and they're not."

"Well," said Harry. "We'd like to do business with you, if we can."

"I'd like to buy a silent partnership."

Harry shook his head, and disappointment gathered above his eyes. "Oh, I'm sorry. I should have figured you'd smell the potential. But we can't sell shares."

"Wait," said Packer. "Explain."

"When we started the island, it wasn't worth anything at all," said Emma. "Now its value is—"

Packer nodded. "Incalculable."

"But the only way we can play this," said Harry, "is to preserve the one thing that makes the place worth anything—that it's a country. So it doesn't have to do what anybody tells it to do. Or not to do."

"Of course. That's why I'm here."

"So we can't have partners in the usual sense. See, when we started out, we hired people to work here. But once there was enough construction to attract attention, we had to start working backwards to clean up our history, and build a few legal fictions."

Packer's eyes widened. "All those people are—"

Emma interrupted. "Citizens. When we knew we had to create the first of the legal fictions, we asked everybody if they wanted in or out. Most of them took the gamble.

You can't pull anything like this off unless you have citizens. We even made one of our partners president."

Harry said, "Look, if you're about to be indicted in the States or something like that, we're having a special today on citizenships. Taking somebody like you is a risk, because we're really not ready for that kind of press reaction, but it's probably worth it."

Packer held up his hand. "No, this is just a business deal. If I can't invest, I'd like to establish a few legal fictions of my own."

"Name one," said Emma.

"I'd like to establish a holding company based here, and move some of my assets."

"That depends," said Harry. "What sorts of assets did you have in mind?"

Packer held up the briefcase. "I'd require about this much space. Transactions that are subject to sales tax, or Federal Reserve reporting requirements, or antitrust laws, or ones that produce a particularly large taxable profit could be carried on by my holding company here."

Harry nodded. "We could do that for a price."

"What did you have in mind?"

"One percent."

"Of the profits?"

"Of the assets."

THE ISLAND

Emma lay on the chaise longue and listened to her own breathing. Her eyes were closed behind her sunglasses, but she knew that if she opened them a little, the high white clouds would have moved to form a different pattern. Maybe the horse's head would be elongated into an alligator by now. She squinted into the sky, but the horse's head was gone already, and the next puff of cloud was still low on the horizon.

She leaned down to the flagstone pavement of the balcony and picked up her glass, then remembered she had to sit up to drink it. Emma looked out over the wall and down at the harbor, and she could see Harry standing far out on the pier, a little figure in jeans and a black T-shirt. He lifted a hand to brush the hair back on his head, and she thought about it again. Harry was going to have to start wearing hats. His hairline had been receding for years, and now the little bald spot in the back was making its way forward. A bald man in this latitude just had to wear a hat. They even called it the Tropic of Cancer, like a warning to people who had the sense to hear it. Emma carried the drink through the open French doors and into the living room, and felt her shoulders cooling as soon as she was out of the sun.

Emma picked up her little leather notebook, leafed through to the section labeled "Shopping list for Kingston," and wrote "Hats for Harry." She'd buy enough of a selection to make it a sure thing: baseball caps, a safari hat, maybe even one of those little captain's hats like Captain Pettigrew hung on a peg in the cabin of his tugboat.

Suddenly Emma's idea shifted into another idea. She took off her bathing suit and put on a sweatshirt and blue jeans, then made her way downstairs to the sidewalk. She could see Vickers' crew already. The yellow bulldozer was moving back and forth beside a big mound of dirt.

She walked in the middle of the wide, curving stretch of grass, stopping once to study the color of the leaves of a big eucalyptus tree. When she reached the end of the meadow, she could hear Vickers barking over the sound of the bulldozer. "Good. Real good. Now spread it back this way." The bulldozer turned and lowered its scoop, then plowed into the mound of dirt and smeared part of it into a flat path. Vickers moved around behind it, and Emma called, "Vickers."

He walked up to her, taking off his gloves and stuffing them into his back pocket.

"I'm here to talk hats."

"Come on," said Vickers. "Let's go where it's a little quieter." They walked a few yards away and sat down under a palm tree. Vickers lit a cigarette and said, "Okay, let's talk hats."

Emma said, "It started with a fraud I want to perpetrate on Harry. I was going to get Harry a hat or two when I make the supply run to Jamaica tomorrow. This island is no place for a man with a shiny head."

"True," said Vickers.

"Then it occurred to me he'd be more likely to wear a hat if it were a big male thing. Like a team uniform. Then I remembered that you could be the world's leading expert on uniforms. That's the first part of the idea. What do you think?"

"About what?"

"I've decided you might want to buy your little army some uniforms. You tell me what you want, and I'll put in an order when I get to Jamaica."

"Probably not."

Vickers glanced over at the men, who were now following the path of the bulldozer and spreading the dirt with shovels. "History gives you a lot of chances to make improvements you'll regret later. This is one of them."

"This isn't history. It's fashion. If people look good, they feel good. Heaven knows, we deserve to feel good. We've worked so hard."

"We're on this little island. If we're going to survive, we need to have a group of men who can handle themselves in a fight, because there's no place to run. We've got that. Now we stop."

"That doesn't sound like you."

"The only strategy that's available is pretty primitive. Everybody is in the army if we need one, and the army is the police force if we need one. As long as we don't start making distinctions, we should be okay."

"What are you worried about?"

Vickers shrugged. "I got tired of little countries where people wear uniforms. That's why I'm here—why I didn't pull out when I saw that this wasn't going to take a few months, or a year, or ten years."

"Forget I said anything." Emma stood up. "I'd better get back to work, or we'll have a golf course and no hotel."

"You said the uniforms were only the first part of the idea."

Emma smiled. "Oh, I almost forgot. The second part

is about uniforms too. When the golf course is finished I want you to pick out a place to put a baseball diamond."

"A baseball diamond? What for?"

"Come on, Vickers," said Emma. "Your mind works like that bulldozer—back and forth, taking a little with it each time. If I'm going to get decent players to come here for winter baseball, I'll need something for them to play on."

"You're doing that so Harry will wear a baseball hat?"

"Don't be ridiculous. I'm doing it to make money."

7

Seven Years

THE ISLAND

Carlos Del Cupido held up his empty right hand, then held the clean white baseball beside it, pinched between the thumb and forefinger of his left hand. He said to the tall, thin, twenty-year-old beside him, "Take it exactly like this." His right hand clenched the ball like an eagle's claw. "Try it." He tossed the ball into the young man's glove.

The pitcher imitated Del Cupido's grip, then slowly completed his windup and pretended to throw.

"Not quite," said Del Cupido. "Shield the ball with your glove until your arm is in motion. If the batter sees your fingers, he'll know what he's in for."

Harry and Emma walked away from them and along the path in front of the gray wooden bleachers toward the dugout.

Emma sat on the bench and watched the pitcher repeat the motion. This time he lost his grip and hurled the ball into the dirt in front of him, and watched it bounce into the backstop. Del Cupido's face showed no surprise. His hand emerged from his jacket pocket with another ball, and he demonstrated the motion again.

"How did you get him?" asked Harry.

"Davey?" said Emma. "He's a prospect for the Orioles. He'll be good if he can pick up something besides his fastball."

"No, Del Cupido. I thought he was dead."

"Well, he's not. He was pitching coach for a team in

the Dominican Republic last winter, so I figured he might like a shot at managing.''

Harry studied Del Cupido. ''What else?''

''He had a season with a Japanese team once, but he couldn't pick up the language. It's hard to coach that way.''

''You know what I'm talking about. I used to own his baseball card. If they ever get around to it he'll be in the Hall of Fame.''

''No he won't,'' said Emma.

''Now we're getting somewhere. Why not?''

''Something to do with bad checks. He can't go back to the United States. There's been a warrant out for him since the early seventies.''

The catcher was now squatting behind the plate with his mitt extended, his right hand between his legs fluttering signals. The pitcher went into his windup, his long left leg kicked forward into the air, and his body followed it, his right arm coming down in a vertical motion like a whip. The white ball flashed in the sunlight, then seemed to dissolve into pure speed. The whip cracked, and the catcher threw the ball back to the mound.

Del Cupido said, ''You'll get it. Just keep throwing it until you like it. Same motion as your fastball.''

Harry stood up. ''Give him anything he wants. The man is a legend.'' He started to walk again, then stopped. ''You write the checks, though.''

NEW YORK

''Stable and substantial?'' Harry said. ''The place is built on rock and steel and concrete. Over that is about twenty feet of the best black soil in the world, washed down to the delta of the Magdalena River in Colombia. You can grow a lawn on it in three days, and we've planted two hundred and fourteen varieties of trees on it without losing one.''

Mr. Maltman shook his head and leaned forward to rest his elbows on his desk. ''That isn't what I meant. I have to answer to the stockholders and directors of Omnibank. What's their assurance that ten years from now there won't be a revolution and a new government that snaps up any investment?''

''None,'' said Harry. ''What's your assurance that eleven years from now a spaceship from Jupiter won't make a crash landing in your hot tub?''

''A hot tub is a limited investment.''

''Not if you're sitting in it. The people who own the island are going to be on it, watching it very closely from now on.''

Mr. Maltman raked his fingers through his white hair in a smooth and fastidious motion that somehow moved it perfectly into place. Harry studied the hair, wondering if it were a toupee. Maltman took a deep breath. ''The bank would like to establish a presence on the island.''

''I'll bet it would,'' Harry agreed.

''But before the bank opens a branch in any foreign country, it has to know something about the climate.''

Harry chuckled. ''Next time you see the bank, tell it the climate is great.''

Mr. Maltman took a yellow legal pad out of his desk and referred to some notes he'd made on it. ''We would require a building, of course.''

''You can build one if it's not an eyesore and isn't too big. We'll lease you the land for a fee.''

Mr. Maltman's eyes widened. ''It's customary for developing countries to offer incentives to attract capital. If you will supply suitable facilities, and perhaps a bond to ensure the—''

Harry held up his hand. ''Hold it. Banks will be allowed to operate on the island under the following conditions. You bring in what you need, and you can stay as long as you're useful.''

''But you're offering nothing at all.''

''That's right. You must be crazy to want to start a bank in a place like that. It's hours from Miami, and there isn't much except a half-finished hotel and a blueprint for a casino. You're the ninth banker who's asked to see me this trip. Maybe you're all crazy.''

Mr. Maltman flipped the pages of his legal pad until he came to a blank sheet, and poised his gold pen over it.

"Let's do this differently. What sort of relationship do you propose to maintain with financial institutions?"

"All right," said Harry. "Here's what I do for you. I don't have time to regulate banks. I'm not interested in printing worthless currency. The standard will be the American dollar. You don't have to worry about getting robbed, because everybody on the island is armed to the teeth, and I control the only ways to come and go. I don't intend to tax anyone, because then people would want me to provide services. I expect to make enough on the island to run the little government we need as a business expense."

Mr. Maltman cleared his throat. "Uh, Mr. Erskine, I hope you'll excuse my curiosity. But how do you intend to do that?"

"Right now there's the hotel, the casino, the business associated with the baseball team. There's the transportation to the island. There will be rental fees for space on the island. Your bank, for instance, would pay me for the right to use up a plot with a building. The prices for things will be high, but I'm not going to rob anybody. It would get around, and screw up the business."

"We'll have to do some studies, of course, but I believe we may come up with a proposal in the next few weeks."

Harry stood. "Don't waste too much time. In another few weeks there will be so many banks setting up dummy corporations to run dirty money through that island that I won't have room for you. As it is, I've had to add five hundred acres this year alone."

"Five hundred acres?" Mr. Maltman repeated. "You mean that when you run out of space you just—"

"Expand," said Harry.

J. Dixon Bacon leaned back in his chair and stared up at the high ceiling above his desk. The long leather chair-back dwarfed him, and his white hair spread out like an aura around his head as the chair tilted back. The chair went back so far that he looked like a strangely over-dressed astronaut strapped in for a particularly rough blast-off.

Harry stared across the desk at him. "I can see up your nose."

"What?" Bacon rocked forward.

Harry said, "This is a nice office. I suppose the paintings came with it. What did you want to see me about?"

"The Federal National Bank is a friendly institution, Harry." Bacon folded his hands on his desk and presented a semblance of a smile.

"It's amazing how friendly banks have been to us this year," said Harry. "There must be fifty who want to move right in and live with us."

"So does the Federal National Bank. Only we're willing to take some responsibility."

"You mean you want to marry us?"

Bacon laughed. "No. We'd like to help pay for the house."

"This is getting too vague." Harry shook his head. "Let's start a new metaphor. Horses, maybe. Or flowers."

Bacon's expression was suddenly earnest. "The Federal National Bank has been a leader in providing funds for developing nations for two decades." He pronounced the word "*dek*-ids." As though to assert his sure persistence, he repeated it. "Two *dek*-ids."

Harry took this opportunity to peer up at the ceiling to see what Bacon had been looking at. "A fat lot of good it's done you," said Harry. "You went into it with the idea that you'd rip them off when natural resources got rare enough to pay, and now every week there's another article saying they're going under and taking you with them."

"We'd like to make one more foreign loan. To you."

"What did you have in mind?" asked Harry.

Bacon clasped and unclasped his hands as he spoke. "We can start you off with fifty million or so. Enough to let you expand to protect our investment. You pay one point below the discount rate. In exchange, we get your business." He wasn't sure that Harry had grasped that part of it, so he rephrased it. "We handle your funds."

"That's it?"

Bacon nodded. "Of course, we'd need to establish a

branch office on the island. We don't just give you a check for fifty million. We pay it out as needed."

Harry shook his head. "No."

Bacon smiled. "Two points below the discount rate."

"No."

"All right then," said Bacon. "We'll call the loan a bad debt after five years and write it off with the rest of them. The government will have to cover them all eventually anyway, or a whole lot of people will lose their shirts."

Harry stood up. "Thanks for the offer, but I've got to run. Someday I hope I won't have to catch the daily 'Rum and Fun' flight to Kingston and take a boat to get home."

"Wait," said Bacon. "We've got papers to sign. Arrangements to make."

"Sorry," said Harry. "I can't make a deal with you. We've got all the banks we need."

"You don't seem to understand," Bacon insisted. "I'm offering you fifty million dollars that you'll probably never have to pay back. Why on earth would you refuse?"

"Because you're dangerous. You've got bad loans out all over South America. You made most of them after you knew you'd never get the first loans back. You did it so you could get into those countries where you could get the authorities by the balls.

"What are you getting at?"

"You've had five managers in Florida and California cited for taking deposits consisting of sacks of hundred-dollar bills that smell like fish and not reporting it."

"That's nothing," said Bacon. "The crime is getting too busy to keep up with the paperwork. And how do you even know about that?"

"It was in the newspapers. You don't have to live here to read the papers. And I check out every company that wants to be on the island. I asked other banks that I deal with."

"Look," said Bacon. "Our branches weren't even charged with a crime. But if they had been, what's that to you? You built that island to attract money. You've got tax evaders, skimmers, money launderers, embezzlers . . ."

"I can afford them. I can't afford you."

"Why not?"

"If you've got our money in your bank, you think you can control us. Things are getting tighter in the States for banks that are staying alive on drug money, and that's bad news for you, because you made all those loans just so you could get into that business."

"I can make this deal sweeter."

"No. I can't have a hundred South American drug dealers blasting away at each other with machine guns in the lobby of my hotel. And I can't have eight or ten beleaguered heads of state blaming the drug trade on my island. Eventually they'd have to get together and close me down." Harry turned and walked to the door. "Goodbye."

Bacon leaned back in his chair again, and stared at his ceiling. When his assistant walked in, he moved his eyes to her without moving his head. "I won't need those papers today. Before we do anything more, I'll have to do some planning."

"We've done quite a profile, sir. Will you be needing it?"

Bacon thought for a moment. "Does it have any pictures in it? You know . . . pictures of the island?"

DOMINICA

Captain Pettigrew sat in the shade of a rubber tree, his eyes half-open. He could hear the constant twittering of birds, and twice a group of little girls came past to stare at him, but otherwise the village seemed uninhabited. Every few minutes he would glance again in the direction of the wooden hut on stilts, but there was no sign of Lord Carnarvon. The place was poor. He decided most of the healthy adults must be off somewhere working at something.

It was when he let his eyes close and forgot about time that he became aware that someone had sat down beside him. He opened his eyes and in his peripheral vision he could see it was an old white-haired Indian, dressed in a bleached cotton shirt and khaki trousers, leaning his back against Captain Pettigrew's rubber tree.

"Good afternoon," said Captain Pettigrew.

"Good afternoon, Captain Pettigrew," the old man answered in an accent that sounded British but wasn't. "I'm Nathaniel Boats. I thought we could have a talk."

"Pleased to meet you," said Captain Pettigrew. Both men leaned toward each other around the trunk of the rubber tree and shook hands.

There was a long silence, and then Boats spoke again. "What do you think of Dominica?"

"It's beautiful. I like the mountains and the lakes. I'm not so sure about the jungle, though. I'd never have found my way here alone, and if I had to go back, I'd have to navigate like a sailor in a fog."

Boats smiled. "The jungle and the mountains are the reason we lasted long enough to get born. The Carib name for Dominica is Waitukubuli. It means 'battlefield.' Caribs used to fight like hell and then hide in the back country where the French and the British wouldn't follow."

"You ever fight?"

"Sure. I was just a lad. Fourteen years old. That was when the British finally decided it was time to round us all up and put us here on the reservation so they wouldn't have to kill us."

"You been here since then?"

"Most of the time. When I was young, I used to go once a year to work the lime orchards. Then, in the late thirties, the lime trees got sick and died. I worked on an American freighter during the war.

"How many Caribs you think are left?"

"I never counted. I suppose they know in Roseau. A few hundred." Boats paused and then handed Pettigrew a photograph.

Captain Pettigrew recognized Lord Carnarvon and his two cousins standing in front of the unfinished entrance to the hotel, with Harry; Vickers, and Emma. "Yeah," he said. "My man Joaquín took that picture."

"Is it what Lord Carnarvon says it is? He's one of the partners in a hotel?"

Pettigrew nodded. "Not just the hotel. The whole island. Me too."

"And you came here to get Caribs to live there?"

Captain Pettigrew nodded. "If anybody wants to come. We need a few real Caribs to make the place look legitimate."

"This fellow Harry Erskine. He's some kind of trickster, isn't he? Maybe a little too smart for ordinary people?"

Captain Pettigrew sighed. "He's that."

"I'd like to meet him."

"Then come to the island with us."

The old man looked across the dusty clearing at the row of thatched huts and plank sheds on stilts. "I don't think so. Maybe next year I'll go stay in the hotel for a week.

"You might like it."

The old man shrugged. "I like it already. Somebody finally thought of a way to use the Caribs. You think the United Nations would let you build a Carib homeland if they knew how few of us were left?"

"I don't know. Maybe that makes you more valuable, like the whooping crane."

"If it works, maybe there'll be a few more."

Lord Carnarvon drove the ancient jeep along a dirt path so narrow that the wet leaves brushed it on both sides, spraying Captain Pettigrew's face and chest with warm rainwater. Every few feet the jeep would bounce wildly, then lean horribly, first to one side, then the other, as it crossed a trough where a rivulet had run through the jungle after a rain. They'd been here a week, and each day it had rained.

"There will be twenty-two people," said Lord Carnarvon. "Can we handle that many besides the crew?"

"Once we're out of sight of land we won't have much choice. They won't be comfortable, but if the weather holds, we'll still have them aboard when we get there." Captain Pettigrew held on to the dashboard as the jeep hobbled over a rut. "You're sure you want to go through with this?"

"It's the only way. Nobody in his right mind is going to move a thousand miles from home because we tell them Harry said it was a good idea."

Captain Pettigrew held on as Lord Carnarvon raced the

engine and urged the jeep up a steep, muddy incline onto the paved highway. He drove on the left side, and Captain Pettigrew considered asking if that was the way things were done here, but then he saw an old truck loaded with bananas approaching on the other side of the road. That was all that seemed important.

A few minutes later Pettigrew saw three women in white cotton dresses walking beside the road, carrying baskets. When they heard the jeep coming up behind them they stepped farther from the road, but didn't look. And then a hundred yards farther Lord Carnarvon pulled the jeep into another, larger village, and stopped in front of a small white church. "This is Salybia," he said, and got out of the jeep. "What time is it?"

Pettigrew glanced at his watch. "About ten minutes to one."

Lord Carnarvon looked around at the small unpainted plank houses on low pilings. A man sat in the doorway of the one across the square. He slowly stood up, moved his chair out of the doorway, and walked down the steps and over to the next house. "We might as well go inside. They'll be coming."

Captain Pettigrew followed Lord Carnarvon up the steps of the little white church. He stopped in the doorway, took off his hat, and clutched it under his left arm. Down the aisle he could see the altar, which was made of a long dugout canoe.

As they walked down the aisle of the empty church, a priest came in through the door behind the altar, adjusting his vestments. He rushed up, shook Lord Carnarvon's hand, then shook Captain Pettigrew's hand, but said only, *"Bonne chance, mon fils."*

Then Captain Pettigrew heard the sounds of people coming into the church. Nearly all were barefoot, so there was only a whisper of cloth and a creaking of floorboards and pews as they came. They all looked to him like Lord Carnarvon, with almond eyes and straight black hair and high cheekbones.

And then Captain Pettigrew knew the bride was coming. There was no music, and no dramatic pause at the threshold. He just saw the priest's eyes focus on a point behind him, and saw his face compose itself in that benevolent, satisfied look that priests had. And he turned to see a young girl with black hair that hung nearly to her waist, wearing the same bleached white dress the other women wore. She had a bouquet of bright purple orchids. Beside her was Nathaniel Boats. As the two walked down the aisle he held her hand.

Captain Pettigrew nodded to Lord Carnarvon and took a step toward the pew.

"Stand fast," said Lord Carnarvon. "You're the best man."

Captain Pettigrew watched the girl and old Nathaniel Boats until they arrived in front of the dugout canoe, and then he looked at the priest.

The priest spoke in French, and Captain Pettigrew didn't understand much French, but there was no point in listening to it anyway. The priest said what Captain Pettigrew assumed were the usual words, and made the gestures that they always made, while Captain Pettigrew watched the young girl and the old man out of the corner of his eye. Nathaniel Boats must be her father, he thought. And it probably wasn't true that all brides were beautiful, but this one was—sort of small and quiet-looking. Captain Pettigrew was, by six or eight inches, the tallest person in the whole church. These people all looked like little Eskimos who somehow got left here in this strange hot backwater a long time ago. These people have been hiding in the woods for about four hundred years, he thought. As the priest droned on, he found himself hoping it was safe for a few of them to come out now.

The priest finished his recitation, and raised his voice in official pronouncement, and then everybody smiled at everybody else for a few seconds, and Captain Pettigrew decided it must be over.

Lord Carnarvon and the young girl walked back down the aisle, and Captain Pettigrew followed at a safe distance. Outside the door, he stood beside Nathaniel Boats. "She's a beautiful girl. What's her name?"

"Lord Carnarvon," Boats answered.

"Before that."

''Esther.'' He studied Captain Pettigrew for a moment. ''I want a favor.''

''What is it?''

The old man looked across the square, and Captain Pettigrew's gaze followed his. The banana truck had been unloaded, and now people from the church were climbing into it. ''Watch them. If they start to die, bring them back here.''

THE ISLAND

''It's a little tough to tell what they think,'' said Captain Pettigrew.

Harry frowned. ''What do you mean by that? Look, we've got to make these people happy here. One of these days somebody from the outside world is going to come here to see what the hell is happening, and then report it to the world.''

''Well, they've only been here a few days, and the place is still a little unfamiliar to them. They came expecting something like Dominica. What we've got here is more like a cross between Key Biscayne and Las Vegas.''

''Well, what the hell do they want?'' asked Harry. ''Did anybody tell you?''

''That's a little tough too. They speak about four languages, and everybody seems to understand all of them, so they go from one to another all the time.''

Harry leaned over the balcony and stared at the sea below. Little waves were moving in slowly, and washing to the foot of the breakwall. He could see Joaquín sitting on a rock waiting for Captain Pettigrew. Joaquín had taken off his shoes and rolled up his pantlegs, and each little wave washed up to the middle of his calf. Harry's mind registered it once again. There would never be a chance to sell surfing as an attraction, but there must be some way to sell its opposite. People went to places because they were hot or cold, high or low, wet or dry. There must be a way to sell no surf. ''Captain, I know this isn't your line but—''

He looked around, but Captain Pettigrew was gone.

Then he heard the door open and close. He walked back through the French doors into the living room. "Captain?"

The Captain was on his way back with Lord Carnarvon beside him. Lord Carnarvon called, "You got a cold beer?"

"Sure. In the refrigerator."

Lord Carnarvon stopped in the kitchen and Harry heard the refrigerator open and close. Then Lord Carnarvon reappeared, sipping a can of beer. "You know, nothing puts strain on the generators more than all these damned refrigerators. I just haven't figured out another way to rig them." He sat down on a lawn chair and propped his feet on the wall of the balcony.

"We'll think of something," said Harry. "We've got sun, wind, tides, and waves. If all of the primal forces can't produce enough power to keep a beer cold, what the hell good are they?"

Lord Carnarvon shrugged. "I figured it was about time to give you a report."

"Good. I was just grilling the Captain. What's this stuff about four languages?"

"That's a good place to start. The people who decided to come with us are sort of old-fashioned. None of them has ever been off the Carib Reserve except for a trip to Maginot now and then, or maybe Roseau. They're six families that lived in remote places, and didn't even spend much time in the villages."

"So we've got six families who speak a bunch of unknown languages? What are we going to do?"

"It's not that bad. They're just a lot more conservative than I thought. The men speak a different dialect from the women. It's an old custom."

"So they can't even understand each other?"

Lord Carnarvon chuckled. "Relax, Harry. Everybody can understand both, and they also understand French and English."

"Thank God," said Harry. "At least I can ask them what they want."

Lord Carnarvon looked uncomfortable. He and Captain Pettigrew exchanged a glance, and Captain Pettigrew cleared his throat. "That's something I didn't get to tell you, Harry. They're a little nervous around white folks."

"What?" Harry shouted. "We went through all this so we can live on this little rock where half the people are 'nervous' every time the other half walk down the street? Or is it just me, personally?"

"It won't be that bad, Harry," said Lord Carnarvon. "They'll get used to it. Most of the people on Dominica are black, so the Caribs are used to people being either Carib or black. It's just the really white-looking whites they're not sure about. All the whites they've seen have been a few tourists. They all heard about the British soldiers from their parents."

Harry sighed. "Okay. I'll try not to snap their pictures or shoot at them. Are they at least getting used to the island?"

Lord Carnarvon nodded. "They like the houses, and they like the hotel, especially the golf course. They love the food. They're glad they came. But they're demanding that I find them something to do."

"Why, that's—" Harry began. "That's—" He paused. "You know, I hadn't thought about it. What did they do before? Did they have jobs?"

"Not exactly. They fished a little, picked bananas. A couple were guides in the back country, which means they were poachers, because hardly anybody ever goes into the back country."

"Poachers?" said Harry. "What did they poach?"

"Rare birds, for their feathers."

"We haven't got any birds that look rare to me, so that's out. And we haven't got room for enough banana trees to stock a supermarket. Anything else occur to anybody?"

Captain Pettigrew said, "Fishing sounds promising."

"What kind of fishing?"

"Probably not what you had in mind. They go out in dugout canoes and net a bunch of fish for supper."

Harry held his head in his hands. "These people are our only pretext for existing." He made both his hands into fists and absentmindedly pounded his knees with them. "They are protecting us from an American aircraft carrier full of tax collectors and subpoena servers. They are protecting us from Cuban MIGs carrying sanitation consultants who majored in the most boring thoughts of Lenin. Tell me something that will help."

Lord Carnarvon sipped his beer. "They sure love baseball."

Harry stood up and paced the length of the balcony. "All right," he muttered. "We will give these people a crash course. We know that they like food, shelter, and baseball, and that's something to build on. Do what you have to to keep them happy until they know what's available and figure out something they want to do."

"Good," said Lord Camarvon. "They're cutting down a couple of the big rubber trees behind the thirteenth green to make canoes."

8

Eight Years

THE ISLAND

Emma watched the Panamanian team run out onto the field. They dug their cleats into the turf and sprinted, their enthusiasm so strong it seemed violent. The Colón Parrots were a good team, as winter teams went. They had the usual roster of desperately eager rookies, who had been told by their coaches that the winter leagues might cut a year off their wait to move up to the majors. But they also had some players of another kind. They had the Yankees' Alvin Ostrow, generally ranked by sportswriters as the twelfth best third baseman of all time. He continued to play all year round even now, because he believed that four months of rest might add a microsecond to his reaction when the ball came down the third baseline. With Ostrow each year came two friends, Pedro Vásquez, the Pirates' starting left fielder, and the fearsome Jim Foot.

Emma could see Del Cupido standing in the visiting team's dugout talking to the Parrots' manager. When he climbed out he was smiling. He walked around the backstop and up to Emma in the bleachers. "We're in for a treat," he said. "Foot is starting."

"Are you a good sport?" asked Emma. "Or are you hoping for a short game?"

Del Cupido held out a can of snuff to Emma, but she shook her head. Then he gazed out at the field. "Winter baseball is all practice. Sometimes I think the only reason we keep score is so we know when to quit. My kids can't get any better practice than facing Jim Foot.''

''I hope they enjoy it as much as you do.''

''Oh, they'll get to test their blood pressure a little. The mound doesn't seem to be sixty-six and a half feet away when Foot is standing on it. But this is what they came down here for.''

''I thought they came down here to learn from you.''

Del Cupido tucked a pinch of snuff under his lip and then shifted it from side to side thoughtfully. ''That's correct. Some of them are going to be surprised at how much they learn today.''

The Parrots were now moving off the field toward their dugout. ''Excuse me, Emma,'' said Del Cupido. ''Time to go to work.'' He clopped down the aisle of the bleachers with both hands in his jacket pockets. As the last of the Parrots crossed the first baseline into foul territory, Del Cupido's team ran out to replace them. They hit fly balls to the outfielders, ran little sprints, fielded grounders, and threw the ball around the infield.

Emma looked out past the center-field fence. There was a row of tall coconut palms, then the long dogleg fairway of the seventh hole of the golf course. And past that, running parallel to it, the fairway of the third, a zigzag that ran nearly to the beach, with big sand traps in the elbows, and a long bunker in the middle. It wasn't just beautiful, it was unsettling. From here the baseball field looked like the base of a giant green fan set in a blue as empty as outer space.

Harry glanced at his watch, then said to Vickers, ''It's almost one o'clock. The game will be starting in a half-hour.''

Vickers gave a loud whistle, and all of the work crew looked up to see his wave except the man driving the bulldozer. When he reached the end of his long, straight path and turned to come back, he saw the others walking toward Harry and Vickers with their shovels and rakes on their shoulders. He raised the arms that held his plow, and made a shallow pass on the return run, then stopped the bulldozer beside Vickers.

"I need gas," he called. "Anybody want a ride to the harbor?"

Two men jumped up and perched behind him, hanging on to the rollbars, and he drove off with them.

Harry looked at the long, straight, level stretch of new ground. "I hope this isn't a mistake."

"It's not," said Vickers. "We can use an airport. When the hotel is finished and we're ready to open the casino, this will pay for itself a hundred times over. The kind of visitor who'll make us rich isn't the kind that spends a couple of days on a boat from Kingston unless he owns it."

Harry and Vickers walked along the rough, broken ground toward the hotel. When they reached the place where the older land began, Harry looked back at the long runway that stretched eastward into the sea. "There are a lot of things about it that worry me in little ways. God, look at the size of it. Half a mile of homemade space that we'll have to cover with asphalt. What a waste."

"Maybe you should have gone with the deal the airlines were offering. They'd have helped cover the cost."

"That's the one part I feel good about," said Harry. "We can't afford to let gigantic companies get set up on the island. All of a sudden there are American interests to protect."

They walked on across the lawn toward the finished wing of the hotel. "So what are you worried about?"

"It's hard to explain," said Harry. "Turning a corner, I guess. Once you've got a runway, you're not an isolated place anymore. People can get here too quickly. And you have to put up with permanent ground crews, and obnoxious pilots, and all kinds of people we haven't thought about."

"And what else?" asked Vickers.

"That's the point," said Harry. "I don't know." As they approached the hotel entrance, Lord Carnarvon came out with Joaquín, Augustino, and Lord Carnarvon's two cousins.

"Going to the game?" asked Vickers.

"Sure," said Lord Carnarvon. "How's Stink Island International coming?"

"We were just talking about that," Harry said. "We'll have the runway finished long before the rains come, and probably the terminal too, if Captain Pettigrew brings enough bricks back with him in the ship tomorrow."

"You don't sound happy about it."

"He's just depressed about the money," said Vickers. "Maybe we can cheer him up by letting him throw in the first ball of the game."

They walked on past the hotel to the main street, where new banks and shops were under construction. The men were putting away tools and ladders, and washing paint-brushes, and moving toward the baseball field. On the first day of each season, Emma had spent the morning walking to every part of the island, reminding everyone she met that the bleachers had been built with great difficulty to hold everyone who chose to sit on them. The island had then fallen into the custom of stopping work on the afternoons of home games.

As they passed the first tee of the golf course, Harry could see four Carib women in the distance, strolling toward the baseball field. One of them was carrying a baby, and a second was followed closely by two little boys. "That's another thing," said Harry. "When we open the airport we'll have to build a big fence around it. We can't have kids wandering onto the runway."

Lord Carnarvon whispered, "Jesus, he's in a bad mood today."

Vickers nodded, and they walked in silence up the path to the baseball field. When they reached the foot of the bleachers, Harry looked at the three hundred men and women and children, some staring intently at the players warming up on the field, some walking up and down the steps to talk to friends or make bets. Many of them waved when they saw Harry, Vickers, and Lord Carnarvon.

Lord Carnarvon said, "Hey, Harry. Did you ever see *Lawrence of Arabia?*"

"Of course I saw it. How could I avoid it all those years?"

"Remember Anthony Quinn? He's made up as this bedouin chieftain, with a rubber nose that looks like it's melting while they sit around the fire, and all of a sudden he jumps up for no reason, and yells, 'I am a river to my people.' "

"What the hell are you talking about?"

"That's us, Harry. Only I guess we're a dirt pile to our people. So cheer up."

"Don't talk like that," said Harry. "It gives me the creeps. This is a business."

"There's Emma," said Lord Carnarvon. "Unless it's George Steinbrenner. It's hard to tell, with all this business going on."

They sat down in Emma's row. She said, "Jim Foot is going to start for the Parrots."

"That's too bad," said Vickers. "I bet Joaquín a hundred that we'd win."

"When was that?" asked Emma.

"About twenty minutes ago. Why?"

"About a half-hour ago he came by to see who was pitching."

The crowd stood while the batting coach of the Parrots slipped a cassette into his portable tape deck and Augustino held his bullhorn next to it, so the national anthem of Panama crackled and hissed over the field. In the second verse, Augustino moved the bullhorn too close, and the bullhorn gave off a piercing shriek, and everyone sat down.

As the players ran out onto the field, Emma said, "You know, we should get a national anthem. Maybe we could hire Randy Newman or somebody to cook one up for us."

"Not you too," Harry muttered. "We are not the founders of a brave little republic. We are a bunch of thieves, remember?"

"Even Disneyland has a national anthem, Harry," said Emma. "So does Del Mar racetrack—something about where the surf meets the turf."

"Maybe we can steal one," said Vickers.

"No," said Emma. "One of the treaties we signed was the international copyright convention."

Augustino's voice blared over the bullhorn. "Pitching for the Caribs will be Denny Colton." Then he said something in Spanish, ending in "Denny Colton." As he spoke there were loud breathing sounds, and numerous clicks and squeaks. He listed the catcher, then ran down the familiar roster of players in order. Every time he said the word ''Caribs,'' all the Caribs in the stands applauded politely. When he announced that Alvin Ostrow would bat first for the Parrots, the rest of the crowd joined in the applause, which grew when a large yellow cat emerged from the dugout and sat on the mound licking his paws.

The three umpires walked to their places, and the home-plate umpire dusted off the plate and crouched behind the catcher. Denny Colton, who played in the summer for the Dodgers' farm team in Albuquerque, performed his wind-up and fired the ball across the inside corner of the plate at knee level.

Ostrow watched it pass, with the look of intense concentration that had been a source of discussion in the box seats of Yankee Stadium for eleven years. Denny Colton had seen it on television since he was in junior high school. When he saw it this time, he remembered that he was pitching to Alvin Ostrow, and that Alvin Ostrow had batted over three hundred in each of the past eleven seasons, and had held three American League batting titles. Colton puffed air out of his lungs in four deep breaths to restore his equanimity, stared hard at the catcher's signals, and threw a pitch that, in Albuquerque, would have broken high and inside. This time it started to do that, but Alvin Ostrow had read the ball's laces as it turned in the air, and now the ball was streaking back at Denny Colton's head. Colton's shoulders drooped a little as he watched the ball bounce in center field. The big yellow cat chased it partway, then lost interest and scrambled over the fence.

Colton lasted three innings, but in the bottom of the third, with one out, there was a Carib runner on first base, and Colton was the next batter.

''What's Del Cupido going to do?'' asked Harry.

''Pull him,'' said Emma. ''Foot walked one man, but he's not going to walk a pitcher.''

Del Cupido sent a pinch hitter in for Colton, and Augustino's voice came over the bullhorn. ''Batting for Colton, number ten, Bill Osborne.'' A second later, another young man trotted out of the dugout toward the bullpen, followed at a distance by a man who was adjusting his catcher's gear.

Jim Foot struck out the pinch hitter in five pitches.

Emma leaned back in her seat and watched the game proceed without really seeing it. What she saw were a lot of figures in white suits on a beautiful green field, performing with precision and competence a narrow and focused drill. It was orderly, and logical, and inevitable. No matter what happened, it would instantly trigger a series of responses that were already practiced as ritual a hundred years ago, because the game was based on simple geometrical measurement.

Jim Foot threw his first pitch to the next Carib batter, who hit a hard ground ball. The first baseman trapped it and whirled to throw the ball at first base. Because this was baseball, Jim Foot had already left the mound by that time and was racing the runner to first base. And because this was baseball, his foot was on the bag while the runner still had a step to go, and his course took him through the trajectory of the ball. It had all been measured a hundred years ago. If nobody hesitated or made a mistake, the runner was always doomed by one step. Emma had watched Del Cupido's pitchers and first basemen practicing this play over and over, to preserve the one-step advantage that was built into the game.

Vickers stood up and said, "I see Joaquín. I'll go try to make a side bet to cover."

It was the middle of the fourth inning, and Emma felt lazy and contented. The sharp, perfect movements on the field were somehow made brighter by the soft inertness of the rest of the visible world. The people in the stands were leaning back on their neighbors' knees, barely moving. The air, as always, moved from east to west at five miles an hour, more a current than a breeze.

Then Emma saw Diane Mowatt striding along in front of the bleachers, holding her hand up to shade her eyes. Diane was still wearing her bank manager's linen suit, but at least she'd come. "Look, Harry. Diane Mowatt at a baseball game. Do you believe it?"

Harry shrugged. "She must have figured out there's no point in keeping the place open if the whole island is here."

Diane Mowatt spotted them and waved her arm.

"Harry," she called, but she wasn't smiling. Harry waved back.

She climbed the steps of the bleachers quickly, and sat down beside Emma. "Hi, everyone," she said, nodding her head at each of them. Then she leaned across Emma and said, "Harry, I've got to talk to you."

"Our team has the red hats, and the Parrots have green hats," said Harry. "It's a tie game."

"Not about games, Harry. I've got trouble."

"What kind?"

"We're having transactions blocked. My bank is being interfered with."

Lord Carnarvon imitated a cheerleader. "Block that transaction. Block that transaction."

Diane turned toward him. "It's not that funny, L.C. You want your checks to bounce?"

"Wait a minute," said Emma. "What's going on?"

Diane spoke calmly, but the calm seemed designed not to counteract her anger, but to preserve it intact. "You know that all of our activity is done by computer. We use a modem and signal to our branch in Jamaica by ship-to-shore telephone. In a way we're just a teller station."

"Of course," said Emma. "But you're so upset. What's happening? If it's a power failure, we can just move in an auxiliary generator."

"It's not a power failure," said Diane. "Somebody is jamming our telephone."

Emma looked puzzled. "Who would jam your telephone?"

"I don't know, but you can be sure I'll find out. I'll bet it's one of the giant pigs of the business—Statecorp or Federal National Bank."

"What would they get out of it?"

"What does a whale get out of gobbling up plankton?"

Vickers came up the aisle to return to his seat, but Diane Mowatt was sitting in it. "I give up," he said. "Does ice cream have bones?"

Emma didn't take her eyes off the game. "Vickers, do you think you can take a look at Diane's phone hookup?"

"Sure," he said. "I just was reminded that Canadians

don't know anything about baseball. Maybe work will take my mind off what I owe Joaquín."

Diane Mowatt followed Vickers down the steps, then along the front of the bleachers. Emma glanced at the two of them. She could see Diane talking with animation and gesturing as they disappeared around the corner.

By the time Vickers reached the branch office of Montego Savings, his brow was beginning to furrow and his jaw muscles were working. He followed Diane inside, past the tellers' windows and into the office. She turned on the computer terminal and punched in her passwords, but Vickers said, "Never mind that." He snatched the telephone receiver out of the modem and put it to his ear. Then he moved to the radio console, adjusted the dials with his free hand, and then set the receiver down again.

Vickers flicked the switch on the computer terminal. "Diane," he said, "I want you to lock everything you're capable of locking in here. Don't take more than five minutes. Then go as quickly as you can to the hotel lobby. If you meet anybody on the way, bring him with you. When you get there, just wait. You won't be alone long."

"All right," she said. "But what is it?"

"Somebody is jamming our radios, but I've got a very strong feeling it isn't all they're doing."

Vickers moved out the door and paused for a moment to look around him. He could see nobody on the little street, but he moved quickly from door to door, peering inside. The buildings were empty, so he turned at the last one, which was only a concrete slab with a frame of two-by-fours raised on it that morning, and began to run.

It was the bottom of the fifth inning and the first two Caribs had struck out. The third man up was wearing an expression that reminded Lord Carnarvon of Harry's. He studied the man, then looked at Harry to compare, but Harry suddenly stood up and said, "Look at Vickers." Lord Carnarvon turned to see Vickers running hard toward them.

Vickers stood at the bottom of the bleachers, his mouth open and his chest heaving from his sprint. Harry, Emma, and Lord Carnarvon scrambled down the aisle and stood around him. Then the four turned and moved off quickly in different directions.

Emma appeared in the dugout and whispered to Del Cupido. Del Cupido ran toward the field, signaling the first-base umpire for a time-out. The umpire spread his arms in the air just as Jim Foot went into his windup. He barked something and the umpire behind home plate stood up, yelling, "Time." Jim Foot threw the ball, the batter took his third swing, and the ball smacked into the umpire's chest protector. The umpire glared at the catcher, who had unaccountably gotten out of the way of the pitch.

By then Del Cupido was whispering to the head umpire, and Harry was running onto the field, dragging Augustino with him. Harry took the bullhorn. "We're going to have to delay the game." He hesitated. "We don't know anything except that somebody is jamming our radio transmissions. Vickers tells me that's one of the things that happens at the start of a military operation. We'd better not all be sitting here in one place."

Augustino took the bullhorn and gave an approximation of Harry's words in Spanish. Suddenly the manager of the Colón Parrots dashed to the head umpire, waved his arms, shouted, stamped his feet, and then took off his hat and hurled it on the ground.

Harry continued. "This will be just like all our practice drills. In fact, it probably *is* just practice."

Vickers trotted onto the infield, followed by Lord Carnarvon and his two cousins. Vickers took the bullhorn and said, "We'll use Winter Defense Without Tourists. If you don't understand, ask the person next to you." The people in the bleachers were standing up. The three Lord Carnarvons fanned out and approached the bleachers, and small groups of men and women began to make their way out of the stands and gather around one or another of them.

Emma spoke quietly with the three umpires. "I'm really sorry about this," she said. "It's like a civil-defense drill. You and the two teams just come with me to the hotel."

"What are we supposed to do if this is real?"

"The bar is always open. I'd order something I could drink through a straw—it keeps your head down."

Emma opened the linen storage in the basement of the hotel, and Esther Lord Carnarvon moved inside and switched on the light. Behind her, the first six men were already in a line taking off their shirts. Emma walked quickly to the next door and unlocked it. People were streaming into the basement now, and she could hear other doors opening behind her.

It was impossible now not to think about Vickers. It was likely that everything now depended on his shrewdness. The eight years of labor and planning and manipulation and outright fraud were over now, and his day had come. She moved to the back stairway and started to climb, her breaths coming in little gasps. At the upper level, she pushed open the door, surprised at how heavy it felt. As she knelt down and set the doorstop, she realized she was angry. It shouldn't have come to this.

Emma ran down the empty corridor. Vickers had coached her on this part of it. She would have to be at the end of the hall with the doors open, or somebody might forget where he was supposed to go. She opened the upper stairwell, and the door to the swimming pool, then stood in the middle of the hall with her arms folded across her chest and her feet planted apart.

The thought of it made her angrier. It felt unfair. There should be some shade of feeling, some time of transition between soft, easy happiness and this. It was like being ambushed in the dark. There ought to be a moment when you see the shadow at the end of the alley, or at least sense something is wrong.

She heard the first six men clattering up the steps at the end of the corridor now. Then they appeared at the open door and trotted up the hallway toward her in single file. They were wearing gray cotton sweatsuits, like joggers, but the first four carried high-powered rifles with big telescopic sights, the fifth carried two of the rifles, and the sixth had four little Ingram submachine guns slung over his back.

Emma waved them up the stairs that led to the roof, as Vickers had told her to, although all of them knew the geography of the hotel as well as she did. Vickers had sounded like Del Cupido when he'd explained it. "Winning is fundamentals,'' he'd said. ''The first six-man team takes the high ground. They have to move out in the first minutes when we probably won't know what's going on, and they may be half-asleep or drunk or terrified. So you stand right here and act like you know exactly what's happened, and wave them up.'' She knew the rest of it too, because Vickers had made a lifelong study of the way people behaved while they were killing each other.

The six were from Vickers' original crew that came in the days of the Sunset Games. They all had little nests on the roof that contained dozens of metal boxes of ammunition, and night scopes, and hand grenades, and food and water. She'd memorized all of it years ago, when Vickers had explained: ''Everything is for their morale. In a fire fight, your whole body tells you to keep your head down. You can't believe that holding your head up in the path of a lot of flying metal and pulling a trigger is going to do any good. But these guys are going to be able to put a bullet into just about any spot for a thousand yards around the hotel. We have to make them think they can do it.''

''Is any of it practical?'' Emma asked.

''All of it,'' Vickers said. ''Each of them will be up there wearing a suit the color of the roof, with a bulletproof vest under it. He's got so much ammo and food that he could hold out for a month. And each one has sighted every square foot he can see from the roof, and knows he can hit it every time he fires. He's invisible, and invulnerable, and devastating.''

''Really?''

''No. An enemy worth worrying about will aim something big and nasty at them—an antitank gun or a grenade launcher or whatever aircraft he's got—and blow them to pieces.''

''So why—''

Vickers shrugged. ''While the enemy is still a long way off, these guys can drop two or three targets a second. If they last ten minutes, the island has already cost more than most commanders would expect to pay for it.''

''So all this ammunition and food and everything is just to fool our own men into thinking they won't die?''

''You never know. Maybe the automatic weapons and

grenades are there because I've noticed that men in the vicinity of machine guns have a greater tendency to fire their rifles. But maybe they're there because the enemy we face will be a few armed robbers trying to storm the hotel, and they'll get cut to shreds coming up the empty beach. The hotel roof is one of the cards dealt to me in the defense of the island. I have to play it without knowing if I'm taking a trick or just forcing the opponent to use a trump card."

"Maybe there will never be a fight," Emma said. "Maybe we'll just have thousands of rounds of live ammunition on the roof, which is a hell of a fire hazard, and, I might add, a hefty expense."

"I hope so," said Vickers. "I really hope I've talked you all into wasting money on a lot of hardware, and made fools of everybody playing cowboys and Indians twice a month for the last few years. I do it because it's what I do best."

Emma watched the next group run up through the corridor and open the doors of the hotel rooms. This group consisted of twelve people. Each carried one of the little submachine guns, and they went in, two to a room, to station themselves at the windows. She recognized some as married couples, and it made her sick to see them crouching low to slip in, then closing the metal doors behind them to protect the corridor from stray shots. But that had been part of Vickers' demonic intelligence too. "Nobody's going to get scared enough to run out on his partner. If the enemy takes a room, he can close this corridor. But he's not going to do it with one shot."

Emma held her arms out and waved the next group out to the lobby, where they'd move up to the second-floor ballroom. Maybe there was no enemy. Maybe it was just another set of war games. Nothing had happened, after all, except some trouble with some radio transmissions. It could just be a storm somewhere out on the ocean, late in the season. Emma directed the next group out the side door into the garden. When the last pair stationed themselves beside the door, she turned and walked toward the lobby. She took long strides, but kept her posture erect.

Now it was time to look for lost sheep. Vickers had

warned her about them. There would be people cut off from their battle stations, people too frightened to remember what they'd practiced. There would be children, and sick people, and all of them would flock to the hotel because it was the biggest thing in sight and because Emma would be there to tell them what to do. Maybe it's a storm out on the ocean, she thought. A big electrical storm.

Harry trotted along the dock, trying to talk through his heavy breathing. "Yes, dammit, you've got to go, Augustino," he gasped.

"But what am I supposed to do?" Augustino asked.

Harry knelt on the dock, untied the rope from the cleat, and tugged it. The boat drifted under the dock, and Augustino stepped onto the deck. Harry spoke through clenched teeth. "You're going to sail out there and use your wits to save our butts, you dumb bastard. No matter what they've got, they can't jam the whole Caribbean. You listen to the radio. When you're forty or fifty miles out, you're sure to be clear. You might hear them talking to each other, you might hear us. In any case you can tell the good guys our communication is cut off, if you can figure out who the good guys are."

"But why me? This isn't my style."

"Because I don't have time to advertise for bilingual heroes," Harry snapped. "Look. You're Superman, the last baby off the planet Krypton. If you can't think of anything better, start broadcasting an SOS, but get going."

Augustino moved to the helm of Lord Carnarvon's sailboat and started the engine. Harry put both feet against the foredeck and gave a hard push. Augustino shifted the engine, and the propeller engaged. He whirled the wheel and moved out of the harbor, giving Harry one last, forlorn look. Harry turned and ran back to the stone quay in front of his house. He could see that four men had already taken their places on the balcony behind the wall. One of them was scanning the horizon with binoculars, and the other three were loading their weapons and moving extra ammunition out to the patio.

At that moment the sight went into a special section of Harry's memory. He saw Horacio Guzmán's brown face, small behind the big black binoculars, and his long, delicate fingers adjusting the focus, the pink palms of his hands visible from below, where Harry stood. Then there was a slight movement. The binoculars jerked upward a few degrees, and Horacio's mouth opened as he squinted into the eyepieces, and then the hands tightened, clutching the binoculars.

Harry turned and looked into the sky. He couldn't see everything Horacio saw, but for the first time he heard it. There was a deep, dull droning of engines. And then he began to run again. His legs were already tired, and his heart was pounding, but he was up the stone steps and on the open ground, sprinting for the old barracks on the point east of the harbor before it occurred to him: I am trying to outrun an airplane.

Lord Carnarvon was sitting at the desk in the office of the clubhouse, looking out the window at the long, straight fairway of the first hole. He could see the first squad running down the right side toward the green. Then he saw three men diverge from the group and move into the grove of trees in the rough. A second later another group crossed the open expanse of grass and moved into the drainage trench that someday would feed the artificial lake that guarded the green of the fifth hole. He glanced at the big electric clock on the wall, which said seven o'clock, and he remembered that the office generator had been left off except when the carpentry crew used power tools. He glanced at his watch, and said to his cousin, "It's twenty after three. We might have a new record for bogeymam drills."

The other Lord Carnarvon said, "There's a certain realism to this one. There's something about seeing Vickers looking serious that freezes your blood."

"I know," said Lord Carnarvon. He stood and lifted his M16 off the desk. "There's nothing like having a professional throat-biting badass around to remind you that you're primarily a lover." He moved to the door. "Is everybody in position here?"

The other Lord Carnarvon clicked his heels. "We'll defend the bar to the last bottle."

"Then I'm off. Don't let anybody go home until we get word from Vickers that it's a false alarm. If everybody looks warlike, he'll feel good for a month."

"Right."

Lord Carnarvon walked out into the main dining room, where his squad of six men were sitting at a long table waiting for him. They were all Caribs, young men who had brought their families to the island at the urging of Esther's father. Two were distant cousins of Esther's, who had always lived in the deep forests around Morne Diablotin, and the others were among their nearest neighbors. Only one of these men had ever been farther from home than a day's walk, and that had been to sell bird feathers in Roseau once a year. When Lord Carnarvon reached the table they stood up, clutching their rifles.

"Do you all have plenty of ammunition?" he asked.

"Yes, of course," said Arthur Boats. "Thank you."

Lord Carnarvon moved toward the door to cover his smile. These were forest people, and there was an odd combination of formality and sincerity about forest people. He had always supposed that it was because they lived in such remote places that speaking to anyone they hadn't always known was a memorable occasion. They followed him out the door and along the paved path toward the back nine of the golf course. As they moved off the pavement, he remembered the first time they'd done this with Vickers.

Vickers had said, "When you come down to it, we don't know much about these guys. We know they're more comfortable outdoors than in. So we've got to send them out in the woods and hope they know more about woods than anybody they meet in there."

The six men faded among the trees, moving at an effortless trot that kept Lord Carnarvon ducking branches and sprinting across clearings. Vickers seemed to think of the Caribs as country boys, only a little different from the Canadians in the Northwest Territories. Vickers should be out here scrambling to keep up with them, he thought. He stepped over a protruding root and remembered that eight years ago this spot had been bare rock. Most of these trees had grown to maturity on the South American mainland.

The place they were going was even more a product of fabrication. The last nine holes of the golf course were built on volcanic rock and dirt stolen from a nameless cay in the shallows off Honduras. I'm running through an imaginary jungle with real natives, he thought. And I'm one of them.

Lord Carnarvon came up with the others at the edge of the fairway, where the trees were tall and the ground was free of underbrush. They moved in the shadows of the trees until they were abreast of the right-field fence of the baseball stadium. Then the point man, David Boats, stopped and looked into the air. Lord Carnarvon saw it too. Far above the island a fat olive-green airplane inched across the sky, then tilted its wings and made a wide turn over the sea. It spiraled lower, and then made a long, straight, lazy pass over the baseball field. Behind it, a line of small white parachutes opened, spreading like little flowers, then swinging gently as they floated downward.

Lord Carnarvon started to run toward the field. He dashed across the fairway, not saying anything to the others, because they could see it as well as he could. As he ran, he could hear them running too, their heavy ammunition clips clicking in the pockets of their jackets, their feet pounding the ground behind him.

In the practices, they'd always moved along in the trees to the edge of the paved path, and then sat down in the thick bushes to wait for Vickers to pass on his inspection tour.

Lord Carnarvon had run so hard that he had to stop himself by pushing against the center-field fence. The others had spread out to keep from bumping each other, and they reached the fence at nearly the same time. Lord Carnarvon peered over the fence onto the field, and the first thing he saw was a red jacket lying on the bench of the home team's dugout. In that instant he realized that he already understood. Someone had known about the baseball game. They'd planned to drop out of the sky and trap everyone in the bleachers—the whole island in one place.

Lord Carnarvon watched as the first three men in jungle fatigues dropped to the grass behind second base, then another landed between the pitcher's mound and home plate. This one sent a little cloud of dust into the air when he hit, then rolled and released his parachute, which drifted almost to first base before it went slack and draped on the ground. Lord Carnarvon steadied his M16 on top of the fence and squeezed the trigger. He couldn't tell whether he'd hit the man or not, because suddenly all the Caribs were firing onto the field, and the men in fatigues were dropping to the ground, and a few seemed to be dead before their feet touched earth.

The man next to Lord Carnarvon had his rifle on automatic. There was a roar, and the brass casings ejected in an arc ,from his rifle and clattered against the fence as though he'd tossed a handful into the air. Then he was inserting another clip, and there was another roar as someone sprayed the third baseline, where four of the men in fatigues were on their feet and dashing toward the visiting team's dugout.

Already there were a dozen bodies sprawled on the field, some tangled in the harnesses of the parachutes, and others just freed long enough to have stood in the line of fire and been cut down.

Lord Carnarvon glanced upward as his thumb flicked the selector on his rifle to full auto.

Vickers moved out of the warehouse on the wharf and heard the shots on the far side of the island. He stepped around the building and saw the C-130 circling the area of the baseball field, and a few parachutes drifting to the grass below it.

"Damn," he muttered, and looked around to see if his men were ready to move, and bumped into Joaquín. Joaquín was staring at the parachutes, and he flinched at each burst of automatic-weapons fire, as though he'd seen some friend hit.

Vickers grasped his arm. "We have to do this the hard way. You only get three men to hold the warehouse."

Joaquín said, "All right."

Vickers said, "You may have to fall back to the hotel. Just try to make the warehouse cost them something."

"All right," said Joaquín. He looked unhappy. "This isn't what you expected."

Vickers shook his head. "I'm sorry."

Already the twelve men were waiting for Vickers, checking their rifles and staring in the direction of the baseball field, and listening to the sharp rattle of gunfire in the distance. Vickers set off at a fast trot, and the others followed.

Vickers tried to goad his mind to clarity as he ran, but it was too early to make sense of the little he knew. Joaquín had been right. He had never expected to defend against a military assault. He'd feared that someday there might be a small incursion by a team intending a robbery at the banks or casino, or an attempt to kidnap a wealthy visitor. But the banks and the casino weren't even operating yet, and only one wing of the hotel was open this winter.

Vickers had studied the island as he'd helped to build it, and he'd made decisions. The strategy had been as simple as he could make it. Everyone on the island had a place he was supposed to go. Every building had a complement of armed men and women, and he'd placed a few nests of young men out in ambush. It was a strategy of fixed strongholds.

It had been a conservative tactic, and he knew it would have worked. If ten armed men had slipped ashore and robbed a bank, they would have found that all the people were suddenly off the streets, and every open space on the island was a fire zone. As the years went by, Vickers had added refinements. He'd spent hundreds of thousands of dollars on equipment his islanders would never need, but which would make them less frightened in an emergency. He had even reinforced some of the snipers' nests with sheets of steel and concrete blocks.

Vickers had never expected a full-scale invasion. The plan had been to move everyone to safe places, and then rush to the disturbance with the twelve men of his flying squad. The strongholds and nests had been intended to deny intruders shelter and keep them pinned down somewhere until he could move in with his little team to arrest them. He'd even bought his squad handcuffs and sidearms.

As he reached the golf course, he saw the C-130 begin its second pass, this time above the seventh fairway. Damn, he thought. A year ago he'd decided against buying three Russian SAM-7 missile launchers that a Nicaraguan had been offering at a discount. He'd told Joaquín, "If we're in the kind of trouble where we need one of those, we'd be better off surrendering."

Vickers saw the string of black specks leave the tailgate of the C-130, then bloom into parachutes. As they did, he heard the pops of the rifles again. This time the noise was coming from somewhere to his left, and he knew it was probably the squad he'd placed in the sand traps at the edge of the first green. It was unlikely they'd hit any of the distant paratroopers, but the sound seemed to make two ends of a circuit suddenly meet.

His mind ran its inventory: His firing stations had no means of communication, because he'd known his people were too inexperienced to be able to carry out simple maneuvers and would have used radios to tell each other how scared they were and spread panic. And now they were all in their positions, armed with simple, reliable weapons, and they wouldn't know what to do except stay there until they were overrun. He looked at the island as the invading commander would, and what he saw was an awful place that had to be taken a yard at a time.

As they moved through the woods, he knew his flying squad would catch up with Lord Carnarvon soon. He would have passed this way only minutes ago, and he and his men would be waiting in the thick bushes on the far end of the fairway. Vickers followed the path he'd plotted for the Caribs. Ahead the firing grew louder, and he changed his course to find it.

Harry walked up the middle of the barracks floor. This building had been one of the first on the island, built on the highest shelf of rock because the low Caribbean tides seldom reached it. The rotating crews of men had lived here in the early days, and later the first groups of stoic tourists came here to spend two weeks in isolation and deprivation.

For years it had been used only for storage. Piled high along the walls now were wooden crates he recognized. They contained pipe fittings that hadn't been used in the hotel plumbing, miles of electrical cable that someday would be used to wire the landing lights at the airport, and tons of supplies for future tourist seasons, most of them bought after dark in places like Cancún or St. Croix from people who worked for large hotels. Now each of the six little windows had a figure beside it holding a rifle.

As Harry passed Althea Simms, she gave him a nervous little smile, and then turned again to stare out her window. It had been five—no, six—years since he'd seen Althea come off Captain Pettigrew's tug at the pier, her little brother beside her. He'd asked Pettigrew, "Are you crazy? Where are their parents?" Pettigrew had answered, "On Grand Cayman. Both dead as fishbait," and walked up the dock to shore. Harry hadn't been able to think of a way to reopen the conversation.

Harry stood beside Althea and asked, "Can you see anything?"

"Just the airplane. And parachutes coming down. Way on the other side of the island."

Then they both heard the hollow, faint sounds of rifles firing, then others, and a couple of long bursts. Harry called to the others, "Everybody do just what Vickers told us, and we'll be okay. Remember, we're not saving ammunition for the holidays." Vickers had told him the sort of thing to say: "None of that 'whites-of-their-eyes' bullshit for the people in the buildings. If they start blasting away as soon as they can see an enemy, maybe they'll have time to calm down and adjust their aims before it gets too dangerous for them. The least they'll do is pump a lot of rounds into the general vicinity. If you hear bullets cracking past your head, you get bogged down thinking about the way you came, and how much faster you can cover it on the way back."

Harry stepped out the door and walked to the next building. Once he and Emma had lived there, but now it too was filled with equipment and supplies. Inside there were two men setting an old Browning fifty-caliber machine gun up on a tripod. The gunner threaded the first rounds of an ammunition belt into the feeder, and pointed the muzzle out to sea.

Harry called, "Is everything okay here?" and Dave, the

gunner, who worked on Captain Pettigrew's boat with Joaquín and had once been in the American navy, answered. "Sounds like the place to be is the baseball field, Harry."

Harry nodded. "If it shapes up that way, Vickers will send for us." He turned and went back out the door in time to see the big olive-green airplane come back over the golf course and drop another line of parachutes. He stepped upon the porch and stared out to sea. It was then that he saw the second airplane. It came in at a high altitude, then flew over the island and turned, making a swooping descent. It came down in a spiral, circling the island. Harry opened the door of the building and shouted, "Dave! Bring that gun out here, quick." He watched the airplane as it came in from the west, this time only a few hundred feet above the water. Harry's breath caught in his throat for a second. What if it was a bomber? He shouted, "Hurry!"

There was a sound of running feet on the boards behind him, but Harry kept his eyes on the airplane. It was fat and clumsy and green, and it was now on a low, straight course toward the island. It passed overhead, and disappeared beyond the hotel as Dave and his partner reached the porch with the machine gun. The long black barrel with the Swiss-cheese ventilation holes in its jacket poked into Harry's peripheral vision, but the sky was empty.

"I guess we'd better get this thing over to the runway," said Dave. "What do you think?"

"I think that damned airport may be more expensive than I thought," said Harry.

Emma made her way back to the hotel basement and into the casino bar. As she entered, she could see Alvin Ostrow lying on the floor. It startled her, until she saw that two of the little Carib boys were rolling a baseball back and forth just out of his reach. He made a grab for it, and the little boys shrieked with delight when they saw he missed.

Both baseball teams and their coaches and unidentifiable hangers-on sat at the tables mixed randomly with a few people from the island. Emma was five steps in before people began to look up and notice her, then stop talking.

By the time she reached the middle of the floor, everyone was waiting for her to speak. Then the batting coach of the Colón Parrots tapped a glass of beer with a swizzle stick from someone else's drink until he noticed that he was making the only sound in the room. Then he shrugged and took a sip.

Emma spoke in a voice that sounded loud to her. "As you know—"

"Louder," came a cry from the back of the room.

Emma took a deep breath. "We seem to be having a national emergency. I apologize for the inconvenience. We don't know yet exactly what is happening, so the main thing is to stay inside the hotel until we do." She hesitated and watched a few of the baseball players exchange glances. "This building is very secure. If, for any reason, we need to leave the building, the exits are clearly marked."

Emma waited again. Some of the faces in the room seemed to be reflecting on the events that might make it necessary to leave the basement. "There will be a lot of activity on these two levels, so don't be alarmed by it. We are now setting up an infirmary on the other end of this level. The hotel is also one of the major storage areas, and of course, there will be a lot of cooking going on in the kitchen upstairs."

A very thin man in a bright Hawaiian shirt that looked too big for him stood up and said, "Point me to the infirmary. I'm the Parrots' team doctor."

Emma pointed to the hallway behind her, and the man left the room. "As soon as we—"

"What can we do?" shouted the Carib second baseman.

Emma said, "For the moment, please stay here. Right now we don't know if this is a false alarm."

Then the sound of shooting reached the basement. It was muffled and distant, but it was unmistakable. Emma said in a hollow little voice, "Thank you." She turned on her heels and sauntered out the door. As soon as she was alone, she began to run. She went up the broad central staircase toward the lobby, and remembered the blueprint for the hotel. "Why on earth would you put fancy rooms like that in a cellar?'' she'd asked. Harry had answered, ''Because I don't want anybody in the casino to know what time it is.''

Emma reached ground level and ran across the foyer to the front doorway, where four men stood staring warily out at the long, broad, empty walk outside.

''What's the shooting?'' she asked.

''Can't see it from here,'' said one of them without turning.

The firing started again, a rapid series of five shots, but they were coming from the roof. She walked toward the back stairway, thinking again about Vickers. She was about to do one of the things Vickers had told her not to do.

Emma opened the steel door to the upper stairway and closed it behind her. The narrow staircase echoed with the sharp cracks of the rifles above, and she clapped her hands over her ears as she climbed toward the roof, seeing nothing but the blue rectangle of the door opening to the sky.

At the top, Emma peered out at the empty roof, then crouched low and scuttled to the chest-high wall where the six men stood, methodically firing and reloading. She cautiously raised her head and peeked over the wall, then lowered her head again, bringing back with her an image like a photograph. In it was the long, flat, dusty stretch of the half-finished airport runway reaching eastward into the sea, and at the end of it, a big four-engine cargo airplane, its propellers turning. A lot of tiny figures were coming out the back of the airplane and dashing off the runway toward the first row of tall palm trees that marked the inhabited part of the island.

She raised her head a second time to look inland, and saw another airplane just like the first, flying over the golf course. There were white swatches on the green grass, and she knew they must be the parachutes of men already on the ground.

Lord Carnarvon crouched at the left-field corner of the baseball-field fence, and looked out at the golf course. He could see nothing but the broad, open fairway, and the woods beyond it. He nervously glanced to both sides, and then behind him, where his companions lay on their bellies in a semicircle. And then, although he knew the plane was gone, he couldn't keep himself from looking up into the sky. He noticed as he lowered his head again that even his neck was shaking.

The open grass he'd crossed to get here looked impossibly dangerous now. But this place felt open and unprotected. He said, "Let's try to get back to the woods."

Daniel Boats said, "It sounds good. How?"

"If we go up the path, we probably won't meet anybody. The only ambush on it was the one we were supposed to set up." He crawled back to the fence, and the others followed, one by one. Then they all got to their feet and ran along the fence until they reached the bleachers, then stopped in the shelter of the little building that held the spectators' lavatories.

Cautiously Daniel Boats slipped in the door marked "Men."

Lord Carnarvon said, "Don't worry. None of them made it off the field." Then he heard the toilet flush.

Vickers moved to the edge of the woods and studied the nearest body. The man had managed to cut himself free of his parachute and make a dash for the shelter of the trees. He'd gotten halfway into the long shadow of a eucalyptus, but he'd been running straight for the thicket where a member of Vickers' flying squad was waiting.

Vickers said, "I've got to check this one out. If anything moves, shoot it." He crawled onto the fairway until he was beside the body. The body was lying facedown, dressed in mottled jungle fatigues. Vickers looked at the shoulders and arms, but there were no insignia of rank, and no unit patches. He could see the man's weapon lying a few feet away in the tall grass. He crawled over to it, and whistled to himself. It was an M16. Quickly he returned to the body, and snatched the hat off. Inside he could find no label, only the number 7½ stenciled inside the sweatband. He clutched the shirt collar and turned it inside out, but there was no label there either. He rolled the body over and tore open the shirt. There were no dog tags, only six horrible, bloody wounds from a burst of an automatic rifle.

Vickers crawled to the feet and looked at the black rubber soles of the combat boots. There had been words stamped in the heel, but they had been worn down too far to be legible. The man was an olive-skinned Caucasian with dark hair. Vickers studied the face, but it was a waste of his ability to control his revulsion. He crawled back to join his men in the woods.

"He's not a regular soldier," said Vickers. "He jumped out of an American plane carrying an American rifle, but damned near everybody in this part of the world has those."

Then Vickers heard the sound of guns at the other end of the island. He stood up and listened. He looked out at the fairway, where fourteen bodies were sprawled. He turned and set off through the woods. The sun had already lost all its ferocity, the light deepening into an orange-yellow through the filtering trees. It would be gone in an hour or two. Where the trees grew farther apart he broke into a run, and heard the others running behind him. It sounded as though the shots were coming from the area around the hotel.

It was the only street on the island, and its purpose was to look like the business section of a prosperous old resort town. Only the few little buildings nearest to the hotel were completed, and the others were in various stages of construction. Harry peered over the pile of lumber down the narrow cobbled street while Dave set his machine gun on the tripod. He could hear someone firing from the roof of the hotel behind them, but it didn't sound any more frantic than it had at first. Harry set his rifle down on the ground beside him, and sat down beside Dave. The long run along the pier carrying the ammunition can had left him exhausted.

"Harry?" said Dave.

"Yeah?"

"Do you have any idea who they are?"

"None." There was a long pause, and Harry began again. "Once, seven years ago, I thought something like this was happening. Then after about thirty seconds, it turned out to be just another load of dirt. I wish—"

"I can see them," whispered Dave. "At the end of the street." Harry rolled onto his belly and looked around the edge of the lumber pile. He could see them too. They were coming up both sides of the street in single file, moving tentatively among the upright skeletons of the new buildings. Harry prepared himself for the deafening roar of the machine gun and waited. After five seconds he turned around. "Dave, will you please shoot the bastards?"

"Now?"

"Yes, now."

Vickers and his squad were on the first fairway in sight of the hotel, when the sound of the big machine gun began. He turned toward it.

When he reached the back wall of Diane Mowatt's bank, he looked around the corner and saw Harry and Dave behind the woodpile. At that moment, Dave flipped open the receiver and threaded another belt of ammunition into the gun. Harry began firing wildly with his rifle.

Vickers waved his arm for his squad to follow, and moved around to the far side of the building. Vickers listened. In a minute or two, the machine gun would jam or Harry and Dave would run out of ammunition. Until then, Vickers wasn't going to assume that they could look down the barrel of a machine gun and recognize an old friend.

Vickers divided his men into groups of three, and sent them into the narrow alleys between the buildings. Then he waited.

Harry watched the end of the belt whip out of the can and disappear through the shuddering machine gun. Dave was still staring down the barrel, a terrible grimace on his face. Instantly Dave's eyes widened, and he said into the silence, "We've got to get out of here."

"Grab the gun," said Harry.

"Barrel's too hot to touch."

"Then screw it up somehow." Harry aimed his rifle at the corner of the nearest building and waited.

"Best I can do," said Dave, and Harry saw him open the receiver and dump a handful of dirt and stones into it, and close it again.

They came to a crouch, then dashed for the corner of the bank. It was only after they reached it that the barrage of firing began again behind them. They didn't need to speak; the gunfire down the street made it absurd not to keep running. As they reached the front door someone opened it, and they found themselves running across the lobby. Near the back stairway Harry came to a stop and leaned against the wall. "Amazing," he muttered. "They never hit within ten feet of us."

There seemed to be no line to mark the boundary between black sea and black sky. Augustino had spent the past six hours under sail, feeling the rise and fall of Lord Carnarvon's boat under him, slower than the swells that came up behind the stern and then lifted the bow afterward. Augustino had used the engine at first, but then it had occurred to him that sometime this voyage might end, and any end more complicated than plowing the prow onto a beach would require gasoline. He was no sailor, but it had occurred to him that the wind probably didn't blow in circles, so it would take him in a straight line. After two hours he had begun to question this, because he remembered seeing a television weather man drawing a chart that showed the wind blowing in circles. At least they were big circles.

He looked at the sail. It seemed to be catching as much breeze as he dared to catch, so he ratified his decision to leave the other sails wrapped up. He moved back into the cabin and tried the radio again.

"This is Augustino Cruz, calling all friendly ships. This is an emergency SOS Mayday call for help. Over."

As before, there was no response. He had been saying the same things in English and Spanish for hours. He had turned the dials to every position, but nothing seemed to work. At first he had picked up nothing but a pattern of whistles and static, but now and then he would hear a voice. He would try to break in, but the voice would go on uninterrupted.

"This is Augustino Cruz. I am a fool lost alone on the ocean, talking to myself. Over."

He felt the boat lean slightly, so he went to the hatch and looked up at the sail. It seemed stable, so he returned.

"This is Augustino Cruz, your all-night madman. I play all the hits all the time, but only I can hear them. Please deposit eighty-five cents for the next three minutes. Over."

He released the transmitter button, and the sound made him jump. "Do not panic. We have you in sight. Keep your cabin lights burning. Do you understand?"

Augustino pressed the microphone button. "Yes, I understand. Who are you?"

"This is the destroyer escort USS *Caliban.* We have been monitoring your Mayday for three hours. The aircraft carrier USS *Barnum* has been diverted with four missile frigates to respond to your island's emergency."

"An aircraft carrier?"

The voice gave an audible sigh. "You will go on deck and strike your sail, and prepare to receive a boarding party. You will commence radio silence. This is the order of Captain Richard Pettigrew, Ninth Task Force."

Augustino stumbled as he rushed to the cabin hatch. He could already see the ship bearing down on him. There were bright lights on the deck and a couple of men looking down at him from the railing of the rusty old freighter Captain Pettigrew had bought at auction in Galveston three years ago.

It was almost four in the morning, and Harry was getting used to making his way through the dark hotel. He found the open door that led up the stairs to the roof by feeling the cool draft. Once he was beside it, the dim glow of the sky made the steps almost visible. It had been an hour since he'd heard the last shots, and they had been so far away that he couldn't tell where they were coming from. This time when he reached the roof, he could hear people talking quietly.

"I wonder what they're doing down there."

"Probably trying not to meet Vickers in the dark."

"They might have gotten Vickers already."

Harry stopped by the door. Lord Carnarvon must have been near the baseball field when the first group had come down. He hoped the Caribs had been able to hide in the woods, but he didn't have much confidence. There had been so much shooting. He heard someone say, "Listen. What's that?"

It was a low, sputtering noise that seemed to quicken and grow into a growl, then climb to a higher pitch. Then it got louder and louder, and it seemed to move. Someone else yelled, "Airplane," and Harry knew it was true. He heard the plane gain speed, then lift itself into the dark sky at the far end of the runway. He heard it climb steadily, but it showed no lights. For a long time he and the others listened, and they could hear the sound of the engines getting fainter.

There was silence after that, as each man held his breath, but the airplane didn't come back. An hour later the sun came up, and Harry could see a small freighter on the horizon. He recognized it, and at the stern, he could see Lord Carnarvon's sailboat.

Emma watched the crew covering the last of the graves. "It seems like a dream," she said. "I still can't believe it."

Vickers stared at the mounds of fresh dirt. "Nine of us killed, eight wounded. It's about three percent of our population." He started to walk. "Let's go."

"Where?"

"To talk it over."

Harry sat back in the bleachers looking down at the baseball field. The groundskeepers were dragging their graders across the infield, where the bodies had been only a few hours ago. "So where do we stand?"

"The umpires have decided that it doesn't count," said Emma. "The last pitch was thrown after time was called, so it's not five complete innings. The game will be listed as a rain-out. Sort of an odd thing to worry about, Harry."

"I was thinking about us."

Lord Carnarvon shrugged. "I guess we play it the way we always have."

"That's not bad," said Harry. "You and Esther go to New York as President and First Lady. Ask the United Nations for help."

Vickers shook his head. "Let's think about what did

happen. We were all sitting here watching a baseball game. Anybody interested could know the schedule. The Parrots have about four players who are celebrities, and there's nothing to do on this island except work or sit with your feet in the water."

"What are you getting at?" asked Emma.

"The first thing that happens is that somebody jams our radio transmissions, and the second is that they drop paratroopers on the field where they expect to catch us all at once. Then a second plane lands soldiers on the brand-new runway, who move inland to take the major buildings."

"We saw it," said Emma. "We don't want to live through it again."

Vickers stared out at the field. "That's what I'm getting at. I keep putting myself in the place of the guy who planned what happened here. It wasn't his day."

"No," said Harry. "It wasn't his day. Twenty-eight of his men killed."

"The thing I keep wondering about is what would have happened if it had been his day. Twenty-eight killed and nobody wounded, Think about that."

"It's awful," said Emma. "We couldn't get out there to help the wounded. They must have bled to death."

"That's right," said Vickers. "But the way it happened was that some of them had their throats cut before the sun came up."

Harry sat up. "Jesus, Vickers. You did that?"

"No, Harry. They did that. I've seen it happen a couple of times, but I was kind of surprised to see it here. These people went to a lot of trouble to make it hard to know who they were."

"But they had guns and planes and uniforms, and—"

"Maybe we'll be able to trace something," said Vickers. "But don't bet on it."

Emma stared at him. "You already have some kind of plan, don't you? You said we should talk about it, but you had something in mind."

Vickers nodded. "We were lucky. Everything they did should have worked, but everything was a disaster. I'd sure hate to go through this a second time."

"Agreed," said Harry. "If we'd known this was going to happen, we'd never have done any of it. There are other ways to get rich. What do you suppose we could get for the place if we sold it?"

Emma said, "It's hard to tell. Nobody's sold a country lately, I mean sold it outright. We've got a lot of loans out for building, and if we sell this place we'd probably have to go to some legitimate country that might not let us skip out on the debts."

"It won't work anyway," said Lord Carnarvon. "It might take months to find a buyer. In the meantime we couldn't leave, because the only claim we've got is that we're here. We're stuck."

"That's probably true," said Emma. "The only thing about the place that's worth much is the fact that it's a separate country. If we sell it, then it's not a phony Carib homeland anymore. It's just a pile of rubbish in the middle of the sea."

Vickers waited in silence, until Emma said to him, "But you're ahead of us, aren't you? Are you waiting for us to go through every option so we'll be desperate enough to do something crazy?"

"I will if you want."

"No, what is it?"

"We don't tell the rest of the world what happened."

"What are you talking about?" asked Harry. "We had two baseball teams and three umpires here."

"Okay," Vickers said. "They were here, but what did they see? They were in the casino, which is underground. And there were no tourists, because the hotel isn't open."

"But what does it accomplish to hush it up?"

"I see it," said Lord Carnarvon. "You want to keep the world in the dark because you're nuts." He turned to Harry. "He wants to go after them."

Vickers frowned. "Hasn't it occurred to you that things like this don't just end? You think somebody buys two military airplanes and outfits a hundred soldiers to have his ass kicked by a bunch of lost souls who are sitting on a potential fortune?"

"That's what happened," said Emma. "It just wasn't their day."

"They picked up Captain Pettigrew's radio signal to Augustino. They thought they might be sitting on the runway when American fighter planes arrived."

"We beat them," said Emma. "We fooled them too, but we beat them.

"We made it very expensive," said Vickers. "Their commander had thought it would be easy, and it wasn't. Now he knows quite a bit more than he did. He still has the planes, and the guns, and if he doesn't have the men, he can get them. Now that the imaginary aircraft carrier is gone, it's only us again, sitting here on what might be the next Las Vegas."

"More than Las Vegas," said Harry. "Maybe a combination of Hong Kong and Hawaii."

"Not Iceland?" asked Lord Carnarvon. "Not Manhattan?"

Vickers stood up. "If we sit here long enough, things will start dropping out of the sky again. They'll just wait long enough to be sure we haven't ceded the island to some serious country. Once they're sure they won't find French marines waiting for them, they'll be back."

Lord Carnarvon said, "So what do you propose to do about it?"

"I'd like to have you organize a crew and have a trench dug across the runway and then covered with plywood and dirt like a tiger trap. And I'd like to have you—"

"What is this?" said Lord Carnarvon. "Are you going somewhere?"

"Yes," he said. "Harry and I are going to hunt these people."

Lord Carnarvon watched as Harry's face began to lose its color.

9

BARRANQUILLA

The Colonel leaned back in his chair and looked out the window at the skyline of Barranquilla. The studied posture of negligent repose brought back to Harry the memory of other policemen in other offices. He recognized the moment when the man behind the desk would turn casually and say, "There's really very little we don't know already."

The Colonel turned and said, "There's really very little we know."

Harry smiled, which seemed to startle the Colonel for a second, but he looked at Vickers. "The Interpol office in Bogotá has been cooperative. The guns with these numbers were consigned, and supposedly shipped, to the Philippine army in 1976. Whether they were, and when they were stolen or bought, is impossible to know. The fingerprints you brought me are only a curiosity."

"A curiosity?" asked Harry.

"It would be extremely unlikely that there would be a record unless these men were convicted of crimes in major cities, or enjoyed some position of great trust, so of course there is none that we can find. It's a curiosity because in one of the prints, the fingers appear in an order other than the order we're accustomed to."

"Oh," said Harry. "I wonder how that happened."

"Some experts might wonder if the subject was alive

when his prints were taken." The Colonel paused, and looked at Vickers again.

Vickers spoke carefully. "We've always dealt with each other on the basis of mutual benefit. As I told you at the beginning, in this case your only benefit is that you may keep some very dangerous people from getting more dangerous, without much risk."

The Colonel raised his eyebrows. "And knowledge might be a risk." The Colonel handed Vickers a sheet of paper. "This is the response to the inquiry about the airplanes."

Vickers took the single sheet of paper, folded it, and put it in his pocket. "I notice it's still sealed in the envelope, and you haven't read it. It's difficult for a man in your position to read everything that comes across his desk."

"What I know won't compromise your case, and what's on that paper won't be enough to build a case. Unless these people still have what they stole, you'll never prove anything to the court. And by the way, I wouldn't show that curious set of fingerprints to the officials when you get to Venezuela."

"We don't expect to see any officials," said Vickers. "It's an informal sort of inquiry."

The Colonel's eyes widened. "You're not talking about a robbery at all, are you? This was some kind of attack."

Vickers shook his head. "Don't be ridiculous. Who would attack an island made of car parts and sediment?"

The Colonel's voice took on an urgency. "You could issue an appeal to the United Nations . . . make defense treaties. You're very good at treaties."

Vickers put his hand on the Colonel's shoulder. "When we know more, we'll make a decision. But it's better if we leave you now."

"This sort of thing is crazy. It's for religious fanatics and ideological lunatics. Give me time. I'll find out enough to take to court."

"You're a soldier," said Vickers. "You know what happens if we waste time making speeches and complaining to foreign courts. We have to hit fast the first time, and it has to hurt them."

The Colonel stared at him helplessly. "I never would have helped you if I'd known."

"You don't know," said Vickers. He turned and pulled Harry out of the room. "Take care."

Harry and Vickers sat on the rear deck of the tugboat as Captain Pettigrew steered away from the row of ships along the wharf.

"Let's talk it over," said Vickers. He slowly scanned the decks of the nearest ship, a Japanese tanker called the *Ashita Maru,* then climbed the steps into the cabin. When Harry came through the door, Vickers closed it and said, "Take us out northward as though we were heading home."

"I guess that means we're not," said Captain Pettigrew. He brought the tug around, and they moved out past the barges and their dredging machinery toward the sea.

Vickers unfolded the sheet of paper again and looked at it. "The Colonel came through for us. The night of the attack, a C-130 landed at El Banco, Colombia, for refueling. It stayed for about twenty minutes and didn't load or unload anything. But one of the ground crew noticed that there were a few bullet holes in the fuselage, and that the tail numbers were painted out, so he figured it had something to do with drugs. He called the cops, and they had it picked up on radar. It came down in Venezuela near Palmarito."

"Are the Colombians doing anything?" asked Captain Pettigrew.

Vickers shook his head. "They didn't load or unload anything, so there wasn't a crime."

"What about Venezuela?"

"The Colombians didn't take it up with them. I guess that's the next logical move."

"Do you really think it is?"

"It s probably what a sane person would do," said Vickers. "It certainly wouldn't do any good."

LAGO DE MARACAIBO

Joaquín jumped from the bow of the dinghy and sank ankle-deep in the mud, then took two labored steps forward, his feet making loud sucking noises. ''I knew you'd pick me,'' he said.

''That's why I picked you,'' said Vickers. ''You're a fatalist.''

''This isn't my doing,'' said Joaquín.

''Then maybe you're right to be a fatalist.''

''And what if I'm killed?''

''It's no worse than you expect.''

Harry stepped into the water. ''Can't you two argue in Spanish?'' He felt himself sinking into the slimy lake bed, so he held onto the gunwale and began to walk, pulling the boat with him until he felt the keel strike harder ground. He turned and looked out onto the dark, calm water of Lago de Maracaibo. In the distance he could see the lights of the oil-drilling platforms stretching across the lake in a line. There was only one place in the middle of his vision where the lights were blotted out by a high, dark shape. He wondered if this was his last look at the tugboat, just as an impression of mass and density in the night.

''Okay,'' said Vickers. ''I've got everything out. Give the rope a few hard jerks.''

Harry stood by the stern of the dinghy, and pulled the rope three times, then held it loosely and waited. He felt the rope tighten, and heard the hull of the boat slide among the reeds. He let go and watched the boat slowly move past him, then fade as Captain Pettigrew's men pulled it back to the tugboat.

He had to take two steps forward to free his feet from the mud without toppling over, so he walked in a little circle to reach the shore.

He heard Vickers hiss, ''Damn.'' Then there was the sound of a hand clapping on flesh. As he stepped out onto firmer ground, he heard more slaps, but by then Harry already knew, because he was crossing into the wall of mosquitoes. They flew into his face in a single swarm, not circling to light in surreptitious raids, but flying straight at him and crashing against his cheeks and forehead, then bouncing off and trying again for a foothold. He slapped at his face and waved his arms wildly as he ran among the weeds. He could hear Vickers and Joaquín ahead of him, crashing through thicker underbrush, so he followed the sound, moving his feet in mad, high steps like a prancing horse. The shrill whining noise of the swarm that had chosen his ears kept him brushing his hands over his face, hair, and neck as fast as he could.

As he ran, he felt a terrible sense of doom. Mosquitoes homed in on sweat, or was it carbon dioxide from breathing, or was it heat? He couldn't remember, but then realized he didn't care, because whatever it was, the more he struggled, the more of it he produced, and he could run the length of the continent to Tierra del Fuego and they'd probably still be feasting on him when he got there.

Harry burst through the bushes and ran into an open space. Then he felt his feet hitting pavement, and saw Vickers and Joaquín squatting beside the knapsacks. He was still flailing his arms and doing a wild, hopping dance as he approached them.

He could see Vickers stand up and raise his arm. Harry said, "It's—" but at that moment Vickers sprayed his head with a wet, poisonous vapor from a hissing aerosol can. Harry closed his eyes, and Vickers spun him around and kept spraying. It took a few seconds for Harry to calm down. The spray dried into a sticky layer on his face and hands, and the smell seemed to change to a stale and metallic perfume. Every few seconds he could hear a mosquito pass close to him, then hover for a moment and then fly away.

"It's a little better out here," said Vickers, "and the repellent helps some." He handed Harry a knapsack and they set off down the dark, empty road.

Harry said to Joaquín, "I thought you'd been here before."

"I have," said Joaquín.

"Why didn't we spray ourselves before we left the tugboat?"

"I did."

As the sun rose, Vickers stopped and opened his map. Then he folded it up and put it back in his knapsack.

"That should be La Solita around the next bend in the lake. Remember, all we want is a bus ride south."

"Don't worry," said Joaquín. "This whole region is full of foreigners who work the oil wells and tankers. If you don't want to be noticed, get drunk and hit someone."

As they walked on, they passed a group of three small shacks beside the road. The three were all painted a fresh white, beginning at the peaks of the roofs, and extending down the walls, to end in a broad red stripe at the foundations. A mile farther they could see the road straighten, and on both sides of it there were sidewalks and low buildings with storefront windows. But the sight that attracted Harry's eye was the line of automobiles parked along the street. Most of them were old, and all were coated with a thick layer of dust from unpaved roads. He said to Vickers, "You know, I haven't driven a car in about five years."

"Do you miss it?" asked Vickers.

"I'm not sure. I'll have to think about it."

Joaquín groaned. "I was hoping we'd have time for breakfast."

Harry stared ahead, and saw what Joaquín was looking at. An old blue bus was just pulling up at the end of the street. As they came closer, a man in a swaybacked garrison hat stepped down from it and began to take money from a little group of people who had collected on the sidewalk.

Joaquín walked up to him. "Where are you going?" he asked in Spanish.

"Mérida." The man didn't look at him.

Joaquín turned to Vickers and said, in English, "We'll have to wait for the next one. We can have breakfast first."

"Pay the man and get in," said Vickers.

For the first two hours, only a dozen people sat in the bus. There were two old men who sat together, both dressed in ancient blue suits with vests, and five women who looked as though they might be three generations of a single family. With them were several boys and girls ranging from ten or twelve years old to less than a year. It was impossible to tell who they belonged to, because they were scolded or comforted by whichever woman happened to be nearest.

They were on a winding highway that climbed steadily into the mountains, and the driver varied his momentum with the uncertain clutch and the worn transmission. Harry wondered if he was saving the brakes for the return trip, and then wondered if he'd see it for himself.

After four hours the driver made a slight miscalculation and had to hit the brakes on a long curve to hold the road. Harry watched as Joaquín's dozing form began to slide across the seat. As the centrifugal force reached its strongest, it pulled Joaquín over and his head thudded against the window. He sat up, looked around, and said, "It's all right. I dreamed that there was a typhoon." After some thought, he added, "I was better off in the dream, because in the dream I was at the helm."

When the bus stopped at Mérida, Vickers stood up and said, "See if you can find out about buses to Palmarito."

Joaquín said, "It may take some time."

Harry suggested, "There's probably a sign."

"No," said Joaquín. "The Venezuelans are the stupidest people in the hemisphere. Some people say in the whole world. A sign would do them no good."

Vickers smiled. "Not that again."

Joaquín gave an earnest look, and shouldered his heavy pack. "I swear. They communicate by grunts and gestures. If it were night, we'd never be able to talk to them."

Vickers and Harry followed him to the front of the bus and out to the street, then watched him through the station doorway as he carried on a long, animated conversation with the man behind the ticket counter, who handed him a printed schedule, then explained it in detail. When he emerged, he said, "It's as I expected."

"What did you expect?" asked Harry.

"I had to tell the man he'd made a mistake in the schedule. He'd forgotten to put a lunch break in before they leave for Palmarito." He moved off toward the other side of the building, and called, "There's a restaurant down the street."

Harry whispered to Vickers, "Are you sure it was a good idea to bring Joaquín?"

"I'm sure," said Vickers. "If it gets ugly, he'll be there. If it doesn't, at least he knows the country."

"Knows the country?"

"Didn't you know he was Venezuelan?"

In the darkness the curves of the road were only flashes of headlights over rock, and then the rock would seem to drift to one side as the bus hurtled downhill.

Harry said, "Joaquín. Have you ever been there before?"

"Fifteen years ago, about. It's different there."

"What's it like?"

"Not like this. There are no mountains, just big trees in jungles that have been there forever. I heard there were Indians, but I never saw any. Palmarito is on a river."

"What river?"

"I don't know. People called it 'the river.' "

"Apure," said Vickers. "It flows into the Orinoco a hundred miles east."

Harry thought about it in silence. He felt a little better. At the worst, there would be some feeling of danger, but then they'd make a quick dash down a jungle path to a waiting speedboat. There'd be thick, protective jungle on both sides, and the sensation of motion. It wouldn't be all that different from the night he and Emma had selected the Caribbean as their permanent residence; there was the discovery that Fat Jimmy knew about the money, and then the dash through the Los Angeles airport, reading the signs on the departure gates, and then the sensation of motion. As he was feeling it, he fell asleep.

When Harry awoke, Joaquín was shaking him. He sat up and looked out the window and saw the sun rising over empty brown plains that rose gradually onto rolling hills. He picked up his knapsack and followed Vickers and Joaquín down the aisle and out to the road. As the bus drove off, his eyes adjusted to the glare. Farther down the road he could see a few buildings, the only variation in the emptiness. "Where are we?"

"Palmarito," said Joaquín. "They cut down the forests since I was here."

"I can see that," said Harry. "It looks like they did a hell of a job."

"Like beavers," Vickers said.

Joaquín shrugged. "It happens. A rich man buys the land and sells the lumber, then lets the peasants live on the land for five years, so they clear it and farm it until it won't grow anything. Then he takes it back and runs cattle on it for a few more years, until it won't even grow grass."

"What do they do then?"

"By then they've built roads deeper into the jungle, so everybody moves on."

"Obviously everybody didn't move on," said Vickers. "Somebody around here has an airfield with a couple of C-130's sitting on it."

"Take your pick," said Harry. "Any direction. You could land a thousand of them within sight of town."

"We'll see them," said Vickers. He started to walk across the road. "Joaquín, is the river down that way?"

"Unless they've siphoned it off and sold it."

Harry caught up with Vickers and walked along beside him. "Do you have a plan?"

"No. Do you?"

"Of course not. I came because you told me if I didn't, I'd wake up a month from now with a gun in my ribs. Right now I'm wondering if this isn't the best way to make that happen."

"Could be," said Vickers. "It might be worth the trip anyway."

"What the hell are you talking about?" Harry's voice rose as he said it.

"If all we manage to do is get our heads blown off, we'll have accomplished what we wanted to. These guys will realize that somebody knows who they are and just might come after them," said Vickers. "For them it's just a business proposition, and that might make the risks unacceptable."

Harry held Vickers' arm. "What do you mean 'for them' it's business? It's business for us. I thought of it, and everybody came into it with the same idea—to get rich."

Vickers walked on, pulling Harry with him. "Things

are what they are, and sometimes it doesn't matter what we say they are."

Harry said to Joaquín, "Listen to him. A few years ago he helped us make up a joke. Now he's starting to believe the joke."

Joaquín said, "The people who made that bus said it was a machine made to turn its wheels. Maybe it's a machine that changes gasoline into smoke."

"Jesus," said Harry. "You too."

Vickers looked ahead at the river, where he could see a few boats clustered around a dock, and a warehouse that looked like a barn that had been pushed there from somewhere else. One wall had buckled, and had been shored up with new white timbers. "Sometimes things change in little ways, without anybody wanting them to. Then one day you take a look at them, and they're something else."

"Do you realize what you're saying?"

"It's not just money anymore, Harry. There are over three hundred people on that island, and most of them don't have anyplace else to go. Nine of them just died fighting in a war."

As they moved across the field, Harry could see four thin and angular cattle grazing near the riverbank on the sparse tufts of grass. "We seem to be into the seven years of lean kine," he said.

They walked along the shore and Harry tried to imagine the way it must have looked before. His imagination wasn't strong enough to cover the scorched brown valley with thick green jungle. It was the same frustration he'd felt the first time he'd seen the La Brea Tar Pits. In order to feel that mammoths and saber-toothed tigers had crossed that ground, he first had to obliterate a twenty-story office building and the Los Angeles County Art Museum, and his mind had neither the will nor the strength to move that much concrete.

"*Llaneros,*" said Joaquín.

"What?"

"*Vaqueros.* Cowboys," said Vickers. Harry could see two men now, walking slowly up from the riverbank to force the cattle to move to another patch of dry brown grass. The two men seemed to notice the visitors at the same time, and they left their cattle without looking back. The cattle stopped as soon as they were left alone, and started grazing again.

The two men were deeply tanned and seemed to be in their thirties. They wore blue jeans and cotton shirts and broad straw hats, and would have gone unnoticed in a bar in Texas, Harry thought.

One of them spoke rapidly, and Joaquín smiled and said in English, "Who are we?"

"We're tourists," said Vickers.

"No," Harry said quickly. "Tell them we work for a large Canadian company, and we're looking for beef. Flash your passport, Vickers."

Vickers held up his Canadian passport, and whispered to Harry, "What's this for?"

"Let me handle it," he said. "The only thing we've seen that's worth anything is those four anorexic cows." He looked at the *llaneros* and smiled.

Joaquín said, "They want to know why anybody would come to this godforsaken place for cattle like those. Why would we?"

"Say exactly what I do," said Harry. "We're looking for very skinny Venezuelan cows to make into hamburgers. It's much better for a person to eat lean meat than fat."

Joaquín translated, and then one of the *llaneros* spoke. As he finished his statement, his companion laughed.

Vickers said, "Careful."

Joaquín said, "He says it's none of his business, but he thinks you want to ship cattle to Canada, fatten them up, and move them across the border to the United States and sell them as domestic beef."

Harry said to Vickers, "See? You just have to find out what the local scam is." To Joaquín he said, "The Metro-Dominion division of the Mr. Food Corporation would never do anything illegal. We're looking for good, healthy Venezuelan beef. Not too healthy, of course."

Joaquín spoke, and the two *llaneros* smirked. One pointed at the four cattle that were now drifting closer. Then Joaquín said, "He says they've got fifty more like those, and you're welcome to take them today."

Harry considered for a moment. "When in doubt, raise. Tell him we've got to deal in bigger lots, and that we'll need special transportation. We can't wait to bring them down the river in boats. We want to fly them out."

Joaquín translated, then said, "Now they're really convinced that we're criminals." But the *llanero* was talking again, and then he pointed up the road.

Vickers didn't wait for the translation. While the man was still describing the place to Joaquín, Vickers whispered to Harry, "Two big green airplanes."

Vickers examined the three backpacks in the darkness, feeling for each object he'd put inside two days before. He said, "Okay. It's time to redistribute everything." He took the short Ingram MAC-11 out of Harry's pack and handed it to him. "All we want in your packs is the food and water. If you have to drop something, pick that. Put your ammunition in your jacket, and carry your weapon. We aren't going to see any people tonight."

"Or perhaps after that," said Joaquín.

Vickers crawled to the top of the little hill and stared across the open field. "I can see lights. We're a lot closer than I thought."

Harry and Joaquín joined him. Harry could see some dim orange lights in windows, but it was impossible to tell how many buildings there were, or the pattern they formed.

Vickers said, "Don't forget to watch for fences. They'll have something to keep the cows off the runway." He studied the lights. "Ready?"

"I can't think of any excuse you'd believe," said Harry.

Vickers stood up and they started to walk in the open field. Harry kept his eye on the lights, but they didn't seem to move any closer. His feet felt light, and it gave him something to think about. They'd been traveling for over forty-eight hours, sleeping on buses and eating at roadside cafés that the drivers never announced in advance, but he felt a strange energy now as he walked through the darkness toward the fixed lights. When he recognized the feeling he felt ashamed of his stupidity. He had been feeling invisible. He heard Vickers whisper, "Stop here."

They sat down and took off their packs. Vickers said,

"We'll get as close as we can and then wait for them to go to sleep. Remember, we've only got two problems. We want the airplanes, but first we want a car. The runway will go east-west and the planes will be at one end of it, so they're easy. But first, the car, and that will be very close to the buildings."

Joaquín said, "You already told us this."

"Just remember everything. We won't be able to talk again before we hit the runway. Make every move as though you had all night to do it."

They waited an hour, then started to walk again. Harry was surprised that he could see the wire fence so far ahead. When they reached it, he and Joaquín examined the places where the wires met the wooden posts, as Vickers had told them. There were no insulators, so it wasn't electrified. He reached out and tapped the wire, still wondering if he'd feel a jolt up his arm, but there was only the cool, tight metal wire.

The three dropped their packs over the fence, then pushed their guns through beside the packs, and moved down the fence a few feet before slipping through it. Then they were walking again, and Harry could make out the shapes of the buildings. There were still lights on, but fewer than before.

Vickers moved ahead slowly, closing all of his senses to the near and immediate, so that he saw and heard only the part of the world in the distant cluster of lights. It was a terrible plan. If he was wrong about one detail, they'd be trapped, and within a few seconds after that, they'd be dead.

Some of it he felt without reasoning. He'd spent much of his life sleeping in barracks with forty or fifty other men. There was always someone waking up to go to the latrine or make his neighbor stop snoring, and there were always those haunted souls who never seemed to sleep for long. He'd seen them get up and drift outside to smoke a cigarette, and maybe stare up at the stars.

He'd described as much as he could to Joaquín and Harry. Whatever vehicles there were would be parked near the buildings. There would be no guards in a place like this, where there was nothing to fear from intruders. He had no tactic except to exploit the certainty that these sleeping men thought they were safe.

Joaquín studied the terrain as he walked. It was exactly as the *llaneros* had said. After the land had been cleared of trees, they'd burned the brush and coaxed a few meager harvests out of the dirt, and now even the cattle were gone. When he'd asked who owned it, they'd shrugged and said, "A rich man in Caracas." It was another way of saying they had no idea.

Joaquín tapped his pocket again and felt the coil of wire. He had already seen the five vehicles parked in a row beside the dirt road, and had chosen the one. He wondered if Harry and Vickers had seen it before the lights had dimmed.

The three men walked slowly and quietly out of the dark field to the edge of the compound. The air seemed thick in Joaquín's lungs, as though there were too much oxygen. He took short, shallow breaths with his mouth open as he moved, concentrating on taking small, slow, noiseless steps.

Then he was beside the car he had chosen, and it still looked right. It was in good condition and was some dark color that could have been blue or black. Maybe there *was* a rich man from Caracas, he thought.

Vickers had been right: the door wasn't locked, because these men had nothing to fear from thieves. He slowly pressed the button on the handle with his thumb and pulled the door open an inch. Then he knelt at the hinge of the door, and moved his knife into the crack until he felt the light button, then nodded to Harry to show he was ready.

Harry opened the door, found the button, and taped it down. Then he got in, released the hand brake, shifted the car into neutral, and waited for Joaquín and Vickers to move to the trunk. The three pushed the car forward slowly, with Harry leaning inside to steer it toward the open field. The tires made a hollow, hissing noise as they turned, picking up little bits of gravel and dropping them.

When Vickers stood up and stopped pushing, Joaquín felt better. He could think about maintaining the slow, easy momentum of the car, and pretend that Vickers could keep the men in the buildings from shooting him in the back. Each step took him deeper into the darkness, and farther away from the guns. He kept his eyes down on the gleaming bumper. Now and then a tuft of grass would appear from under the car and sweep away behind, and he got used to watching for them until all at once the car picked up speed and there was a dark, smooth pavement under his feet. He stood erect and looked ahead. They were on the runway.

Harry steered the car down the paved surface away from the buildings. Already he could see the two dark shapes in the distance. He sensed a recurrence of the distaste for the airplanes that he'd felt the day they'd appeared over his island. They had the shape of something alive and predatory.

Vickers moved forward suddenly, and Harry heard him exhale in frustration. Then he walked across the tarmac alone. There were three objects gleaming in the darkness beyond the airplanes, and he stopped at the nose of the first one. It was new and shiny, not yet fitted with weapons, but even without them unambiguous in its purpose. He understood the commander, and wondered if he was sleeping now in one of the low wooden buildings across the field. The man had dropped airborne troops on what he'd thought was a defenseless tropical resort. This time he knew the island's defenses, and the tactic was like a reflex. Three helicopters armed with rockets and machine guns would take out the fixed positions Vickers had set up on the island in a few minutes, and send the inexperienced construction workers and gardeners and sailors and misfits running for nonexistent cover.

But where was all the money coming from? He moved closer to the helicopters. They still had the bright yellow factory paint on them. What did they cost—half a million each? They'd have to be bought by a legitimate customer and smuggled here, so it might cost twice that. Vickers heard a faint creak behind him, and he knew Joaquín must have opened the hood of the car. He turned and trotted up to him. "Don't start it yet," he whispered. "I've got to look around for a minute."

"What's wrong?" asked Harry.

"I wasn't prepared for this. I brought six grenades to

screw up the C-130's and make a lot of noise. But we've got to do better than that."

"I don't suppose you can fly a helicopter."

"I sure as hell can't fly three of them," said Vickers. "Look around for fuel trucks."

"There's one on the other side of the buildings," said Joaquín. Then he took off his shirt and started ripping it into strips.

"What the hell are you doing?"

"I have a very stupid idea. It will probably get us all killed."

"What is it?" said Harry.

"We can't push a fuel truck out here, and if we start its engine near the buildings we'll be killed. I don't even know where the fuel tanks are on these airplanes, but I know where it is on this car. If we start an airplane's engine on fire, I'm sure the fuel tank will tell us where it is."

Vickers said, "You were right—this probably will get us killed." He slipped off his jacket and tore open his shirt. He said to Harry, "I'd like the wicks as long as possible."

Harry took off his shirt. He watched Joaquín move to the side of the car and unscrew the gas cap. "It's full," he whispered. "This should be a fine, bright spectacle."

Vickers looked back at the three helicopters. Each had a long, wet rag tied to the base of its tail rotor and another to the main rotor, drooping to the ground. He'd also opened the hatch door on each one, and tossed a wet, reeking rag inside the cockpit.

He joined the others at the car, and helped push it out into the field. The three used one of their canteens to wash the gasoline off their hands. Joaquín lay across the front seat of the car, working under the dashboard with his knife and wire. Then the engine turned over and started. He held his breath as the engine settled into a strong, steady idle.

Then they walked back down the runway to the flight-line, and took their positions. Vickers crouched behind the last helicopter and watched. He saw, under the wing of one of the big cargo planes, the flash of Harry's cigarette lighter and the uneasy flicker of the flame cupped in his hands. Then there was a light at the second airplane, and he knew it was time. First he lit the two long, thin rags that ran together along the ground. Then he raced the flame to the helicopter and tossed a match into the open cockpit. The fumes in the unventilated dome caught with a hot puff that sent a bright orange claw of flame to grasp the air over his head. He turned and ran to the next two helicopters.

Vickers was halfway to the car before he dared to look back. Inside the canopies of the three helicopters he could see flames, and the flames illuminated thick smoke that rose out of the hatches. The rag he'd tied to the main rotor of the first helicopter was almost to the engine now, and he could see that it had ignited some grease on the shaft.

Across the flightline the flames were brighter. Long rags hanging from under the wings of each plane were now burning up into the engines, and in the glow he saw Joaquín and Harry sprinting toward him. Then he saw a long, flaming segment of one of the rags burn through. It was on the left inboard engine of the nearest airplane. As it fell, it illuminated the pavement beneath it. Vickers pivoted so fast he had to take a long step to keep from twisting his ankle. He took four more steps, watching the ground in front of him getting brighter and thinking about the pool of liquid on the pavement and the flaming cloth dropping toward its own reflection. He hadn't seen the pool in the dark, and he didn't know if Joaquín had found some kind of fuel valve, but he hoped that he had the sense to keep running.

Vickers ducked behind the open door of the car, then crawled into the back seat. Within seconds he heard the others reach the car. One of them opened the passenger door, so the light went on. It didn't matter, because the interior of the car was already bright as the flames burned higher and started to crawl along under the fuselage of the airplane.

Vickers sat up and reached for the little submachine gun on the floor. As he picked it up, the car began to move. Harry was in the driver's seat, and he was accelerating across the field toward the five low wooden buildings. Joaquín had picked up the gun under the passenger seat, and was clutching it in front of him. Vickers said, "Joaquín, when we get near the cars and the building, open up. Don't bother to aim, just hose everything down."

"I'm not cruising along while you guys shoot cars," said Harry.

"Just make sure you don't spin out when you get to the road. You're the one who hasn't driven a car in five years."

The car was crossing the runway now, and Harry used the smooth surface to gain speed. Suddenly there was a flash that made the little cluster of buildings in front of them look white, and then two seconds later a deep boom as the fuel tank of the big cargo airplane exploded. Then the lights went on in the buildings, and Vickers could see men running behind the windows.

The car was approaching the building now, and Harry could see men spilling out into the courtyard, some of them in underwear and others in fatigue trousers and carrying boots they hadn't had time to put on. A group of them milled about in the spot he would have to cross to reach the road.

Harry leaned on the horn and turned on his headlights. For a moment the group seemed paralyzed in the glare, but then they scattered, just as Joaquín's Ingram roared. When Vickers started to fire behind Harry's head, it startled him and his foot stomped down on the gas pedal. Then there was a brush of something behind Harry's neck, and some loud yelling that faded as he passed.

Harry hit the brakes and turned right onto the highway and the car began to gain speed. Then he heard a second sharp thump as Vickers' hand grenade went off in the courtyard.

As the car moved along the highway, Vickers looked out the back window. He could see men running in several directions at once. But far beyond them, at the end of the runway, there were now big, billowing yellow flames rolling into the sky. The three helicopters were engulfed, and one of the C-130's was tilted at an angle with one wing tip pointing toward the ground. As he watched, the plane's belly seemed to tear outward and spill glowing debris along the pavement. He counted four seconds before the sound of the explosion reached his ears. ''Drive like hell for the border,'' said Vickers. ''I want time to booby-trap the car with grenades when we dump it.''

''You'd punch a dead man,'' said Joaquín.

''It's not much, but after what they've seen tonight, it shouldn't take much.''

''Won't take much?'' said Harry.

''To give them a superstitious feeling every time they think about that island out there.''

THE ISLAND

Emma opened her eyes and saw Harry's silhouette as he walked into the bedroom. She watched him for a moment drifting in the darkness, trying to be quiet. When she spoke, the shape jumped a little. ''Is everybody okay?''

''Yeah,'' said Harry. ''How about you?''

''A little worried, but I guess I'll get over it now. Everybody here has had trouble sleeping since the airplanes came. Was Vickers right?''

''I guess so. We found the planes.'' He sat on the bed and put his hand on her hip, and it defined the rest of her body in the darkness.

''Where were they?''

''Venezuela. Way in the outback someplace. I forget the name of it. It's one of those places where you wonder why it ever could have needed to have a name. We shot up the place, burned the planes, that sort of thing.''

''Is Vickers happy?''

''Sure. He loves these undergraduate high jinks.''

''You don't sound good, Harry. Come lie down with me.''

As Harry lay beside her, he let out his familiar groan. For the last week, she'd missed the groan. It had something to do with exhaustion and relief, and at the same time, it was a comment on the human condition in the most general terms Harry was able to formulate. ''You don't sound like the whole thing was such a roaring success.''

"The Fat Man wasn't there. It was just a bunch of soldiers or bandits or whatever they are."

"Fat Jimmy? You thought Fat Jimmy was in Venezuela?"

"He's everywhere," Harry muttered. "And we stole his money."

"But it's been years. It must be eight years."

"The Fat Man never forgets."

Harry lay on the couch in the living room and felt the breeze coming in through the French doors. He decided it felt best when his eyes were closed and he could feel the air on his eyelids. He wondered whether it would be possible to sleep intermittently for five or six days without being sick, just moving from the bed to the couch to the chaise on the patio to keep his circulation going. He decided it would, but that it would require a superhuman lack of curiosity. Even now, as he heard Emma walking quietly across the room, he was forced to open his eyes. "Do me a favor, baby?"

"You don't look like you're up to it," said Emma. She picked his leg up and laid it across the other at the ankle so she'd have room to sit beside him. "Besides, we've got guests coming up the sidewalk. Lord Carnarvon, the Captain, Vickers . . ."

"Good. I want to settle this nonsense once and for all. That man has been haunting me like a big fat ghost since before we came here."

"Not that again. Fat Jimmy is a small-time criminal."

"So am I."

"He's not capable of mounting an invasion from an airfield in Venezuela. His idea of a soldier is a guy with greasy hair who drives by in his car and shoots at you with a shotgun if the price is right."

"It's been a long time. Maybe he's gotten more sophisticated too. He's after us, Emma. He wants us dead."

Emma shook her head slowly, a soft, pitying expression in her eyes. "We're out of that league now. We're already too big for him."

"It's him. I can feel him every time he thinks about me." There was a knock on the door and Harry jumped.

"If only it were Fat Jimmy . . ." Emma patted Harry's chest and walked to the door.

Harry sat up and watched Lord Carnarvon, Captain Pettigrew, and Vickers walk in and settle into chairs around the room. Lord Carnarvon said, "Welcome home, Harry."

Harry nodded. "I never want to go anyplace with Vickers again. He's always telling you what to do."

Lord Carnarvon glanced at Vickers, then offered, "At least you won. You did it."

Vickers shrugged, his long arms hanging limp, almost to the floor in the low leather armchair. "Moral victories aren't worth a whole lot in the long run, but it might be enough for now. We did break some airplanes."

Harry stared at the floor and shook his head. "We brought all these suckers out here to this barren piece of rock and worked them half to death and then got some of them killed. Now we've got to keep the rest of them alive. That was the deal."

"I know in a minute I'm going to regret saying this," said Lord Carnarvon, "but Harry's right. If we can't do that much, we can't do anything. I've been searching my mind for people who might have set this whole thing up. I know Vickers probably has whole countries for enemies, and I've got a few enemies, and—"

"It was a man named Fat Jimmy," said Harry.

"You're both crazy." Emma paced the room. "I've been thinking too. This isn't some personal grudge."

"I agree with Emma," Captain Pettigrew said sagely. "It's a criminal conspiracy. A few years ago some men from the Ku Klux Klan tried the same thing in Antigua. It didn't work that time either."

"Tried what?" asked Harry.

"They tried to take over an independent island with military weapons," he said. "I guess they wanted to make the Invisible Empire visible."

"Wrong gene pool," said Emma. "Those paratroopers looked Latin American. There wasn't an Anglo-Saxon among them. Why doesn't anybody look at the most obvious things around them? We're in the middle of a poor, volatile area, full of revolutionaries and guerrillas who'd love to have an offshore base."

Vickers looked up at the ceiling. "This is interesting. You're all right." He stood up and walked toward the door. "When the Colonel has managed to track down who owns the land in Venezuela, we'll see who was most right. Then we'll figure out what to do about it."

"I'll buy that," said Captain Pettigrew. "I don't think I have any enemies with enough money to buy airplanes, and I know I don't have any with enough to buy them twice. We'll just wait and see."

Emma walked Vickers and Captain Pettigrew to the door, and Harry stood up. "Well, it's been a nice little vacation, but I guess I'd better get packed."

"Where are you going?"

"Los Angeles."

"What's in Los Angeles?"

But Emma was already back in the living room, standing with her arms folded. She answered for him. "Fat Jimmy."

Harry spoke to Lord Carnarvon, but he was looking at Emma. "I've got to see Fat Jimmy."

Lord Carnarvon didn't bother to look for a chair. He sat down on the floor without taking his eyes off Harry. "This is crazy. You don't know if he did it."

Harry shrugged. "No, but I want to see him anyway."

Lord Carnarvon looked at Emma, who was on her way into the bedroom. After a few seconds he heard the door close behind her. "For all these years you waited for him to come and get you. Whenever anything happened, somewhere in the back of your mind, you were saying, 'Uh-oh. The Fat Man.' Well, he never came, never sent anybody, never did anything at all, did he?"

Harry propped himself on the arm of the couch. "Lord Carnarvon, you are not a stupid man. In spite of having known you for some years now, I can say that you probably could have learned to do simple tasks, balance a checkbook, and ride a bicycle. But don't try to be sensible."

"Harry, you've got this all backwards. After all this time, you've forgotten. He never did anything to you. You're the one who robbed him."

"That makes it worse. All these years, he's been sitting

there hating me, storing his hatred like a bucket of acid. The fact that he's perfectly justified makes him hate me more.''

''You're right, Harry. He deserves whatever he gets for being dumb enough to let you and Emma get away with his money.''

''This isn't a joke. I did what I did. But there's still a very mean, powerful, devious man out there who never forgets. And someday he's going to do something to get even. Maybe he's behind what just happened to us.''

''If you still believe that, then going after him alone is an idea you might want to talk over with a psychiatrist.''

''It's an idea I got from Vickers.''

''It would be.''

''I realized that Vickers was right about this stuff all along. You don't just sit there waiting to see if they're cleverer than you are the next time out, because if they are, you're dead. You think a man like Fat Jimmy cares about the measly pittance we took from him?''

''If he doesn't, then what are we talking about?''

''Even in those days, he made that much a week. He wants to put my head in a duck press.''

''Some people will eat anything.''

''I'm not going to put up with this anymore. I'm not going to spend the rest of my life waiting for somebody to stick a gun up my nose. Fat Jimmy is, and always has been, the one most likely to do that.''

''All right,'' said Lord Carnarvon. ''I'll go pack. Vickers reminded me on the way over that it's my turn to watch you.''

Harry walked into the bedroom and sat on the bed beside Emma. She was curled up under the blanket, making a small and fragile lump in the middle of the bed. He could see only the top of her head, and when he reached down to touch her hair, she shrank farther into the covers.

''Lord Carnarvon is going with me,'' said Harry.

The small lump moved a little, but there was no response. Harry stood up and walked to the closet to look for his suitcase, and he heard her voice. ''You're stupid, Harry.''

He turned to look at Emma, and now she was sitting up in the bed. "Why is that?"

"We already beat them. They're sorry they ever tried it."

"This isn't just about that. It's about Fat Jimmy."

"We can't afford Fat Jimmy anymore, Harry. You can't have him."

"What are you talking about?"

"You have to let him go. That was another time, another place, another life. You can't go back now and make it come out right. And you can't choose to have him be your enemy just because he's the one you're used to."

Harry stood in the doorway and looked at her for a moment. Then he walked back out to the living room. He was a little surprised to see Lord Carnarvon still sitting there. "Hold up on the arrangements for L.A.," he said. "Emma thinks we should wait and see."

10

Nine Years

THE ISLAND

Vickers drove the roller over the fresh tarmac, following the straight, endless tracks of the tires that had spread the black stuff on the ground. It was slow and hot, and watching the lines on the new pavement began to hypnotize him. It amused him for a moment to think, This might have been my life. He might have been there now, driving a slow tractor in a long, straight line in British Columbia, pulling a harvester or a manure spreader or a tiller, up one line, down the other. Then it occurred to him, This is my life. Only this field was going to be an airport. It was nearly finished, and it would be one of a hundred things he looked at as he walked around the island that he felt comfortable with. This one would take longer to get used to because of what had happened on this ground. But it was safe now. A fly couldn't land on it without passing into a free-fire zone, and it wouldn't survive more than a minute or two without convincing the eyes that scrutinized it through gun sights that it was, after all, only a fly. That much Vickers knew how to do. There were others who could drive a straighter furrow because maybe they'd stayed longer on the farm. But Vickers had learned his own trade well enough.

Vickers heard a whine over the sound of the roller's diesel engine and wondered for an instant whether a stone had been kicked up into the fan, but then the whine grew and dropped into a lower register, and then it was a deep, throaty growl, and the shadow of the apparition slipped over him like an eyeblink, and fluttered down the runway away from him, followed by the apparition itself, an impossible sight that was all bright, burnished silver and a glimpse of orange afterburners, all suddenly obscured by the airplane's drag chute popping open to slow its momentum and display a gaudy red star and the single word "Cuba."

The airplane didn't seem to Vickers to be slowing down fast enough on the runway, and he watched wide-eyed as the brakes on the main landing gear emitted a couple of puffs of hot smoke, then did it again, while the nose gear rattled up and down onto the half-paved final four thousand feet, shaking the silver airplane and making its wings wobble, and very likely rattling the pilot around in the cockpit like a Ping-Pong ball in a keno basket.

Vickers cut the throttle on his roller and ran for the margin of the runway just as the dusty blue pickup truck bounced across the grass into his path. The truck stopped and the driver waited for him to climb into the bed with the three other men, but Vickers opened the cab door and said, "Slide over," as he slipped in behind the wheel.

Vickers drove toward the airplane, which had exhausted its momentum a few feet from the end of the runway. Now it was making a sharp right turn on the grass to push its nose back onto the pavement. As the truck approached, the pilot cut his engines and began to raise his canopy. Vickers said to the man beside him, "I know you can drive as well as I can, but doing it is quicker than explaining. There's only one place to park when you're on a welcoming committee. If you're behind the engines, you risk getting fried. If you're in front, whatever weapons are on board are aimed at you when the bastard tries to climb out and bumps against a switch. If you're beside this one, your chances are probably worse."

"Why's that?" asked the man.

Suddenly there was a loud bang, as the overheated left tire of the main landing gear exploded. Shreds of rubber and red-hot bolts and strips of unidentifiable metal shot outward and bounced on the runway a hundred feet to the side, and the plane listed horribly, resting on one tire and one partial metal rim.

"Because he made a 'pray-to-Jesus' landing," said Vickers superfluously. Then the other tire blew, spewing fragments outward from the other side of the plane. "Well," said Vickers, "at least we got that over with."

Vickers stopped the truck on a diagonal a hundred feet in front of the plane and just to the right side, and got out onto the rough gravel surface. He said to the men in the bed of the truck, "Get out on this side and stay low. Then spread out and walk toward the plane."

As the four men began to converge on the disabled airplane, Vickers called, "When you're close to him, be friendly, but pat him down. Sidearms are standard issue for fighter pilots going out over foreign territory."

Fifty feet ahead, Vickers saw the pilot disengage himself from his restraining belts and stand up on his seat. There was a broad grin on his face as he waved his arms.

"It seems he's an idiot," said Vickers. "Make sure he doesn't hurt himself getting down from there."

Vickers stopped the truck at the rear entrance of the hotel and said to the Cuban in Spanish, "We've got to walk the rest of the way. The road ends here."

The Cuban answered in English, "Who are we going to see? Is it Harry and Emma?"

Vickers turned toward the young pilot and scrutinized his face. Its expression was cheerful and curious, almost guileless. "You've heard of them, eh?"

The two climbed out of the truck, and the pilot, still holding his helmet under his left arm, fell into step with the taller Vickers. As they crossed the open lawn beside the hotel, Del Cupido and his first-base coach, Marco Méndez, stepped out of the hotel lobby. Del Cupido stopped and put on his sunglasses, then grabbed Méndez's arm. "Look. Look at that kid with Vickers."

"What the hell is he wearing? He looks like one of those guys they shoot out of cannons."

"No," said Del Cupido. "I've seen him someplace."

* * *

The pilot sat on the balcony of Harry and Emma's house, still wearing his flight suit. His helmet lay on the floor a few feet inside the living room. He sat with his left leg crossed so his ankle rested on his right knee, and he wrapped the lace of his boot around his index finger nervously as he spoke. "I have decided to be a stockbroker," he announced.

"You took a fighter plane here so you could be a stockbroker?" asked Emma. "I don't think I follow this."

He nodded. "I've studied economics for five years, and English for eight. I'm ready, and now I'm on my way."

"What the hell are you talking about?" asked Harry. "Haven't you heard of sneaking around?"

"It was the only way out," the pilot protested. "When you see the trend in the market, you've got to make your move. I was losing an incredible amount of money every day, and they wouldn't let me out. It's a bad system. 'The Evil Empire,' they call it in Washington."

"That's Russia," said Harry.

"Same thing. I'm a political refugee asking for asylum, having escaped from behind the Iron Curtain."

"That's East Germany," said Harry. "This island isn't a place you can defect to, you know."

The pilot threw up his hands. "It's not my first choice. But how would you like to try to fly a Cuban fighter-bomber into Miami? I'd have made it about halfway."

"He's got a point," said Vickers. "We don't have the wherewithal for shooting down fighter planes." Then he added, perhaps for the benefit of the Cuban, "Yet."

"Look," said the Cuban. "Let's start this all over again. My name is Mariano Rojas. I was born to play the stock market. But I was born in the wrong place. There's no stock market in Cuba, and there's no money. Okay? Thank you."

Emma looked at the small, wiry young man. His bright black eyes seemed to flick from person to person with, if not intelligence, at least alertness. "Have you thought about what your little visit here might do to us?"

He smiled at her shrewdly. "Don't worry. By the time they know where I am, it will be too late."

Harry moved closer. "What are you talking about?"

"I told them a false course on the radio, then flew in at about five meters' altitude all the way. They don't know where I am."

"How can you be sure it worked?" Vickers sensed something. There was a part of it he wasn't telling.

"I gave them a false image on their radar. There's a device."

Harry and Emma looked at each other, then at Vickers, who shrugged his shoulders. Vickers stared at Rojas, wondering if he was lying. He'd never, in all his years of fighting, spent any time near the more sophisticated species of military aircraft. His most vivid memories of jet fighters involved crouching in underbrush and wishing his side had more than the other side. The little he knew was mostly alarming. "There's no munitions placard on your plane. What have you got aboard that we need to worry about?"

"Nothing," said Rojas. "Too much weight."

Vickers sighed. "Harry, let's find some clothes that will fit this guy. He's not going to be able to fly that thing out of here, so there's no reason for him to sit around dressed like Captain Midnight. It makes people nervous to look at him."

Harry nodded. "He looks about the size of Lord Carnarvon." As Vickers led the Cuban out, Harry whispered, "Maybe they're both from the same planet."

It was eight-thirty when Harry and Emma entered the hotel dining room. They walked across the quiet, carpeted space, its high ceiling barely visible above the muted light of the antique chandeliers, and Emma thought about the room. It was an accident of proportion and shape of a sort that sometimes happened without warning, when a theater had perfect acoustics or a swimming pool was always calm. Emma had been in many rooms that gave an impression of isolation from the world outside, but the hotel dining room had an effect that was stronger than that. This room conveyed a sense that the world outside was unreal, that the jarring show of time and change was only a meaningless and ephemeral series of images flashing and noises crashing and then passing without reverberation, the entire effect being itself a constant, and therefore of little interest and no consequence.

Harry stopped suddenly. Emma glanced up at him, then followed his gaze to a table in the far corner of the room. Seated there was Mariano Rojas, wearing a fresh white *guayabera* shirt. The man sitting across the table from him was coach Del Cupido, and he was holding what looked to Emma like a contract. Harry said softly, ''Figure that one out.''

As Harry and Emma approached their table, Del Cupido glanced up and spotted them. He stood up and reached their table before they did. He picked up the little sign on it that said ''Reserved for Mr. and Mrs. Erskine,'' and looked around for a place to put it, then handed it to Harry and sat down.

''Nice of you to join us,'' said Emma.

Harry set the sign on the one remaining empty chair, but Del Cupido picked it up again. ''We're going to need that,'' he said.

''For whom?'' asked Emma. Her eyes betrayed an amusement that Del Cupido's feral alertness caught instantly.

''You don't know, do you?''

''No,'' said Harry.

''That kid over there is Mariano Rojas.''

Harry nodded. ''He told us that. If you know his name, then you probably know how he got here. And that is a fact that we're not mentioning in restaurants in front of a bunch of corporate officers who still get Roosevelt and Lenin mixed up in their nightmares. Get it?''

''You really don't know,'' said Del Cupido. He leaned close to Emma and spoke with a fevered urgency. ''Emma, get me this kid.''

''We've got him already. We don't know what to do with him.''

He whispered, ''Mariano Rojas,'' then looked around to assure himself that nobody had heard, ''is the best natural shortstop south of wherever Ozzie Smith is playing today, and he's about twelve years younger. He can hit for average and hit for power to all fields, which Smith, God bless him, can't do.''

"You've got him mixed up with somebody else," said Harry. "This kid is a pilot for the sort of airline where you can't buy a ticket."

"That's part of the irony," said Del Cupido. "They take a kid with reflexes like a cobra and eyes that can track a bullet in a basement, and the only use they can make of him is driving a damned fighter plane in circles over the sugarcane."

"How do you know about him?" asked Emma. "Where has he played?"

"No place," said Del Cupido. "Cuba. It's the same thing. His team did an exhibition series in Mexico two years ago, and another one in Managua this year."

Harry touched Del Cupido's sleeve and said quietly, "There are some names that cause digestive problems, remember."

"Harry, I'm trying to tell you something here," said Del Cupido. "It's bigger than saying 'fuck' in front of the children. This kid is a major talent, and if the news gets out tonight, there's going to be a scout from Pittsburgh here tomorrow. The fact that he didn't arrive on the number-ten bus makes it worse. He's going to be news."

Emma sighed. "Bring him over here."

Del Cupido got up and moved to the distant table, where Mariano Rojas was just beginning his *mousse au chocolat*. He picked it up and carried the *mousse* and a spoon to Harry and Emma's table.

Harry said, "Mariano, we'd like to talk business with you."

Mariano stopped his spoon in the air, looked at Harry, then looked at the chocolate on the spoon, and put it in his mouth. Then he said, "Okay."

"Do you like to play baseball?" Emma asked. Del Cupido stared at the ceiling and worked his jaw muscles.

"I love it," said Mariano.

"You can play shortstop for the Caribs," said Emma. "Mr. Del Cupido will sign you up tonight as soon as we reach a financial agreement, and you can play tomorrow if he thinks you're ready."

"I won't have time," said Mariano. "I've got to get to

Wall Street to look over the big board. I've got a lot to do."

Harry felt a tingle in the back of his neck, and his breathing slowed.

Emma looked at Harry, and noticed that the expression was on his face again. His features were bland, friendly, and curious. He smells blood in the water, she thought. The kid said something, and it told Harry his weakness.

Harry said, "We have some connections in New York, and most of the other financial centers too, come to think of it. Maybe we can help."

Del Cupido looked at Harry with mute horror, but Harry went on. "What will you need?"

Mariano shrugged. "First, I've got to get there. Then, I'll have to get an office, and a ticker-tape machine, and a telephone."

Harry nodded sagely. "I see. And then you buy and sell stock. Do you have enough money?"

Mariano smirked. "That's the simple part. I think fast, and I work fast. I'll start out buying on margin, and then sell out as some of my holdings go up. When I get far enough ahead, I'll buy a seat on the exchange and start taking on customers."

"I see," said Harry. He resisted the temptation to glance at Emma.

Emma's eyes focused on a table across the room. "There's Sam Fish," she said. "Sam Fish is the president of a very large corporation that has its headquarters on the island. Have you ever heard of him?"

"No," said Mariano.

"Have you ever heard of Nat Packer?"

"No."

"He's what you want to be," said Harry. "We'll introduce you to him, and you two can talk stocks and bonds over drinks later, okay?"

Mariano grinned. "What an opportunity. I've got to catch up on things." He stood up. "You've got to take advantage of the experienced animals."

"What?" said Emma.

"The bulls, the bears."

"Come on," she said, and took his arm. "You're going to meet the fish."

Sam Fish knocked on the door of Harry and Emma's house, but Emma was already on her way. "Be right there, Sam," she called. When she opened the door, his brow was furrowed, as though he were thinking about something very difficult, and his eyes didn't meet Emma's. As he walked in, Harry handed him a glass filled with ice and something that Fish decided was Scotch, but didn't taste.

"Sorry about the hour," he said. "I had to take enough time to be sure."

"Well?" asked Harry.

"He's amazing," said Fish.

"Does he know anything about the stock exchange?"

"Everything," said Fish. "Not a thing."

"You've got us," Emma said. "You haven't got us."

Fish considered. "I was going to tell you this in a sensible, logical way. I sat by myself for a few minutes after he left, and I even practiced. But it's the kind of thing where you have to know all of it before any of it makes sense."

"Forget the logic, then," said Emma. "We'll ride it out."

"What you've got there," Fish began, "is a kid who probably has the shrewdness and the concentration to make himself a good living somewhere in the financial world. And he's well educated, to a point."

"What point?" asked Harry.

"I'm not sure." Fish stared at a spot high on the wall as he calculated. "I can say he's firmly grounded up to late 1933. Really knows his stuff. After that, he drops off."

Emma looked at Harry, and then at Fish. "Why?"

"As near as I can tell, it's a problem with education in economics in Cuba. Some political problem. He can quote Ricardo's *Principles of Political Economy and Taxation.* Written in eighteen for-God's-sake seventeen. And of course, he's got Marx like he was reading it off a tattoo on your forehead." Fish rubbed his own forehead in an unconscious gesture. "You want to talk Keynes, he'll talk early Keynes. On the American economic system, he's fine . . . to a point. This kid has studied the Pecora Committee reports on Wall Street."

"The what reports?" asked Harry.

"It's the commission that tried to figure out what caused the stock-market crash of twenty-nine. I can see why that stuff was available in Cuba. It pretty clearly makes the case that a whole lot of rich guys got that way by screwing poor people."

"You mean it's propaganda?" said Emma. "I never heard of it."

"No, it's all true. But the good guys won. Or they had a semi-successful holding action, anyway. The next year the Securities Act was passed, setting up the SEC. The rules changed. Or maybe I should say that for the first time there were some rules. We're talking nineteen for-God's-sake thirty-four."

"Mariano doesn't know all this?"

"No. He has a very sketchy notion of what happened after about the time Batista came to power."

"When was that?" asked Emma.

"Just before—1933. Batista didn't much care about educating ordinary people. After 1959 the Cubans were very interested in educating people, but they have a real preference for political theory and whatever's specifically practical. It was politically important to know what's wrong with capitalism. But the changes since the thirties are just footnotes to these people. The American stock market's got nothing to do with them."

"What are we going to do with Mariano?" asked Harry.

"What do you want to do with him?"

Harry turned to Emma. "What do we want to do with him?"

"We want him to play baseball. Maybe we should send him to school or something. He can't play baseball forever."

"Oh, I forgot," said Fish. He reached into his coat pocket and produced the contract Del Cupido had given Mariano. "He asked me to witness his signature and give this to you. When he found out you need capital to be a capitalist, he took a look at the salary."

Emma took the contract and glanced at it. "What are we offering?" Her lips pursed, and a tiny sound came out. "Oh."

Vickers awoke, alert, listening for the sound again, but when it came, it wasn't the same. The first sound was just the static tickling the telephone bell as the connection was made, and the second was the ring. It was like an indrawn breath, and then the shout. Vickers sat up and lifted the receiver. "Yeah. Vickers."

Through the wiring and then the radio receiver that picked up the words that pulsed over the sea came a familiar voice. "Vickers. This is Gordon."

Vickers felt something like an electric shock in his spine, and he noticed that he was standing up beside the bed, and the telephone was about to slide off the night table. "Chinese. Where are you?" And the voice, calm and quiet and uninfected by his surprise, said, "L.A."

It had been ten years since he'd heard that voice. That day Vickers had tossed his duffel bag into the open gun-bay door of the chopper, and he remembered he'd tipped the mini-gun on its mounting so its bundle of six barrels had aimed upward, and then Chinese Gordon had pointed at it. "When you're up, don't forget to push that out over the hills. If you don't, we'll see it in the rematch." And then a voice had yelled, "Incoming," and the helicopter pilot had lost his patience and started his blades swirling, at first slowly and then speeding up to a scream, so the sound of the approaching mortar round was inaudible until it thumped into the trees across the compound. And then Vickers' helicopter was sweeping upward, swaying from side to side, and Vickers clung to the doorway to watch. He'd lingered there long enough to watch Chinese Gordon trotting toward the next machine, its rotors already beginning to turn slowly above it. Vickers had always thought of that as the last helicopter out of Luanda, maybe the last out of all of Angola. In any case, it was the last that Vickers had seen.

Chinese Gordon said, "It sounds like you're on a field telephone. Can you tell it's me?"

"Yes," said Vickers. "It's the best connection we can get. You have something to tell me."

"I do. I'm calling about what happened there yesterday."

"What about it?"

"A man came to see me today. He'll come to you soon. Talk to him. He's a serious man."

"Who is he?"

"Whoever they want him to be."

"Why are you calling for them? Have you taken a job?"

"No. I'm calling for you. I made a deal with him once, and he stuck to it. Talk to him." Vickers heard the click of the telephone disconnecting. He stood in the darkness, wondering if the place where the click had come from was Los Angeles, the island, or somewhere in between.

Vickers sat down on the bed and put the telephone back in its cradle. He picked up his watch from the nightstand and cupped it in his hands so the green radium on the face would glow brighter. It was four in the morning. Before long the sky would start to turn that odd purple color, and there would be no way to go back to sleep. Then he admitted to himself that there already was no way to go back to sleep.

He walked to the bathroom and turned on the shower, then waited for the water to heat up. How had Chinese Gordon managed to find him after all these years? He hadn't. They'd found Gordon. They probably hadn't needed to do anything special to accomplish it, either. They probably watched the island like cops watching a whorehouse.

He stayed in the shower for a long time, letting the water slowly wake him by heating his skin until it felt desensitized, and it made no difference to step out of the hot water of the tiled cubicle into the hot steam of the bathroom.

He made coffee on the stove while he dressed. Then he poured some into a cup and walked to the door, where he stopped. Vickers walked back to the bedroom and pulled a shoulder holster out of the closet, where it hung among his belts and neckties. Then he went to the gun cabinet and selected his old Browning nine-millimeter pistol. It was bulky under his jacket, but the weight of it was comforting in the lonely dawn.

He sipped his coffee as he walked along the deserted breakwall toward the airport. The sun would be up before long, and already he could see lights in the cabins of some of the boats in the harbor. In the hotel kitchen they'd be breaking eggs into little bowls to save time later, when the day began. On another day he might have stopped there to have breakfast with the chefs and waiters, but not today. He wanted to go out to look at the airplane. Everything else in his world made sense and seemed to be tending in the right direction, and he wanted to check the one thing that wasn't, as he might have run a hand over his head to touch an unruly strand of hair, for no reason except to assure himself that it was still out of place.

When he stepped onto the apron of the airfield, he already could see in the dim light the shape of the Cuban fighter plane, covered now with the camouflage netting he'd bought for a machine-gun emplacement he was planning for the end of the runway. It looked long and shapeless, like a cat burrowing under a blanket. As he moved closer, he saw a figure standing alone, just beyond the spot where the net was tethered down, and staring at the belly of the plane. He studied the figure as he walked toward it. It wasn't the kid who'd flown it here, come alone to stare at it in triumph or regret before there was anyone awake to see him. The figure was shorter and broader, a middle-aged man in a dark gray suit.

His next step had a hitch to it, because as he pushed forward on the ball of his foot, he knew that this was the man Chinese Gordon had called for, and he hadn't decided whether the call was an introduction or a warning. "This is a serious man." It was a cryptic remark between two men who shared the unspoken assumption that someone would be listening. "Talk to him."

Vickers walked on. He sipped his coffee without taking his eyes off the man, then moved the cup to his left hand and held it away from his body, as though he were afraid of spilling it. The gesture kept his jacket hanging loose on the left side of his body, so he could reach the gun quickly, leave the cup hanging in midair, and dive away from it in one motion.

The man was watching him, waiting for him without moving. He looked about fifty years old, with graying brown hair that was beginning to show the sparseness that sometimes came with age. He had the barrel-shaped torso that might indicate he was out of shape, but Vickers knew he couldn't count on it.

When Vickers was within ten feet of the man, he stopped. "Good morning."

"Good morning," said the man. Vickers detected a tired cheerfulness in the voice. "You're John Vickers."

Vickers nodded. Neither man moved closer.

"My name is Porterfield. Maybe you got a call to let you know I was coming."

"You know I did. He didn't say you were here already or what you'd be calling yourself this time out."

Porterfield shrugged. "It's all right. I'm here on a straightforward business deal."

"What do you want?"

Porterfield nodded at the airplane under the netting.

"I'm not sure it's ours," said Vickers. "I don't think it is, actually. And I know damned well it's not mine."

"You were the easiest one to talk to."

Vickers sipped his coffee. "What do you want a MIG for? If they gave it to the Cubans, it can't be state-of-the-art."

"It's not a MIG," said Porterfield. "It's a Sukhoi SU-24. I'll give you two million for it, and have it off your hands within twelve hours."

"Two million? The going rate for fighter planes is more like thirty."

Porterfield shook his head. "They've been building these since 1974. We know all about it. Besides, there's no other customer."

"The French, the British, the Germans—"

Porterfield shook his head. "We've foreclosed the possibility of an auction."

"You have?"

Porterfield nodded. "You can't deal with the Cubans. They're not going to buy back their own property from somebody they're not afraid of. You might work something out with the Chinese, but they wouldn't pay much."

Vickers looked at Porterfield for a moment. "Let's go for a walk."

Porterfield strode along in silence. Vickers would take him to see the others eventually. Porterfield was a patient man. The papers he carried in the breast pocket of his suit identified him as the president of the Seyell Foundation, a nonprofit charitable trust based in New York. Before that he'd been the vice-president of the Mr. Food Corporation, and before that the chief operating officer of a small Florida airline. He was still listed on the board of directors of the corporation that had unwittingly bought the airline. They had wondered why such a profitable, well-conducted little company had come onto the market at all. They hadn't paid much attention to the fact that the airline had given up its route to Honduras at just about the time when a new government had been elected there. The route hadn't been particularly profitable: judging from the cargo manifests, the planes had often flown there nearly empty. There had been rumors that the airline had begun to solicit bids for a buy-out because Porterfield had a heart condition. The rumors had been unfounded. Porterfield's heart was as sound as it had been in Guatemala in 1954, when the knife stuck in his back had missed it by an inch. Porterfield had spent his life taking care of problems that kept his heart active. And today there was the airplane.

He'd chosen Vickers because in the hasty background investigations of the major players on the island, the researchers had turned up nothing promising except that Vickers had served in three mercenary armies that had also attracted a number of former American soldiers. In the twelve years Porterfield had spent in Special Ops, he'd seen enough to know that two foreign mercenary officers who spoke the same language would inevitably know each other. They might hate each other, but the two foreigners would be brought together repeatedly by their common acquaintances. It was particularly true in Africa, where it would be assumed that two white men in a remote war zone who spoke English would react the same as two black men who spoke Dinka or Luo meeting in the tube station at Hyde Park Corner.

He'd had only twenty-four hours to act on the assignment of the airplane. It had been a gamble to take the time to fly to Los Angeles, but he'd known that Chinese Gordon would never get involved unless he saw Porterfield. The gun under Vickers' coat had reassured him. Vickers wasn't stupid, and his mind wasn't the sort that would waste Porterfield's time with obfuscation and indirection. Vickers led him out to a point of land beyond the woods that lined the golf course and stopped, letting Porterfield look for himself.

"Graves," said Porterfield. "They don't look like you dug them one at a time."

"We had a bad day a while back," Vickers said. "You want that airplane. What I want is not to have to dig more graves." He studied Porterfield. "We had an invasion here. They had American weapons, C-130's. The works."

"We didn't do it."

"I figured. None of the bodies had anything on him to put the blame on anybody else." Vickers shrugged and walked on.

"What are you asking for?"

"I'd like to have you guys find out who tried to take the island. Then I'd like help making sure it doesn't happen again."

Porterfield considered as he followed Vickers down to the beach. They walked along the hard edge of the wet sand above the surf, and Porterfield made a decision. "We've already tried."

Vickers stopped and frowned at him. "You have?"

"We didn't have any luck. There are all kinds of people who might want the place. You wrecked the cargo planes in Venezuela?"

Vickers nodded. "We had to do something fast, and that was all we could manage at the time."

"I'd have done the same. But it killed the trail. They abandoned the cattle ranch they were using as a staging area. The planes had been floating around from one owner to another for twenty years. The last owner that went bankrupt lost them to his creditors and the bank sold them at auction to the nonexistent cattle company in Venezuela. The whole thing was designed to avoid using any names."

"How did you people find out about it?"

"The Colombian police made some discreet inquiries to various other countries, and we have some friends in those countries."

"And you bothered to check it out. Why?"

"It was the guns, really. The Colombians were interested in some serial numbers on M16's. That always piques our imaginations. The guns were supposed to have been shipped to the Filipino army ten, twelve years ago. No telling whether they ever were."

Vickers grabbed Porterfield's arm. "Then what the hell would you do now if you were me?"

"Damned if I know."

Harry and Emma sat on their balcony looking out at the harbor. The dock extended like a pointer a hundred yards into the blue, as though it had been built to mark the direction of the two Netherlands cruise ships anchored a quarter-mile out. Emma poured more coffee into Harry's mug, and he acknowledged it with a nod. She set the coffeepot on the glass-topped table and Harry could see a little aura of steam form under it, like a puff of breath on the glass. "Harry," she said, "it's time to talk about Mariano Rojas. He'll be awake soon."

"I thought he was settled," said Harry. "He's going to play baseball for a few years. That ought to hold him."

"It'll hold him for the winters. But it doesn't get him what he wants. We've got to get him what he wants."

"I'm not sure I follow this."

"He's going to be famous. Or at least, notorious. He's a defector. I'd have to look into it, but I think he's our first. The wire services are going to give him a good week."

"Easily," said Harry. "I've been trying to think of a way to translate the attention into money. The baseball team can always use the publicity, I know. But there must be a way to pick up some immediate cash on him."

"Harry," said Emma. "He took an amazing gamble just for the privilege of living the dullest life imaginable in the twentieth century—buying things he'll only see on paper. It seems to me that this is one of those times when we have to decide what we stand for."

"We stand for what we always stood for," said Harry. "Creating an environment where we make big bucks without working for them except on special occasions."

"Harry, it's not like that anymore. This place has started to outgrow us."

"It never has to," said Harry. "We just have to learn to juggle more information, and stay alert."

"We're not a pair of hungry kids anymore, trying to get away with a rake-off on the Fat Man's take. We're getting middle-aged, and we're millionaires."

"That's right," said Harry. "And you know why? Because every morning, I get up and greet the day like I meant it. I look at you while you're sleeping and I say, 'This woman has probably got the finest ass in the hemisphere,' and, 'None but the brave deserve the fair.' I look out over this balcony and say, 'Today, not a sparrow will fall to the earth that Harry Erskine won't pick up and sell as a fresh squab.' "

"But you're not really like that," said Emma. "You're just trying to be a pain—" She stopped. "Did you hear that?" There was a loud rap on the door.

"Not the first time," said Harry. He set his coffee cup on the table and walked into the living room. The knock came again as he reached the front door. Harry swung the door wide, and smiled at Vickers, who didn't smile back. Then Harry saw the other man. "Hello," he said. "Come on in."

Vickers said, "Harry Erskine, Ben Porterfield." Then he saw Emma look in from the balcony. "And Emma Erskine."

As they filed through the living room, Harry noticed that Porterfield didn't appear to look to either side. He had learned that an apparent absence of normal curiosity was actually its opposite. He also noticed that Porterfield had the hint of a limp when his weight shifted to his left leg. He was wearing an expensive suit, probably English and probably tailor-made, and rubber-soled shoes that looked as though they were made of Italian glove leather. It was an interesting combination in someone who had the face of a man who had put in twenty or thirty years worrying about mortgage payments.

As they sat down around the table on the balcony, Emma asked, "What brings you to the island, Mr. Porterfield?"

"He's a spook," said Vickers.

If Emma was surprised, it was impossible to detect it. Without hesitation, she picked up another cup and handed it to Porterfield. "What do spooks like in their coffee?"

"Now that your cover is blown," said Harry, "what else can we do for you?"

"It's not a secret," said Vickers.

Porterfield nodded. "If you thought I was a private party making an offer for that airplane, you'd waste time trying to get a better price from the United States."

"He knows you," said Emma, and patted Harry's arm.

"You want the Cuban airplane?" Harry asked. He turned to Emma. "See? Not a sparrow falls . . ."

"I'll give you two million in cash, and get it out of here for you a few hours from now."

"It's not in shape to fly," said Harry. "In fact, if you go out and kick the tires, it'll fall over on you."

"I saw it," said Porterfield. "We'll haul it to the harbor and load it on a ship with a crane."

"You have a ship with you?" asked Harry.

"There's one on its way."

Harry pursed his lips. "Fair enough. Tell me why you want the airplane."

Porterfield thought: this is a man who has spent his life assuming names and titles and pretending to do one thing while working feverishly to accomplish another. He's giving me a lie-detector test. Aloud he said, "I'll be as honest as I can. I don't really know what they'll do with the airplane. Probably the air force will fix it and fly it in Nevada for adversary drills."

"You're here for something else," Emma observed.

Porterfield reviewed his own words in his mind. Had he already said it? "Yes, ma'am."

Harry smiled smugly at Emma. "The kid."

Emma returned his smile. "No way. He's not for sale."

"I'm sorry," said Porterfield. "I don't understand."

"You can't have the pilot," said Emma. "He's not going to spend the next ten years on truth serum in some military base in the desert."

"No," said Porterfield. "We just want the hardware."

"What hardware?" asked Vickers. "You were out there. If there were any weapons, he jettisoned them over the sea to lose the weight."

"I'd better explain," said Porterfield. "I'm here in the first place because our analysts determined that he probably would have been shot down by his own side unless he were carrying an ECM pod. I looked, and they were right."

"ECM? What's that?" asked Emma.

"Electronic countermeasures. It's a device that fools radar."

Harry's eyes glittered. "So this plane is carrying a sophisticated machine that makes it invulnerable?"

"Not sophisticated," said Porterfield. "The plane is a good catch. The Russians are still using that model all over the world. But if they have anything new in electronic countermeasures they wouldn't give it to the Cubans."

"It's got to be worth more than two million, though, don't you think?"

Porterfield sipped his coffee. "It all depends on context. Mr. Vickers has undoubtedly known intelligence officers. He can tell you. We're like collectors. We pick things up—bits of junk, rumors, names, numbers. Someday it might be useful, but probably it won't."

Harry turned to Vickers. "Is there any point in keeping the plane?"

Vickers shrugged. "It would be great to have our own fighter plane, but there's no way in the world we can fix it, maintain it, or fly it. The only place to get parts, weapons, or technicians is the same place we got the plane."

"Is the offer fair?" asked Emma.

"It's not what the plane would cost to buy, if they were for sale," said Vickers. "But there are no other likely buyers, and the clock is running."

Emma frowned. "You mean we absolutely have to decide now?"

Vickers said, "If we sell it, the Cubans can't come and

take it back. It didn't belong to the kid who flew it here, and we have to remember that. He stole it."

Porterfield spoke kindly to Emma. "It's not such a bad offer. You have some trouble you never wanted. We'll make it go away, and give you some money."

Harry sighed. "We'll deal. I want a quiet agreement about the pilot, though. He's going to live here for a time. Eventually, I want to set him up in New York. He'll need the legal right to live there and do business as a stock-broker or a financial analyst or whatever he decides to call himself. If he gets deported, it's not to Cuba, it's back here."

"Simple," said Porterfield. He studied Harry. "Tell me. What's he going to use for money?"

"He gets half the money for the plane," said Harry. He caught Porterfield's intrigued expression. "Hey, I'm greedy, but I'm not a vampire. Now get that goddamned piece of crap off my island before I'm up to my armpits in fur-faced Cubans." He wandered to the wall of the balcony.

Porterfield rose and said, "I'd better get started."

"I suppose so," said Harry. "Oh yeah. The money. When you marked it, you didn't put some damned chemical on it, did you?"

"No," said Porterfield. "They just made a list of the serial numbers.

Harry nodded. "Have a good trip."

"Thanks."

Porterfield walked along the dock, waiting for the launch to come in from the freighter in the harbor. Vickers came abreast of him and muttered, "What are you smiling at?"

"I was just thinking about this island. Does the Cuban pilot know yet what it is to have a million dollars?"

Vickers shook his head. "It seems he's also the best shortstop in this part of the world, so he'll have to get used to it."

Porterfield grinned. "The next one will have the formula for synthetic diamonds sewn into the seat of his pants."

Vickers shrugged. "Maybe not. But we've got Harry and Emma."

"It must be hard to figure out just when to trust them."

"If Emma came up to me and said Harry could eat his own head, I'd know enough by now to say he couldn't. But I'd also know enough not to bet on it, because when I got up the next morning there'd be twenty-three people who'd swear they saw him do it."

Porterfield chuckled, but Vickers noticed that his face had a tired, pained expression. "I just wish sometimes that history didn't erase things so completely." He paused. "I guess that's just part of getting old. I just hope . . ."

Vickers put his hand on Porterfield's shoulder. "One time I was in a poker game that went on for thirty-six hours. At the end of it I backed the second-best hand for all I had, and came out busted. You know what the guy who staked me said? 'We sure got a lot of play for our money.' And we did."

"Harry likes power."

"He just likes to keep things controlled."

"First you build a high tower so you can stand up there and see that everything is going the way it should, and pretty soon you're dropping peanut shells on the heads of the people who aren't doing what they should. After a while they get used to the peanut shells, so the only thing that will do is rocks." Porterfield stared out at the sea. "Keep an eye on Harry."

Vickers shook his head. "Harry's not like that. He just wants to see how far he can walk before his shoes wear out."

11

Ten Years

WASHINGTON

The Assistant Secretary leaned forward at his desk and contemplated the tan file folder in front of him. The island again, he thought. What's old Harry up to now? The island had been responsible for his two accelerated promotions, and was, indirectly, the source of the money for the house in Georgetown. It had brought him to the attention of the Senator. As long as the Senator kept getting reelected and maintained his seniority, anything was possible. Four presidents who hadn't agreed on anything had come and gone during his years in the State Department. But year after year when someone from State or the Pentagon or the CIA walked into the hearing room to appear before the Senate Foreign Relations Committee, the first face he'd see was the Senator's.

He closed the folder and lifted the telephone. "I'll be at the Senate Office Building for about an hour, and then I'm going home." He picked up the folder and put it into his attaché case. The island was the best demonstration he'd seen of the Senator's character, and there were quite a few people in Washington at the moment who would have felt a chill if they'd known about it. Roughly once a year the Senator would call and say, "I'm curious. See what you've got on the island."

The first time it had happened he'd almost been able to believe in the sincerity of it. The term was accurate and precise. The island was a curiosity. After the second time, the Assistant Secretary had understood. There was some kind of scheduling system at work, and the island was going to come up in its regular turn.

The Senator hadn't ever forgotten about the island. He was keeping his attention on it with the ferocious intensity that he devoted to major crises. But that attention was gauged to a sense of time so slow that only he perceived its continuity. It was as though his mind were engaged in time-lapse photography. It was only after the Assistant Secretary had contemplated the process that he began to notice that the Senator looked at people the way he looked at the island. He watched and waited, and sometimes he quietly shifted his immense influence to one side or another.

As he walked into the Senator's reception room, he heard one secretary say to another, "Our man in Havana." The receptionist heard it too, and said into the telephone, "The Assistant Secretary of State."

He moved toward the door as it opened from the inside and the Senator came out. The Senator's right hand was already extended, and he performed the effortless gesture that must have been a reflex from his six successful campaigns. As the right hand shook his, the left grasped his elbow and pulled him into the office.

"Come on in here," said the Senator. The greeting seemed redundant, because the Assistant Secretary was already being steered into the office and couldn't have strayed off course without somehow breaking the armhold.

The Assistant Secretary let himself be propelled toward the only chair he'd ever occupied in the room, and paused there to wait for the Senator to make his way around the desk so they could sit down simultaneously. The Senator settled back in his chair and asked, "How is history treating our friends?"

The Assistant Secretary opened his file folder, but answered without looking at it. "The same trends, only they seem to be speeding up a little. There was that ugly accident a couple of years ago, of course. Harry Erskine is still a small-time confidence man at heart, but he's getting rich, so he's able to keep everybody happy."

"Have they made any moves toward an actual government?"

The Assistant Secretary shook his head. "Lord Carnarvon is still the President, to keep up the legal fiction that the island is the last homeland of the Carib Indians. But the structure is still essentially corporate. Harry, Emma, Lord Carnarvon, Vickers, and Pettigrew seem to act as board of directors. They seem to ask other people about things now and then, but the founding five are still in charge."

The Senator thought for a moment, then said, "It's amazing they lasted this long. It must be eight or nine years."

"Ten," the Assistant Secretary said. He paused, then decided that the safe way to speak to the Senator was to offer neutral observations. "You've been watching these people for a long time. You're waiting for something."

"Of course."

The Assistant Secretary waited, then said, "If I knew what it was, I might be more helpful."

"Change. I'm watching for change."

THE ISLAND

Harry straightened his black tie and studied his reflection in the window that overlooked the sea. The cummerbund didn't quite conceal the beginning of a middle-aged belly, and the light from the chandelier glinted off his bald spot. He decided he looked like the restaurant reviewer for a regional newspaper. Last night he'd decided he looked like the executive in charge of offering personal banking services to people who had inherited money.

There was a knock on the door, and he heard Emma call, "I'll get it." As she crossed the living room she said, "Don't you look nice?"

"No," he said to the window.

He heard Augustino Cruz say, "Sorry, Emma. A little problem at the casino," and Emma answer, "Harry will handle it. He's just trying to suck in his gut for the mirror."

Augustino came in as Harry turned away from the window. "Hi, Harry. I didn't know when you'd be in the hotel, and—"

"It's okay. She was right. That's all I was doing."

"It's the damned Caribs in the casino again."

"Who is it?"

"Charlie Wellington and Sullivan Boats."

"Let's go assess the damage." Harry stopped at the door and called down the hallway, "Emma, I'll meet you over there."

He followed Augustino down the flagstone walk and along the breakwall above the sea. The narrow pathway beside the high stone wall had been broadened, and the tourists had made it a custom to stroll there in the evening, so the breakwall had taken on the look of an ancient promenade in an Italian city. They passed three sidewalk cafés in the two hundred yards from Harry's house to the hotel. None of the people who sat at their outdoor tables drinking wine and eating confections could have known that they were sitting in shore batteries designed by Vickers after the Baseball War.

Emma had glanced at the piles of cut stone blocks waiting to be set into the earth to protect the crews who would operate the mortars and machine guns, and said, "Those little peninsulas are going to be the best views on this side of the island."

Harry had said, "That's the idea."

Emma had squinted her eyes along the wavering shoreline and announced, "We'll use them somehow." Then, after a minute, she'd begun again. "Make sure you leave enough room for a good-size kitchen in back. In this climate the indoor dining rooms can be small, but I don't see any reason to cramp the kitchens."

Harry glanced at the people sitting on the stone patios. The evening breeze moved over them and lifted smoke from cigarettes up out of the light into the black sky at the constant acute angle that seemed by now to be a special law of nature here. Some of them were within thirty feet of a vault of munitions big enough to turn the café into a crater. Vickers had insisted it couldn't happen, but Harry had ordered signs that said "Fireworks Display" and

"Danger! Demolition Project" to be tacked up after an accident, the choice to be dictated by the size of the explosion.

Harry and Augustino crossed the paved square before the hotel and turned to take the shortcut through the labyrinth. The labyrinth had been Esther Lord Carnarvon's first project on the island. She'd seen an article somewhere about the maze at Hampton Court, and had begun transplanting cuttings from shrubs in a complicated pattern on a bare open plot of ground beyond the tennis courts. Once rooted in the black soil Vickers had dredged from the mouth of the Magdalena River, the plants had grown with a ferocious energy, and the walls of green reached the height of a man's head in three years. About once a month someone would look down from a hotel window and see a visitor wandering aimlessly in the labyrinth, miserably lost within a few yards of the nearest path out. It was a tropical version of the formal garden; the geometrically trimmed hedges that made an amusing puzzle in England were replaced by impenetrable barriers of leaves and flowers, and woven lianas of creeping and climbing vegetation that overwhelmed and threatened a little human being. From some of the deeper recesses of the puzzle the overshadowing trees made it impossible to see more than a thin strip of characterless blue sky overhead.

Harry unerringly chose his path through the labyrinth, weaving in the dark as Esther had shown him. Augustino emerged after him, and the two moved between two tennis courts, then skirted the huge irregularly shaped swimming pool with its artificial island and waterfall, and entered the hotel.

They hurried down the back stairwell to the casino level, and Harry stopped. He could see the two Caribs standing beside the roulette table on the other side of the cavernous room. As he started to walk again, he watched the croupier, an enigmatic old professional Harry had recruited from a casino in Puerto Rico who seemed to be French and refused any name but Jean Le Croupier. With the graceful efficiency of a magician, Jean passed his long white fingers over the rack of chips, deposited two perfectly cylindrical pink stacks on the table, pushed them to the two Caribs with his rake, and in the same motion harvested a big pile of chips of every color except pink.

Harry let out his breath in relief and for the first time recognized that he hadn't been able to take a full breath since Augustino had arrived at his door. It hadn't happened yet. Some night there would be a stranger who happened to watch the Caribs, and he'd notice. If he were smart enough, he'd realize that what he was seeing wasn't a run of luck. It was a genuine phenomenon that had something to do with nature but seemed to obliterate the notion of probability, like the discovery of a ten-pound diamond. If the stranger bet on every number the Caribs chose, he'd own the hotel in about an hour and a half. Harry strolled up to the roulette table and forced himself to smile. "Evening, gentlemen." Then he turned to the croupier. "Jean, how is it going?"

Without moving his cold green eyes from the table, he muttered, "As always, Harry. In Singapore we would have cut their throats."

The two Caribs grinned at Harry, their perfect white upper teeth just touching their lower lips. Sullivan Boats said to Charlie Wellington, "How much have we got?" Charlie glanced at the stack of pink chips, and answered, "Ten thousand, eight hundred. That ought to be enough."

"Good," said Sullivan Boats. "Let's buy Harry a drink."

"It's on me," Harry insisted. "Here. Want to cash in these chips first?"

"No," said Charlie. "Jean will hold them for us. Won't you? We're just going for a drink with Harry."

Jean Le Croupier didn't deny it. He merely announced, "In Beirut, we would have mixed you a special drink."

Harry patted Charlie and Sullivan on their shoulders as Jean pulled their mound of chips toward the rack and said, "See if you can remember the recipe."

The three men made their way across the busy casino, Harry a head taller than the two brown Caribs. As they entered the bar overlooking the casino, they passed a table where a woman in her thirties with long, straight brown hair sat alone. Her still, watchful eyes had a look of repose as she stared out over the scores of blackjack tables ranked before her. But as Harry and Sullivan and Charlie passed, her eyes shifted to the mirrored surface of the column a few feet away, studied them in reflection, and then drifted back over the casino.

A voice above her said, ''Debbie, isn't it?''

''No. It's Deborah,'' she said. ''How are you, Mr. Baldwin?''

''Can I sit down for a minute?''

''Suit yourself.''

''Then I'm fine, thanks. And you?'' He was a tall, thin man about her age, with the slightly sloping shoulders of a scholar, but the cut of his tuxedo made his torso look square.

''I've been well. I assume you're here to take a look around.''

Baldwin spoke very quietly. ''It's a hard place for Treasury to ignore. You can jog the whole island without working up a sweat, and there are a hundred and seventeen banks. If just the Americans who are supposedly residents of this place showed up at once, there wouldn't be room for all of them to stand.''

She nodded. ''If it makes you feel better, it's not just Americans.''

''Maybe if you get around to it, you can tell me when it's going to end.''

Deborah said nothing. She sipped her martini and glanced at the mirrored column again, then put down the glass.

Baldwin leaned forward. ''You are still with the Company, aren't you?''

''We stopped calling it that when everybody else started. It wasn't fun anymore.''

''What do you call it?''

''None of your business.''

Baldwin whispered, ''Look, Debbie. It's a hell of a fortuitous accident that we're here at the same time.''

''Is it?''

''All you have to do is give us two hours before anything happens, and we'll be set.''

She looked at him. ''Set for what?''

His eyes widened. ''To save the financial records. There

are literally thousands of accounts in those banks that are full of money moved offshore to evade taxes. There are laundry accounts full of money from drugs, prostitution, political kickbacks, all kinds of secret—'' He stopped. He sat with his eyes closed and his jaw muscles working, as though he had suddenly felt a sharp pain in his stomach.

Deborah looked at the mirror again and satisfied herself that Harry and the two Indians were still at their table.

Baldwin spoke through clenched teeth. ''Deborah, there are graves on the island. Do you people know what's been going on here? Down by the eucalyptus trees—about thirty, all with the same date on them.''

''Thirty-seven,'' she said. ''We knew about it at the time. It was self-defense.''

Baldwin frowned. ''You've been watching them all these years?''

''Haven't you?'' She glanced at him over her glass.

He gazed out at the casino. ''Look out there. I count fifty blackjack tables, all full, all hundred-dollar minimum. If you figure they play a hand every two minutes, that's a minimum of twenty-one thousand bet every hour at every table. If no player ever makes a stupid bet, and the house is absolutely honest, the vigorish is five-point-six percent. Every hour, every table is making a minimum of eleven hundred and seventy-six dollars. Every hour, every day, every year, and none of it is taxed, and none of the interest on it is taxed, and—''

Deborah studied him. ''If you want to go try your luck, I won't tell anybody what you win.''

Baldwin shook his head. ''I don't understand you people.''

Deborah touched his arm and left her hand there. ''Sometimes it pays to be patient, just watch and wait, and go slowly. What you can't get by grabbing and pushing will come to you when it's ready.''

Baldwin brightened. ''What are you saying?''

Deborah spoke softly. ''This has all happened before. This is the sixteenth century—a few cutthroats, a few people with a flair for outmaneuvering the major powers, a few runaway slaves. It will pass.''

"All I ask is that you tell me two hours before you move in."

She looked disappointed. "Pay attention. In an average year there are seven hurricanes in the Caribbean. In all these years not one has crossed this island. Once in a while there's a tidal wave. Can you imagine what a sixty-foot wave would do to this place?"

"You're waiting for an act of God. Like Sodom and Gomorrah." He looked astonished.

Deborah grinned. "It's in the middle of our immediate sphere of influence. If someone else shows signs of moving in and digging missile silos, of course we'll act. But they won't. Something else will happen first."

Baldwin sighed. "I want another drink. I suppose you people have expense accounts that aren't audited for liquor."

Deborah was staring into the mirror at the three men at the table behind her. "Get me one too."

Baldwin looked around for a waiter, and Deborah listened to the men behind her, who were talking louder now.

Harry said, "It's not because it's costing us money. It's because it's driving me crazy."

Sullivan Boats sipped his drink. "We'd hate to have that happen, Harry."

"So what is it?"

"We pick the right number," said Charlie Wellington.

Harry leaned forward. "I know that, you savage. I want to know how, before some guy from Las Vegas learns to do it too."

"Don't worry about that. There aren't any Caribs in Las Vegas," said Sullivan Boats. Then he turned to Charlie Wellington, "Are there?"

"Nobody I know of."

Harry said, "Now we're getting somewhere. I read someplace that American Indians can see better than other people. The average person can see seven thousand stars without a telescope and an Indian can see eight thousand. It's your eyesight, isn't it?"

"We're not American Indians."

"Exactly," said Harry triumphantly. "How many stars can you see? Nine thousand? Ten?"

Sullivan Boats said, "Who sits around trying to count stars? You'd lose your place after about five minutes."

"But you can see better than we can, can't you?"

Charlie Wellington looked at him. "How the hell would we know that? Harry, do you think about stuff like this a lot?"

Jean Le Croupier walked into the bar, his small, bright eyes scanning. He stood with his abnormally straight posture in his archaic tuxedo, then half-turned on his heel and moved to the table. "There you are," he said. "It was time for my break, so I cashed you out." He produced a neat stack of bills with a paper band around it, and handed it to Sullivan Boats.

"Thanks, Jean," said Charlie Wellington. "Sit down and we'll buy you a drink."

Jean Le Croupier sat in the empty chair, and Harry noticed that his back didn't touch it. He lit a short, fat cigarette and exhaled the smoke through his nostrils. "Mineral water. I work until three."

Harry said, "How do they do it? Is it their eyes?"

Jean glared at the two Caribs. "In Las Vegas we would have experimented to see if it had to do with their kneecaps."

"Well, what is it?" said Harry. "Every time one of them comes in here he milks the roulette wheel like a cow. Are they cheating somehow?"

Jean turned his icy eyes on Harry. He contemplated him with disdain for a moment, then seemed to soften slightly. "The Caribs are, without exception, incapable of dishonesty. And no one can cheat Jean Le Croupier."

"But you know something, don't you?"

"Of course."

"Is it their reflexes? Do they see what's going to happen and then bet on it quickly?"

"No. Lord Carnarvon bets without looking."

Harry gritted his teeth. "Don't tell me there's a system for roulette. It's ridiculous."

Jean shook his head. "Three months ago I brought Esther Lord Carnarvon and her little daughter in here before my shift. Little Emma is three, and had never seen a wheel.''

''You brought Emma into a casino? A baby in a casino?''

''I had to know. She was no worse at it than her mother, who had never gambled either. They were both the same as these two.'' He leaned closer to Harry and scowled as he said the three words slowly. ''They never lose.''

Sullivan Boats smiled. ''If you really liked us you'd think positively: 'They always win.' ''

Harry glanced at Jean. ''In Monte Carlo—''

Jean seemed to enjoy the thought. ''—we'd have displayed your jewels in the national treasury.''

Harry stared at Jean. ''You have some theory, don't you?''

''They're God's curse. God kept them isolated in a remote place for hundreds of years, where they would never see a roulette wheel. He only brought them out now, to the one place on earth where they would be part-owners of a casino, and winning would do them no good, to show that He can do as He pleases.

''You're giving me the creeps,'' said Sullivan Boats.

Jean Le Croupier sighed with resignation, then pointed at the roulette wheel he'd just left. ''Where will the ball stop?''

''Double zero,'' said Charlie Wellington.

There was a clattering of the ball as the wheel slowed, and they could see Raul Martínez, Jean's replacement, move his marker to the top of the board and pull his rake down the ranks of numbers to clear the chips away.

Across the bar, Deborah studied Harry's face in the mirror. She didn't move her eyes until Baldwin returned and asked, ''Can you tell what they're talking about?''

She pushed her empty glass aside and lifted the new one. ''Every time one of the Caribs comes in here, Erskine coaxes him away from the gambling tables. I guess he's afraid they'll lose all their money.

Baldwin said, ''Would you like to join me for dinner? The food here is incredible.''

''I usually go to the restaurant after Harry and Emma are seated.''

"I saw her come in a few minutes ago. She's over on the other side of the casino talking to somebody. They can have one dinner without being watched."

Deborah shook her head. "That isn't why. I just wait to see what they order."

Out on the floor of the casino two tall men, one white and the other black, spotted Harry and started to move through the crowd of gamblers toward the bar.

"Vickers and Pettigrew," said Deborah.

"Pettigrew I know about," said Baldwin. "Who's Vickers?"

Deborah smiled. "Let's go get a table before they all decide to do the same." She stood up and said quietly, "It'll give me a chance to explain some things you might need to know."

Baldwin rose and followed her into the empty corridor. "What might I need to know?"

"Vickers is a good place to start. He's Canadian, a professional soldier. He was in eight or ten pretty nasty little wars before he met Harry Erskine. He even did a couple of things for us."

"What does he do now?"

She shrugged. "One of the things is, he makes invading this place just to roll in a few tax evaders a very stupid idea."

"You mean to say we're afraid?"

"Of course not," said Deborah. "If they want to, the navy can turn the place into empty ocean from twenty miles out. That would kill four or five hundred innocent tourists, all rich; about thirty professional baseball players, maybe a dozen of them well known in the United States; and any number of surprise guests. Considering the prices here, that would include six famous actors, the band that has that week's number-one song, and the President's niece." Deborah stopped to take a breath. "The quick commando-style invasion has been tried here."

"The graves. Who are they?"

"Oddly enough, we haven't been able to find out," said Deborah. "The question isn't whether a raid would be disastrous. Judging from what they spend on weapons, it would. The real question is whether afterwards they'd protest to the UN, or Vickers would find his way into the office of whoever ordered it and blow his head off.''

In the casino, Harry was saying to Vickers, ''It would be incredibly simple. We get five or six of them passports from an Oriental country—maybe Japan. We make a reservation at Caesar's Palace in the name of Mitsui Bank or Mitsubishi or something, like they were a bunch of executives on a holiday. If they just talk Carib to each other, I figure they're good for a whole evening. You and I can pretend we're their limousine drivers or something.''

Baldwin stirred slightly in the bed, and some part of him noted that it was daylight, but there was nothing about the placement of the furniture to remind him that he was in the wrong room. He dozed off again, and whatever had awakened him the first time happened again. He heard it, and then realized it wouldn't fit into the fabric of his dream. There was a metallic click, and an electronic whir, and another click.

He opened his eyes, and for an instant nothing made sense. There was a naked woman standing in the sunlight at the French window to the balcony, doing something. Then he remembered it was Deborah, and remembered what had happened the night before. It was her hotel room, so whatever she was doing was probably normal, but what the hell was that noise?

''Good morning,'' he said. ''You're beautiful.''

''Yes,'' she answered. ''And to think I was a sixty-year-old Cuban man until the surgeons at Langley did a few cuts and sutures.''

He raised himself on one elbow and looked at her. She was aiming a camera out the window. There was the click of the shutter and the hum of the automatic rewind. ''Do you do a lot of that?''

''Second roll of the morning.''

''What's out there?''

''None of your business.''

''About last night—''

''Have you noticed that nobody ever starts sentences with 'About' except that one? It was as good for me, and I know that you still respect me now that it's morning.''

He lay back in the bed and closed his eyes. He heard the camera click again. ''It probably wasn't as good for you.''

''Have it your way.''

''Do I have to leave right now?''

''No.'' She set the camera in a dresser drawer and looked at him for the first time. ''It helps my image around here to have a little fun, and how much golf can you play?'' She walked back to the bed and crawled in beside him.

''Deborah,'' he said. He could feel her hand slowly moving up his thigh.

''What?''

''Is that your real name?''

''Of course not.''

''Who are you really?''

''Deborah.''

Emma watched Del Cupido walk out toward the pitcher's mound. He seemed to be on his way across the field on a morning stroll, looking around him at the grass, the stadium, and even up at the sky. He looked a little surprised when he found himself in the middle of the diamond. He seemed to find it fortuitous that there happened to be a pitcher standing there, and one he happened to know very well. He patted the pitcher's shoulder as a greeting. Then, from Emma's seat above the dugout it looked as though he were saying, ''What the hell. As long as I'm here anyway, let me show you something.'' He took the baseball, gripped it, held it up for the pitcher to see. Then he went into his windup, and he looked to Emma as though he were twenty years old again. His left leg kicked high in the air, and his right arm extended behind him. There was the giant step forward and his arm came down in a perfect vertical swath. The ball jumped up four inches just before it reached the plate, and the catcher rocked back on his heels to trap it. Del Cupido chatted with the pitcher for a few seconds, then walked back to join Emma.

''You ought to pitch the next game,'' she said.

''I already know how to pitch,'' Del Cupido answered.

''That's what I . . . Oh, forget it.''

''What brings you out this early, Emma?''

"I got a phone call from the commissioner of La Liga Puertorriqueña de Beisbol Profesional."

"Oh," he said, and looked down at the ground. He happened to see a small stone there that might get caught in somebody's spikes and cause him to stumble, so he concentrated on digging it out with his heel.

"He said he'd asked for an assurance from you that we'd go to the Serie del Caribe in February with no more than six players from the American major leagues."

"Yeah," said Del Cupido. "I talked to him." He glanced at her. "That's the rule."

Emma nodded. "He happened to mention that you'd told him to pound salt up his ass."

"He told you that?" asked Del Cupido. "Then he's no gentleman."

"He seems quite polite except when he's quoting," she said. "We only have six big-league players, don't we?"

"That's right. For this year."

"You mean you're getting ready to make your move?"

Del Cupido picked up the stone and examined it, as though he were looking for a vein of platinum.

"Great," she said. "I've been waiting for this."

"It's not exactly going to happen like we planned," he said. "The whole of professional baseball isn't going to pack up the day after the World Series each year and move south."

"Enough for five or six teams?"

"Easily."

"You know what the Dodgers are getting this year from television, Harry?" Emma waited. "Take a guess."

"A hundred trillion dollars and they get to pick the City Council and have sex with all the actresses in Hollywood," said Harry. "Or the reverse."

"That's only if they're in the pennant race," Emma answered. "The figure is twelve million dollars. That's if they stink this year."

Captain Pettigrew nodded. "I've always been a Dodger fan. Lots of people held it against them when they moved to a better climate, but fifty-eight was about the time I did the same, and I don't think either of us has ever regretted it. The criticism rolled right off us."

"What I'm getting at is that we've got a chance this year to make some deals."

Lord Carnarvon asked, "What deals?"

"Del Cupido and I worked it all out two years ago. Winter baseball has always been impossible, because you can't sell enough tickets in this part of the world, and you can't play on the mainland. So we go completely to television, live by satellite, and sell the games to a cable company."

"Pretty ambitious," Harry said.

"Of course it is. It's absolutely crazy. And major-league players who make a million dollars in the summer won't come down here in the winter, except they do already," Emma said. "A lot of them were born near here."

"What do you do for competition?" asked Harry. "Nobody wants to see a bunch of vacationing all-stars beat the shit out of some local team."

"We're taking care of that already," said Emma. "We're going to do this in the open, a year in advance. We're telling everybody we're getting a whole roster of big-league players and giving them a chance to keep up with us."

"You'll get thrown out of the legitimate leagues," said Lord Carnarvon.

"Or we'll pull out and take the six or eight best teams with us. Think about it. You have a tight World Series in October. The center fielder for the Astros hits a grand slam in the bottom of the ninth and destroys a two-hit seventh game for the Red Sox pitcher. In November or December that pitcher and that batter face each other again, here. You think people in the States won't watch that?"

"You may have a point," said Harry. "Is there any way to get a satellite hook up without paying for it?"

Deborah's head was cradled in Baldwin's arm. She looked up at the ceiling, which now glowed with light reflected from the ocean below. "My favorite so far is Harry's Marriage Registration Act."

"What was that?"

"He decided he'd solve several problems at once. A few years ago, when people from the island started going other places on business and vacations, Harry realized that he was going to have to start doing one of the things governments do, which is to keep a record of citizens and issue them passports. Once he got started, he was in trouble. He had to keep records of who was related to whom, and what shots they'd had."

Baldwin shook his head. "That should have shown him what it is to be a government. These days every bunch of lunatics with a sewage system and a manifesto thinks they've got it licked. Wait until he has to give them something they don't want and then charge them for it."

Deborah went on. "Harry didn't have the patience for it, so he realized he'd have to pay someone to do it. But Harry always tries to be reasonable. He decided it wasn't right to tax people who didn't want the service. So he bundled all the census costs into a Marriage Registration Act."

"That's not bad," Baldwin admitted. "At least it takes the long view.

"He tried to," she said. "He said the island would not recognize marriages performed in other countries unless they were registered here and a fifty-dollar fee paid. He figured most of the rich adults who had moved here from elsewhere to evade taxes would pay the fifty and cover his costs. They'd also be the ones who wanted passports and naturalization papers that would look good in foreign courts, and want to be sure their children inherited."

"I can see the reasoning," said Baldwin. "Your customers come to you only when they need to set the record straight."

"Oh, Harry worked out the effects of people following the rule. But Harry didn't bother to figure out all the implications of noncompliance. If a person moved all of his assets here, and didn't bother to pay the fifty bucks, he had a quickie divorce with no need for a settlement: *ex post facto* annulment."

"My God. What happened?"

"What happened was a very quiet gold rush. Only this

time the prospectors brought the gold with them. The nearest we can tell, in the first year, the Marriage Registration Act brought five hundred new citizens, and that included twenty-two really major fortunes. You people think everybody is here to get away from you. Actually, a lot of them laugh at you—they have so many kinds of write-offs you barely scrape their skin. But a vengeful ex-wife gets half."

"Then a lot of these people are fugitives already."

"Nobody with a hundred million dollars is a fugitive. They go where they please. As long as they don't stay more than a month or two, they can even go back to their old hometowns."

Baldwin sat up and stared at the wall. "Why is that your favorite story?"

"It shows that history gets more interesting if you manipulate it a little."

"You would like that. How can you know each step of this?"

"None of your business."

"All right," Baldwin said carefully. "You have a cover identity. It's not my fault that I know you're in the CIA. I didn't ask to be, but I was there during that little incident in the Federal Reserve in Miami. Okay, so that's over, and you still won't tell me about you. What about her? What are you pretending to be?"

"I'm a television executive," she said. "I'm one of those girls who would slit your throat to get ahead."

"But you really are one of those girls who would," said Baldwin. "I mean really."

"See how good at this we are?" Deborah grinned.

"Why is it you're never anything normal—waiters or bank tellers or something? It's always journalists or big executives or jet-set socialites. It's like a game thought up by children."

The telephone rang, and Baldwin jumped. Deborah studied him with amusement for a moment, then crawled off the end of the bed and walked around to the nightstand to answer it. "Hello, Mrs. Erskine. What a nice surprise." There was a pause as she listened. Then she said, "Yes. Ultraworld. We're not the biggest, but we're backed by a gigantic organization with almost forty years of experience."

Baldwin climbed out of bed and walked toward the bureau where his clothes lay crumpled. As he turned, he saw Deborah sitting primly on the edge of the bed listening. Slowly the corners of her mouth began to turn up. "Yes. That's definitely something I'd like to talk about. Tonight? Absolutely. See you then."

Baldwin was just beginning to separate his shirt from his trousers. "Was that *the* Mrs. Erskine?"

"The same."

"What's she up to?"

"It's a business deal," said Deborah. "She wants to broadcast winter baseball games to the United States by satellite."

"There." He smirked. "If you had been here as a secretary or a fourth-grade teacher from Cleveland, she'd have left you alone."

"Exactly."

"So what are you going to do now?"

"Get her a satellite hookup."

"What?"

"Who has more satellites than we have?"

"Deborah," he said, "you're going to make these petty crooks into billionaires."

Her back straightened and she picked up the alarm clock beside the telephone. "Wow. It's almost noon. We'd better get moving."

"Lunch?"

She frowned. "No, I'm sorry. We won't have time. You've got to be at the airport in an hour."

"I'm not going anywhere."

She walked up and put her arms around him. "I'm sorry, sweetie, but you are. When you get to your room you'll find that your boss has been calling for hours. But you can think of an excuse for him."

His face seemed to freeze in an expression of dismay. Next it slowly changed to anger. He freed himself and returned to the task of sorting out his clothes.

"Don't pout. I just can't have you around to distract me. I'm not allowed."

As he spoke, his head bounced rhythmically up and down like a puppet's. "You don't have to flatter me. I'm a big boy. The thing that bothers me is what you're doing down here. This island is—"

"A duck," she said softly.

His head tilted. "A what?"

"It's a duck. And the United States is a big sleepy old alligator. It looks like it's not even alive, lying in the water so still. But everybody knows what happens when the alligator gets hungry. It's a law of nature."

"Then why are you getting rid of me?"

"Because the alligator isn't hungry, and down here if you scare the ducks you might get killed. And I like you." She put her arms around his neck and kissed him. Deborah gave a little sigh of pleasure.

12

THE ISLAND

Joaquín and Vickers walked along the beach toward the northeast point where the Carib canoes were pulled high up on the sand. From here they looked like a row of torpedoes aimed out to sea. Vickers wore his usual costume, which Lord Carnarvon called "Vickers Amphibious-Maneuvers Mufti." He wore opaque aviator glasses, a khaki shirt with military epaulets from some long-disbanded army, and a faded canvas belt that had loops for pistol ammunition. From the belt down, the martial figure disappeared. He wore bright yellow swimming trunks and a pair of disreputable straw sandals.

Joaquín pulled two cigars from his breast pocket and the two men stopped to light them from the six-inch flame of Vickers' tarnished lighter. "You ever wonder why a man who makes two or three hundred thousand a year still paddles out on the ocean in a hollowed-out log?"

"It crossed my mind," said Vickers. The two walked on, puffing thoughtfully on their cigars. "Is that what a share is worth these days?"

"You don't know?"

"Why should I? What am I going to do—go visit my money in the bank?"

"You should at least know that most of it's not in the bank. Harry's been buying land and paper in other countries for years." Joaquín watched Vickers studying his cigar ash as they walked along. "You don't look happy about it."

"I was just thinking. That makes us the richest country, per capita, in the world. It means we're getting ripe for another invasion."

"I'm not," said Joaquín.

"You know, it's the worst failure of my life. I tried to find out more. I'm still trying, but I've never gotten anywhere. I always thought the Colonel would figure it out, but he never did."

"El Presidente."

"Right. The President. He's a pretty good one, too, isn't he?"

"He has very few peers."

"I always thought he was crazy to give up the army for politics. There's not much security in this part of the world for a politician unless he's got something else going for him."

"In this part of the world we get nervous about politicians with something else going for them—particularly armies."

"I talked to him the other day on the phone, and that's about what he said."

Joaquín looked at him through the corner of his eye. "You really do think it's not over, don't you? That's why you called him."

Vickers stopped and sat on the sand and stared out at the vast, empty blue sea. "I just had a feeling, and I wondered if he'd heard anything that might help me give a name to it. Presidents of serious countries have all sorts of information we don't."

"So that's why you've spent the past two weeks bothering people about grenade launchers and rifles." Joaquín sat down beside him.

"I've looked to see if we've gotten too fat and prosperous." He stared back at the shore along the bay, stretching in a long arc from the hotel to the point. Here and there he could see bright red, blue, and yellow beach umbrellas like little flowers sprouting in the white sand. "We haven't added an inch to this island that isn't a death trap to a landing force."

"But?" asked Joaquín.

"It's two years and I don't know who they were. I've been waking up at night with a funny feeling in the back of my neck. I had this strange urge to walk the island again—go all around the perimeter, just to see if everything was where it should be, and everybody was okay."

Joaquín squinted upward at the sun, and stood up, brushing the sand off his white trousers. "Then we'd better get at it, don't you think?"

When they reached the point, Vickers wandered among the Carib canoes, puffing on his cigar. Then he stopped and looked along the shore. "Nice morning," he said. "It doesn't look like anybody's gone out."

Joaquín stopped too. "There's a baseball game this afternoon, but that's not for hours."

A voice came from behind one of the canoes. "Lord Carnarvon took everybody out to the golf course."

Vickers walked around the canoe and looked down at the figure on the sand. It was Nathaniel Boats, Esther Lord Carnarvon's father. He was sitting beside the overturned canoe with a mallet and chisel, sighting along the keel. "There's a man from California coming tomorrow to decide if he wants his tournament here, so they're doing some gardening while the sun is low."

"Hello, Nathaniel," said Joaquín.

Nathaniel said only, "Joaquín, go to the stern and tell me if the spine is straight."

Joaquín knelt at the other end of the canoe. "Yes."

Nathaniel Boats sat up. "I thought so. My grandson made this boat." He gave a sly look at Joaquin. "I came to see if it needed a touch of the chisel while his daddy had him away."

Joaquín stood up and looked at the sand. "I don't see any chips."

Nathaniel Boats smiled. "No."

Vickers sat down beside the old man, who was putting his mallet and chisel into an old canvas bag. "Nathaniel, have you seen anything strange lately?"

"Everything here is strange."

"I mean out on the sea. Maybe more airplanes than usual, or a ship that wasn't going anywhere."

"Only the boat out there right now."

"Where?" asked Vickers.

Nathaniel Boats nodded at a grove of palm trees on the peninsula. "I've been watching it since dawn. It's very slow, drifting out there beyond the reef. Maybe once an hour I walk around the point and take a look, and it's closer."

Vickers stood up quickly. "Let's go look now."

Nathaniel Boats took Joaquin and Vickers along the beach and through the palm trees. When they were halfway through, he stopped and pointed. "I should have kept an eye on it," he said.

Joaquín stared out to sea and said, "We'd better get out there."

Vickers saw it too. It was an old, high-sided fishing boat with peeling white paint and a short, thick mast with a board ladder nailed to it and a crow's nest on top. It was rolling with its side to the waves, and he could see at least a dozen men on the deck. "There's a bunker up the bluff with guns and ammunition. I can hold them off while you get help."

"They're not attacking," said Joaquín. "They're getting ready to drown. They need to be saved."

Nathaniel Boats was already moving toward the row of Carib canoes with stiff, bowlegged strides. He said, "There are paddles in the canoes. We'll each paddle one out there and tow another one. It's not much, but it's the best we can do."

Joaquín and Vickers broke into a run and passed him. When Vickers reached the canoes, Joaquín was threading the bowline of one canoe under the seat of the one behind it. He worked quickly, expertly tying the familiar sailor's knots without looking.

Vickers pushed the first canoe toward the water, dragging the second behind it. "You're a seaman," he said. "Give me some quick pointers."

Joaquín finished tethering two more canoes together, and pushed them after Vickers. "Keep it aimed at the waves, paddle like hell, and don't lean over if you can help it."

"Got it," said Vickers.

"At least if you don't get swamped until you're out there, the poor bastards can hang on to your canoe." Joaquín turned and sprinted back up the beach, where Nathaniel Boats was beginning to push the third pair of canoes to the water.

Vickers watched the two moving toward him for a second, then looked down at the hollowed-out log at his feet. He felt a terrible despair, and a knowledge that what he was doing was stupid, and an inability to think of a way not to do it. He pushed his canoes into the water and ran two strides into the surf before he flopped his body across one of them and rolled into it. He felt it surge upward on a wave as he lay on his back feeling for the paddle. He sat up and grasped the smooth blade, twirled it around, and jabbed it into the water. He paddled hard, chopping at the water a dozen times before the canoe seemed to go anywhere. Then he felt the sharp tug backward as the rope tightened and the second canoe spun around and followed.

After a few more strokes he found himself moving to the left, so he switched hands and paddled on the other side. He knew he must be zigzagging from side to side, but he sensed that four strokes on each side of the canoe gave him the greatest illusion of progress, so he counted them to himself as he struggled out to sea.

As Nathaniel Boats passed Vickers he felt a little pang of worry. Vickers was a stone man; a man with great strength in his arms and shoulders, alien to the sea. If he fell in, he would swim by pounding the sea with his fists and fighting it, as he was fighting it now, and the sea would wait until he had used up his life and then swallow him.

Nathaniel Boats paddled on, aware of Joaquín behind him to his right, watching him and matching his strokes. As Nathaniel skirted the point he watched the endangered boat and judged the distance. It was no more than a quarter-mile, but the boat was wallowing broadside to the waves now, the mast swinging back and forth in an arc that seemed to widen with each roll. It would be on the reef soon, and capsize or break up. As the fishing boat tilted toward him again he saw the decks clearly, and felt puzzled. The boards were crowded with people, clinging to the rails and to each other and to the mast.

Joaquín watched the old man ahead of him and tried to narrow the distance, but it wasn't possible. He had worked on blue-water ships for half his life, but he hadn't been in a canoe since he was a child, and he had never thought of taking one out on salt water. As he too passed Vickers, he wondered about him. He probably didn't imagine the danger he was moving into. Joaquín had been on a tanker that broke in half in a storm off Panama. Maybe it was good that Joaquín and the old Carib would reach the fishing boat first. Vickers would have time to see the panic, the desperate men jumping into the water and flailing to the canoes that represented safety, and probably swamping them in the scramble to get aboard. Joaquín studied the pattern of the waves boiling over the submerged reef. There were low points that the Caribs crossed each day to get out of the lagoon, and the old man would be heading for one of them.

Joaquín glanced at the fishing boat again, and let out a low whistle. It was already happening. A wave lifted the clumsy old boat a couple of feet and pushed it onto the reef. The wave receded and the boat came down so hard on the reef that Joaquín heard the crunch, and then the squeal as it slipped backward, tearing a seam in the boards. The next wave slapped the side of the trapped vessel and threw white water a dozen feet in the air. The boat settled again, but the third wave pounded it into the impassable barrier.

Vickers counted his strokes, straining for more speed. He knew he was doing better now, because the others seemed no farther ahead. He knew there was something strange going on. He was used to hearing Lord Carnarvon and Joaquín, and especially Captain Pettigrew, laughing at the seamanship of some of the millionaires who bumped expensive yachts into each other in the harbor. But even Vickers could see the boat out there was no rich man's vanity. It looked ancient and weather-beaten, and as graceless as a garbage truck. Anybody who owned such a thing would have some practical use for it, and ought to be capable of steering it into the harbor instead of crashing it into a rock pile on the wrong side of the island. And there seemed to be too many people on it. There was something ghostly and frightening about it. There was no sound of an engine, and nobody yelling for help, and it was obvious the damned thing already had a big hole in it and would be on the bottom in a minute or two.

Vickers watched the boat, and as he watched, he paddled faster. A solitary black man appeared on the stern of the boat and walked off it into the water. As Vickers paddled, people lined up on the main deck and, one by one, walked to the stern and into the sea. The fourth one up was a woman carrying a child in her arms. "No!" Vickers shouted. "Wait." The scene was so orderly and quiet that when Vickers yelled, a thin coffee-colored woman turned her smooth, pretty face toward him and seemed to smile at him before she jumped.

Nathaniel Boats was within fifty yards of the wreck and he could see the heads of the survivors bobbing in the water. One of them swam to meet him, and Nathaniel veered toward the man, then felt the drag as the man pulled himself into the canoe. Nathaniel glided for a moment, and silently asked, "And what will you do now that you're safe? What are you?" He took another stroke and felt the answer. The man had freed the second canoe and was now reaching for the paddle. In a few strokes the man was ahead of him, moving back to the reef. But Nathaniel had no more time to watch, because now he was surrounded by people treading water. Two men held on to the canoe, but neither showed any inclination to climb aboard. One waved his arm high above his head and shouted, *"Étienne! Ici! Vite!"*

A man who was obviously Étienne bobbed toward the canoe holding a baby in his arms as he floated on his back. The first man took the baby and gently laid it in the stern. Then a woman boosted a child about three years old into the boat. After that, the woman and three men came out of the sea, sprawling to keep from overturning the vessel. They held out their hands to pull others to the canoe, and soon the gunwales were covered with the clutching fingers of survivors.

Nathaniel Boats looked for the other canoes, and he saw

that four were filled now with black men and women and children, and others were clinging to the sides. The fifth was moving toward shore with six strong men in it. He caught sight of four paddles, and that appalled him. There couldn't have been more than two paddles in each of the beached canoes. There were dozens of people out here. How could six men, who seemed to be the strongest, abandon them? He felt disgust as he watched them reach shore and leap from the canoe. When he saw them sprint up the beach and begin to drag the other Carib canoes down to the sea, he smiled. He shouted to the people in the water, *"Sois tranquil, mes enfants!"*

He heard a loud, wrenching crack and turned his head in time to see the fishing boat break apart on the rocks. The bow section washed over the reef, and the stern, heavy with the useless metal of the engine, lolled backward and sank in the deep water beyond.

In the water beside his canoe he saw a single white face. Vickers looked up at him and gasped, "Even the girls are better in a canoe than I am. I couldn't get the hang of it."

Nathaniel Boats nodded. "You're a very large fellow."

Harry arrived at the old wooden barracks just as Captain Pettigrew and Emma and Dr. Pentifecky emerged. As the door slowly swung shut, he could see them standing on the porch, the glow of the light from inside illuminating them, then narrowing to a thin beam, and then disappearing. Emma looked calm, and that was a good sign. Dr. Pentifecky looked tired, but that could mean anything. They might have called him off the seventeenth hole of the golf course and worked him for the next sixteen hours.

Emma saw his familiar silhouette in the moonlight. "Harry," she called. "How did things go in Houston?"

"We own a cattle ranch, and no cattle. I got the call from Vickers before I could see the broker."

"What?" asked Dr. Pentifecky.

Emma patted his arm. "I'll tell you about it later. It takes an hour to describe it."

Harry put a foot on the bottom step and clutched the railing. "Vickers didn't tell me much. What have we got?"

"They're pretty healthy, all things considered," said the

doctor. "I got the lab work back only about an hour ago. No significant pathology, only malnutrition."

"You didn't say anything about that before." There was annoyance in Emma's voice.

Dr. Pentifecky sighed. "It's nothing more than you'd expect."

"They were on that boat for a couple of weeks," said Emma. "At least it's over now."

"I didn't mean that," said Dr. Pentifecky. "They probably did better on the boat than an equivalent number of fat Swiss lawyers would have. They know how to share short rations so nobody actually dies."

Harry tried unsuccessfully to feign patience. But in the dark his voice sounded tense. "I don't know what you're talking about. Vickers had an operator break into a call, said it was an emergency, and then started telling me about a dream or something. I just got off an airplane."

"What we've got in there," Emma began, "is fifty-six survivors of a shipwreck. Vickers and Joaquin and Nathaniel Boats pulled them out of the water near the reef. The part that's like a dream is that they apparently saved all of them."

"My God," said Harry. "Who are they?"

"I don't know what to call them," said Emma. "They're immigrants or refugees, I guess. There were fifty-six of them, all crammed in a fishing boat no bigger than Lord Carnarvon's sailboat. They made it most of the way here, and ran out of gas."

"If 'refugees' means people without credit cards, we'd better think this over," said Harry. "Where did they come from?"

"Haiti," Captain Pettigrew answered.

"Haiti?" Harry's voice was strained. "They came all the way here?"

There was no need to answer. The others waited while Harry tapped his foot nervously on the wooden step. At last he said, "I assume by now we're way beyond the food-clothing-and-shelter stage."

"You'd have been proud of everybody, Harry," Emma said. "People really come through in an emergency."

"Good. Doc, the next thing I'd like is for you to place a quarantine on the building starting right now."

The doctor seemed amused. "Oh, that won't be necessary, Harry. Vitamin deficiencies aren't communicable."

"I'm glad," said Harry. "Please, just do it anyway. I want time to work this out. We'll all be able to think more clearly in a day or so."

The doctor's voice was puzzled. "But there's no pretext."

Harry snapped. "I've got to have time to figure this out. These people need to eat, sleep, and relax, don't they?"

"All right," said the doctor. "I'll pronounce some mumbo-jumbo to the people taking care of them, and put up some frightening proclamation if you want. A couple of days of rest won't harm anyone. It might be the first some of them have ever had, judging from the calluses and musculature."

"Wonderful," said Harry. "Now, if anyone knows where Vickers and Lord Carnarvon are, I'd like to talk to both of them."

"They're in the hotel," said Emma.

"Good. Come on," said Harry.

"You and the Captain can go ahead. I'll help Doc with the con game."

Harry hesitated, pondering the tone of her voice. "Fine," he said, and set off down the walk. A moment later he heard Captain Pettigrew following him, and he slowed to let the older man catch up, then walked on in silence.

Captain Pettigrew spoke deliberately. "Harry, you're a smart man."

"Thanks. So are you."

They turned onto the broad avenue lined with shops that ended at the brightly lit hotel entrance. "That's sometimes been a problem for me," the Captain said. "It hasn't always made me happy."

Harry stopped beside the window of a jewelry store and leaned against the wall. "You too?"

"I'd just like to be able to let some things go by without

having to think about them. These people today, for instance."

"What about them?"

The Captain looked at the diamond necklace on a black velvet stand in the window as though he'd never seen it before. "They're poor black folks from Haiti. They'll take a couple of days of hard thinking. There are all kinds of choices and options and implications to be considered."

"That's true," said Harry. "This is a whole new problem. We've never had a genuine immigrant before."

"What I keep wondering is this, Harry. If it was fifty-six blond Swedes that came here in a Princess cruise liner, would we still have as much to think about?"

"Yes. Absolutely. You've known me forever, and you know I'm no racist. It's not the way my mind works."

"I just want to believe that if it were Swedes, or maybe the Swiss lawyers the doctor was talking about, they'd be quarantined in that barracks while we think, and not sitting in the bar of the hotel watching the floorshow."

Harry nodded his head. "They'd be quarantined. I've got to know what's going on. I just spent the day getting on and off airplanes because I got a lunatic phone call from a man I know isn't afraid of anything, but sounded like he'd seen a ghost." He held his wrist up to the lighted display case and glanced at his watch. "I'm stopping time so I can catch up."

The Captain started to walk, and Harry walked with him. "Emma was right," Pettigrew said. "Everybody reacted well today. They came through in an emergency, without hesitation. You'd have been proud of them. I know you don't want to admit that, but you're proud as hell of them right now."

Harry followed Captain Pettigrew into the hotel lobby, and down the side stairway into the casino. As they walked past the tables, Harry scanned the faces, as he always did. At the end of a roulette table was a very thin, intense Frenchwoman he'd met shortly after her arrival, who was some kind of model, and beside her the elderly man who seemed to make his living by studying her plate at dinner and harpooning the objectionable morsels with his fork before they could do her harm. Tonight, at least, there were no Caribs.

Captain Pettigrew walked up to the bartender and asked, "Have you seen Vickers or Lord Carnarvon?"

The bartender nodded. "They're down the hall in one of the private dining rooms. We've been shipping beer down there since I came on at six."

Captain Pettigrew and Harry left the bar and moved down the quiet, carpeted hallway. As they reached the door of the third dining room, they heard a loud burst of laughter, and then feet stamping.

Harry swung the door open just as Joaquin emerged carrying a large metal tray filled with empty bottles and glasses. "Harry. Captain," he said. Then he looked very serious. "Good. You can go for the next round. I'm going for this one, but the next one is yours."

Harry and Captain Pettigrew moved inside. There was a large conference table with dirty dishes piled on the far end, and half-covered with a white tablecloth. Around the table sat Lord Carnarvon, Vickers, and six unfamiliar black men, all drinking beer and laughing and talking.

Lord Carnarvon beckoned to Harry and Pettigrew, and his gesture caught Vickers' attention. Vickers shouted, "Harry. You finally made it."

"I just got in," said Harry, looking at the glazed eyes around the table. Everyone seemed to be drunk except Lord Carnarvon.

Vickers stood up, but as he stood, he put his free arm around the shoulders of a thin black man beside him and lifted him out of his chair. "You can help us celebrate. This here is Étienne, and he's a fucking hero. You ever try to swim carrying a baby?"

"No," said Harry. "Pleased to meet you, Étienne."

The man smiled, but he was so intoxicated that his eyes seemed to be focused on the wall behind Harry.

Vickers said, "He doesn't speak much English. And this is Jean-Pierre, and Felix, and Gustave, and Charles, and Gregoire. Did I miss anybody? No."

Harry and Captain Pettigrew circled the table shaking hands with the Haitians. Then Harry said to Vickers, "I'm really tired, so I'd better get home. I just wanted to let you know I was back.''

''Noted, verified, and recorded,'' said Vickers. ''Tomorrow I'll want to talk to you about this while I'm nursing my hangover.''

''Good idea,'' said Harry. Then he added, ''And can you make sure they get back to the barracks tonight? The others might get worried if six men vanish.''

''Right,'' said Vickers. ''We'll all stagger over there shortly.''

Harry turned to leave, and Lord Carnarvon stood up. ''I'd better get home too, before the kids have to go to bed.''

Harry and Captain Pettigrew and Lord Carnarvon stopped in the hallway. Captain Pettigrew looked at Harry. ''Things sure do get complicated fast. You should have stopped time sooner, so we could figure out what to do.''

Vickers walked into Harry's house with his sunglasses on, and if there was surprise behind them when he saw that Captain Pettigrew and Lord Carnarvon and Emma and Harry were waiting for him, it was invisible. He sat down on the couch and accepted a cup of coffee. ''Thanks, Emma. I was up a little late last night.''

''Augustino told me,'' she said. ''I hope you didn't make any of those fellows sick. They've been on a boat for two weeks.''

''We took care of the dehydration, I think.''

Harry walked to the counter and refilled his coffee cup. ''What we'd better do is try to sort out the facts. Anybody know any?''

Emma said, ''They're from an island off Haiti. There are fifty-six of them, and they're very poor. What else is there to know?''

''They're fishermen,'' said Vickers. ''Or they used to be until yesterday. Their boat is on both sides of the reef.''

Harry walked back to his chair, and Lord Carnarvon said, ''I got most of the story last night. They lived in one village, just scraping by on the island. On a trip to the main island a year ago, somebody heard two guys talking about a newspaper with an article about us. He couldn't read, so he bought it from them and took it home to have somebody else read it."

"I wonder what the article said." Harry sipped his coffee.

"It said we were making a lot of money," Lord Carnarvon answered. "It also had a map with latitude and longitude."

"Whatever happened to censorship?" said Harry. "They've really let things slip since Papa Doc died."

"It was a Paris newspaper," said Lord Carnarvon. "Anyway, this year was a bad one for them, so a couple of weeks ago they just piled everybody into their best boat, spent the last of their money on provisions and gas, and headed here."

"What the hell did they think was going to happen?"

"The artist in Paris took some liberties. He was trying to convey the curvature of the earth, so he had Jamaica on one side looking small, and the mainland on the other looking small, so they figured there was plenty of space here."

"I'd like to find that artist."

"So would they," said Lord Carnarvon. "Because the island was so big, he put our coast about sixty miles north of here. When they got there it was empty sea, so they crisscrossed until they ran out of gas, then drifted two days before they washed up on the reef."

Harry put down his coffee cup and folded his hands. "Well, we've got troubles now."

"I'm not sure I understand," said Vickers.

"They read an article in an old foreign paper that said there was a place where they just might be able to get by. If they're fishermen they must have known how dangerous it was to put so many people on that boat. They must have been pretty desperate."

"That's true," said Captain Pettigrew.

"That's trouble," said Harry. "This island is the same as that fishing boat. It's got limits. I just don't know what they are."

"What are you talking about?" asked Vickers.

Harry sighed. "I suppose we were going to have to face this someday. We built this place from nothing. Everybody we brought here was part of the scheme. We jacked the prices up so high that only the rich would even visit. Now all of a sudden we've got something we can't handle. So what do we do?''

''Of course we can handle it,'' said Vickers. ''There must be five or six hundred people a day coming into the airport.''

''And they pay eight hundred a night for hotel rooms, and gamble, and eat, and drink, and buy things. And then they leave.''

Emma looked amazed. ''Oh, Harry. Lighten up. Starving immigrants make lousy suckers. Give them a year and they'll be dumb and rich like the rest of us.''

''Exactly my point,'' said Harry. ''We haven't worked this out yet. We haven't decided if there will be such a thing as a genuine immigrant on this island.''

''There's an issue of decency here,'' Emma insisted.

''The issue is control,'' said Harry. ''Decency was pulling them out of the drink. I just don't know what to do next.''

''What are you afraid of?'' asked Captain Pettigrew.

''We are a tiny dot of synthetic land surrounded by millions and millions of the poorest people on earth. Almost all of them live under governments that consist of three equestrian statues and a battalion of stormtroopers. Yesterday we got fifty-six people.'' He glanced at his watch. ''It's still early. By lunchtime we might get fifty-six more. In two weeks we could double our population.''

Vickers looked confused. ''Harry, these are special people. They knew the risk, but they came here anyway. Even if their boat weren't in pieces on the bottom of the sea, we couldn't herd them all back onto it and send them away. It's a miracle they made the trip once.''

Harry shrugged. ''It's a detail. We could fly them to Port-au-Prince, or give them a boat, or something. The problem is that I don't think we'll survive if we ignore the issue of immigration and let everybody stay who wants to. The island will load up the way the fishing boat did, with the same result.''

''If that gets to be a problem, we'll handle it,'' said Lord Carnarvon. ''We're adding an acre a week now.''

Vickers took off his sunglasses and rubbed his eyes. "These people are brave, strong, resourceful. They're exactly the sort of people this country needs."

Harry slowly shook his head. "This isn't a country. You're starting to believe our own lies. We'll have to say no sometime. They'll all be brave and admirable."

"I think we should keep them," said Vickers.

Lord Carnarvon turned to Harry. "If space is the problem, we could tie immigration to land. Everybody who comes here has to contribute work or money to extend the land a little. We've got hundreds of square miles of reefs and sandbars all around us."

"Captain?" said Harry. "You haven't said a word."

"Well, I just don't know. All this time we've managed to stay out of each other's way."

"Meaning?" asked Emma.

The Captain shrugged. "Do you see any way we're going to be able to figure this out on our own? Harry might be right about the problems."

Harry shook his head. "I know it sounds like I'm suggesting we boot them off the island. What I'm really asking is that whatever we do, it be something we decided to do, not something that happened to us."

"But if we can't decide, how is that going to happen?" asked Lord Carnarvon.

Harry's face had a look of sincerity. "I say we ask everybody to vote on it. I can live with just about anything, as long as it was decided on the island."

"Good idea," said Vickers. "It's the only way."

"Right," said Lord Carnarvon.

"Harry—" said Emma.

Harry held up his hands and asked the others, "How can there be anything wrong with that? We'll just extend the quarantine two more days, and then vote in the stadium on Thursday. That'll give us time to present the issues and talk to people."

"Harry—" Emma began again, but the others were already moving toward the door.

Harry returned to the living room, and walked to the balcony overlooking the sea. Emma followed him out, and held his arm. "You just can't resist, can you?"

"Resist what?"

"Fooling people."

"It's a habit," said Harry.

"What do you want to do?"

"Retain control."

"Harry," said Emma. "Fooling large numbers of people instead of getting to them one at a time isn't exactly a step up in the world."

"I know that. I never thought I'd stoop to becoming a politician. I've never been anything worse than a simple crook."

"Don't worry," said Emma. "You're still not a politician. I just don't understand why you're worried. The Haitians are very nice. Once they're settled, I'm sure you can manipulate them as easily as you do everyone else."

"I'm worried because this is the first time anything changed on the island without my thinking of it, or at least agreeing to it. We didn't invent this. It just happened. I don't want things just happening. I don't want to be at the mercy of nature or probability or something. I want a scheme."

Emma smiled and kissed him. "Poor you."

"Harry Erskine is a great man," said Augustino Cruz. "A few years ago this spot was underwater. Now it's the home stadium of one of the best baseball teams the world has ever seen. And more to the point, there's not one of us who hasn't gotten rich because of him. He's—" There was an explosion of applause, and Augustino waited for it to subside.

Harry slipped out of the stadium and walked along the pathway toward the golf course. He passed a poster that read "A Few Thoughts on an Immigration Policy by Harry Erskine." Augustino would handle them. There was no point in hanging around to listen to people getting up, one after another, to tell each other how much they liked Harry. The whole campaign had gotten a little bit out of hand, especially in the last twenty-four hours. He'd talked to everyone he could corner, and nearly all of them had been reached by Augustino already.

Three days ago he'd started the campaign, assuming that

by now he'd have an immigration policy to present. He'd done everything he could to remind people who Harry Erskine was. He'd built up his credibility, so that this afternoon he could walk into the stadium, tell the inhabitants of the island what he was going to do, and then walk out with their unanimous assent. If there were trouble later, nobody could blame Harry Erskine. By the end of the first day, Harry had been satisfied that they'd vote for anything he wanted.

But this satisfaction had been tempered with a mild discomfort. He'd gone to meet the Haitians and talked to the few who could speak English. They were exactly what Vickers had said they were: decent, kind, honorable, admirable people who had suffered terribly through no fault of their own. He liked them. He had thought about them constantly for hours at a time, however, and he couldn't imagine what he was going to do with fifty-six people who did not know how to steal, fight, or gamble. And he had never yet invited anyone to share in his plans who wasn't of use to him. These were good, deserving people, but if he started letting people come in on that basis, the island might as well be Greenland for all the good it would do Harry Erskine. What bothered Harry most was that if he could simply vote like anyone else, without influencing the entire populace, he'd vote to let them stay.

On the second day, Harry had begun to worry. He knew he had the votes, but he didn't have a policy. But he'd decided that the campaign would lose its momentum unless he kept adding to it. People were already beginning to find excuses to evade the bogus quarantine and visit the Haitians in their barracks. It was then that he had designed the posters. On them he'd stated everything he knew about the Haitians, about immigration, and about the island's capacity for absorbing additional citizens. No matter what he decided to do, he would be seen as having been fair, deliberate, and honest.

By this morning, Harry had known that he had won. No opinion could possibly prevail against his when the people met at the stadium to vote. It was only then that Harry's worry turned to panic. He awoke feeling dizzy and disoriented. By ten o'clock he still didn't have a decision, and his palms began to sweat. For the twentieth time he asked Emma what she thought. This time he'd said, "If we let them in, what do they bring to us?"

Emma had said, "They bring what immigrants always bring to a country: children and grandchildren."

Harry had said through his clenched teeth, "This is not a country. Our product is not future physicists. It's money."

"I don't know why you ask me," said Emma.

Finally Harry had given up. It was time to go to the stadium, and he had no policy. He went to the hotel and found Augustino in his office. "There's a change in the plan."

"What's that?" said Augustino.

"I'm not going to make a speech. Don't introduce me, just let whoever wants to talk have the mike, and then let them vote."

"What's the plan? Harry, if you're just going to fake the count—"

"I'm not."

"Well, at least tell me how you want it to go?"

Harry closed his eyes to ease the headache. "I don't know."

Augustino studied him. "Harry, are you okay?"

"I'm tired, that's all. I honestly don't have an answer. If we ship these people back to Haiti, they'll starve to death. They don't even have a boat anymore. If we don't, we may be up to our armpits in refugees in a year."

"You mean you're not rigging this thing in any way?"

"No. I don't know the answer, so I've got to let this one go by. Just use the opportunity to remind them what a great guy I am. No sense wasting all our efforts."

Harry walked along the edge of the golf course, past another poster that was tacked to a tree. He heard the crowd give another roar in the stadium. He stepped off the path and pulled down the big white poster, folded it up, and took it with him.

He found a garbage can behind one of the shops along the walkway that led to the hotel. By now he'd taken down two more posters. Above the garbage can was another poster he'd had printed years before. It was called

"Thoughts on Garbage." In it he reminded the island that organic waste made good fertilizer, and that metal, shells, brick, stone, and even some plastics could be used to build up the island's size. ". . . Any archaeologist will tell you," he'd written, "that ancient cities no bigger than ours sit on top of thick layers of broken pottery, armor, clay tablets, household implements, and trinkets. We can learn a lot from the ancients." He had seen the need for this exhortation very early. Most of the citizens had recent experience of poverty, and were accustomed to living with such frugality that garbage production was a fraction of his optimistic projections. He'd considered instituting inverted sumptuary laws, and had drafted some: wasteful products with a great mass of packaging were to be bought, and unprocessed bulk products outlawed, as well as durable goods that were really durable. But he'd lost interest before he'd shown the new regulations to anyone but Emma. Her reaction had been, "It makes you sound like you're insane." A short time later the hotel had opened, and the island had been overrun by people who didn't need Harry Erskine to teach them. If the island lasted long enough, there would be an acre of land built on a foundation of nine irons thrown into the sea from the approach to the diabolical thirteenth green of the golf course.

Harry took down the old poster over the garbage can too. For the last few years he'd had agents from the island traveling the hemisphere making offers for commodities that would raise the level of the surrounding Rosalind Banks a few feet to produce more dry land. Harry's scavengers had gotten the rubble of old stone buildings after an earthquake in Guayaquil in exchange for the trouble of clearing it away. He'd bought shiploads of mine tailings, slag from steel mills, slabs of concrete and asphalt from roads that went to places nobody wanted to go anymore.

He walked back out to the street, and turned toward the hotel. He heard another roar, the shouting voices of the assembled islanders in the stadium. This time it went on for ten or twelve seconds before it changed into another sound. The crowd was chanting now. "Harry! Harry! Harry!"

Harry kept his head down as he hurried into the hotel.

The campaign definitely had been a mistake. He just hoped the tourists on the rest of the island thought somebody named Harry had just hit a home run in the stadium. Harry headed for the bar overlooking the casino. At least if someone did recognize the word the island's inhabitants were screaming, he was going to have an alibi.

He carried a very large glass of Scotch to the far table, where he could watch Jean Le Croupier's polished and efficient movements, and took a big gulp of his drink.

The first people to return from the meeting were Sullivan Boats and Charlie Wellington. They often stopped in the casino in time for Jean Le Croupier's first break of the day, so Harry assumed they had gotten bored and decided to return to their usual routine.

When they walked to the roulette wheel, Jean Le Croupier nodded to the pit boss, and left his post. Harry watched the two Caribs and the tall, thin Frenchman talking with animation in French as they walked below his table. Then Jean Le Croupier said in English, "In London, we would have shown you something about razors."

Sullivan looked up and noticed Harry, then nudged the others. The three walked to the railing and looked up at him. "Good show, Harry," said Charlie. And Jean, his thin lips in an unaccustomed smile, moved closer. It was disconcerting, because for the first time Harry recognized that Jean looked a lot like a picture he'd seen of Voltaire. Harry leaned back in his chair, but it was to move his face farther from the bright, small eyes of Jean, which seemed to be closer to him than he could bear.

"I'm surprised at you, Harry," he said. "I thought you were going to wait for the guillotine."

"What?" said Harry. But Jean and Charlie and Sullivan were moving off through the crowd. "What?" said Harry, louder now.

A hand touched his arm, and he turned his head to see Augustino standing over him. Augustino was sweating, and there was a strange look on his face.

Harry asked, "What the hell is he talking about? We weren't going to kill anybody."

Augustino's eyes moved to Jean Le Croupier, but Harry could see the question was only a momentary distraction.

Augustino said, "Don't listen to him. You know he's crazy."

Harry said, "What happened?"

"I guess I might have overdone it a little. I reminded them of all the things you've done for them, and how hard it is to keep track of everybody, and make sure they're happy and healthy."

Harry considered. "Sometime it might pay off. We'll just lower our profile again until we want to cash in on the gratitude."

Augustino looked pained. He said, "Things may have gotten a little out of hand."

Harry said, "Tell me." He felt two small spots of cold beginning to develop on both sides of his spine.

"They bought it. People started getting up and asking the crowd what they could do for you and Emma and Vickers and Lord Carnarvon and the Captain. But mostly you."

"That's nice of them," said Harry. "But it's a lousy idea. It's a business, and we've all gotten very rich. And of course, I can always steal more."

"Uh . . ." Augustino began. "It's not anymore."

"Not what?" asked Harry.

"A business. After they voted on the Haitians, they decided to give you a rest. We're going to have a regular government."

"They love us, so they're going to rob us of the island we built? It's insane." Harry was angry now. "What kind of government?"

"A democracy. They'll keep Lord Carnarvon as President, and vote for representatives to make policy."

"Democracy?" Harry realized he was shouting, and made an effort to hold down his voice. "They're not ready for democracy."

Augustino shrugged. "Half of them came from democracies."

"But those were democracies where other people ran the government. Come to think of it, I'm not ready for democracy. Nobody is."

"It's too late," said Augustino. "You should have heard them."

"But they were shouting my name."

"That's because they thought you were giving them a hint that it was time for them to take the weight off you and take care of themselves. It's like Churchill, after the war. They were so grateful they voted him out of office."

"But that's England, the most civilized country on earth. They even spell it without a Z because everybody is born knowing how to say it." He sat scowling at Augustino for a moment. "Tell me. How did our government decide to treat the Haitians?"

"Full citizenship. You're their guardian until they're settled."

13

THE ISLAND

"I have asked Lord Carnarvon to translate for those of you who only speak French," said Harry. He paused and looked around the large living room of his house. There were people sitting on the three long couches, and others sitting in the overstuffed chairs and on the arms of the chairs, and a row of people sitting on the bar with their feet not touching the ground. They all seemed to be listening.

"The most important rule for getting along on the island is this: No Weirdness." He said it slowly, and then waited while Lord Carnarvon translated. He studied the faces, and saw the same sequence of expressions cross the faces of several Haitians. First there was concentration, then confusion, then an effort to let the facial muscles relax so that nothing would be revealed. Others had so much presence of mind that they were able to shift to the enigmatic, empty, attentive look without effort.

Harry wondered if they had actually stopped listening. "What do I mean by 'No Weirdness'? This doesn't mean you can't practice your religion if you feel like it." He wondered if Lord Carnarvon would screw up the double negative and make it sound like a prohibition, so he added, "You can. On this island everyone tolerates everyone else."

He let Lord Carnarvon sort out his negatives and catch up. "What I mean is, we've made arrangements to buy you a couple of new fishing boats. If you catch a blowfish, throw it back." There were a few raised eyebrows, but Harry pressed on. "In every community, from time to time someone will die." He studied the faces again. "When it happens here, we are unhappy. We're so unhappy that we have several doctors try very hard to revive them. After that we perform an autopsy." Harry held up the palms of his hands. "It's very simple. No weirdness."

When the Haitians had left, Harry asked, "Do you think everybody understands?"

I'm not sure if I do," said Lord Carnarvon.

Harry said, "If we're in the immigrant business now, we're going to have to give people something for their effort. The first thing they get is immunity to whatever kept them in line in their hometowns."

Lord Carnarvon said, "It's usually just thugs." He remembered something with pleasure. "The first day one of them got a look at Vickers in his shades and asked if he was a Tonton Macoute. You could give him your 'No Weirdness' speech."

Harry muttered, "I like these people, and I want them to be happy. Do they seem happy to you? As happy as they should be?"

"What is it you're actually worried about?"

Harry shook his head. "With Americans I usually worry about them robbing each other. I'm comfortable with that."

"No problem. Nobody risks his life to save some woman's baby and then snatches her purse."

"See?" asked Harry. "That's exactly what I mean. These people are far too well behaved. It's almost as though somebody is controlling them without our seeing it."

Lord Carnarvon patted Harry's shoulder. "I guess you're right, Harry. One of them is a voodoo houngan who gave them all blowfish poison and turned them into zombies. I think it's one of the babies."

"A houngan wouldn't do that. A bocor might, and it would keep everybody scared shitless."

"Have we got either one?"

"They come from an isolated village on the Ile de la

Gonâve, the poorest, most primitive part of Haiti. There's never been anything there but them and some giant iguanas. I'll bet we've got at least one of everything."

"No iguanas so far," said Lord Carnarvon. "But I'll keep checking."

Harry and Lord Carnarvon walked across the golf course to the ocean, then moved up the rocky shoreline. Lord Carnarvon pointed to a spot sixty feet beyond the breakers, where the gentle swells rolled over a dark rock. "There. You can see it now."

"I see it," said Harry. "Is it just an outcropping or is it enough to anchor some land?"

"It's just the highest part of a little ridge. We can extend a hook, like a miniature Cape Cod, right over the top of it, close off the end, drain it, and we've got another freshwater lake."

"Looks good to me."

Lord Carnarvon shook his head. "There was a time when you'd have been looking for a phone to call for concrete by now."

"I'm sorry," said Harry. "A lot has happened in the last month or two, and I guess I'm a little distracted."

"Our new government? It had to happen sooner or later, or somebody would have used it as an excuse for gobbling us up."

"It's not that I object to democracy," said Harry. "It's that we're losing control."

Lord Carnarvon waited for Harry to walk on, then matched his steps to Harry's. "It's the Haitians, isn't it?"

"Look," said Harry. "I'm not a racist. The day they came, the Captain was taking my measurements for a white sheet. Most of the people here are black or brown, and I recruited them."

"We seem to be walking toward the Haitian village, or suburb, or whatever it is."

Harry's voice hardened. "It's not my segregation. They asked to be set up like that to start. And it worries me as much as anything else. How can you feel like one of the boys if you live in a separate neighborhood?"

"Why are we going there?"

Harry seemed to be reciting something he'd said to himself in advance. "You know what this was when we started. It was a variation on the 'open-city' idea. And I found the ideal place for it, like a state line, where fifteen kinds of police forces were all around us, but couldn't touch us for fear of the others. And there were fifty more around them that we managed to bribe or fool with the Carib-homeland thing."

"All that still works, Harry. Why are we going to see the Haitians?"

Harry said angrily, "Because everything is falling apart. We're not recruiting shills for the con anymore; we're taking in raggedy refugees. And a simple strategy discussion turned into a damned constitutional convention." He scowled. "We used to split the take from the suckers because that's the way the con works." He walked on, and muttered, "Now we're a bunch of socialists. And instead of scouring the Caribbean for booty, I'm worried to death that somebody's picking on these honest settlers."

They reached the point and climbed the stone steps up to the plateau of new land. As they climbed to the higher level, the sounds of hammers and saws were audible over the sea. Across the clearing a row of ten concrete foundations had been set into the ground. Bare white wooden frames had already been erected on four of the foundations, and farther down, men knelt on the grass nailing studs to the frame of the first wall of the fifth.

Harry and Lord Carnarvon moved to the end of the row of houses. They could see now that each house had a crew consisting of four or five Haitian men and women and six or seven people from other parts of the island.

"That's one thing about this place," said Harry. "By the time you leave here, you have a hell of an education in the construction trades."

"Somebody's leaving?"

Harry didn't answer. The two stood watching the men raise the wall frame on the foundation, then moved toward the houses that were closer to completion. "Right along here," Harry began, "we'll put a meandering path that's about a foot lower than the houses and ten feet wide, all the way to the ocean. If we get serious rain this year, the runoff won't take anything with it. I'm sick of losing topsoil."

They moved closer to the first foundation, and Harry stopped. He stared out to sea, and whispered, "Don't make it obvious, but take a look at the front entrance."

Lord Carnarvon held his hand above his eyes as though he were shielding them from the sun, and glanced beneath the empty doorframe. There was a small white china bowl sitting on the wooden floor where the door would soon go. "The bowl? It looks like oatmeal."

"It's an offering for the loas."

"Loas must have lousy teeth or ulcers. I assume they're something we're against?"

"They're gods. Voodoo. I wonder if that's the problem?"

Lord Carnarvon shrugged. "You told them we had freedom of religion. Nobody around here cares if they practice voodoo."

"And after they heard that, they told me they were Catholics. Something's up here. Why would they lie about it?"

There was a flapping sound, and a tall, thin young woman walked around the house wearing sandals and balancing a baby on her hip. She smiled shyly at them, then sat on the threshold. She picked up the bowl and set it on her lap. Then she transferred a spoon from the hand that held the baby, and cooed softly while she shoveled a spoonful into the baby's mouth, then expertly caught the dribble of mush from its lower lip with the spoon.

Lord Carnarvon took Harry's arm and pulled him toward the next house. "Chilling, isn't it?"

Harry shrugged. "Maybe I'm crazy. But if I'm not, then it is chilling. The only reason they'd hide it is if someone told them to. These people aren't liars. I know, because I am."

They walked past the last of the foundations and set off toward the old barracks where the Haitians had lived for the past two months. Harry went on. "If it were just a straightforward religious thing they'd have built the hounfort out in the open. They want to be out on the point so nobody hears them beating the rada on Saturday nights."

As they came around the corner of the building they could see Emma sitting on the lawn with two boys and a girl, each about six years old. They were drawing pictures on pads of paper with colored markers. Emma stood up and said, "I'll be right back. When you're finished, come show me." She walked up to Harry and gave him a little kiss on the cheek. "They're beautiful children, aren't they?"

"They sure picked up English fast," said Lord Carnarvon.

"They don't understand much yet," said Emma. "But if you talk as though they did, they will. Their Spanish is about as good. Kids just take everything in when they're young, and don't waste time worrying about how hard it is."

One of the little boys tossed his marker down on the grass where the others could reach it, and got to his feet. He trotted up to Emma and held out his pad. There was a circular geometric design, with swirls and flourishes inside it.

"Why, that's beautiful, Jacques. *Trés bon.* What a wonderful design. Like a flower."

Harry took the pad, knelt down beside Jacques, and said, "It's very good, Jacques. You do learn fast." He stood up and said to Lord Carnarvon, "Ask the kids if they'll show us around."

Emma whispered, "Harry, you're up to something."

"Humor me," he answered, then turned to the three children. *"Les bateaux?"*

The children set off toward the beach in the sheltered cove. They scampered ahead a few yards, then came back to urge the slower adults forward, then moved ahead again.

The two fishing boats had been hauled up on the beach and set on blocks. They looked ungainly and tall out of the water. Their hulls had already been scraped and sanded, so there was a mottled, derelict look to them. "I guess they knocked off for lunch," said Emma. "What's the attraction?"

Harry said, "The design on the pad isn't a flower." He led the children around to the ladder leaning against the hull of the boat, and climbed aboard. A few seconds later, he appeared at the stern and called, "Lord Carnarvon, can you come with Jacques, and make sure he doesn't fall off the ladder?"

Lord Carnarvon followed the little boy up to the deck of the fishing boat, but Harry had disappeared.

"In the cabin," came Harry's voice, and Jacques trotted to it.

When Lord Carnarvon entered the hot, cramped cabin, he could see that the glass in the front window had been replaced that morning. There was a border of fresh putty around the two panes. He could smell a faint odor of wet paint, so he stayed away from the walls and fixtures, but he couldn't see any surfaces that looked wet in the dim light.

Harry was looking up at the ceiling, and little Jacques was beside him.

Lord Carnarvon glanced up at the ceiling too, not bothering to fight the irresistible reflex. Above him was a painting, a picture of a woman in a blue dress, with a bright red heart on the chest, and beside her, a long green snake. The painting was shiny, and Lord Carnarvon realized it must be the source of the paint smell.

Harry pointed at the woman and asked, "Erzulie Freda?"

Little Jacques happily repeated, "Erzulie Freda."

Harry then pointed at the snake. "Damballa Wedo."

Jacques studied the snake and said, "Damballa Wedo." He seemed fascinated. "Damballa Wedo," he said, then hissed portentously, "Sssssst."

Harry walked around the cabin and out onto the deck, where he studied the winch that would soon pull the new net out of the sea. Then he said, "Come on. Let's get some lunch."

Emma and the two children were waiting below when Jacques joined them. Lord Carnarvon explained to them in French that they must be hungry. The three children ran ahead again, looking back now and then.

"What was that all about?" asked Lord Carnarvon.

"It was about voodoo," said Harry. He said to Emma, "Children have a certain honesty. First Jacques draws a vevey—"

Emma interrupted. "It was just a pretty design."

"Next time you see it, they'll have it chalked on a floor and sacrifice a chicken in the middle of it. And in the cabin of the boat somebody just did some very good portraits. Jacques tells me they're Erzulie Freda and Damballa Wedo."

"Did he say that?" Emma asked Lord Carnarvon.

"Sort of." Lord Carnarvon turned to Harry. "Actually, the first one to say that was you. A six-year-old isn't going to tell you you're wrong." He was silent for a few paces, then asked, "What are they, anyway?"

Emma said, "Erzulie Freda is the goddess of love. She's a bit of a flirt, and is sometimes fickle, and she likes a lot of attention. Damballa Wedo is the rain god, and he behaves like all rain gods. One minute he's bestowing blessings, and the next you wish he'd go drown himself."

"Why do you two know so much about voodoo?"

Emma's lips turned up in a mysterious smile. "In my first ten years with Harry, I learned a lot."

"You never said that before," said Harry.

"Harry does all the world's major religions," said Emma. "His voodoo was always one of my favorites."

"You used voodoo to rob people?" asked Lord Carnarvon. "You should feel great about this."

Harry shook his head. "In Chicago we were good enough to get some money out of rich white women who thought science was having your horoscope plotted instead of reading it in the papers."

Emma chuckled. "Harry had it worked out with two friends of ours. One of them had worked as a female impersonator in a bar, and he was good. He'd be the cheval. He'd go into a trance and get possessed by Erzulie Freda."

"What did the other one do?"

"Make sure the offerings miraculously vanished. Oh, he had hands . . ."

Harry was still frowning. "We made a lot of money out of Erzulie Freda. But that stuff won't work with these people. It's like selling a talking cow to a farmer. And if somebody is victimizing these people, it won't help to have me bully them some more. We've got to find the bocor and kick his butt off the island."

* * *

Harry stood in the living room and stared out at the sea. Captain Pettigrew sat in the chair to his right, his posture stiff and erect.

Harry said, "Nobody knows anything about it. I must have talked to seventy people."

"Doesn't that mean that whatever they're doing isn't bothering anyone?" asked the Captain.

"It worries me." Harry walked to the couch and sat down. "Why would they keep it a secret if there wasn't something to worry about?"

"You'll think of a reason."

Harry leaned forward. "All right. There's the shipwreck. Just tell me one thing. Is there any chance that it was intentional?"

"Some chance. We could send divers down to see if we can learn something from the wreck. But what does that have to do with voodoo?"

Harry stood up again and paced the room. "I'm not sure. I can't help wondering if things might not be different from the way they look."

"Tell me a story."

Harry stared at the floor, then said, "All right. There's a remote, poor village on an island off Haiti. For a couple of hundred years everything's stable because there's no way it can get any better. They practice voodoo, as most people do. But at some point this generation's houngan dies. Or maybe one day a new guy shows up, only he's not a houngan. He's a gangan, a bocor, and he kills the houngan."

"Light and darkness?" asked Captain Pettigrew. "Good and evil, old and new. Or is it white and black?"

Harry gave him a sharp look. "You wanted a story. The bocor has the whole village terrified, completely under his control. He's smart enough to know that there's not much profit in bullying people who have nothing, so he brings the whole lot of them here."

"Then he's Moses," said Captain Pettigrew. "He's done them a big favor."

"Not Moses," said Harry. "Now he's got fifty-some people with real prospects. How does he keep them obedient? The same way he always has. And what's the difference? Now he has to keep it all secret. He has to convince them they'll die if anyone finds out."

"I see," said Captain Pettigrew. "On the evidence, do you think your little story is true?"

"No. But everything else that occurs to me is just as scary."

Harry walked to the window again and looked out toward the sea. He could see the lights of the Panamanian ship anchored far out in the harbor, waiting for dawn to unload. As he started to turn, his gaze lowered and ran along the pier in front of the house. Harry stopped, his neck muscles stiffening. He said to Captain Pettigrew, "Don't stand up yet." He turned his head as though he were staring along the shoreline, but kept his eyes on the dock. "He's out there."

As Harry looked, he felt the cold, stiff feeling at the back of his scalp slowly move down his spine. There was a solitary black man standing out on the dock and looking up at Harry's window. He stood motionless with his arms down at his sides, and his legs slightly apart, as though he had been standing there in the darkness for hours, and could stand there as long as he needed to. Harry sensed the force of malevolent concentration that was focused on him.

"Who's out there?" asked Captain Pettigrew.

Harry moved away from the window before he answered. "It's somebody watching me."

"The bocor?"

"Who else? I can't explain it, but I feel something. He's just standing there like a statue, and I feel his eyes, his resentment."

The Captain said, "You're starting to believe in the power of voodoo?"

Harry walked to the desk on the far side of the room, and opened the bottom drawer. The Captain watched him reach in and take out a heavy automatic pistol, slide a clip into the handle, and turn around. "I believe in the power of logic."

"You're going out there?"

Suddenly there was a knock on the door. Harry handed

the gun to Captain Pettigrew and whispered, "He must not have seen you. Go into the bedroom and see what happens."

"Then what?"

"If it's what I think it is, don't wait too long. And don't worry. I'll clean up the mess."

Harry took a deep breath and let it out slowly, considering how his voice should sound. At least Emma was at the hotel with Esther. Whatever happened, she wasn't going to have to watch it. He planted his feet, and pulled the door open. On the doorstep was a tall, muscular young Haitian. "Étienne," said Harry.

Étienne's eyes flickered for an instant. "Yes," he said. He stood still in the dim light, his hands empty at his sides. Harry recognized the stance of the lone man on the dock.

"Come in," said Harry, and stepped aside, keeping his body half-shielded by the heavy wooden door. As Étienne walked into the lighted room, Harry looked at the place where his loose white shirt hung over his waistband. If there were a gun or a knife, it would probably be there. Then he remembered that a gangan capable of holding a village in bondage couldn't do it with a gun or a knife. "What can I do for you?"

Étienne said quietly, "There are five of us here. The others are out in the darkness, waiting."

Harry felt the cold on the back of his neck again. "Why?"

Étienne said, "We're angry."

"You speak better English than you let anyone know."

"People speak more freely if they think you don't understand. We came here knowing very little. I stayed quiet and learned you don't like us."

"It's not true," Harry began. Then he wondered. If he knew the rest of it, maybe he wouldn't like them. He formulated his position carefully. "I want to know more about you." He waited, then said, "You're here now because you're angry at me."

Étienne stared at him ominously. "Voodoo."

In the silence, Harry listened for Captain Pettigrew stirring in the next room. Would Étienne hear the sound of the pistol's safety catch being disengaged? "What about voodoo?"

"We trusted you with our children and you tried to teach them voodoo. Today you told my son that the Virgin Mary was Erzulie Freda."

"What?" said Harry.

Étienne's eyes were filled with contempt. "You're frightening our children with magic, and turning them away from God."

"No," said Harry. "Wait."

Étienne went on. "And you said the English word for a snake was Damballa Wedo." His fists were clenched, and his rage was building.

"I didn't," Harry protested. "I just—"

"You did," said Étienne. "You don't believe in voodoo yourself, but you use it to frighten poor children." He turned. "It won't work. I came to tell you that."

"I wasn't—"

Étienne was already at the door. "The others didn't want to come and talk to you. They want to leave the island now. But I wasn't afraid in Haiti, and I'm not afraid now." He stepped out onto the doorstep and bellowed, "No weirdness!" then slammed the door.

Harry sat down on the couch and stared at the wall across the room. In a moment he was aware of Captain Pettigrew, who had removed the ammunition clip from the pistol, and was gently replacing it in the desk drawer.

"I can explain it to them," said the Captain.

Harry sighed. "Maybe you can explain it to me." He walked to the window and tried to look out at the vast, dark sea, but instead he saw only his own reflection in the glass. There was a pitiful, small, solitary figure staring out at his own parchment-colored, sad face with a wrinkled brow and squinting, afflicted eyes. It was the face of a careless driver who had crashed his car into someone, and was only now beginning to search his fragmentary memories to find an excuse for it. As he watched, he saw the front door open and close behind his reflection, and Emma appeared beside Captain Pettigrew in the background. The two reflections talked quietly, but Harry didn't listen.

He watched the reflection, and heard his own mind formulating phrases and reformulating them. ''It happened too fast. I only saw little flashes of it.'' But as his mind moved back and forth over the parts he'd seen, trying to fit them together without seams that bumped and jarred him, he sensed that things were in motion again. There was no time to linger. He walked into the bedroom and pulled his suitcase out of the closet.

Emma walked in, sat down on the bed, and watched him pulling shirts out of the closet and scrutinizing them. ''Where are we going this time?''

''Europe, I guess,'' said Harry.

''Why?''

''I've got to get out of here, and it'll make me feel better about it if I can tell myself I'm doing something smart. We'll go look at a few investments.''

Emma stood up and walked to her closet. ''How long will we be gone?''

''I don't know.''

''Why are we really going? Because you're embarrassed?''

Harry shook his head. ''I need a vacation, Emma. I've spent all of my life using my imagination to work out ways to screw people out of what I needed. Now my control is shot. My imagination is turning around on me and eating me up.''

Emma gave a little smile. ''You always exaggerate.''

He looked at her, and an expression of understanding appeared on his face. ''That's true. I do. That's probably connected somehow.'' He went back to his packing. ''Tonight I realized that I've been driving myself and everybody else crazy imagining things about a bunch of poor harmless people. My only consolation is that I also tripped some warning signal in the collective psyche that said, 'We'd better make our own decisions.' So now I can go away.''

''Are you sure that's the right thing to do?''

''Yes,'' he said judiciously. ''I'm not sharp, and I can't resist the temptation to run things—a bad combo, you'll have to admit. I'm jumpy and suspicious. If I try to hang in here now, I'll end up like one of those crazy old dictators running around in a comic-opera uniform and sending spies out to make sure nobody's saying bad things about me."

"What about the Haitians? They're hardly settled."

"I figured out how to fix them up."

"How?"

"Stay out of their way."

NEW YORK

J. Dixon Bacon sat with his board of directors in a long row behind the table on the stage of the auditorium. As George Staunton, the executive vice-president of NewFed, formerly Federal National Bank, read the annual report of the bank's holding corporation verbatim from a blown-up copy of the company's brochure, Bacon stared out at the audience, looking for familiar faces. The ones he was looking for would have their eyes on him. They were the investors who handled the accounts of large insurance companies, major pensions, and mutual funds. They'd have read the report weeks ago, discounted the claims and projections that had no numbers attached to them, and they'd be waiting for him to speak.

Staunton was approaching the end of his recitation now. His words, measured and clipped and polished by his prep-school accent, sounded to Bacon like silver coins dropping into a bucket. Much of the audience would be satisfied at the end of it. Some of them, people from wealthy families who had held stock in the company for a half-century and retained the vanity of pretending to take personal responsibility for their investments, were already beginning to contemplate small, quiet lunches at their clubs that would stretch on long enough to make any activity in the afternoon inconvenient, and a drink respectable.

They already felt that what they'd heard was enough to constitute an annual stockholders' meeting, and they were beginning to study the adjacent aisles for like-minded acquaintances. But Bacon's eyes slipped over these people, searching for the others, the dull little men who had no personal wealth, but held fiduciary responsibility for a union pension fund or a brokerage, and had a billion dollars' worth of NewFed stock to drop on the market if they felt a tremor of anxiety.

He spotted a face in the back of the room that made his mind work rapidly, turning over the implications. It was Sam Fish, president of the Nat Packer's holding company. Bacon wrote a note to himself in the margin of his annual report to find out how many shares of NewFed Nat Packer owned. Packer wasn't the sort who bought bank stock. He was the sort who bought companies he could control. As Bacon finished his note, he heard applause, and was compelled to put down his pencil and add to it. Nothing should mar the tranquillity and monotony of this performance. If he seemed distracted or overly busy, one of the dull little men, the professional gamblers who handled the big blocks of stock, might get a hunch it was time to cash out. He stood up and shook George Staunton's sweaty palm, then stepped to the podium.

He leaned into the microphone and said, "Thank you, George. Now, if there are no questions, I'd like to—"

Four hands shot up in the audience, and Bacon judged he could ignore them. "—entertain a motion to accept the annual report from management."

"Wait!" came a call. There were cries from all over the room. "Question! Over here."

Bacon squinted. "Sorry. It's the lights. Couldn't see you out there." He turned his head toward the wings. "Could we turn these lights down a little, please?" The immediate dimming of the lights made him feel powerful and invulnerable again. "Now. Question?"

One of the dull little men was already standing. "I move that the report be rejected until a separate audit of investments in foreign countries is presented to the stockholders."

"Well, I don't know that that requires a full vote," said Bacon. "That information is already available. If you'll turn to page seventeen of the report, you'll see that we've got seventeen billion, eight hundred million loaned with an annual return of nine-point-six percent, and real-estate investments amounting to two billion, seven hundred million."

The dull little man said, "Has the bank received any actual interest payments on the loans during this fiscal year?"

Bacon turned to George Staunton, who said, "Yes," and sat down.

"How much?"

Staunton stood up again, and pretended to consult some notes. "Approximately thirty million dollars."

As the audience computed the percentage, a murmur of dismay moved through the aisles.

"I'd like to explain that figure," said Bacon. "We all know that many Third World countries have experienced a recession brought on by a decrease in oil prices, et cetera. They have been unable to make cash payments, but the interest continues to accrue. We are not going to have any bad debts, and have, in fact, accepted some valuable real assets in some cases, in lieu of cash."

"Such as?"

"Oh, cattle land in Venezuela, oil leases in Brazil, and so on. We'd be happy to provide a list, if you'll leave your name with one of the people at the registration desk. Now. May we vote?"

As the voice votes were taken, Bacon said, "The 'Ayes' have it. Thank you," and he was on his way off the stage, and then out the door in the wings.

Bacon walked across the cavernous lobby of the hotel, his jaw set in a brittle grimace that people too timid to venture a close approach might have accepted as a smile. But Crossley, the factotum who carried Bacon's briefcase and opened doors for him, was the sort of man who ran in Central Park every morning to keep himself looking young, in case an opportunity should arise that his superiors felt required energy. He recognized the look. Bacon's was the face of a man in the last few yards of a five-thousand-meter race, his teeth displayed only because he was blowing hot air out through his teeth, like a steam engine.

As they reached the street where his car was waiting at the curb, Bacon said, without turning his head, "Have McManus in my office when I get there."

The factotum panicked. "McManus, sir?"

Bacon's eyes shot to his face and burned into it for a moment, but Pullman, the second vice-president, answered. "I've already called him, and he's on his way." They both got into the car, and Pullman slammed the door.

The driver pulled the car away from the curb and into traffic, leaving the factotum standing in front of the hotel. He stared at the car as it moved down the street. The doorman said to him, "Can I get you a cab, sir?" He turned and looked past the doorman at the groups of stockholders beginning to stream out of the entrance. "Yes, and please make it fast."

The doorman thought the factotum was trying to impress him with the tightness of his schedule, but he wasn't. He was measuring the dwindling seconds before Bacon realized that he didn't have his briefcase. Whoever McManus was, the factotum prayed that he be someone Bacon didn't want to impress with the figures in the briefcase. . . . "Please, God, let it be some pal of his from the club."

Bacon walked into his office and closed the door. McManus was already standing by the window, looking out at the park. Bacon noticed that McManus had bought another new suit, and that this didn't look any better than the others. There was something about the man that made him look as though none of his clothes belonged to him. Somehow his thick pink neck, abraded by the barber's razor and jutting from his shirt collar, made him look like he'd borrowed the clothes from a smaller man.

"Well?" said Bacon. "Fill me in."

"I've found enough people to do it," said McManus. "We have the ship and the equipment."

"I know that," said Bacon. "I'm paying for all of it. Every cent, every day. When do I see results?"

"This isn't going to be a walk in the park," said McManus. "The men will need a little more training, and we've got to get the logistics right before we send them out there."

Bacon stifled his urge to shout. "I know it's not easy. Nobody knows better than I do. You got the men you wanted, every one of them handpicked, you said. Now they need more training."

"It's that old problem again," said McManus. "If only you'd come to me the first time, I could have handled this years ago. But that fellow you hired—Herrera—well, he just didn't know how to do this kind of thing. He wasn't much more than a drug smuggler."

"We've been through all that."

"But it doesn't make it go away. You taught these people something about reality, and now they're dangerous, and they're dug in. I know Vickers, and he's got a long memory, and he's smart enough to know that right now, when he's shitting in tall cotton, is when he's most likely to attract this kind of attention."

"Look, McManus. I just came out of a stockholders' meeting where people were on the edge of shaking out my pockets. They're mad, and they're scared. I've got to have something to show them next quarter, or this bank is going belly-up like a dead whale. I haven't got time."

McManus walked to the window again. "I've got people there watching. When the time comes, I'll move."

"When?" asked Bacon. "I've got to have something I can turn into cash."

"They'll drop their guard, even if it's only for a day."

"What's going to change? What's ever going to be different from the way it is now?"

McManus shrugged. "A falling-out among the leaders, a chance to turn one faction against the others, something I can use to get things started."

"I've been taking all these expenses—millions of dollars—from a discretionary account. It's for investments that have to be kept secret for a few weeks. This has gone on for years. Dozens of people know I'm onto something that's going to be profitable. It's got to come through, or I'm ruined, and so are a lot of other people."

"What can I do to cover that?" asked McManus. "I'm no accountant."

"You can get me Harry Erskine with a rope around his neck and a pen in his hand. And then you can get me that island."

14

WASHINGTON

100A UNI 463 JFK
1000P Heathrow

The Assistant Secretary stared at the dark, smudged photocopy of an airline ticket clipped to the file folder and frowned. He lifted the sheet and glanced under it to be sure this new item hadn't been misfiled. It looked like one of his own travel vouchers. Then he saw the names: "H. Erskine. E. Erskine."

He looked at the date again, then dug down to the page beneath and read it carefully. Beneath that was a second copy of a report from the British Foreign Office.

He didn't bother to ask his secretary to place the call for him. He dialed it himself, then thought about the date. That was over two months ago. When the Senator took his call, he said, "Harry and Emma have left the island."

"I know," said the Senator.

The Assistant Secretary felt a sudden tension in his diaphragm. His breaths came in shallow little puffs that seemed inadequate for speech. At first he had trouble isolating the stimulus that had caused the feeling, but then he recognized it. The old man had other sources of information. His own importance was at stake. Maybe he was only a confirming source, a redundancy. The Assistant Secretary heard himself demand, "Well, what are they doing?" and was disappointed in himself. He should have had the patience to find out through channels. It could only have taken a week or two, but he was letting things fall apart. He'd thrived as a supplier, and suddenly he was a consumer.

"Don't know yet," said the Senator. The voice was untroubled, but the Assistant Secretary's imagination tumbled into the space where the pronoun should have been: *I* don't know? . . . *We?* . . . *They?*

The Assistant Secretary reasserted his self-discipline. "I'll try to find out, Senator."

The Senator's voice was enigmatic. "Thanks." Then he added, "They're in Paris now."

PARIS

Harry lay on his back on the balcony of the hotel. At first he seemed to be asleep, but then Emma saw his lips move as he muttered something. She walked up to him.

"You're lying on cement, Harry."

"I'm getting the famous Paris sun. Why don't you go shopping?"

"The sun is brighter on the island, and you don't have to lie on cement. There are probably people in those windows across the way who think you're dead."

Harry slowly and laboriously rolled over and did a push-up, then got to his hands and knees. "I am a little stiff."

"When are we going home, Harry?"

"You've done this as long as I have. You know the inside man decides."

"You're the inside man, Harry. When?"

"When I'm sharp again. It only works as long as nobody gets tense and starts to blow it."

"You don't get sharp by lying on cement."

"No."

"I suppose I'd better make use of this time while you're moping and punishing yourself."

"That sounds like a good idea."

"So you admit it."

"No."

* * *

Emma sat across the table from Harry, and it seemed to him that a vast expanse of white linen and a clutter of gleaming silver and glass separated them. She lifted her crystal tulip goblet and sipped the champagne, then set it down somewhere behind the candelabrum. The three candle flames never wavered, and it was impossible to look through them at her face without squinting.

When she spoke, her voice sounded surprisingly near. "This is the best food we've had since we came to Paris.

"The article said it would be," said Harry.

"What are you going to do about it?"

Harry looked among the vertical obstacles on the table and picked out his glass. "I'm satisfied with the investment. We did the right thing."

"You've got to get over this. It's getting annoying." Emma lifted her left hand six inches off the table, and one of the waiters glided to her side. "I'll speak with the chef."

"Madame?" said the waiter. "Surely everything was—"

"You know it was. I want to see the chef."

The waiter bowed and hurried off to the dark corridor that led to the distant place where the business of cooking proceeded in noiseless isolation. Harry studied his glass in silence.

Emma whispered, "You're sitting there thinking it's unseemly. Well, to pay up and leave would be inhuman."

"I don't want to make things harder," said Harry.

The tall, thin waiter returned like a gendarme, escorting a young black woman in a gleaming white tunic. As they emerged from the corridor, the woman ran her hand through her hair to confirm her belief that the chef's toque had tangled it, and then shook her head. When she looked into the dining room, she gasped and rushed forward. "Harry and Emma." Her mouth shaped the words, and her next step would have been a run, but she caught herself and only skipped once, then crossed the floor at a fast walk. When she reached the table she said aloud, "Harry and Emma," and she kissed Emma's cheek, then Harry's. "This is wonderful. Just wonderful."

"Please sit down, Althea," said Emma. "Just for a few minutes."

Harry said, "We missed you."

"Not as much as I missed you," said Althea. Her shoulders squeezed up tight to her neck. "This is the best surprise I've ever had."

Harry said, "Join us, then."

Althea Simms glanced around the room. "I'm not the master chef here, you know. I'm still sort of an apprentice."

"I remember you in that shack on the point the day the paratroopers came. You weren't afraid of anything then," said Harry. "You'd have taken on six or seven master chefs and thrown in a restaurant critic or two for practice."

Althea sat down. "You're right," she said. "And it's not every day, is it?"

"Besides," Emma said, "you're getting to be a celebrity. We've been reading about you."

Althea stared at the table. "Paris is really a very small town. I mean the part that cares about three-star restaurants."

"We read it in an American magazine. One of the twelve most-promising chefs of your generation."

"Oh, that," said Althea. Then she smiled again. "It's really you two who should be in a magazine. Only I guess you are, a lot, aren't you? When I was at the hotel school at Cornell, ours was just about the only country that was still paying to send people away to colleges."

"The Arabs are still doing it. That's where we got the idea." Emma paused. "Anyway, we wanted to tell you how proud we are that you've done so well."

"I'm ready to leave now," said Althea. "I can't wait."

"That's right," said Harry. "If you're ready to set up your own restaurant, here or anywhere else, the island will always be ready to make up any extra money not covered by your annual dividends. It's not a loan."

Althea Simms looked alarmed, and tears began to form in her eyes. "I thought you were here to say I was ready to go home."

"You want to go back to the island?" Harry asked.

"That was the whole idea, Harry. Not just for me, for everybody who was sent away. We don't want to stay in places like this. We have our own country."

* * *

The hotel room was awash in a terrible white light from the lamps on tall stands that had been placed along the ancient Chinese screen, and the Persian rugs were covered with cables that had been taped to them. The television camera was on a cart that was wedged between two heavy leather chairs to keep it from moving.

The man's ears stuck out from his head impossibly, as though he were a specimen pressed between two glass slides. He held a microphone that wasn't connected to anything, but served as his scepter of authority. He leaned forward in his chair and shouted in a thick cockney accent.

"This is Nolan Stankey, in a rare—" Then he slumped. "I'm sorry. Let's try again." He took a deep breath. "This is celebrity interviewer Nolan Stankey, and I'm in a sumptuous hotel suite somewhere in Paris, for a quiet discussion with Mr. and Mrs. Harrison J. Erskine. That's right. You know them as Harry and Emma, perhaps the most elusive couple in the world of high finance."

He smiled for a full three seconds, then turned to Emma. "That's the teaser, leading into the commercial. In the countries where they have commercials. In the others we'll edit it so we go right into the first question."

"We're not elusive," said Harry. "We just don't leave the island much."

Stankey said, "Let's begin," and nodded to the man behind the camera. He intoned, "Last year three different publications called you the richest couple in the Caribbean. You have untold millions invested all over the world. Do you have any idea of the size of your fortune?"

"Let's keep it untold," said Harry.

"It is true that your corporation is a silent partner in both Tiffany and Cartier?"

"No, it's not," said Emma.

Nolan Stankey clenched his jaw muscles, and said to a man with a clipboard, "Tell Dave I appreciate his research." He turned to Emma. "We'll take a different tack. You are perhaps the richest couple in the Caribbean, and yet I'm told you live simply, without many of the accoutrements of great wealth. No furs or Rolls-Royces."

Emma looked puzzled. "You don't wear a fur coat on a tropical island. You'd die."

"There's only one road, and it's two hundred yards long," Harry said.

Nolan Stankey looked desperate. He aimed his useless microphone at Harry. "What are you doing in Europe?"

"We're here to check some investments, see some people."

Stankey's face assumed a look of triumph. "You were in Paris yesterday, and so was Sheik Yamani. So you were talking about oil. You've formed a cartel with the desert princes."

"We were talking to a girl we know named Althea Simms," said Harry. "About dessert. Anyway, Yamani isn't the Saudi oil minister anymore. I'd have thought you, of all people—"

"Let's talk about the island," said Stankey. He turned to the camera. "The island. Tax haven for the very rich, gambling den for the high rollers. And for those who have it all, a place to get away from it all. A place that didn't exist twenty years ago, a new paradise wrested from the sea and parlayed into a billion-dollar money machine."

"And the second home for the last of the Carib Indians," said Harry. "Don't forget that."

Stankey went on. "The home dugout for the Caribs, winter baseball's all-star team, bringing in millions a year in television royalties and endorsements for this couple." He pointed his microphone at them like a baton, and intoned, "But also the home hideout for some very strange bedfellows, according to reports I've seen."

"Strange bedfellows?" Emma said.

Nolan Stankey glanced at a piece of paper. "Undercover agents from all over the world have flocked to the island to follow people they keep an eye on."

"If they pay their own way, we don't discriminate," said Harry.

"Indeed you don't," said Nolan Stankey. "I only need to mention a Mr. Altmeyer who was spotted several times on the island. Just one name out of dozens of names of people who—"

"What do you mean, 'spotted'?" asked Emma. "He

owns a house there. His wife, Rachel, is a friend of mine. They're not hiding."

"Surely you know where their wealth comes from."

"He's an importer," said Harry. "Or he was. He's retired."

Nolan Stankey turned to the camera again. "The mysterious Mr. Altmeyer, gunrunner to the elite, merchant of death."

"Gunrunner to the elite?" Emma laughed.

"And there are others," Stankey continued. "People who might have come out of a Hollywood movie, sharing caviar and champagne with the superstars who play them on the screen. Socialites from the jet set, hobnobbing with—"

"Gamblers from the bet set?" asked Emma.

"And fishermen from the net set," said Harry. "Or are they the wet set?"

Emma shrugged. "Depends. Dogs are from the pet set, but they could be from the vet set."

Nolan Stankey's ears reddened at the tops. "The well-to-do mingling on the silver sands, where this couple, known to their friends as Harry and Emma, hold court. But it wasn't always that way, I'm told." He pointed his microphone at them. "It was rags to riches. What made you leave the United States for the good life in the sun?"

Emma smiled. "There were some people who wanted to talk to Harry."

"Oh?" said Nolan Stankey. "So a simple business call from an acquaintance in the tropics lured you to your destiny."

"No," said Emma. "The ones who wanted Harry were in the United States. We stole their money."

Stankey lowered his microphone. "I can't put that on television. I can't put any of it on television."

Emma patted his arm. "I'm sorry. But we didn't know you were going to make it all up."

"Of course I am," said Stankey. "People want to know about you, and they want you to seem glamorous. They want to hear about money and jewels and gold falling from the sky."

"It didn't fall from the sky," said Harry. "We stole

enough to get started, and then charged ridiculous prices for ten years and figured out ways to avoid paying for things."

"I can't do anything with that," said Stankey. "They want to think it just comes. They don't want to have to steal it."

"We could try again," said Emma. "I'll make Harry behave."

"I've got a better idea," Harry said. "You've already got some film of us in fancy places. And you can show this interview without the sound. Just record whatever you like over it."

"Sure," Emma said. "Tell them something that sounds exciting. We don't mind. Send us a tape of it here at the hotel."

"That's all you want?" said Stankey.

"Oh yes. Say something about winter baseball. We're broadcasting some games this year, and a plug would be nice."

"A deal," said Stankey.

Harry pursed his lips, then added, "It might also be smart to stay away from that stuff about surprising people who come to the island. One of them owns the syndicate that distributes your program in the United States."

"Really?" asked Stankey.

"Other than that, just have a good time. Make up whatever you want about us. It'll make a nice surprise."

There were shots of the island from the air, and then a panoramic view of the south beach, with its broad strips of pink sand from Mexico and black sand from Hawaii and white sand from Chile and green sand from an island Harry couldn't remember near New Guinea. Then there was a sequence showing Emma's baseball players in action, with subtitles listing their famous names and their major-league teams. There was a moment from the last golf tournament, in case anyone had missed Marty Palestrina's hole-in-one when it had been televised six months ago. As the camera moved to follow the ball in the air, it swept across the distant ocean and the white yachts resting in the harbor. Then the scene changed to the hotel garden, the casino, and a montage of various houses, including Lord Carnarvon's, which the narrator called "The Presidential Palace."

The narrator said, "And who are the geniuses behind this paradise for celebrity millionaires?" and Harry and Emma appeared on the screen, walking on the Champs Élysées.

"I look like the Bulgarian Minister of Agriculture," said Harry. "Is that the way I look?"

"It's special effects," said Emma. "You really look like the mayor of a small town in Oklahoma."

Nolan Stankey's face replaced theirs. "If you guessed Harry and Emma, you're absolutely right. They're rumored to be the richest couple in the western hemisphere, and live like the Emperor Montezuma and his queen in a compound surrounded by guards and devoted servants."

"Servants?" said Harry.

"This is fun," Emma laughed. "We told him to do what he wanted."

Stankey continued. "Harry has been asked by no fewer than six foreign governments to take over their finances. But why not? Corporations compete for executives, but only countries have enough complexity or enough money to interest a man like Harry Erskine. His gorgeous wife, Emma, has turned down numerous movie roles to remain on the island with her husband. We were told by a film-industry source that Emma Erskine is the most-sought-after woman in the world, but no studio could possibly meet her demands. And what are they? To accommodate her entourage of twenty-six personal assistants, each of whom flies back and forth to the island to arrange her social engagements. She also has her own wardrobe staff, who travel the world to find just the right gown for every occasion."

"Just the right sweatshirt for every occasion," said Emma. "And matching sneakers."

"I caught up with them at Cannes," said Stankey, "where they'd arrived three weeks early for the film festival. They were being given private screenings of the major entries, and as usual, Emma was being wooed by the world's producers."

There was a clip from the interview. Emma was shaking her head and saying "No." Beside her, Harry was looking appalled.

"I look like the papal envoy to Port Said," said Harry. "I can't understand it."

The telephone beside the bed rang, and Harry stood up and walked away. "Where are you going?" asked Emma.

"I'll answer it in the bathroom. I just hope this thing hasn't been on the air yet. It could be somebody calling to ask me if I'm sick."

Emma heard Harry answer and then walk back to kick the door shut. She heard him say "Lord Carnarvon" before his voice subsided into mumbles. She looked at the television set. Stankey was in a room similar to theirs. He stared past the camera as though she and Harry were in the room with him, and said, "I've been told that when you're on the island you often wear jewelry worth over five million dollars." Emma heard herself answer, "You don't wear a fur coat on a tropical island."

Harry sat on the edge of the bathtub. "We're watching ourselves on television. Wait'll you see it. We look like the last of the Hapsburgs."

"I hope I'm around to catch it when it's on."

"What's up?"

"It's trouble, Harry. We just found a secret cache of guns on the island. Machine guns, mortars, everything."

"Are you sure Vickers isn't stocking up? You know he's psychotic."

"I'm positive. They were all smuggled in with a load of topsoil for the land around the Haitian village."

"You found it on the ship?"

"No, Harry. It's a long story. A couple of weeks after you left, we started finding signs of voodoo again. Some mornings there were those curvy designs and blood like somebody cut up a chicken. The first time was in the visiting-baseball-team dugout, so we thought, Oh, what the hell. They're just rooting for the team, and it's probably a good sign. But it's been getting weirder every day, and this gun thing is scary." He waited, but Harry said nothing. "Harry . . ."

"Let me think for a minute." There was another pause, and Harry's voice came back. "Where's Vickers?"

"He's visiting his old pal the Colombian politician. He got an invitation yesterday."

"Did he actually talk to the Colonel?".

"I guess so . . . No. I think it was a telex. Who cares?"

Harry's voice suddenly carried an urgency. "Listen, L.C., because there probably isn't much time. Emma and I will head for home and try to work something out on the way, but don't hold your breath."

"What are you saying?"

"It's the Haitians, and that voodoo stuff. One of the few things I'm sure about is the Haitians. They aren't doing voodoo. I don't have time to explain, so ask Captain Pettigrew."

"He's not here either. He's on a run to Panama."

"Then I've really got to go. But trust me about the Haitians. And dig up anybody you saw shoot a gun in the last invasion, because I think you're about to have another one."

"What the hell am I supposed to do about it?"

"Whatever occurs to you. I've got to go roust Emma. If they suckered Vickers and Pettigrew, they're probably about to put us in a bag."

"What are you going to do?"

"You know me. Save my ass first, and think about yours later." He hung up the telephone, and moved quickly to the bathroom door.

When he swung the door open, the first sight was the tall, dark, bearded man standing in front of him pointing the little machine pistol at his chest. He almost lost control and pushed him out of the way, but contained himself and only craned his neck to look over the man's shoulder at Emma. She sat as she had when he'd last seen her, in front of the television set. But now she shrugged her shoulders, and he could see the muzzle of the other man's gun was pressed against the back of her neck. She smiled a forlorn little smile. "Do you suppose all the publicity was a mistake?"

BOGOTÁ

Vickers carried his suitcase across the lobby of the Bogotá airport. Out of the corner of his eye, he thought he saw the little man to his right nod at someone, but when he looked at him, the little man was walking quickly across the floor waving and smiling at someone in a crowd of arriving passengers. He could hardly have been more conspicuous.

Then two men in gray Italian suits materialized in his path. They seemed always to have been there, and their sudden visibility was not because they arrived, but because other people left. He started to step around them, but that made him see that the closest man had a wire coming up out of his collar to a little pink earphone above his left ear. As soon as he saw it, he heard a faint crackle of static that must have been deafening to the man.

The man winced. "Mr. Vickers?" He put his hand to his ear, but didn't remove the device. Now he pawed at it like a tortured beast.

"That's right," said Vickers. Of course they were secret-service, and he decided he'd make a point of telling the Colonel to spend a few bucks to get them decent radios. This guy was probably having the control tower's landing instructions hammered into his brain.

The second man, who had enough rank to be free of a radio, flashed a plastic identification card. It looked like a laminated old British pound note with his face plastered over the Queen's. "We've been asked to take you to the President. Your passport, please."

Vickers handed him the passport. "I've already been through customs."

The man examined the passport, then said, "Very good. Come with us, please." He kept the passport in his hand, and led Vickers to the glass doors, then held the right one open to let Vickers out to the drive, where a plain black Mercedes waited at the curb.

The first man took his suitcase and put it in the trunk, and then ushered Vickers around to the back door. Then he grimaced as a shrill whistle came from the earphone. "I'm sorry to ask, Mr. Vickers, but you understand. Any weapons?"

"No," said Vickers. "I just got off a plane."

The second man moved up with a portable metal detector and held it six inches from Vickers' body, then moved it slowly up to his shoulder, then down to his shoes. "Thank you, sir."

"Quite all right," he said. "The first time I met the man, I not only got frisked but I had to wear handcuffs."

The two didn't smile. The first man opened the door for him, and the second got into the front seat beside the driver. Vickers settled in the back seat and watched the man beside him pop the earphone out of his ear as the car cruised into the traffic.

After a few minutes Vickers sensed that there were fewer cars around them. The car speeded up. "Are we going out to the country?"

"Yes," the man beside him said. "I'm afraid you'll have to wear this blindfold from here on."

"That's not necessary," said Vickers. "I'll feel like an idiot."

Then the little pistol appeared over the top of the front seat. "That's not entirely inappropriate."

PANAMA

"Do you know what it costs to bring a ship this size from the Caribbean, through the canal, and up the coast this far?" Captain Pettigrew scowled.

"No," said Señor Cabazón. "I'm sure it must be considerable." He tugged at his immaculate white cuffs one at a time so that his small onyx cufflinks would show. "But I never sent these letters, and I don't have any"—he examined the top sheet—"concrete blocks with steel reinforcements." He shook his head. "Not one. If I did, I'm sure I'd be happy to have you rid me of them."

Joaquín studied Señor Cabazón. "It's a great pity," he said in Spanish. "As you can see, we were asked to bring our own labor to move the blocks. We've spent a great deal of money to give seventy-five men an unpleasant cruise to your malaria-ridden country.

Señor Cabazón's eyes narrowed. "Perhaps they can find something for you in Nicaragua or El Salvador."

"Let's go," said Captain Pettigrew. He took Joaquin's arm and guided him from the office. They walked in silence down the worn tile staircase, past an old woman who sat on a wooden bench in the lobby, knitting a narrow red strip that was too long to be any article of human clothing.

The sunshine in the plaza seemed to revive Joaquín. "It's what Vickers said would happen. People know we're small and rich. Now they stand in line to rob us."

"I don't understand it," said Captain Pettigrew. "He didn't say he needed a bribe, or he had unexpected expenses, or there was a new tax on exporting rubbish from the country. He didn't have a cargo."

Joaquín shrugged. "So we don't get the extra few acres of land this trip. If Rubio keeps hitting foul balls into the sea, we'll have a beach made of baseballs by spring."

"I didn't come to the damned Pacific Ocean to go home with an empty ship. I'm going to make a few calls."

"What the island has always needed is an active volcano," said Joaquín. "It could add a couple of shiploads of rock a week for free. Call Hawaii."

Captain Pettigrew ignored him. "They're tearing down a block of hotels in Acapulco to build new ones. Maybe they'll let us pick up something from the wreckage."

"How far are you willing to go just to salvage this trip?" asked Joaquín.

"Not as far as Hong Kong."

THE ISLAND

Lord Carnarvon stared at the telephone, then walked through the empty house. As he passed the first doorway, he stopped. Little Lord Carnarvon's baseball glove hung from the bedpost, and on the rack on the wall were two bats and a canoe paddle. He glanced at his watch. Maybe they could evacuate some of the children. It would take a few hours, and then what? Would they be safe in a hotel in Miami?

He heard Esther come in the front door, talking to someone. There was a crackle of paper bags. Lord Carnarvon took a deep breath and then went to meet her. "Esther?"

"I'm back," she called. "And I brought an old man to carry my bags."

Lord Carnarvon walked into the living room and saw

Nathaniel Boats moving into the kitchen with two grocery bags in his arms. When the American supermarket opened on the island Lord Carnarvon had laughed at it. It had been a part of the veneer for the tourists. But then the islanders had gotten used to the shopping carts and the cash registers and the broad, air-conditioned aisles. His father-in-law, Nathaniel, had been one of the most outspoken advocates of the store. ''You want to live in a hut and swat flies off your plate, go ahead. I've done it. The rest of the world has a supermarket.''

They came out of the kitchen together, and Lord Carnarvon thought how different they were. The leathery, wrinkled man seemed at least a generation too old to be Esther's father. ''You look awful,'' Esther said.

''I think we've got trouble. No, I'm sure we do.''

''Tell me,'' said Nathaniel Boats.

''This morning we found a bunch of heavy weapons that were being buried near the Haitians' houses. There were a lot of voodoo symbols around. I called Harry and he says they don't believe in voodoo, and that they're not hiding guns. What I see doesn't make sense, and having Harry tell me I don't see it doesn't make sense either.''

Nathaniel looked out the window at the ocean. ''They're Roman Catholic,'' he said.

Lord Carnarvon sighed. ''I mean nobody cares what they are. I care if they're planning some violent revolution or something. Harry thinks it's not them at all.''

''Harry's a smart man,'' said Esther.

''I know. And so is Vickers, and so is Captain Pettigrew. None of them is here. Half the island is off somewhere or other. I'm up to my armpits in tourists, and now somebody is getting ready to murder us in our sleep.''

''We'd better get started,'' said Nathaniel.

''That's right,'' Lord Carnarvon agreed. ''Started doing what?''

''You're the President.''

Lord Carnarvon shook his head. ''Isn't that amazing?'' He took a deep breath and said, ''But we're it this time. We're all there is.''

''What do we do?'' asked Esther.

''Talk to everybody you know you can trust, but nobody

else. Tell them I think Vickers and Harry and Emma and Captain Pettigrew have been lured away, and we're about to be invaded. Don't use the telephone or write anything down. Make sure they understand that."

Lord Carnarvon walked toward the door.

"Where are you going?" asked Nathaniel Boats.

"If this is what Harry says it is, then all I can do is the opposite of what I'm supposed to do."

Lord Carnarvon walked to the front door of Étienne's house and knocked. There was no answer, so he made his way around the house to the patio. Étienne's baby girl was pushing herself to her feet using a yellow plastic sand pail as a prop, but then it slid a few inches and she sat down abruptly. Her eyes widened with her indrawn breath, and she prepared to scream. Lord Carnarvon lifted her up and swung her to his shoulder just in time to confuse her. The scream turned into a puzzled little moan.

Étienne and Maribel were on their hands and knees scrubbing the patio when Lord Carnarvon approached. Étienne stood up to turn on the hose and saw Lord Carnarvon holding his baby. "Look at this," he said angrily. He pointed to a large circular whitewashed design on the pavement, then sprayed it with the hose, but that only rinsed the soap off. The design seemed to clarify and sharpen as he washed it.

"A vevey?" asked Lord Carnarvon.

"It's somebody's way of telling me to get off the island. There must have been twenty of these all over the place in the past three weeks. You're saying you haven't seen them?"

"I have," said Lord Carnarvon. He set the baby down beside her sand pail. "It's one of the things I wanted to ask you about."

"It's the white people," said Étienne. "First it was Harry himself, and now he's gone away so the others can do it. They hate us."

"Harry doesn't hate you," said Lord Carnarvon. "I just talked to him on the telephone in France, and he wanted me to see if I could get your help. He said you were just about the only one we could trust with this problem."

"Harry said that?"

"That's right," said Lord Carnarvon. He took a chance. "He said you'd proven yourself." Lord Carnarvon watched Étienne's face as he thought about that. It almost broke his heart to see the man's mind move from suspicion to a kind of noble hope that this time it would be different. Lord Carnarvon formed an image, and it was a politician lying to a poor man to get him to risk his life.

"What do you want me to do?" asked Étienne.

"I think that everyone on the island may be in danger," said Lord Carnarvon. "And the only way we can survive is by being better than we were yesterday."

"People here have been very kind to us. That's why I don't understand all this." Étienne pointed at the ornate design on his patio.

"I don't understand it either," said Lord Carnarvon. "It may be that someone wants us to distrust each other, and maybe actually fight. I'd like to fool them."

Étienne's expression changed. "I suppose then that you want to keep us apart. Just lock us up for the moment until things calm down. Is that it?"

"No," said Lord Carnarvon. "I want to give you all the weapons I can find and hope we can save each other."

"Weapons?"

"There's a big pile of guns in the food storehouse down the beach. They were hidden in a load of dirt. I'm not sure if they're here because somebody wanted me to think you were hiding them or they wanted to use them themselves."

"We're not soldiers," said Étienne. "John Vickers tried to teach us, but—"

"I'll tell you what to do," said Lord Carnarvon. Where the hell was Vickers? "Whatever these people are doing, I believe this is where they'll come first to do it. If it starts before I can get everyone else ready, you'll have to buy us time."

15

THE ISLAND

Lord Carnarvon walked along the edge of the dark golf course, inside the line of tall trees. He felt breathless and supernaturally alert. He wanted to run, but maybe the bushes were full of waiting enemies. He regretted being alone. He could die here in the darkness, drop into a black pocket, and it would be hours before anyone suspected it.

"Lord Carnarvon." It wasn't even a whisper. It could have been his own thought. "We're right here."

Lord Carnarvon stopped. "Who?" he asked.

Five men came out of the bushes, and he discerned from their short stocky silhouettes that they were Caribs. Any of them could be me, he thought. We're such near relatives we're all like each other's ghosts. "What did you find?" He spoke aloud, and then realized he'd done it to dispel the sense of terror he felt at the strangeness.

"Dynamite," said Sullivan Boats. "There were bombs in the ammo under the two sidewalk cafés."

"And on the roof of the hotel." It was so much like Lord Carnarvon's own voice that he knew it was one of his cousins.

"Time bombs?"

"No such luck. They had little radio antennas, so somebody could push a button somewhere else whenever he felt like it."

Lord Carnarvon shook his head. "I guess Harry wasn't

imagining it. I wonder if we've got anybody who can disarm a bomb. I'll bet Esteban Ruiz—"

"Hell with that," said Sullivan Boats. "We just moved them."

"Moved them?" Lord Carnarvon's voice rose.

"Sure. We buried them on the beach for now. I'm not going to sit around saying, 'What happens if I pull the blue wire?' You think I'm nuts?"

"Wait a minute," said Lord Carnarvon. "I think I figured something out."

"Good for you," said Sullivan Boats.

"It's Vickers' firepoint system. They figure if we're in trouble we'll put people in all the same spots as we did years ago, and they'll just blow them up.

"What can we do about it?"

"Keep moving bombs."

As Lord Carnarvon ran through the woods, he felt his own voice chanting in his throat, "What else? What else? Everything else." First it all seemed impossible, but then it occurred to him that already he was ahead. When the sun came up there would be a hundred little changes all over the island. People who were usually asleep would be awake and armed. Bombs that were supposed to demolish positions would be gone. "What else? Everything else."

He could see the lights of the hotel in the distance, and then under his feet was the paved path that wound out of the woods to the tennis courts. As he looked at the high chain-link fences and bright white spotlights on the tall poles around them, his eye transformed them. He realized he was looking at his own concentration camp. The tennis courts would be where the enemy commander would herd the captured islanders and hold them. Then he remembered it wasn't his own camp, but his children's. He'd already be dead, and so would Esther, probably. They'd announce to the world that the prisoners were being treated well: there were even showers in the locker rooms on the other side.

Where was Vickers? Even if somebody had lured him away, he'd still be going to a place where he had powerful friends. He was an absolutely remorseless homicidal maniac in a place where the authorities would quietly congratulate him if he did something illegal to get home. But maybe it was better that Vickers and the others were gone. Harry was ransom; Vickers was revenge.

Lord Carnarvon moved to the kitchen door of the hotel and knocked. The heavy steel door opened an inch, then swung wide to admit him.

"Lord Carnarvon," said Jean Le Croupier. "Of course."

"What are you doing here?" asked Lord Carnarvon.

"I have experience with detonators," said Jean, "and some dexterity with my hands."

"There's one here too?"

"Not in the kitchen. You can't hide anything in a hotel kitchen. It was taped to the methane tank outside."

"Where is it now?"

"In Oran we would have—"

"What about here?"

Jean clenched his jaw. "It's buried under the hedge about sixty meters east." He pointed at the wall of the kitchen, and Lord Carnarvon didn't even try to orient himself to where that would be on the outside of the hotel.

"What else has been done?"

Jean Le Croupier shrugged. "They're searching the island for more. The front desk is studying the guest list to look for saboteurs. Augustino has people walking the island to waken *les vieux.*"

"The—" And then Lord Carnarvon's brain had switched to French. "Of course."

"The Caribs already knew," said Jean. "They're clairvoyant. But you knew that too, because you are a Carib."

"Of course." The old man was mad. Lord Carnarvon said, "Keep up the good work," and patted his bony shoulder, then moved through the kitchen to the pantry, where already men and women who worked in the hotel were moving military assault rifles and ammunition clips onto carts and covering them with towels and tablecloths.

He moved to the door opening into the restaurant, then peeked out at the tables. There were a few pairs of tourists sharing a late supper, and from the far corner of the room he heard a familiar laugh. He opened the door a little farther and beckoned to a waiter. The man recognized him and entered the kitchen.

"Do you want me to clear the dining room?" the waiter asked.

"Not unless you hear guns," said Lord Carnarvon. "Right now I'd like you to bring Del Cupido in here if you can."

"What should I say?"

"Just tell him I've got to talk to him privately, and I can't go in there like this without stampeding the tourists."

"Right," said the waiter. As he turned, Lord Carnarvon could see the pistol stuck in his cummerbund.

"Wait a minute," said Lord Carnarvon. He carefully pulled the gun out and stuck it in the man's inner coat pocket. "I know you've got to carry it, but don't let it show." As the man left, he thought, These people aren't fighters. They came here because Harry's deranged mind invented places for them. Where the hell is Harry?

He was glad he'd thought of the baseball players. They were above suspicion. They were all too rich to steal, and everybody deserved a chance to fight or run. A few had even become citizens of the island when their own countries had degenerated into some form of chaos or hopelessness. He'd let Del Cupido decide how to tell them.

Del Cupido strutted into the kitchen behind the waiter. "All right, chief. What's the—" He glanced around the kitchen at the chefs and sauciers and busboys, all rushing back and forth carrying weapons and ammunition. "Aw, shit," he said. "We were going to win tomorrow."

Lord Carnarvon walked up the back hallway of the hotel's basement level and made his way to Augustino's office. He opened the door without knocking, and four men whirled to stare at him, then went back to making marks on the map of the island that Augustino had tacked to the wall. Lord Carnarvon could see that the marks were the places where dynamite had been planted, and little arrows showing where they'd been moved. The map was extremely detailed, with little drawings of buildings and paths and groves of trees. Across the top was Augustino's most recent promotional slogan, "The Place Made of Dreams."

Augustino appeared at his elbow. "We'll have an update from the airport soon, Mr. President."

"Mr. President?" he whispered. "What is this?"

Augustino drew him farther from the other men. "A lot of people are going to be scared if this goes on very long. I'm trying to plant the idea that this isn't a half-assed operation."

"They all know it is. They live here."

"It's times like this that you get the payoff on your public-relations investment. In fact, I can open up the men's shop on the first floor while you take a shower."

"I haven't got time for a costume party. I've got to play general."

"Don't worry, L. C. I called Vickers' buddy in Colombia. As soon as he gets there they'll turn him around. I told him we've got a tight vote on a major issue."

"What the hell does that mean?"

"Nothing, but Vickers will get it."

"He probably will," said Lord Carnarvon. "Any word from Harry and Emma or Captain Pettigrew?"

"Not yet, but soon."

Lord Carnarvon sighed. "Get word to some people we can trust who have boats. I want as many as possible heavily armed with full tanks moved out of the harbor."

"Great idea, Mr. President," he said loudly. Then he whispered, "If it's okay with you I'd rather not be in a boat this time."

"Don't worry," said Lord Carnarvon. He turned to go.

"Wait a minute," said Augustino. "What's the rest of the strategy?"

"Anything you can think of. The best thing would be if by tomorrow nothing is the same as it was today."

Esther Lord Carnarvon stood in the living room of her father's house. Her ears could distinguish three breathing patterns. Her father's breaths came so slowly that sometimes she wondered if he were just getting used to the boundary between sleep and death. Her son and her daughter were like little animals, their breathing fast and eager. She went out and closed the door behind her. Lord Carnarvon would want her. She knew that by now he'd be settling in the hotel, where people could look at him and feel safer.

She thought about Emma as she walked down the path toward the hotel. She could feel that Emma was alive somewhere. There was a dull, nagging sensation of tension, but no terror yet. When Emma's face floated into her mind there was a look of watchful, calm, the wise eyes studying something that was happening. That meant Harry was alive too. Lord Carnarvon would be pleased.

PARIS

Emma felt the steady pressure of a man's hand on her shoulder blade, pushing her forward. The blindfold was too big for her, so it pressed on her nose and made it hard to breathe. Her ears seemed to pick up every sound, and she could feel tiny differences in the air around her. She went up a ramp made of concrete, and through a doorway that she knew must be very wide, because the hand didn't limit her lateral movement. She heard Harry cough to let her know he was still there, and she cleared her throat to answer.

Suddenly the street noises were gone, and now they were in a cavernous, empty space. There was an echo when someone walked a few paces to her right. There were a few loose hairs above her forehead that had been disarranged by the blindfold, and when she stood still, she could feel a soft, steady breeze move them slightly. There was some kind of ventilation system, and the room was huge and empty, and the floor was smooth, like polished stone.

Pictures floated into the darkness behind Emma's blindfold: a theater, a library, a post office, a museum. They were all impossible. Maybe it was a prison.

BOGOTÁ

He hadn't had to wear the blindfold after all. Vickers focused on the driver's shoulder, keeping the man in the front seat in the corner of his vision at the same time. The man beside him was getting overconfident, letting the miles of highway erode his alertness. It was the man in front who would get him. The man was still half-turned, resting the gun on the top of the seat so that it always pointed at Vickers' chest. The position was too uncomfortable to allow him to lose his edge, and he never looked away at the window. The only hope was that his cramped position had allowed the circulation in his side to slow, so there would be no authority in the muscles when he had to move quickly.

Vickers would have to make two moves. They would be timed perfectly so that they were opposed to the way the world worked. He learned them as he sat there, his eyes staring past the driver's right shoulder. When he was satisfied that his body would perform them without thought, he waited. He set his mind on the three men in the car with him. He let his body slump down in repose to communicate a false sense of his size and strength.

He judged the strength of the man beside him, and the speed of the man in the front seat. As he contemplated their weaknesses and the exact attitudes of their bodies, he recognized that the feeling was coming on him. It was the cold calm that meant he was ready. He could shape time and control these men absolutely. They would struggle to make moves that would be of no use to them.

He held himself in repose as the car turned off the highway onto a narrower street in the suburbs. Vickers stared past the driver's shoulder to watch for the right vehicle to appear in the left lane. He saw it, and then the driver saw it. "Truck coming," the driver muttered.

The man in the front seat lowered the pistol, and the man beside Vickers seemed to wake up. He started to lift his own pistol, and Vickers decided to let him.

When the two men were thinking about the problems the truck driver might cause them, Vickers' hand jabbed to the left and pushed the car door open. The man in the front seat raised his pistol in that direction, but Vickers had thrown his body against the man beside him. The man was big enough to have put up a struggle, but his left arm was pinned against his body, and his right hand held the useless pistol. In a frightened reflex, the man's chubby finger tightened on the trigger, and fired a shot through the roof of the car. The roar was deafening, a sound the other men didn't hear but felt, as though the shot had been an explosion.

The driver panicked and stomped on the brake just as the truck in the other lane crashed into the open door. There was a bang and a shower of broken glass, and the car spun around. The driver and the man in the front seat were pressed by centrifugal force into the right half of the seat.

At that moment, the big man beside Vickers used all his strength to push Vickers away from him. In the spinning car his struggling was useless, but when the car stopped, Vickers combined his own strength with the man's and helped the man propel him through the empty doorframe into the street.

Vickers had known this much before it had happened, and he'd known that the man would sense too late that he was pushing his captive out of the car, and try to follow. Vickers rolled on the street and prepared to divert the clumsy weight of his charging opponent.

The man lunged toward him, his body filling the empty doorframe just as the man in the front seat fired at Vickers. The bullet tore through the man's shoulder, and Vickers caught the look of horrified surprise and pain on the man's face, then turned and ran toward the truck. The driver had stopped after the car door had smashed into his left headlight, and now he was standing beside the detached door with an injured expression. As Vickers ran toward him, the expression turned to terror, and he turned and ran too. Vickers dashed to the cab of the truck and had it moving before the man looked back, and as Vickers drove past him the man hadn't slowed down at all.

THE PACIFIC OCEAN

Captain Pettigrew dreamed of a time that must have been when he was a child, or maybe it was the way things would be after he was dead. He'd never been able to decide about that, but they were probably the same. But he was in that swimming pool again. It was so large it was like the reservoir of a dam. There were hundreds, maybe thousands of people in it, but the pool was so vast that they weren't bothering each other. And Pettigrew was swimming underwater, gliding effortlessly like a fish. He passed lots of people, some floating above him, their arms and legs fanning in that strange, slow, graceful way, and some bobbing on their toes like ballet dancers. There were so many that the bright colors of their bathing suits and the various tones of their skins, like all the colors of polished wood, made the quiet place where he swam seem unbearably beautiful. And then, slowly, he began to feel the pressure in his chest that meant he would have to breathe again. He arched his back and looped upward to the silver border of the surface, and broke through, feeling the warm fresh air in his lungs. Then he took another stroke, as he always did in this dream, and kept gliding upward, above the surface. He soared a few feet upward and then leveled off. And as always in this dream, as he floated in the warm air above the swimming pool, he thought, Isn't this something? And the people he passed looked up at him and smiled and waved.

Then the wind came up, and it was very dark, and Joaquín's voice said, "Captain." And he was Captain Pettigrew again, lying in his cabin. He sat up and breathed deeply, and looked at Joaquín sitting in the chair across the room.

"Why are you in my cabin?" he asked.

"I knew you couldn't sleep either."

"What made you think that?"

"Because I was coming to wake you up."

"All right," said the Captain. "We'll go home."

PARIS

Emma waited for fifteen minutes after she heard Harry taken out. She knew it was fifteen minutes because she counted. Then she took off the blindfold. She saw the thick metal bars gleaming in the dim light, and then the rows of numbers on little brass plates on the wall, and thought: I'm in a bank. I know everything that is happening to me, and I could have avoided it, but I can't now. I might as well put the blindfold back on, and wear it until they come back, because seeing—knowing—is only to remind myself that we were just like cattle in a feed lot. They were always going to do this. They were always among us, waiting until we were fat enough to butcher.

She heard them walking toward her on the bank's marble floor. She listened carefully for Harry's voice.

BOGOTÁ

Vickers studied the Presidential Palace from across the broad plaza. He knew that there was very little chance that any of the guards would recognize him, and he had no identification. He also knew that somewhere in the crowds crossing the plaza on their way to work, there would be men like the ones who had met him at the airport. They knew he had to come here. There was nobody else who could help him. He couldn't even leave the city without papers. Soon the sidewalk café would close to clean up after the early breakfast crowd.

He looked up at the waiter and said in Spanish, "I would like to use the telephone."

The waiter pointed to the pay telephone in the inside dining room.

"I'd like something more private. I'll pay twice the cost of the call."

The waiter shook his head. "That's the only one. The pig is afraid I'll talk to my wife and not the customers."

Vickers reached into his pocket and pulled out an American ten-dollar bill. "Then give me some coins."

The waiter looked at the bill suspiciously and said, "I'll have to see about this."

Vickers waited, and watched the plaza. It had a terrible look of normalcy. There were families dressed for a holiday in the capital, the children scrubbed and starched, little girls like dolls, wearing tiny gold earrings in their ears and ribbons in their hair.

The waiter returned, but he was carrying a tray full of food for another table. Vickers held up his finger, and the waiter nodded, then rushed off to the kitchen.

Vickers looked out at the plaza again, and spotted the short man. He was with a woman who was wheeling a baby in a stroller, and they were coming toward him through the crowd. Vickers stood up and walked into the café. He stopped beside the kitchen door, and when the waiter came out, he grabbed his arm.

"I'm in a terrible hurry," Vickers said. "Please."

"I'm sorry," the waiter muttered, and set his tray on an empty table. "Here." He reached into his pocket and handed Vickers his American bill.

"No, keep it. Just give me money for the telephone."

The waiter pointed to the telephone, and Vickers saw the paper taped across the coin slot. "It's broken." As Vickers took the bill, he laughed. The waiter's eyes brightened, and he laughed too.

In a minute someone would be coming through the back door of the café, and the others would gather in the front, and Vickers would die. He said, "It's not my day. Take the money, my friend," and walked out onto the plaza. He kept his eye on the short man, and chose a group of young government workers walking quickly across the plaza to their jobs. He moved close to them and changed his position every ten steps to make it difficult for the unseen killers to choose positions. He knew that if there were a rifle with a scope somewhere, one of his own shifts would bring him into the cross hairs.

He stayed with them until they began to veer toward a side street. He gauged the distance to the gate, and set off alone. He made eight steps before he heard the shot. He was only fifty yards from the palace now, and the shot had sounded way off the mark, so he decided it was time to gamble everything.

Vickers broke into a run. When he heard the second shot, he knew he was going to make it. The man must be firing from hallway across the plaza. There wasn't even a ricochet near him. Vickers sprinted across the open space, fists clenched, and now people were moving to clear a path as he approached them, but he didn't care, because in seconds he'd be there. Now he could see the guards gathering at the gate, their rifles held high across their chests, ready for their opportunity, their eyes squinting at the crowd in the plaza.

Then he heard the third shot, and at first it made no sense to him. A guard dropped his rifle, and Vickers heard it clatter, and then the guard fell on it. They're shooting at the guards, he thought. Vickers saw the guard next to the fallen man grimace and yell something. Then he saw him snap his rifle to his shoulder and take aim. Vickers even heard the report of the rifle, but it sounded like an explosion in his own body. As the bullet passed through him, he only thought, *Not me.*

16

THE ISLAND

Lord Carnarvon stood on the roof of the hotel and watched the men preparing their snipers' nests in the afternoon sunshine. The last time, these men on the roof had made a difference. They might make a difference again. But unless the enemy had learned nothing, they would do something besides plant a bomb to clear the roof, and these men might die. All he had been able to think of to protect them was to place other snipers at the windows of the floor below, to make the roof cost twice as much.

He heard the metal fire door open and slam shut, and then he felt the presence of Esther beside him. "Lord Carnarvon," she said.

He put his arm around her. "Did you go through the reservation lists?"

"Yes," she said. "Things are all wrong."

"I know. We don't have time to evacuate that many people from the island. We'll just have to try to keep them safe."

"No. There are two hundred and fifty men who registered with credit cards from the same bank."

"You mean the same exact bank? Same branch?"

"No, of course not. They're from all over, but all of these men are traveling without women, in twos or threes. All of the cards are from NewFed."

Lord Carnarvon thought for a moment, then smiled wearily. "Either you've figured out what's happening to us, or we're about to harass a whole lot of innocent gay men."

"Two of the cards have numbers in sequence. Twelve-digit numbers."

"Warn everybody you can get to." He stepped into the stairwell, and glanced at his watch. The sun would set in a couple of hours, and two hundred and fifty men could be anywhere out there, or in the hotel, in the restaurants, or . . .

He moved down the stairs two at a time, and the combinations began to form themselves in his mind. Of course it could be a bank. A country would fall into Harry's traps, afraid of being involved in a war over a speck of artificial land. But banks thrived on wars, and this one had branches and subsidiaries all over the world. Why not a bank? Lord Carnarvon turned the corner into the back hallway and stopped to keep from bumping into Augustino.

"It's starting again," said Augustino. "The telephones are dead, and the radios are being jammed from somewhere offshore." Augustino started to move past him, and Lord Carnarvon felt an impulse to block the hallway. Then he realized that Augustino, at least, seemed to know where he wanted to go.

He said to Augustino's back, "They're tourists. Some are in the hotel."

Augustino waved his hand. "I know, I know, and if they think they can get out of here paying with phony credit cards, they're crazy. I've got people in the corridors."

Lord Carnarvon turned and hurried off in the other direction. He reached the service entrance behind the kitchen and moved outside. He was in the back of the hotel where the garbage bins sat like the buildings of a miniature city surrounded by high hedges, when he heard the first shots, far in the distance. Lord Carnarvon turned to run back into the hotel, but the next sound stopped him. It was like a deep indrawn breath, then a sigh that went on for several seconds. As it went on, his heart began to beat in his chest so hard that he felt it in his ribs.

He ran through the opening in the hedge, and stared in the direction of the baseball stadium. He could see people in the top row of the stands, staring over the edge toward the eastern point of the island. There were actually people in the stadium waiting for the game to begin. How could there be anyone who didn't know? How had he let this happen?

He started to trot toward the baseball stadium, when he heard more shots. There were two, then five more from another weapon, and then, for the first time in years, he heard the staccato rattle of several automatic weapons firing at once. He changed his course in mid-stride, and nearly twisted his ankle. Then he stopped. "I'm alone, and I never bothered to pick up a gun. Now it's starting, and I'm running as fast as I can for five steps in one direction, then five steps in the other direction, like a frightened parrot. Which way? It doesn't matter. This one. You're committed now, so punch hard. Too late to duck."

He broke into a run, taking the path to the point, where the Haitians had built their houses. He'd decided yesterday that this was where it would begin, and now the gunfire was coming from there. Lord Carnarvon forced himself to stop that train of thought. He was justifying himself to someone, and nobody had asked. He dashed across the open space behind the street of shops, and headed for the golf course. His breaths were coming hard now, and his mouth was dry and tasted like metal.

He made it to the woods behind the ninth fairway, and paused. There were guns here someplace. He remembered Vickers pointing them out on the map to groups of new citizens. "On this island, you'll always be within a few minutes' walk of enough guns to arm a squad of guerrillas. The locations of these weapons drops are our only military secret. Never talk about it, never write it down, just remember where you're supposed to go if the time ever comes. One word of warning. You get pissed off at your neighbor, cut his throat, and you'll have a trial. But nobody who misuses our military weapons is going to live to reload. Is that clear?" It had always been clear.

Lord Carnarvon searched the ground for the marker. They all looked the same, like access boxes for turning on a water valve for a buried sprinkler system or a filter trap for a sewer. When you raised the heavy lid, under it would be a little concrete bunker with clean, oiled rifles and dull black ammunition clips. Lord Carnarvon stubbed his toe on the cover just as the firing began again. He knelt and lifted the heavy steel panel and peered inside.

There were only two rifles and six ammunition clips. He lay on the ground and reached down to pull up a rifle, then fished the magazines out one by one, putting them in his pockets. Then he replaced the cover. He decided to believe that the islanders who were supposed to find the weapons had been here and moved into the woods. He would find them. He stood and began to run.

Lord Carnarvon heard the sound of running feet and ducked behind a bush to fire. As he waited, six young men ran up the path in single file. The point man sensed his presence, and his hand went behind his back. As though a wind had blown them away, the six disappeared into the brush beside the path.

"It's me," he called. "Lord Carnarvon."

The point man reappeared, much closer than he'd anticipated. He recognized Julio Cardenas, the son of one of Vickers' original flying squad. The boy looked at him. "It is," he called. "It's okay." The others stepped back onto the path. Cardenas said, "We heard the guns. Where do you want us?"

Lord Carnarvon said, "They look like tourists. The Haitians will be trying to hold them off."

Lord Carnarvon set off at a trot, and the six young men followed. At the end of the path, Lord Carnarvon stopped and listened. In front of him was the broad, open lawn that the Haitians had planted for their children to play on, and then the first of the houses. It all looked terribly quiet. He waved his arm to signal the others to spread out, and he heard them move forward on both sides of him. Then he waited.

Suddenly the house at the end of the row spewed out a volley of shots, a short, steady roar that seemed to come from several places at once, as though the house itself were erupting. Lord Carnarvon sprinted from house to house toward the sound. He could see that each house he passed was unoccupied, and he knew that the Haitians must all have gathered in one building to make their stand.

As he reached the last abandoned house, he slowed his

pace, then crawled to the corner and peered across the lawn. There were two dead men sprawled in the garden. One of them wore an Irish fishing hat, and it had somehow been pushed down tighter on his head when he fell, so that he looked as though he'd been shot in the middle of some strange comic impersonation. The other was wearing a Bahamas T-shirt. Lord Carnarvon wondered if it were his own, or part of a plan to costume the invaders as tourists. The man's head had a small bald spot like a monk's tonsure. Neither seemed to be armed. What the hell was going on here?

Lord Carnarvon saw something move in the periphery of his vision, and he froze. A small, thin stream of smoke rose from the side of the house. As he watched, it grew. One of the windows of the house opened, and a black arm tossed a pan of water toward the smoke, but it splashed on the grass three feet short. As the pan was withdrawn, the window seemed to disintegrate, shattering inward as though bullets had hit it everywhere at once.

The shots were returned from inside, and Lord Carnarvon's eye followed the only barrel he could see. It rested on the windowsill, and pointed somewhere to his left. He ducked back and made his way to the rear of the house as quietly as he could. He flipped his selector lever to full automatic, took a breath, and then stepped into the open.

As he did, he came face-to-face with a man in a green golf shirt with a kangaroo above the pocket. The muzzle of his rifle nearly touched the little badge as he fired. At the same time, he saw three other men crouching along the side of the house. They all turned as he fired, and one got off a shot that hit the awning over Lord Carnarvon's head. Lord Carnarvon sprayed across all three at shoulder level, stepping away from the first man as he fell.

Then Lord Carnarvon heard more gunfire to his left, and the sounds of men crashing through the brush toward the golf course. Scattered shots went on for thirty seconds, and then he saw one of his flying squad step into the open and wave his hand. Lord Carnarvon moved toward the house where the Haitians were gathered. A man was already stepping toward the back of the house, pulling a green plastic garden hose.

Étienne sprayed the charred white siding of his house and the water hissed and boiled upward in a cloud of steam. He half-turned his face toward Lord Carnarvon, and then nodded.

Now other people slowly ventured outside, all of them scanning the woods, their guns held high as though they were afraid it might start again.

On the hotel roof, Esther Lord Carnarvon listened to the sharp cracks of the guns at the point. She sang a little song that made Lord Carnarvon impervious to arrows and the bites of sharks. It had been in her family since time began, but she'd never sung it since her marriage.

Then she looked out across the beach below the two sidewalk cafés, and wondered what it was that she was supposed to see at such a spot. As she watched, a great cloud of sand flew into the air, and two breaths later, the sound reached her. It was a deep thud, and she understood that the bomb they'd found in the café had been detonated. Then the other one went, a hundred yards farther down, and the same sound reached her.

She turned to the men in the snipers' nests and cooed, "Be calm, be brave. They're just moving sand."

Then she returned her attention to the fighting in the distance. There was something happening at the baseball field. She could see that there were lots of people in the stands, and then she saw a man in a baseball uniform run out of the stadium and into the woods. It made her angry that the baseball player should have to be afraid. Esther walked to the nearest pile of weapons, and selected a nine-millimeter pistol. It took her a moment to find the ammunition for it, but she took three loaded magazines, and slid one into the handle.

She thought about Emma as she made her way to the stairwell. When women were captured in wars, it usually didn't go well for them. But Emma was special. Once she'd been looking strange, staring out at the sea with a sad look, and Esther had asked her what was wrong. She'd answered that it was an old hurt. "I was gut-shot by a policeman, dear. Don't ever let a man take you where you'll be shot at unless you really love him. It hurts like hell.'' Esther sent Emma some strength as she descended.

As Esther moved through the hotel lobby, a few people stared at the big pistol in her hand. When she reached the door, there were four men standing in front of it, staring out at the broad stone walkway.

''Excuse me,'' she said, and started out. Two of the men turned, and she saw that one was Sullivan Boats, her cousin, and the other was Lord Carnarvon, her husband's cousin. He said, ''Esther, you can't go out there alone.''

''Come with me.''

The two looked at each other, picked up their rifles, and followed her. She led them through the tall hedges of the maze, and beside the tennis courts, where the roses she'd bought in the United States were already climbing toward the top of the fence.

''This has been a good island,'' she said. ''Things are growing.''

''We're going to the baseball field?'' asked Sullivan.

''Yes,'' said Esther.

As they made their way down the winding paved walk beside the golf course, Esther heard a loud clopping, like a horse. The two men stopped and held up their rifles, but Esther said, ''Wait.''

Then a man in a baseball uniform ran around the bend and into sight. He stopped and held his hands in the air.

''Hello, Farley,'' said Esther. The man recognized her and lowered his hands. ''What's going on?''

Farley Atkins took a deep breath, and let it out. ''Guys in a boat landed on the beach, and took over the field. I was there to warm up, and nobody else showed up. They just came over the fence pointing guns at the fans, and that was that.''

''How did you get away?''

''I was in the bullpen waiting for other players to show up. By now those guys with the guns will be herding everybody into the stands, just like that soccer place in Chile.''

''Did anybody else get away?''

''A couple of the television people got out when I did.''

''Are you afraid?'' she asked.

''Damn straight,'' said Farley.

"We're going to do something. Would you like to help us?"

"Yes, ma'am." His eyes narrowed slightly, and she saw that he was aware that he might die.

"You can probably shoot this better than I can." She handed him the pistol, and he checked the load. "Here," she said, and gave him the extra ammunition she'd brought.

They walked along the path until they found the four television technicians hiding in the woods. They thought they couldn't be seen, but Esther stopped and called, "Come out and join us."

One of the men was sitting beside a small camera. As he came forward, Esther called, "Bring your equipment." The four men stepped onto the path, and Esther waited. Then she said, "What's wrong with the one behind the tree?"

The person came out, and Esther could see it was Deborah. "Hello, Esther," she said. "The guys decided I should hide until they were sure who it was." She smiled. "Excess male hormones or something. Well, what'll it be? Do we get the hell out of here or hide?"

"I think," said Esther, "that the best thing we can do is go to the stadium."

Deborah's eyes widened. "Wait. Didn't he tell you?"

"Yes," said Esther. "Come with me."

WASHINGTON

The Assistant Secretary pushed the cassette tape into the recorder and pressed a button. "This is the first one," he said. "The woman is Arlene Gold, CIA. Her cover name is Deborah Wilson, so don't get confused if they call her that."

"Turn the volume up," said the Senator.

He watched as a hand-held camera panned across the outside of a baseball stadium. He could see the heads of a few people in the top rows, but nothing more. There was a female voice saying, "A few minutes ago, there was quite a bit of firing from inside the stadium, but now the shots you hear are from other parts of the island." Then the face of Deborah appeared. "As you can see, today's baseball game between the Caribs and the Aztecs did not start on schedule, because the island has been invaded. We have no idea yet of the casualties. Here with me is Carib pitcher Farley Atkins, who bravely made his escape from the stadium so that he could broadcast the truth about what has happened."

Farley Atkins stepped into the frame of the camera, and it was clear that the room they were in was very small and had whitewashed walls. "Well, it ain't over," said Atkins. "The people on the island are fighting for their lives, and they sure could use some help. And then there's the baseball team. I don't know if I'm the only one who got caught, or the only one who got out . . ."

The Senator lifted the telephone and said, "Get me the President, right away." Then he hung up and said to the Assistant Secretary, "How many people are watching this?"

The Assistant Secretary knotted his brows. "It's a satellite transmission to the cable system. Their regular subscription audience might be five million tops. But the networks are subscribers, and this is news. Farley Atkins was Most Valuable Player in—"

"I know that. Tell me about this Gold woman. What does she think she's up to?"

"They won't say."

"What conclusion am I supposed to draw from that?"

The Assistant Secretary studied his hand and tugged one finger as he named each possibility. "They might be using the island as an excuse to do something in the region, depending on who it is they plan to blame. They might have someone or something on the island that they don't want to write off. It would have to be something bigger than a field operative like Deborah, of course."

"You mean we don't know?" the Senator snapped. He picked up the telephone, and his tone changed. Now he was gentle, conspiratorial. "How are we doing on that call?" He listened for a moment. "Then get him on the plane." Then he hung up and looked at the Assistant Secretary, who was staring at him over his hand, holding on to his third finger.

The Assistant Secretary said, "The problem is that the people who keep track of things like that are supposed to work for the director of Central Intelligence, but some of them don't, or don't really. So 'we' certainly know, but in either case, unless we're talking Russians or something, 'we' might not tell us."

The Senator nodded, and the Assistant Secretary was surprised. He actually seemed to understand. He stared at the Assistant Secretary shrewdly, and the Assistant Secretary sensed another huge moment in his career was about to occur. The Senator said, "He'll be calling in a second. What's your best guess?"

The Assistant Secretary clenched his teeth, and said, "I think she's gone native."

"Reasons?"

"These people sometimes turn into anthropologists. They spend five years spying on people who eat tree bark, and then spend the next five convincing their superiors to help the bark-eaters."

"No coercion?"

"They won't tell us much about her. But she's been Special Ops and Clandestine Services only, almost all of it away from home. At the very least she's been trained and psychologically prepared for situations where she'd disappear and nobody would ever know what happened to her."

The Senator paused. "You believe she's acting on her own, without a gun at her head, and probably without orders from Langley. And she has some philosophical reason for what she's doing."

The Assistant Secretary felt a terrible need to qualify and complicate the Senator's summary, but he restrained himself. "Yes. You can't force a woman like her to make a satellite transmission against her will. It's too easy to flip the wrong switch or pull a plug."

"All right," said the Senator. "I'm going to make my move now. Go back to your office and pretend this never happened."

The Assistant Secretary stood up. "I'll try to find out whatever I can, and get back to you."

"No," said the Senator. "It won't do any good to know more now. I won't talk to you again for a few days."

The Assistant Secretary turned and walked through the outer office. He heard the buzz, and he even heard the receptionist say, "Senator, it's the President."

Inside the office, the Senator studied a list of names on a single sheet of paper as he spoke. "Mr. President, there are a few fellows that I'd like to have you talk to off the record . . . That's right, a little lobbying and arm-twisting as a special favor to me. It might even turn them back from a fatal course of action, and unless I'm mistaken, you already know some of them." There was a pause as he listened. Then he said, "That's right. That's what it's about." Then a tiny sliver of steel seemed to enter his voice. "They'll feel flattered if they hear it from you. If you've got to hear a history lesson, it's a lot cozier to hear it from the President in private than from some redneck circuit judge in public." He listened, then a smile crept across his face. "No, sir. It won't be necessary. I'm going to be down at the Washington *Post* for the next few hours talking with some old friends, and it'd be better if they weren't around to overhear a phone call from the President. I'll know everything's okay when I see it on television like everybody else."

THE ISLAND

Nathaniel Boats lay in his canoe and stared up at the sky. The sun was halfway down in the ocean, and the two helicopters looked as though they were flying out of the fire on the edge of the earth. But he could feel the presence of the ship over the horizon.

The two helicopters swept over his canoe, but kept the same altitude and direction. They were probably on some kind of schedule, he decided. The ship would be heading toward the island now. Probably there would be hundreds of men aboard, ready to swarm onto the beaches, but almost certainly there would be a man who dressed like Vickers but had lost his soul.

He remembered the terror of the day in 1930 when the British warships had appeared off the coast of Dominica. His father had carefully unwrapped the ancient revolver from the oilcloth, loaded it, and stuck it in his belt with his serrated fish knife. Then he'd gone out to the middle of the village and joined the other men. And then the sun had gone down just like this, and the English gunners on the ships had aimed their cannon, and fired the first volley of star shells over the Carib compound.

The men had stood for a moment listening to the whistle, and then there was a deafening boom, and everyone had looked up into the sky, and known the Carib uprising was over. Many of them scattered at the first horrible sound, running back to their houses to throw themselves over their children, as though their bodies could fend off an artillery shell as big as a man. But Nathaniel's father had stood still. Then he'd turned in the direction where the ships lay, miles offshore, aimed his pistol at a forty-five-degree angle, and fired a single shot into the night sky.

Nathaniel Boats remembered the artillery. He sat up and gauged the angle of the helicopters' course. The ship that had brought them would be out there to the west, and soon after dark it would move toward shore. He judged it could be done with one or two other men. He lifted his paddle and turned his prow toward the marina.

Esther and Deborah sat quietly and listened to Farley Atkins. The cameraman had propped his camera on the table, and was now peering out the window of the trailer with an M16 rifle in his hands.

Atkins was saying into the microphone, "The helicopters are still circling around above us, but they don't seem to be firing at anything. When you get here—and I'm talking to the marines now—watch out for those babies."

Esther turned to Deborah. "How long do you think it will take for marines to come from Florida?"

Deborah looked at her. Deborah's eyes were sad and sympathetic. "There probably won't be any marines, Esther."

Esther thought for a moment. "Don't you think they heard us?"

"That I'm sure of. But Harry set this place up so that nobody could intervene without upsetting all your neighbors."

"Then why did you help us?"

Deborah smiled. "I don't know. I guess it was easier for me than not doing it would have been."

"Will the CIA fire you?"

Deborah hesitated, then seemed to make a decision. "How long have you known?"

"Emma always knew. She said it was a good idea to make a deal with you, because your television company couldn't go broke."

Deborah stood up. "Okay, honey. Let's go find your husband and see if he's got any ideas about springing those poor folks in the stadium."

Lord Carnarvon edged into the players' entrance to the stadium, then moved through the Carib locker room, past the showers, and then out to the hallway that led to the dugout. He waited and listened, but all he could hear was the sound of his friends carrying the boxes of guns and ammunition up behind him.

"This hall leads to the other dugout," he said, and watched while eight men filed down the hall. He had already sent snipers to the electronic scoreboard in center field, and under the stands, and out along the fences. Maybe one of his strategies would work. If Vickers had been here, he'd have known how to do this simply, efficiently, and quickly, like a bird snatching a bug out of the air. But he was only Lord Carnarvon, and he had to try everything at once.

Lord Carnarvon stuck his pistol in his inner coat pocket, and crawled through the doorway into the dugout. He could see there was nobody on the baseball field, so he slowly craned his neck and looked out at the bleachers.

What he saw astounded him. There were at least a hundred island people in the bleachers, but they weren't prisoners. They were armed. They weren't baseball fans surprised by a party of invaders. They'd come to lie in wait. They had captured two dozen men in jungle fatigues, and now they were engaged in a lively debate about what to do with them. As Lord Carnarvon stepped forward to settle the question, he heard a growl of engines and a sound like giant wings flapping, then saw the bellies of two helicopters sweep overhead.

Augustino Cruz saw the helicopters before he heard them. He already had everyone off the roof of the hotel when they passed overhead. As they came closer, the people in the top-floor windows opened fire, and he could see sparks where the bullets hit their metal sides. He fired at the glass windshield of the first helicopter, but he couldn't detect any damage.

The helicopters never varied their course toward the hotel. They flew down toward the roof like old-fashioned dive bombers, fired a salvo of rockets that streaked downward and pounded into the roof, and then they swooped up and away. When Augustino opened the metal door and ventured out onto the roof again, he could see that it was a disaster. There were holes in the roof that a man couldn't jump across. He could see a small fire burning on the tar at the far corner, so he ran back inside and pulled the extinguisher off the wall, then dashed along the edge of the roof to put it out. As he sprayed the flames he could hear the helicopters turning. As the sputter of their engines grew louder, he threw himself down on the tar and covered his head. The roof felt hot, and the fire seemed to inch closer to him as he lay there. He reached for his fire extinguisher.

Then the sound seemed to diminish. He lifted his head and saw the helicopters flying off over the sea. It was just as well for them, he decided. During the day he'd managed to trap over a hundred of the bogus tourists in their hotel rooms. If the helicopters had opened fire on the lower floors of the hotel, it would have made a sickening sight to open the doors of those rooms.

Nathaniel Boats paddled his canoe under the black shape of the anchored ship, never taking his eyes off the dim lights in the pilothouse. It was big, with a clear deck for the helicopters in the middle, but not as big as the British battleships when he was a child. He listened for the other canoe, and he could hear the sound of a paddle behind him. He knew it wasn't Charlie Wellington's paddle. It had to be Esteban, the other man. It was a strong, eager swish, like a child might make before he was taught properly. Nathaniel listened for four more strokes. There was no hesitation or flutter; perhaps a lack of restraint.

He stopped paddling and let a long, rolling wave slow his glide until the second canoe came up beside him. He held on to their canoe with his hand and leaned his head so close to Esteban that he could feel the warmth of his face in the cool air. ''Don't paddle any more. I'll find you when it's done.''

He heard Esteban put his paddle in the bottom of the canoe and pick up his rifle. Then Nathaniel maneuvered his way backward to Charlie Wellington. He said in Carib, ''Pick me up at the bow. Esteban is too loud.''

Nathaniel slowly glided to the stern of the ship. Under the surface he could sense the huge propellers waiting to chop his canoe up. The rudder, bigger than the wall of a room in his house, loomed above him. He gave a stroke, and was beside it.

Nathaniel moved to the center of his canoe and rolled the first heavy oil drum over the side, leaning away from it just enough to to keep his canoe from capsizing. Then he grasped the rope and lashed the barrel to the rudder. Esteban had set the timer inside an hour ago on the island. Nathaniel judged that there were at least a hundred pounds of explosives inside the barrel, so he wished Esteban great intelligence and a sure hand, knowing his wish came thirty years too late to ensure the proper explosion.

He paddled toward the bow and looked along the sides of the ship as he went. He found nothing as he went that would serve his purpose. He glided under the big anchor chain and up to the bow. There had to be something below the waterline, where the rust did its work. He ran his hands along the edge of the submerged prow, and it came to his hand as easily as the thought of it. There was a rivet that had loosened, and as he touched it, he felt it turn. He pulled on it, and it came out two inches. He held it with his left hand as he felt for the bowline, then tied the rope to the big rivet under the surface.

Nathaniel slipped quietly into the cold water, and slowly swam away from the ship. He managed only five or six strokes before Charlie Wellington found him on the dark ocean, and placed the canoe in front of him.

As Nathaniel hoisted himself up out of the water, he heard the two helicopters. He lay in the canoe and watched them swoop overhead, their red and green running lights blinking. When they came over the ship, big spotlights on their bellies flashed on, and formed huge pools of light on the ship's deck. As the first helicopter eased slowly downward onto the empty deck, Nathaniel Boats smiled.

He got to his knees in the canoe and picked up his paddle. He plied the paddle as he'd done when he was a young man. His strokes were long and smooth, and the canoe moved toward the island, coasting on the swells.

After a half-hour he could see the island, and he smiled a second time. The island was blazing with electric lights. At this distance, they seemed to waver and twinkle in the vast darkness, like stars. The canoe rode a rolling wave over the reef, and a moment later, Nathaniel Boats heard a dull thud somewhere in the distance. He thought at first that he had only wished it, but then in front of him Esteban raised his paddle in the air and let out an ear-piercing whoop. It was unseemly, but it made him think of his father, who would have loved to hear it.

Esther Lord Carnarvon sat beside her husband in Augustino's office in the basement of the hotel. He grasped the telephone receiver hard as he spoke, so his brown knuckles whitened.

"Thank you," he said. "I don't think there's anything you can do here at the moment. But thank you." He hung up, and Esther studied him.

She asked, "Why is Vickers in prison?"

"It's not a prison," said Lord Carnarvon. "It's a military hospital. They shot him by accident, and he wants to fight. That's what you're feeling."

"Oh," she said.

Lord Carnarvon pressed a button on the telephone. "Get me Paris, France. I want Althea Simms. I don't know what time it is there, so try all the numbers you have. There's a restaurant, and an apartment, and I don't remember what else."

17

PARIS

Althea Simms walked across the vast marble floor of the bank toward the row of tellers. There were only a few other customers in the bank, mostly business people like her, coming in to get cash for the day's transactions. She even recognized other restaurateurs she'd seen many times at the big markets before dawn, competing for the best, freshest fish and vegetables off the backs of trucks that had just arrived in the city.

She waited her turn in the line in front of the teller. When she was standing before him she lifted the heavy bag onto the counter. The barrel of the gun protruded only an inch through the slit bottom of the bag toward his stomach.

She saw the look of dismay on his face and she felt a little wave of regret. He looked so frightened he might forget what he was supposed to do. She said in her flawless French, "If I hear an alarm, you will be dead. You will give me all the money in your drawer. Put it in a bag."

Althea watched the man's jaw muscles tighten as he stepped on the silent alarm button. If Lord Carnarvon has made a mistake, she thought, I will be in prison for a very long time. Then she said, "You're doing a terrible job. Open the gate and let me inside. If you don't, I'll start shooting." That didn't sound convincing to her own ears, but the man obeyed. He came around the counter and pushed open the little door, then stepped back to let her enter.

Now that she was in the protected space behind the counter, she didn't mind waiting for the police to arrive. The teller seemed happier too. He set about filling canvas bags with money, in a transparent attempt to keep her waiting.

In the distance, she heard the sirens, a faint "Wah-wah" sound, and then they cut off. The teller must have heard them too, because he tried to talk over them. "If you'll put down your gun and walk away, we can forget this happened," he said. "It's a mistake."

"No," she answered. "All the other tellers know."

She could tell that the police had arrived outside the bank, because there was silence. There were no cars driving past the bank anymore. Althea knew that she'd done her job. In a minute they'd storm the bank, pouring in all the doors at once with guns drawn.

"I've changed my mind," she said. "I've decided that I'm never going to get out of here. But there's no reason for you to be frightened. Go away."

The man looked at her a little sadly, then turned and walked out through the door to the wide marble floor. At first he walked slowly and a little stiffly, but once he was out, he moved faster and faster toward the door, his hope of survival rising in him.

Althea glanced in the other direction, and saw that the other tellers had already slipped away. She went to a desk and put her bag on top of it, then sat down in the chair to wait for the police to get their men and cars arranged as well as they could. As she waited, she tried to imagine them closing the streets, placing men at each door and each window, so that no human being, however strong or cunning, could ever escape from the bank.

They'd definitely arrived. Althea could hear the terrible artificial silence that must be the sound of a large number of men making no sound. She stood up and looked around her, wishing there had been some other way. Lord Carnarvon had just said, "That's who's got Harry and Emma. You're the only one we have in Paris right now. I'm not saying you can do it. I'm just saying that if you don't, nobody else will."

She regretted that she'd been able to think of nothing better to do. There was only one building in Paris that belonged to NewFed, and here it was, within blocks of the hotel where Harry and Emma had been staying. She had surprised herself by being able to see that part of it so clearly. If these people wanted the island's money and business holdings, the simplest way would be to kidnap Harry and Emma. It was possible that Harry was the only one who even knew where all the money was. Althea knew there were numbered accounts in Switzerland and London and Hong Kong and probably everywhere, and hundreds of investments made in the names of shelter companies. The only way anyone could get them was to force Harry to bring them all together and sign them over. And the only way they could hope to gather the funds without raising suspicion was through their own bank. And it had to be done in a brief period while the island was under siege, and nobody could yet know that Harry and Emma had been taken.

They had to be in the bank, and it was time now to find them. As soon as she turned her back, the last of the innocent tellers and customers would slip outside into the arms of the police. And when they did, the police would come in to get Althea. She just had to make sure that when they found her, they'd also find Harry and Emma.

She peered into the bank vault, through the steel cage at the rows of safe-deposit boxes. She moved past it, but then she realized that something had changed. When she identified it, her heart began to pound in her chest. The change was that she had stopped smelling Emma's perfume. She pressed her face against the bars and sniffed. Emma had been in the vault. In the dead, stale air of the closed vault, there lingered a tiny hint of Emma's special scent. No bank employee could possibly afford to wear Emma's perfume.

Althea's breathing slowed, and came out in little nervous puffs. Could they have taken Harry and Emma somewhere else, maybe killed them? No. It would take days to complete so many large transactions, and Harry and Emma would have to be there, available during business hours and safe, in a place that was built to keep people out, but would just as effectively keep people in.

Althea ran along the row of tellers' windows toward the big oak door that led to the offices. Somewhere in the building Harry and Emma would be waiting for her.

The rooms on the corridor were all open, but the inhabitants had fled. There was a coffee cup on one desk, and she could see steam rising from it. There was a silence that seemed to invite her to make a noise, to reveal her position to some hostile intelligence that was waiting to obliterate her.

She rushed on to the end of the corridor, where she passed beyond a plain metal door with no markings, and entered the narrow brick stairwell. She cautiously moved up to the next floor, and opened the door she found there. This time she was in a broad hallway with thick red carpets covered with long Oriental runners, so her feet made no sound as she walked on. The rooms here were empty too. They were big, dark, old-fashioned offices with wood paneling and brass lamps topped with green glass shades. Farther down the corridor, there was a turn. As she made her way around the corner, she smiled.

At the end of the corridor was a carpenter's sawhorse with a sign on it that said "FERMÉ" bold red letters, and the excuse, "Renovation," in small, apologetic black letters. There was only one door past it. She felt an overwhelming sense of love and longing when she saw it. Beyond that simple door, twenty feet away, were Harry and Emma.

Althea hesitated. Even with the gun, she couldn't hope to dash heroically in and declare them rescued. She had to frighten the captors. She moved back to the end of the corridor, walked out into the stairwell, and closed the door behind her. Then she aimed the pistol down the stairs and pulled the trigger. There was a loud, sharp crack that echoed in the closed space, so she could barely pick out the sound of the ricochets. She fired the gun again twice, rapidly, then waited.

She heard the door on the far end of the corridor swing open, then heard the muffled, hurried voices, and an elevator door opening. After a moment she heard it close again. She stepped cautiously back into the corridor. She could see that the carpenter's sawhorse had been moved aside, and the door of the mysterious room was open. She walked inside and looked around her. There were croissants on the desk, and coffee cups, and bottled water. Beside them were several blank sheets of paper with Harry Erskine's signature on them. She set her gun down and walked back out into the hallway.

Althea looked at the panel above the elevator and watched the numbered lights, When the elevator reached the ground floor, she listened anxiously for gunshots. When they didn't come, she wondered for a moment whether that was a good sign or a bad one. But when she saw the lighted numbers recording the elevator's slow, inexorable progress as it brought the policemen up to her floor, she smiled again. She stood with her hands empty and open as the elevator doors parted, her arms extended from her sides as though inviting an embrace.

At the rear of the building, Armand Gautier of the Sûreté, dressed as a cabdriver, watched the door of the bank. He had two uniformed policemen stationed beside the door, but his own function was grimmer. This might be more than a robbery. He was to ensure that, in the worst circumstances, no armed person would make it to the street. He hoped to do nothing. But the authorities were disturbed that Paris had lately become the killing ground for terrorists of all kinds and the secret death squads for half the world's dictatorships. French citizens were being shot in cars and blown up in cafés by foreign lunatics. That was going to stop.

Gautier held his rifle in his lap and watched as the door swung open. A middle-aged couple came out onto the sidewalk, shielding their eyes from the sun as though they'd been hiding in a closet. He congratulated them silently. But then the door swung open again, and two men carrying pistols stepped into view. He snapped the rifle to his shoulder, but then he saw that the two gendarmes were alert.

In a few quick, silent moves, the gendarmes had the

two men disarmed and lying flat on the street, waiting to be taken away.

Gautier waited and watched. The next person out the door was a police sergeant wearing a bulletproof vest, so Gautier began to disassemble his rifle. The sergeant took charge of the two former hostages.

When Gautier looked up again, two more policemen were coming out the back entrance, escorting a young black woman, who looked very happy to be alive. He was surprised to see the two hostages rush up to the girl, as though they knew her.

Gautier started his engine, then turned it off again. He put the rifle in its case, and shoved it under the seat. He saw the older white woman throw her arms around the little black woman and kiss her.

WASHINGTON

In his office, the Senator looked out the window and spoke affably into the telephone. "I don't know what you're talking about. The President doesn't ask me about anything but foreign policy, and then all he wants is a vote count. If he told you to stop doing something, though, I'd take his advice." He paused and listened. "Well, hell. If you've already done what he said, I can't imagine why you're calling me. We're not even in the same branch of government. You remember—the Constitution and all that stuff. What's all this about, anyway? The Foreign Relations Committee hasn't got much to do with domestic banks."

18

Eleven Years

WASHINGTON

The Assistant Secretary picked up the newspaper on his desk and read the article again.

> NEW YORK—In a press conference today, Police Commissioner David Bozeman admitted that there are still no leads in the bizarre disappearance of the board of directors of the NewFed Bank two weeks ago. The air-sea search for the remains of the private jet which disappeared over the Pacific has found nothing to date.
>
> The eight-man board had been in ultrasecret negotiations with a cartel of Asian businessmen in the Pierre Hotel until early this month, according to Marianne Penton, executive assistant to J. Dixon Bacon, chairman of NewFed. On Thursday of last week, Bacon and the other directors boarded a Lear jet at La Guardia Airport with five men representing the Far Eastern interests. She said the names of the men had never been revealed to her, and that they spoke a language she couldn't identify although she believes it may have been Tagalog, a language of the Philippines. The plane stopped in Los Angeles for refueling, and filed a flight plan for Honolulu, but never reached its destination.
>
> The *Wall Street Journal* has reported that according to insiders, the destination of the flight was probably Hong Kong, where certain powerful Asian interests have been assembling billions in liquid assets in preparation

for the reversion of the Crown Colony to mainland China in 1999. Official State Department inquiries have so far not revealed the names of the five Asians. Sources in brokerage houses here assert that this is to be expected in deals of this magnitude. It is believed that the reason for the secrecy was that the Asians had been bidding for a controlling interest in the ailing New York banking giant, which had recently been forced to write off major loans to Mexico, Brazil, and Argentina. This setback came less than a year after the revocation of the charter of the bank's Paris branch, a move which crippled NewFed's ability to attract European business. In a statement issued at the time, French officials accused the bank's employees of allowing the branch's premises to be used in the kidnapping of Harry and Emma Erskine, wealthy American émigrés now residing in the Caribbean. Insiders believe that bankruptcy has been stalking the bank for some time, and a buy-out offer would have been welcome.

So far the only clue to the identity of the missing Asian financiers was a monogram on a briefcase carried by one of them on the trip to La Guardia Airport. According to Mr. Bacon's chauffeur, the briefcase bore the gold letters "L.C."

19

LOS ANGELES

Lord Carnarvon came back into the drawing room of Harry's hotel suite. "That's it, Harry. The Captain says they're all back home. Sullivan Boats got off the plane from Mexico City an hour ago. That leaves us."

Harry lay back on the couch and stared at the ceiling. "I'll see you there in a few days."

"A few days?" asked Lord Carnarvon. "Where are you going to be?"

"Here."

"Here? You're just going to stay in a hotel in Los Angeles instead of going home? What for?"

Harry pursed his lips, then looked at Lord Carnarvon. "Because Fat Jimmy lives here. I've spent half my life wondering about him, and now I'm going to find him."

"Why now?"

"Because I never got around to it. There we were in that Paris hotel, and all of a sudden I'm looking at two guys with guns. One of them's got his gun pressed against the back of Emma's neck, and she's got this sad little smile on her face. I could tell she thought it was a bunch of out-of-work terrorists who saw us on TV and decided to pick up a few extra bucks. Not me. I thought: The Fat Man. He's finally made his move."

"But he hadn't."

"No. And now he's finally lost his chance. I'm never going to be scared again. Look, I know everything you're going to say. It's been eleven years. He's not going to be sitting where I left him. He might be powerful, surrounded by people I can't get past. He might even have moved away. But I'm going to find him. And then I'm going to hold him up to the light and look at him."

"All right," said Lord Carnarvon.

"What?"

"Yes," Lord Carnarvon answered. "Sure, I'll go."

Harry drove the Cadillac up the San Diego Freeway, past the lights of Westwood and upward onto the long incline that led to the San Fernando Valley. "This has changed," he said. "They added lanes. Lots of lanes in eleven years, just like rings on a tree trunk." It was still as dark on this stretch as it had been when he and Emma ran with the Fat Man's money, the taillights of the cars ahead like hundreds of little red stars leading him up into the pass.

Lord Carnarvon stared ahead. Cars were still the oddest part of the place. It seemed to be all roads, and the buildings were just places where you stopped your car to rest, or stopped to get gas, or to get your car fixed or traded it in for another car, and then got back on the road, trying to make up for the time you'd lost. In the village on Dominica, growing up had meant going out alone into the vast, lonely world. The challenge was being alone on foot in the forest, or after that, alone on a small boat in the middle of the dark, empty sea. Here it seemed to be going out to struggle to make your way against thousands of other people, all moving as fast as they could to get there before you did and take your place before you found it. If they did, they'd get your job and your money, your house, your food, and your woman, and there'd be nothing left for you. You'd never get an identity; you'd never exist at all. "Where does Fat Jimmy live?"

"Way out in the Valley." Lord Carnarvon imagined a grassy plain. But then they reached the top of the hill and he could see the huge expanse of the San Fernando Valley, the rows of lights stretching ahead of them into infinity.

Harry stepped harder on the gas pedal, and the car picked up speed going down the hill, as he moved two lanes to the left. But there was the blare of a horn, and then a car that Harry had narrowly missed moved up beside them. A young man was driving, and he rolled down his window and screamed at Harry, "You asshole! Can't you drive?" Lord Carnarvon was shocked. Nobody talked to Harry that way on the island. He studied Harry for a reaction.

"He's got a point," said Harry. "It's been a long time, and I'm a little rusty."

"Just don't get arrested," said Lord Carnarvon. "I don't want to get arrested."

Harry sighed, and Lord Carnarvon felt the car slowing down. "Sorry." After a few seconds he announced, "This is the exit coming up. We're not far from the street. Get ready, burn incense, sacrifice somebody, do whatever you do."

"I usually hold my breath until I pass out." Lord Carnarvon picked up the little square machine pistol and slipped a clip into it as Harry guided the car onto the ramp and stopped at a streetlight. There was a blast of music, mostly drums, and a pickup truck pulled up beside them. Lord Carnarvon watched as a big blond boy with a fat face shrugged his little dark girlfriend's arms off his neck so he could lean forward to assess the traffic flow before he roared his pickup truck off to the right. Lord Carnarvon could see she'd draped herself over him again before he'd shifted into third gear fifty yards down the street. Then the green light went on, and the Cadillac was moving again. He wondered what Harry had looked like as a teenager. He sensed that Harry and Emma hadn't looked much like the beefy boy and his girlfriend, but he couldn't imagine what they had looked like, or what they'd been.

"Here's the street," said Harry. He pulled into a dark, quiet suburban lane, lined with long, low houses with big multiple-car garages attached to them. "It's different. The Fat Man owned most of these lots when we left. He never admitted it, but nobody ever built on them, and I went downtown once and looked it up."

"You mean you and Emma wanted to live here?" It was almost sad—Harry and Emma living in a nice American suburb in a house with a built-in barbecue in the back. Maybe just by living here they would have, by force of the atmosphere—one part charcoal smoke, one part smog, one part lawn fertilizer—become normal like the people around them.

"No. It never occurred to me. I just figured that knowing more about the Fat Man might be worth something someday. Here. Here it is." Harry stopped the car and turned off the lights. "I'll go around to the front. You go to that window. It covers the living room, unless he's put in a wall. If anything weird happens, open fire and keep firing until there's nobody standing up." Harry got out of the car and stuck his gun inside his coat, under his left arm. "I'll wait until you're set."

Lord Carnarvon spent a few seconds regretting that he'd never learned how to drive. If something happened to Harry, he would be alone on foot, fifty miles from the sea. He made his way up the lawn to the side of the house and peered in the window. He could see a blue glow in the darkened room where the television projected dim ripples on the walls and ceiling like the reflection of sunlight on water. He heard the doorbell, and a young man in a T-shirt that said "Ensenada" stood up and moved to the front door.

At the front of the house, Harry held himself ready. He could sense from the delay that somebody was looking at him through the fish-eye lens set in the door. Then the door swung open, and Harry gasped. The man before him was no older than some of the baseball players at home. He was barefoot and unarmed. "Yeah?" said the man. "Can I help you?"

Harry contained his surprise. Of course by now people like Benny Costa would have graduated to managing the Fat Man's interests, and the Fat Man would have hired younger men. "Is Jimmy around?"

The young man started to close the door. "Sorry. Wrong address."

"Mr. Albano?" Harry ventured.

There was a woman's voice inside. "Wait a minute, Dave. Did he say Albano?"

The young man turned his head, and a woman joined him. She was holding a little girl about two years old in her arms, bouncing her up and down as the child eyed Harry with evident distaste, sucking her thumb with her index finger curled over the bridge of her nose. The woman said, "That was one of the names on the papers when we bought the house. Don't you remember?"

Dave shrugged.

"You're too late," she said to Harry.

"About six or seven years," said Dave. "We bought it from the one after him, I think."

Harry smiled weakly. "I've just got to learn to keep in touch with people. Thanks." He hurried to the car, where Lord Carnarvon was waiting for him. "What the hell are you doing here?" asked Harry. "You were supposed to cover me."

"I saw toys on the floor. Where next?"

"The bar where he hangs out. It's off Sunset. It's red meat and pasta with sauce that tastes Mexican and beer in pitchers you can't lift with one hand."

"We're going to shoot up a bar?"

"I don't think so. We'll lure him out and corner him or something."

They stood across the street from the small stucco building for a moment while Harry studied it. There were two young men parking cars for the customers who pulled up in the street in front of the restaurant, but Harry couldn't tell if they were armed. "All right, this is it," he concluded. "This is Filippo's."

"It's not called Filippo's anymore, Harry. The sign says 'Grenouille Japonaise.' "

"It looks the same, it's got to be the same. Look at all those fancy cars in this neighborhood. They may have named it the Japanese Frog, but I know damned well who's in there. It's a dive, and they won't know me, so be ready for anything.

Just inside the door was an emaciated, stern-eyed man who studied them for a second, then seemed to adopt the hopeless cheerfulness of a dentist. "Two for dinner?" But Harry was staring beyond him at the bar. "Holy shit," he muttered.

Lord Carnarvon followed his gaze into the bar. There

were huge abstract paintings on bare white walls, and prosperous-looking young couples seated at black tables large enough to hold only two glasses and a tiny ashtray that seemed to be a diminished vestige of the days when people in bars smoked. The maître d' said quietly, "If you'd like to have a drink in the bar before dinner, I can take your names."

"What the hell happened to this place?" asked Harry. "It looks like a psychiatrist's office."

The maître d' cocked his head and smiled attentively. "The art on the walls changes every week, sir."

"I used to come here when it was Filippo's."

"Did you, sir? That must have been some time ago."

Harry and Lord Carnarvon walked to the bar, dodging very thin waiters who looked as though they spent their days auditioning for acting jobs, but now scurried about carrying plates decorated with tiny slices of fish and poultry and colorful dwarf vegetables. "There," said Lord Carnarvon. "I see one with pasta on it."

"I didn't mean a spoonful of angel hair with corn and fish on it. I meant a big sloppy red dish of linguine. This place has been gutted and hosed out."

The elderly bartender leaned close to them. His faded, rheumy blue eyes narrowed. "Harry?"

Harry whirled and stared at him. "Thank God. They missed something. You're—"

"Bobby," the bartender said.

"Of course. Bobby." Harry shook hands with the bartender. "This is a friend of mine," he said, nodding toward Lord Carnarvon. "His name is Joe."

The bartender smiled. "Glad to meet you, José."

"*Sí,*" said Lord Carnarvon.

"The place looks pretty good, doesn't it? Where have you been? It must be—what? Ten years. Nobody would have recognized you but me."

"I moved out of town," said Harry. "Where is everybody?"

"Like who?"

Harry leaned closer and said in a tense, quiet voice, "You know who."

Bobby shrugged his shoulders, and snatched up a rag in

the compulsive defensive movement bartenders use when they might need to be too busy to talk. "No I don't."

"Fat Jimmy."

Bobby looked relieved. "The Fat Man? He's dead."

"Dead?" said Harry. "How is that possible?"

Bobby's smile opened to emit a laugh. "That's just what I said when it happened. It's what everybody said. I guess people figured if there was a way to kill him, somebody should have thought of it sooner. He was a human disease."

"A boil on the ass of the human race," said Harry.

"A malignant pissant of the first water," said Lord Carnarvon. "I'd drink to him if I had a drink."

Harry ignored him. "Are you sure he's dead? Really sure?"

"Certainly. He's been dead for a couple of years. That's too long for a practical joke."

"Did you see him die?"

"Hell, I can't take a day off just for the fun of it like that. You've got to trust the papers for some things. He had a heart attack followed by a ride to Forest Lawn."

Harry looked from side to side, scrutinizing the young lawyers and store managers around him. Then he whispered, "If you didn't see it, I wouldn't say anything too loud. Unless Benny Costa died with him."

"No," Bobby admitted. "Benny Costa lives like a king in Arizona. They say he didn't wait until the doctor left the body. He just went to Fat Jimmy's house long enough to clean out the cash and got back on the freeway. You have to be a damned speed fiend to beat the doctor down the driveway when somebody dies, but there never were any flies on Benny Costa. Maybe it was force of habit. It wouldn't be the first time somebody died and Benny Costa hit the freeway."

Harry pursed his lips and nodded. "Arizona. The Fat Man used to have a place outside Scottsdale."

ARIZONA

Harry and Lord Carnarvon sat in the Cadillac and watched the front door of the house open. A middle-aged man with a thick, barrel chest walked down the sidewalk. He was wearing leather slippers and Bermuda shorts, so his feet looked small and delicate as he scuffled to the end of the driveway and bent down to pick up the morning newspaper. Harry muttered, "That's our boy," as he started the car and slipped it into gear. But instead of driving off, he wheeled into the driveway and squealed to a halt between the man and the house.

A look of terror appeared on the man's face, and he started to run, clutching the newspaper under one arm. Harry was out of the car now, and sprinting after him. It was only ten or twelve steps before he caught up with him. Then, as Lord Carnarvon watched, he simply tapped the man on the shoulder and said, "Benny, cut it out," and they both stopped. Costa bent over with his hands on his knees and caught his breath, as Harry talked. "I'm just here to see the Fat Man."

Costa stood up and folded his newspaper. "He's dead, Harry. Go see him at Forest Lawn in L.A."

"I did," said Harry. "Only looking at the grave wasn't enough. The Fat Man and I were close. So I dug him up."

Costa looked at him suspiciously. "The hell you did."

Harry shrugged. "I want to see him, Benny."

Costa sighed. "You got a gun?"

Harry opened his coat and showed Costa the pistol grip of the Ingram MAC-10.

Benny Costa, still carrying his newspaper, led Harry and Lord Carnarvon around to the back of the big brick house. There was a large patio, made of broad slabs of pink sandstone, that led up to the edge of the clear blue swimming pool. "There he is," said Benny. "That's him."

Harry stared, then squinted his eyes. The man sitting in the sun beside the swimming pool was brown and leathery and skinny, his knees like thick little knots, wider than the thighs above them. The man held his face up into the sun, his eyes closed in an idiot reverie, savoring the warmth on his skin like a wrinkled old lizard. ''What's wrong with him? Cancer?''

''No. He had a checkup last week. He's fine.''

''Then what squeezed the juice out of him?''

''Time, disappointment.''

Harry's voice dropped to a whisper. ''What's he doing here? He looks like a desiccated crocodile.''

''I didn't let you in here to insult Fat Jimmy.''

Harry shook his head in amazement. ''What do you say to insult Fat Jimmy?''

The old man heard something, opened his eyes, then stood up and walked toward them. Harry could see the skin stretched over his ribs like the skin of a turkey left in the oven too long. His bony legs were bowed, and the fret pointed inward as he walked. ''Hello, Harry,'' said Fat Jimmy. ''What did you bring me?''

''He doesn't work for you anymore, Jimmy,'' said Benny Costa. ''Not for a long time.''

The old man's eyes glowed, but not with curiosity, or even greed. He was amused. ''He brought me a present. I know he did.''

''Jimmy—'' Benny Costa began.

''He's right,'' said Harry. ''I did.''

The old man looked at Lord Carnarvon for a few seconds. ''You a Navajo?''

''No,'' said Lord Carnarvon. ''I'm not from around here.''

''Do you know anything about physical culture?''

''Physical culture?''

''Health. What to eat, sweat baths, that kind of thing.''

''No. There aren't enough of us left to fill up a decent aerobics class,'' said Lord Carnarvon.

The old man shook his head in disappointment. ''That's probably why. The Indians in this part of the country knew their gastroenterology. They ate pine nuts and acorns. They shit like heroes, and lived to be a hundred.''

''Good for them,'' said Lord Carnarvon.

''Good for all of us. I live like they did now. I'm a better man for it.'' He turned to Harry and asked, ''What's the present, Harry?''

"That depends," said Harry. He moved close to the old man's tanned, wrinkled face. "Have you been trying to kill me?"

Fat Jimmy looked at Harry as though he were trying to remember him. Then he smiled and shook his head. "Not for years. I had people looking for you in Chicago, New York, all over the place, but you were gone. Then, when you turned up with your own island, it was too late. The Commission wouldn't let me do anything down there."

"Why not?" asked Harry.

Fat Jimmy's eyes glittered. "They didn't know who I was. Fifty years of sending them their cut. I never shorted them, either. Like everybody else, I thought they'd know and come after me. There wouldn't be anyplace I could hide. But they didn't even know I existed. They must have had so many little guys like Fat Jimmy sending in their nut each week for so many years that they stopped paying attention and keeping them straight in their minds."

Harry chuckled. "This is a joke, isn't it?"

"Yeah," said Fat Jimmy. "It was. I went to New York and asked for a meeting, and nobody would see me. For years I'd heard it: 'Mr. Garbanzo thinks you're doing a great job, Jimmy. He's got something in mind for you.' 'Mr. Fettuccine wants to come west next year, Fat Man. He'll need a guy like you.' But when I got to New York, nobody had ever heard of me. I sat for three weeks in a hotel room calling people up. God, it was embarrassing."

"But you finally saw them?"

"Sort of. I hung around an Italian restaurant where these guys ate, and one day one of them came in. I made it as far as his table before his soldiers stopped me. I showed him an article about you and your island. I had a bunch of Xerox copies with me in case the Commission wanted a special meeting right away, and I had a plan."

Harry sat down on the nearest lawn chair, and Fat Jimmy sat across from him, leaning forward to stare into Harry's eyes. Harry smirked. "That's a plan? You wanted the whole Mafia to come down on me?"

"You?" said Fat Jimmy. He slapped his bony knee with the heel of his hand. "It wasn't about you. What did you steal from me? A lousy two, three hundred grand? It was the island I was after. In the right hands, a place like that would have made so much money that they'd have had to think of new numbers to count it."

"You weren't stupid, Jimmy," said Harry. "Even we made a lot on it, and most of the stuff you'd have done there would have made us throw up."

The old man stared at the sparkling, clear surface of the swimming pool. "Yeah," he muttered, almost to himself. "It was a dandy plan."

"But what happened?" asked Lord Carnarvon. "What did this potentate say?"

Fat Jimmy spat. "Oh, nothing. He just gave a look at one of his guys—kind of a tired, disgusted look—and they threw me out on my ass. I weighed three-fifty or so in those days, but I remember getting hauled across that restaurant at about thirty miles an hour. I hit the doors with my face, and then I was on the pavement. While I was lying there I was already waving a hundred-dollar bill at a cabdriver to get me to the airport."

Benny Costa shook his head. "I think that was the low point of his life."

"No," said Fat Jimmy. "The low point came later, during that tax-evasion thing. That was when those morons finally found out who I was. There was a story in the newspapers in New York. 'Gangland Figure Arrested in L.A.' They sent a couple of guys to talk to me. They weren't there to offer big lawyers or help with the fine, just to see if I could do them any damage. The big thing they wanted was to be sure I wasn't doing anything about that island on my own. They'd gotten burned on that stuff about trying to snuff Fidel Castro years ago, and about drug smuggling, and they just weren't up to another scandal."

Harry leaned forward and looked into Fat Jimmy's eyes. They were strangely calm. "What happened then?"

"Right about then I had my heart attack. The doctors thought it was tension about the tax thing, but it was depression. See, the tax problem was that a cop found four hundred thousand in cash in my garage. I pleaded guilty to betting on football games, gave the IRS half the money, and paid another quarter of it in bribes and fines. It was nothing. I was going through a mid-life crisis, and that was something. You know what I did?"

Lord Carnarvon held up his hand. "You became a priest. You had a sex change. You—"

"Who is this guy?" asked Benny Costa.

"He's the President of our island."

Benny surveyed Lord Carnarvon from toe to hairline. "It figures."

"I took stock," said Fat Jimmy. "I asked myself: 'What am I doing and why am I doing it?' "

"Face it, Jimmy," said Harry. "You did it because you have the values of a python. You're the human equivalent of athlete's foot."

Fat Jimmy nodded. "That's true. I was." He paused. "Pay attention to what I'm saying, Harry. When you realize you won't need any more money, it's stupid to waste your time getting it. You should keep an eye on the mirror, Harry. You remind me of myself at your age."

Harry's hand went to his waist, and he sat up straighter. "That would be libel if you said it in public."

"I don't go out anymore, Harry. I guess I could, but I had enough of that."

Harry reached into his pocket and handed Fat Jimmy a key. "That's the key to a locker in L.A. airport. There's money in a suitcase."

"Ah . . . the present. I figured that's what it was—the money you stole from me. That's nice." He handed the key to Benny Costa. "Here, Benny." Costa took the key and put it in his pocket without looking at it.

The old man stood up and walked to the edge of the pool, and then jumped into the water. After a moment his head reappeared at the surface. "Your conscience is clear. I'm happy. Benny's happy. So go away."

He bent his knees so that he submerged again. When he came up, he swam in slow, unhurried strokes the length of the pool. At the far end he made his turn, then pushed off and glided to a stop. He lifted his head, blinked his eyes, and called, "It's over. I forgive you."

20

Fifteen Years

THE ISLAND

Harry sat in the lawn chair on the balcony and looked out at the sea. Far off in the distance he could see waves from the four days of storms off Cuba arriving in ranks to smash against the new seawall a mile out. The waves would cause an upwelling and shift tons of sand and shells and silt up to the barrier, and leave it there. By the end of the year, the seawall would be a sandy hook, another arm of land reaching out and across the horizon to surround a bit of the sea and eventually wipe it away. The new generation of engineers was better than the last, and someday they'd master the process completely. They'd make the sea do everything. The crushing forces of water and wind would be directed to keep adding land, and they would do it.

On the other side of the house, it was no longer possible to see the end of the land. The only vantage from which the water was visible was the upper floors of the hotel. But Harry had resisted for years the impulse to put land between his house and the harbor, until Augustino had suggested a network of canals. He'd accepted the idea, not so much because he had any inclination to live on a canal, but because he had begun to separate himself from decisions about the future of the island. Any day now, a new idea might occur to him, something better.

He stood up and walked into the house. It was time to put on a respectable suit and prepare for the evening's festivities. He looked down at the thin, spindly legs that stuck out from his khaki shorts. They were late-middle-age legs. If he were to walk outside now, he would be mistaken for just one more retired automobile executive from Detroit, down for an expensive holiday during Augustino Cruz's World's Fair because the little woman already had two minks and a Caddy, and this year she wanted a place where she could wear all the jewelry he'd given her for thirty anniversaries without getting them both killed.

He walked past the television set, and stopped to watch the new pitcher Emma had found in Mexico strike out a Yankee batter in the day's exhibition game. Then the screen went blue and the camera panned above the skyline of New York until it came to the top floor of a huge new building. It zoomed in on a slim, dark-haired man looking out across Central Park. A deep British voice with an accent that came from a social class so refined and rarefied that no children had been born into it for three generations said, "This is the man with the best hands ever to work on a baseball diamond. He's willing to make investments for you. Of course, if you prefer, you can put your money in the second-best set of hands . . . or the third . . . or the fourth . . ." The voice trailed off, presumably back across the Atlantic. Then an American voice came on. "The name is now Rojas-NewFed. But the address is still Wall Street." Harry picked up the remote-control switch and turned off the television set. Mariano had done a good job with the NewFed Bank over the past couple of years, and Harry felt the merger had made sense. Mariano had been the tactician behind the unfriendly takeover in the confusion after the bank's board of directors had disappeared, so he'd earned the chance to run it as a subsidiary.

The finger on the doorbell pushed down and held its place, as though there were some terrible urgency. Harry sighed. It was probably Lord Carnarvon's son, Lord Carnarvon. He always did that. Harry opened the door, and saw the face he still thought of as the original Lord Carnarvon. "Same gene pool," said Harry.

Lord Carnarvon knitted his brows. "What?"

"Come in."

Lord Carnarvon entered, and Harry began to push the

door closed, but there was a call from a distance. ''Hold that door.'' Harry glanced across the lawn and saw two men making their way toward him. One was a tall, thin man with coal-black hair and a mustache, who held himself with a posture so straight that, as Lord Carnarvon had once said, ''You could hang a plumb line from the back of his head to his heels and it wouldn't touch his ass.'' But he was walking very slowly, measuring his steps in a cadence that seemed stately even for a former President of Colombia.

He was gauging his pace to the labored hobble of his friend Vickers. His poise was of such potency that it looked from a distance as though he were actually delaying Vickers, making his listener pause to concentrate on some anecdote he was telling. And Vickers, when he was with the Colonel, looked as though he too were a man at his ease, as though stopping now and then to lean on his thick wooden cane were part of his natural swagger. But Harry couldn't look at him without feeling the strangeness of it: Vickers, of all people, stiffened like this for years now, because a young soldier was being fired upon, and he'd seen only one possible explanation over his rifle sight, a tall, dangerous-looking foreigner sprinting toward him out of a crowd.

As the Colonel helped Vickers up the steps, Harry said, ''Hi there, Colonel. I didn't think you'd go in for this kind of circus. Augustino's just trying to rob a few extra tourists.''

The Colonel smiled. ''My country has an exhibit. All former presidents can do is open new highways, speak at universities, and go to trade exhibitions. Some can go back to their old occupations, but not soldiers.''

''Lord Carnarvon's gone back to being a cannibal,'' said Vickers. ''We don't mind.''

''You're all early,'' said Harry. ''Emma's not ready yet.''

Lord Carnarvon's eyes swept from Harry's face to his bare feet. ''You, on the other hand, are.''

''It'll just take a few minutes. You guys can fix yourselves a drink. Make me one too. I'll be back before the glass starts to sweat.''

Harry slipped into the bedroom, and walked up behind Emma. She was standing before the full-length mirror, wearing a long pale yellow dress. Their eyes met in the mirror.

"You think it's too much yellow, don't you?"

"No," said Harry. "Never."

She looked puzzled. "What?"

"Everybody's here but Captain Pettigrew and Joaquin. If we're going to get there during our lifetime, we'll have to leave in a few minutes. Vickers walked over."

"They're going to meet us at the restaurant. The Captain wanted to talk to Althea about something."

Harry put on a dark blue suit quickly, glancing now and then at Emma, who was now at the mirror in her dressing room, carefully putting the last delicate touches to her makeup. He'd lived with Emma for about twenty-five years, and he'd seen her do this thousands of times, but it suddenly occurred to him that he didn't know what makeup was made of. He looked away to tie his necktie. "You know what he wants to talk to Althea about, don't you?"

Harry watched as Emma studied the effect of her work, turning her face first to one side, then the other under the lights. She said, "Of course. He's going to tell her it's okay to marry Étienne's nephew."

"Oh. Is it?"

"Yes," said Emma. "Étienne says he's a terrific kid."

"He's supposed to be a terrific doctor. By the way, why do you know all this?" He watched her beginning to formulate an answer. "Never mind. It's okay."

He followed Emma out into the living room, then watched her greet the men who waited for them on the balcony. In the fading sunlight, with the sky on this side of the island already turning purple, the yellow dress was perfect, and she was more than just a beautiful woman, but a spectacle, like a flower or a star. As they made their way to the door, the men seemed actually to be happier because they could see her.

They gathered again on the lawn, and strolled at Vickers' pace down the broad walkway above the seawall toward Althea Simms's restaurant on the point. Suddenly, from a barge in the harbor, the first of the evening fireworks streaked upward into the sky and exploded into a glittering shower of orange and green fragments that floated for a moment, and blossomed before they fluttered down toward the sea.

As though it were the signal that the sun had set, a man a hundred yards ahead of them stood beneath the tall metal pole and started to tug the pulley rope to lower the simple blue flag with a single star on it. The people who were passing on their way to the hotel from the baseball stadium stopped and watched him pull the rope until the little strip of cloth came down into his hands.

Harry turned to Emma. "We did it, Emma. Look at the silly bastards. They think it's a country."

Emma hung on Harry's arm so he leaned toward her. She kissed his cheek, and said sweetly, "That's right, Harry. We fooled them." And she glanced past him, across the broad expanse of grass toward the hotel. All along the commercial street beyond the hotel entrance, in the yards of the houses near the point, and the paths toward the woods, people of the island stood motionless for a moment.

In the next breath, the world changed again, and people were already moving, going in different directions, forming new patterns with their arrangement and disparate velocities and individual desires.